KISS TO Belong

ANNA B. DOE

Text copyright © 2021 Anna B. Doe
All Rights Reserved
ISBN: 9798428651416
Copyediting and proofreading by Once Upon a Typo
Cover Design by Najla Qamber Designs
Cover Photo by By Braadyn
Cover Models: Hailey and Caleb

This is a work of fiction. Names, characters, places, and incidents are the products of the author's imagination or are used fictitiously and are not to be construed as real. Any resemblance to actual events, locales, organizations, or persons, living or dead, is entirely coincidental.

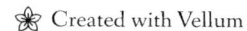

❋ Created with Vellum

"I want to be with you, it is as simple, and as complicated as that."
– Charles Bukowski

BLURB

He loved her his whole life.

New Year has kicked off on a rough start for Alyssa Martinez. Pregnant, homeless, and alone, she has to figure out how to start over before her baby arrives.

Maddox Anderson has always been a brainiac. If only confessing to his best friend he has been in love with her his whole life would be as easy as coding.

But she always saw him just as a friend.

When Maddox finds out what's going on with Alyssa, he demands that she move in with him. When sharing a bed turns into late-night snuggles, and movie nights end up with Alyssa straddling his lap, something will have to give.

But can Maddox prove to her they belong together when Alyssa is convinced that he deserves somebody better than her?

Chapter 1

ALYSSA

"What the hell is wrong with me?"

Coco, my three-year-old Yorkshire terrier, tilts her fluffy light brown head to the side as if she's wondering the very same thing herself. I wipe my mouth with the back of my hand, the stale taste of puke still lingering on my tongue.

It might just make me throw up all over again.

Coco rubs her body along the side of my leg, demanding attention, so I extend my puke-free hand toward her and give her a scratch over her back.

I've been feeling off for a few weeks now. At first, I thought it was something I ate, but when I kept throwing up even after a few days, I knew it had to be a stomach bug of some sort. I was just in the middle of my midterms, so I didn't have much choice but to suck it up. But now it's been at least an entire month. I'm pretty sure stomach bugs don't last this long.

Sighing, I push to my feet. The process is slow, every bone in my body protesting the movement as I flush the toilet and go toward the mirror to wash my hands. While I'm at it, I splash cold water over my face, too, letting it cool down my flushed skin.

When I lift my head, I catch the sight of myself in the mirror. My skin is even paler than usual, and I'm naturally fair since I've been gifted with my nanna Edith's genes. Ginger hair, ivory skin, and freckles, lots and lots of freckles.

Big, dark bags are prominent under my blue eyes. And my usually smooth hair is a mess. I'm not even sure when was the last time I washed it, probably last week on that one day when I actually felt human.

I reach for the towel but find the rack empty, so I crouch down in front of the cupboard and grab a fresh towel. Just as I'm ready to get up, my gaze stops on the box of tampons me and my roommates always keep stashed inside.

I look at the box, almost in a daze, as I tap the towel over my face.

When was the last...

I'm not sure how much time passes before it hits me.

"No." My fingers tighten around the towel that's still pressed against my cheek as the cold sweat washes over me. "No, no, no."

This is a mistake.

It has to be.

Pushing to my feet, I hurry into my bedroom, looking around the space until my gaze falls on my phone that I left charging next to my bed. I yank it off the cord, quickly entering my code before opening my calendar.

Different boxes are colored with the dates for my school assignments, but that's it.

This can't be happening, dammit.

I swipe my finger over the screen looking back at November.

Nothing.

October...

There.

Three little red squares. I tap one of them. Spotting. Seeing the words on the screen jogs my memory. My period usually lasts at least five days, and it's pretty heavy the first couple at least, but this time it was only a slight spotting. I waved it off, attributing it to stress. I had a big project due, and I just had a fight with my mom.

My fingers wobble, and I tighten my grip on my phone, so it doesn't fall out of my grasp. My knuckles turn white, but I barely notice it because I'm frantically swiping back toward the present, hoping more red squares will appear, but it's useless.

My last period was almost *three months* ago.

"Maybe I just didn't put it on my calendar?"

Even before the words are out, I know I'm being foolish. If I had my period, I'd have put it on the calendar. I've done it every month since I got it for the first time when I was eleven. You don't suddenly forget a decade-old habit.

Finally, my legs give out on me, and I fall back on my bed.

"This can't be happening," I murmur out loud as if saying the words will somehow make them true.

But it doesn't change the fact that I haven't had my period for the last two months.

That I've been throwing up for the last few weeks.

Because whether I want to admit it out loud or not, deep down, I already know the answer.

I'm pregnant.

The warm air hits me as I slip inside my house, a shiver running down my spine.

As soon as the first shock washed away, I grabbed my bag, put on my jacket, and boots and was out of the house.

At this point, it was all just speculation. Maybe I really caught some mutated form of a stomach bug that's been plaguing me for the past few weeks; you could never be sure of such things.

Either that or I was pregnant.

I have to know, and I have to know *now*.

The whole trip to the store took longer than expected. While a big chunk of students had already left campus for the holidays, the locals were still here, and it felt like every person in a twenty-mile radius was doing some last-minute Christmas shopping. Still, I got what I was looking for, and now it was time to find out the truth.

My phone buzzes. I pull it out of my pocket, scanning the screen before picking up.

"Hey, you. Just wanted to see how you're doing. Feeling any better?" Yasmin asks on the other side of the line as I go to the bathroom.

"Fine, still a bit off, but hopefully, I'll feel better soon." I turn the bag upside down and let the box fall on the counter.

Or I might just feel even sicker. The jury is still out.

"You should seriously go and see a doctor. You've been feeling off for how long now?"

Weeks.

"A while now," I admit non-committedly. "I really think it's just some bug."

"Bugs don't last that long, and you know it," Yasmin says sternly, and I can totally hear her rolling her eyes at me.

Yes, *hear*. It's all in the tone of her voice.

I met Yasmin through a mutual friend. Last year she started dating Nixon, one of my best friend's roommates. And although I've barely known her for about a year, we really hit it off, and lately, I've been hanging out more and more with Yasmin and her friends Callie, Kate, and Chloe than my own friends.

"Alyssa?" Yasmin calls, breaking me out of my thoughts.

"I'm here. Just thinking."

"I hope that thinking involves getting your ass into the doctor's office."

The test on the counter draws my attention. It's a tool that serves in medical diagnostics. That counts, right?

"Maybe?"

Somebody, probably Nixon, calls Yasmin's name in the background.

"You should go. I'll be fine."

"Of course you will. Please promise me you'll call if you don't feel well. And go to the damn doctor, Aly."

"I'll be fine." When she clears her throat, I give in. "But if I don't feel well, I'll go to the doctor, I promise. Talk soon?"

"Sure, take care of yourself."

I chuckle. "I love you too."

"Yeah, yeah."

We say our goodbyes, and I hang up. I look at the screen and notice all the red bubbles on my apps. Skipping the social media notifications, I go straight for the messages. A friend sent a picture of her and her boyfriend at some ski resort in the mountains, while the other is on the beach in Mexico. I quickly reply, wishing them fun. Then there's my mom's message.

Mom: Please wear something appropriate for the party tonight.

Mom: And for all that's holy, try not to be late.

"Thanks a bunch, mom," I mutter, rolling my eyes.

I open my boyfriend's message last, my heart picking up speed as I do.

Chad: Pick you up at six?

The pregnancy test mocks me from the counter. Chad and I've been dating for a year now. He's a nice guy—handsome, smart, from a good family. My parents love him, which is definitely not easy to find. Some days I wonder if they even like themselves.

What will he think if I'm pregnant?

Just like me, he's a senior at Blairwood, on his way to law school once he's done. And while we did talk a little about the future, it's always been in general terms, nothing specific, which suited me just fine.

But what if there is no time left?

I look at the clock—still two hours to go.

Me: Sure. See you soon. Xo

Putting the phone on the counter, I pick up the box, tentatively flipping it on the other side to read the instructions.

A lump forms in my throat, but I push it down and rip the box open. Coco's ears perk at the rustling sound.

"It's now or never, Coco."

Chapter 2

MADDOX

I tug at my collar as I enter the stuffy ballroom, the warm air suffocating me almost instantly. Or maybe it's this damn tie.

This is the last place I want to be, but as my mother likes to point out, attendance is non-negotiable for the members of the Anderson family. After all, she's the one organizing this Christmas charity gala to raise funds for children suffering from cancer. The least I can do, according to her, is show up and play nice. However, while I support her causes one hundred percent, I could do without actually having to come to the party and mingle with other people. I tried to point it out, but of course, she didn't want to hear about it.

Lucky me.

Keeping my head low, I slide through the crowd of overly dressed people and head straight for the bar. Maybe if I keep a low profile, I'll be able to...

"I thought we agreed you'd come on time."

Busted.

Probably in record time, too.

Sighing, I push the metal frames up my nose before turning

around and facing my mother. "Mom," I greet, bending down to place a kiss on her cheek.

Caroline Anderson's dark red lips are spread in a smile, always the perfect senator's wife, but I can see the disapproval in her dark eyes as she takes me in.

"Didn't have time for a haircut either? Honestly, Maddox," she tsks, shaking her head slightly.

I run my fingers through my curls, pushing them back. Not that it helps, if it's to be judged by the narrowing of her eyes. "I was busy working on my current project. I told you that, but you insisted I should come regardless."

"This is a family event, Maddox. You have to support your family. Besides, it's Christmas."

I nod since it's easier than fighting with her. There's no way I'm going to come out as a winner. She's a lawyer's daughter and a wife, and it shows. So instead, I change the subject.

"Where's Dad?" I take a sweep of the room, searching for my father's tall frame. People are divided into groups, chatting between themselves, but a few eyes are on us.

"Schmoozing." Mom waves her hand. "You know how your father can get."

"Yeah, I do."

They might be doing this for charity and giving back to the community, and they might even mean it, but that doesn't make it any less of a stage set up to support my father's political career.

"Come on, walk with me around the room." Mom loops her arm through mine and tugs me away from the bar and toward a group of people. "Everybody's been asking about you."

I groan inwardly but let her pull me along like the good son I am.

For the next thirty minutes, I let my mom drag me from group to group, doing my best to pay attention and show interest as we stop to talk to different high-profile people attending this event.

I'm in the middle of a conversation with the governor of New York when I see a flash of the familiar red hair, but before I can catch her eyes, she's already gone.

Dammit.

I nod at whatever the man is saying, but all my attention is on finding my best friend.

Mom must notice that I'm distracted because she excuses us after a couple of minutes and pulls me away.

"Alyssa is here," I comment, still searching for her.

Mom makes a sweep of the room, smiling at people watching. "She came with her boyfriend earlier."

Of course, she did.

My body turns stiff as it always does at the mention of her boyfriend. Aly has dated in the past, but never this long, and never a guy her parents actually approved of.

Is this it? Is he the one for her, and I finally lost my chance?

My throat wobbles as I struggle to swallow the lump that formed.

All these years...

My eyes land on her just as the song ends. Aly pulls away from her preppy boyfriend, smiling up at him, and my jaw clenches. It's an instinctual reaction. Then again, I've had it with every guy she's ever been with, but there is something particularly sleazy about, what's his name again? Chuck? Chase? Something like that. He puts his hand on the small of her back, leaning down to whisper in her ear, as he leads her back to their seats.

Mom stops and turns around to face me. "When do *you* plan to bring a girlfriend, Maddox?"

If I can't have her, I don't want anybody else.

I force myself to look away from Aly. "Sorry to disappoint, Mom."

"I'm not disappointed." She straightens my collar and tie. "I just want you to be happy."

"I know."

But it's hard to achieve happiness when the girl you're in love with and have been in love with all your life is in love with somebody else.

ALYSSA

"Champagne?" Chad asks but doesn't wait for an answer before grabbing a couple of glasses from a passing server and handing me one.

I take it, curling my fingers around the delicate crystal.

Chad's free hand slides to the small of my back. "You've been quiet tonight."

I notice one of my mother's friends watching me, so I paste a smile on my lips. "Just a lot on my mind."

Like the fact that I'm carrying your baby.

The words appear in my mind, and the need to gulp down the champagne is strong, but no more alcohol for me—a shame since I could use it right about now.

God, how many times have I drunk in the last few months? I was definitely not partying as hard as I used to in my freshman and sophomore years of college, but I live for an occasional drink with my girls.

My fingers itch to rub over my belly, but I clench them harder around the glass. Did I unknowingly harm the baby? Was there something else except drinking that I might have done that could have put it at risk?

A wave of heat hits me out of nowhere as panic spreads through my body. I force myself to take in a shaky breath, not that it helps much.

"C-can we go out on the terrace?"

Chad glances at me for a moment, a contemplative look on his face. I don't know if he can see something's wrong or if it's all in my head.

After taking the test that turned positive, I pushed everything to the back of my mind because I needed to prepare for tonight. I looked awful, and there was no way I could come to the gala like that. Not coming wasn't optional either, so I had to suck it up.

Compartmentalizing was something I was good at. My mother taught me that from an early age, and I mastered it.

Chad takes a step to the side. "Sure."

Nodding, I turn and go for the door, discarding the flute at the first available surface before slipping outside in the chilly night. A shiver runs through my body, but finally, *finally*, my lungs open up, and the sweet air fills my body.

Hands land on my shoulders, making me jump in surprise.

I look over my shoulder to find Chad's serious eyes on me. "Are you okay?"

"Y-yeah, it was just hot inside."

Chad slowly turns me around to face him. His finger slides under my chin, and he tips my head back to look at me.

Chad Kennedy is gorgeous. I bet if he wanted to, he could easily be a model. His dark blond hair is neatly styled away from his face, his bright blue eyes surrounded by thick eyelashes are staring into mine. His lips are full, and he must have shaved before leaving because his square jaw is baby smooth.

Chad slides his fingers over my cheekbone. "You look a little pale. Do you still have that bug?"

I close my eyes, unable to look at him.

This is it—my chance to tell him.

I mean, I knew I'd have to tell him. It's not like I can hide that I'm pregnant from my boyfriend and expect him not to notice, but I'm not sure I'm ready.

How does one do that, anyway?

Do I just blurt it out? Ask him to sit and explain? But how? Is there a guide for this shit? Because it certainly would come in handy right about now.

A lump grows in my throat. My stomach rolls, and for a moment, I think I might throw up once again.

Closing my eyes, I brush my clammy palms against the sides of my legs, feeling the rapid pounding of my heart in my eardrums as sweat coats my body.

"Alyssa?" There's a soft, nervous chuckle as his hands smooth down my arm. "Are you okay? You're scaring me."

I'm scaring myself.

I slide my tongue over my dry lips and open my mouth to explain, but I end up just blurting out: "I'm pregnant."

I'm pregnant.

I'm pregnant.

I'm pregnant.

The silence that falls over us is almost deafening. I slowly open my eyes and look at Chad's expressionless face.

He doesn't say anything, doesn't blink, just stares at me.

"C-Chad, did you—"

"You have to be joking." He pulls back abruptly like I burned him. It's like my words snapped him out of the daze he was under. "Please tell me you're joking."

I wrap my arms around myself, the cold finally getting to me. "I'm not. The bug... it wasn't really a bug."

He narrows his eyes at me suspiciously. "How long did you know?"

Is he serious?

"I just found out earlier tonight."

"And you decided to tell me now?" his voice raises. He looks around, running his fingers over his face.

"When was I supposed to tell you?" I yell right back, tightening my grip around myself. This is so not going as I expected. Not that I'm sure what I thought in the first place. "I know this is a surprise, and you haven't expected it, but neither have I..."

"Is it?" he bites out. "A surprise?"

I blink, unsure where he's getting at with this. "What?"

Chad stalks closer. "You said you were on the pill."

"I was." I remember the little pill I popped into my mouth like clockwork this morning. "I am."

Shit, just another thing I should probably stop doing.

"Then how the fuck did this happen?" Chad demands.

My head snaps up, and I see the irritation on his face.

It takes me a moment for his words to register in my mind. He can't mean...

"It happened the old-fashioned way, Chad. No protection is one hundred percent foolproof, and you know it. Besides," I jab my finger in his chest forcefully, "it was *you* who insisted we get rid of condoms because you don't like them."

"Because I thought we were protected!" He lifts his arms in the air and lets them fall by his side, clearly exasperated.

I shake my head. I can't believe he's actually serious about this. "Of course, it's my fault."

"I'm not saying..."

"You're not?" I lift my brow at him. "Because it sure seems like you are."

Chad rubs his hand over his face. "Are you sure?"

"Well, as sure as I can be with a missed period and a positive pregnancy test in my bathroom trash."

"Fuck." He rubs his hand over his face, ensuring he doesn't

mess his hair. Because God forbid, he looks anything but perfect.

"I called my doctor. They scheduled me in after the holidays for a checkup."

I watch him, waiting for some kind of reaction, but I don't get anything. Chad smooths his hand over his head and nods. "Good. That's good."

Good?

I don't see how anything about this entire situation is good, far from it. We're in our senior year of college, the last thing I need is a baby right now.

"Maybe the test was wrong." The hope in his voice is hard to miss.

I press my lips in a tight line. Highly unlikely, but I'm not going to point it out.

He looks around. "Listen, I have to go."

"What?"

He can't be serious, can he?

Chad turns his attention to me, but he's not looking at me. Not really. "You're going to your parent's house anyway, right?"

"Yeah, but..."

"Then I should go. Call me after you hear back from the doctor about..." He waves his hand in the general direction of my mid-section. "Okay?"

I nod my head, at a loss for words.

I can't believe he's leaving just after I've told him I'm pregnant.

"Okay. We'll talk soon." With another nod, Chad turns around and runs back inside like the devil is at his feet.

We'll talk soon? That's the best he has? *We'll talk soon?*

Tears that I've been pushing back from the moment I realized what's happening come rushing back to the surface. Tears of frustration, anger, fear, disappointment, loneliness, *fear*... it all hits me at once.

"Aly?"

I look up and find Maddox standing in the doorway and watching me worriedly. I'm not sure how long I've been standing here, just staring into nothingness. Probably awhile.

"Are you okay?" Maddox asks, observing me in that quiet, intense way of his.

I try to cover a sniffle and force out a smile. "Sure."

But, of course, my best friend sees right through it. "You don't look fine." He moves closer, his eyes taking me in from head to toe. "You're freezing."

"I needed some fresh air, but I forgot to take my jacket." I wipe under my eyes, brushing my tears away quickly, so he doesn't see them.

Maddox shakes his head and starts unbuttoning his jacket.

"You don't have—"

Before I can even finish, he takes the jacket off and puts it over my shoulders, closing it gently. He cups my face, brushing his thumb over my cheekbone. "Why are you crying here?"

"I'm not crying," I protest, looking away.

Maddox's gaze darts to the ballroom before coming back to me. "Did I just see Chuck leave?"

"It's *Chad*," I correct; I'm not even sure why. "And yeah, he just left."

"Do I need to go after him and teach him a lesson?"

A chuckle, a real one this time, escapes me. "You wouldn't hurt a fly."

Maddox is one of the best, *kindest* people I know. When we were little, he'd be the one going around our neighborhood, saving hurt animals and helping kids in need.

Maddox pushes his glasses up the bridge of his nose. His

hand reaches up, and he slowly tucks a strand of my hair behind my ear, the tips of his fingers grazing my skin.

A shiver runs through me.

Damn, he was right. It is cold.

"Don't be so sure. If he made you cry, I'd punch him in the face without blinking an eye." Those dark eyes stare into mine for a moment. "C'mon, let's get you inside before you freeze to death."

He throws his arm around me, pulling me into his side. His warmth envelopes me, so I snuggle closer. I hadn't even realized how cold I was up until this moment.

"Or..." I look up at him. "Want to ditch this thing?"

A crooked smile forms on his lips. "I thought you'd never ask."

"A *Harry Potter* marathon?"

If it's possible, his smile grows even brighter. "You know it, Aly."

I press my head against his chest, letting out a long sigh. "You're the best friend a girl can ask for; you know that?"

"Yeah," he lets out a long breath. "Yeah, I know that."

"C'mon, let's get out of here." A cacophony of noises slams into us the moment we're back into the ballroom. I glance over my shoulder at Maddox following behind. "Let's stick to the side and hope no—"

"Where do you think you're going?"

Maddox and I both come to a sudden stop, our wide eyes meeting.

Dammit, we're so busted.

Plastering a smile on my face, I turn around to find no other than Mrs. Anderson standing behind us, arms leisurely crossed over her chest, one eyebrow raised in silent question. She shifts her attention from me to Maddox.

"Well? What are you two up to?"

"We were just going out to get some fresh air?" I offer, the answer coming out more like a question.

Mrs. Anderson's dark eyes shift to me. "You were just outside."

"Fine," I roll my eyes, throwing away any pretense. "We're getting out of here. Happy?"

"Aly," Maddox chastises.

"What?" I look over my shoulder at him. "It's not like she doesn't know it."

"What am I going to do with you two?" Mrs. Anderson shakes her head. "One would think you'd take this seriously since you're not children any longer."

Maddox and I exchange sheepish looks, and I have to bite the inside of my cheek to prevent myself from laughing out loud. God only knows how many times we've done the exact same thing in the past.

"Fine," Mrs. Anderson sighs. "Off with you, just be careful nobody else sees you."

I lean in to hug her, pressing a soft kiss to her cheek. "You're the best, Mrs. A."

"Yeah, yeah, you only say that when I let you off the hook."

"That's what makes you the best."

Sliding my fingers into Maddox's firm hand, I give him a tug and murmur, so only he can hear me, "Run, before she changes her mind."

So we do just that. Laughing until we're out of the ballroom, and if only for a moment, my heart feels lighter. Things might be changing, but there's always going to be one constant in my life.

Maddox.

Chapter 3

ALYSSA

"Based on the measurements, you're fourteen weeks along," Doctor Jeremy says, her eyes fixed on the screen.

My tummy clenches at her words. Nervousness, unease, hope, fear are all mixing inside of me and making my stomach roll.

Fourteen weeks.

I've been growing another human inside me for fourteen weeks, and I haven't even known for most of that time.

My gaze darts toward the screen as I hold onto the edge of the exam table to steady myself. The image on the monitor is a mix of blacks, grays, and whites. I'm not sure what it should represent, but she seems to know what she's looking at—at least, I hope so.

"How have you been feeling?"

"Nauseous?" I say, but it comes out more like a question. The woman chuckles. "Yeah, I remember that phase."

"You have kids?"

I guess it makes sense; she has at least fifteen years on me, if not more. But up until this moment, I've never thought too much about pregnancy and children.

"Two boys and a girl. Couldn't keep anything down with any of them for the first three months." She looks at me, a kind smile on her lips. "Would you like to hear your baby's heartbeat?"

My baby's heartbeat.

My own heart does a flip in my chest.

I open my mouth, but no words come out, so instead, I simply nod.

Doctor Jeremy turns her attention back to the screen and presses a button. A quick *whooshing* sound fills the small room, and my throat goes dry. The sound is extremely fast, like the flutter of a bird's wings.

Thump-thump-thump-thump.

"Is that normal?" I ask, my teeth sinking into my lower lip.

"Completely. Babies usually have a much faster heartbeat than adults do."

Babies.

Warmth spreads through my chest as her words sink in.

I'm going to have a baby.

My baby.

Rationally, I knew that, but somehow hearing it from the mouth of a professional makes this whole situation real.

I'm going to have a baby.

Sitting in a little white convertible my parents bought me for my sweet sixteenth, I look at the house in front of me.

I guess now I know why Chad couldn't bother to pick up any of my calls or return my messages earlier today. He and his friends are having a damn party.

My fingers clench around the steering wheel as a wave of irritation hits me.

I could understand that the news was a shock. And in retrospect, blurting it like that in a room full of people during a charity gala wasn't one of my best decisions, but damn him. I was surprised and scared, too. I expected him to call and check in during the winter break. I wanted him with me today for support, but he's been MIA all this time.

Screw that.

Screw *him*.

I gave Chad more than enough time to process everything; now it was time to talk and figure out what the hell we were going to do about this situation because, ready or not, this baby was coming.

Just thinking about it makes a wave of nausea hit me all over again.

Cracking open a window to let some fresh air inside, I press my palm over my low belly. "You think you can give me a break, little one? Just for a teeny-tiny bit?"

How can a baby be growing inside me? You'd think that at fourteen weeks you'd be able to see something, *feel* something, but nope. My stomach is still as flat as it was before, and the only sign that something's going on is the constant puking. Oh, and tiredness. I don't remember the last time I slept so much in my life.

The doctor assured me that both things were completely normal, and I should start feeling better in the second trimester.

With one final rub over my belly, I push open my car door and get out.

The lights are on in every room of the house, and although it's cold outside, somebody left the front door wide open for people to come and go as they please. The music is playing loudly, making my ears ache.

I enter the foyer, my eyes scanning the space for my boyfriend, but no luck.

"Alyssa."

I turn around at the sound of my name and see Lucas, one of Chad's roommates, tugging at the hem of his shirt as he descends the stairs. His clothes are rumpled, a smear of lipstick is on his neck, telling me exactly what he's been up to just moments ago.

"What are you doing here?"

"Lucas," I tilt my head to the side in greeting. Blairwood might not have fraternities, but that didn't mean we didn't have our own equivalent of frat houses, this being one of them. "I'm looking for Chad. Have you seen him?"

"No idea." He rubs at his nape. "He was around here the last I saw him."

No shit. I want to roll my eyes but hold it in. "I'll go look for him."

Without waiting for an answer, I continue down the hall. There are more people than I expected for a Tuesday evening, but I guess students are trying to use the fact that it's still early in the semester and enjoy their freedom before the classes really start.

I nod at a few people I know but don't bother stopping to chat. I came here to talk to Chad, and that's precisely what I'm going to do.

I'm just reaching the end of the hallway when I spot a figure in the kitchen. No, not a figure. *Two* figures. They're hunched together, softly chuckling at something.

"Chad?" I narrow my eyes as I shift my attention from my boyfriend to the girl he's with. "Jennifer?"

They both pull apart so quickly you'd think I'd thrown a bucket of cold water over them.

Chad looks up. His eyes are wide, hair disheveled. "Alyssa. Hey. What are you doing here?"

Jennifer takes a step back, tucking a strand of her hair behind her ear as I enter the kitchen.

"I came here to talk," I say, not bothering with a greeting. I'm tired, irritated, and I just want to go home and sleep undisturbed for the next few days, preferably. "I tried calling first, but you weren't answering." I look from my boyfriend to my roommate and back. "But I guess you were otherwise occupied." I tip my chin toward them. "What's going on here?"

"We were just talking." Jennifer tries to smile, but it's clearly forced.

"Talking, huh? The last time I checked, talking didn't include my friend being pressed against my boyfriend."

Okay, maybe I'm just a little passive-aggressive, but can you really blame me?

What the hell is she doing here? And what were they talking about?

"I... We..." Jennifer's mouth falls open, but no words come out.

"Jennifer just came to check in on me since she didn't see me at the gym."

"Exactly." Jennifer lets out a little sigh of relief. I lift my brow, and her eyes drop down to avoid my questioning gaze. "I guess I'll leave you two to it."

I watch her as she leaves the kitchen, that unsettling feeling growing bigger by the second. I'm missing something, I'm sure of it. I just don't know what.

"You want to g—"

"Gym?" I ask before he can finish.

Chad seems surprised by the interruption. "Well, yeah. I go to the gym."

I raise my brow. "With Jennifer?"

"She was there one day, and we worked out together.

What's the big deal?" He crosses his arms over his chest defensively. "What did you need?"

He's hiding something. I can see it clearly now. It's in the way he avoids meeting my eyes. His throat bobs, his fingers clenching around his bicep.

And what's with Jennifer? I don't think that girl has ever lost the ability to speak. Besides, since when is Jennifer going to the gym? She hates it, and I've never heard her mention it before.

Is... Is something happening between the two of them?

"Alyssa?"

Chad's irritated tone snaps me out of my thoughts. "What?"

"Was there a point to you coming here? Do you want to talk or not?"

The need to act like a bitch, stomp my foot, and say no is strong. Instead, I squeeze my fingers and nod.

Just then, a group of clearly drunk people passes by the kitchen, talking and laughing loudly.

Chad's hand brushes against the small of my back, startling me. "Let's go up to my room."

I turn on the balls of my feet and go toward the stairs, passing a confused Lucas on my way up.

Chad's room is the first on the left, so I push open the door and flick on the light.

"What's up?" Chad asks as soon as the door is closed.

I turn around and glare at him.

What's up? Seriously? That's the best he's got? What's up?

"I'm pregnant," I say curtly, completely done with this conversation. "Not that it's anything new, really. Which you'd know if you either answered my call or, I don't know, maybe offered to come with me when I told you a couple of weeks ago?"

He rubs the back of his neck. "So the test was correct?"

I blink, but nope, he's still staring at me, waiting for an answer.

"We live in the twenty-first century, Chad!" I yell, exasperated with him. "And while there is a small chance the test could be wrong, let's be real. If it's positive, it means I'm pregnant."

Chad narrows his eyes at me. "You don't have to be such a bitch about it."

"I'm being a bitch?" I grit my teeth, trying to keep my cool.

"Yes, you're being a bitch, Alyssa!" He runs his fingers through his hair, making it stick in all directions. "I didn't want any of this."

I take a step back like he slapped me. In a way, he did. "And you think I did? I never imagined I'd be a mom before I finish college."

"Oh, please. Didn't you just complain a few weeks ago that you don't know what the fuck you're doing with your life? I have a career waiting for me, Alyssa. *Law school.* I've been accepted to Harvard. I can't have a kid now."

"Well, this kid is coming whether you want it or not, Chad!" I yell, letting my hands fall by my sides.

"You're keeping it?"

What?

My hand flies to cover my stomach. "Of course, I'm keeping it! What the fuck, Chad?"

The silence falls over us, heavy with all the things left unsaid. We just stare at one another, both of us panting hard, but neither saying a word for what feels like forever.

Slowly, Chad shakes his head. "You can't be serious."

I wrap my arms around myself tighter, as if I can protect the baby, *my baby*, if I hold it close enough. "Of course, I'm serious."

Chad just stares at me, unblinking. "I'm not doing this." He shakes his head. "You want to keep it? Fine, but I want no part in it."

"So that's it, huh?" I bite the inside of my cheek to stop the tears blurring my vision from spilling. "You don't want any part in this, and we're what? Breaking up?"

How is this happening?

"No, I never signed up for this." Chad rubs his palms over his face. "I fucking don't want any part in this. I don't get how *you* do!"

"And I did?" I move closer to the man I've been dating for the past year. I actually look at him, and the only thing I find is a scared little boy. "It might not have been my first choice, but it's my *life* now. And I'm not about to walk away from my responsibility just because it hasn't been planned, and it's easier that way."

Shaking my head, I walk around him, stopping just in the doorway, my back to him. Closing my eyes, I take a step forward. "Goodbye, Chad."

Chapter 4

MADDOX

"Yo, Mad, you coming or what?" Hayden's irritated voice greets me through the Bluetooth as soon as the call connects.

"On my way," I mutter, my eyes fixed on the road ahead.

"That's what you said thirty minutes ago," he grumbles, clearly unhappy with the situation.

"I got sidetracked in the lab. I'm in the car now."

I slow down as I come to the part of the road where there are different cars parked on the front lawn and haphazardly along the curb, blocking the traffic. The white two-story house is completely lit, loud music coming out through the open windows.

Are they for real? It's the middle of the week.

One vehicle is practically parked in the middle of the street, making it hard for me to slip by without scratching my car.

Seriously, who gave this idiot...

My thoughts drift away when I see a flash of red in my peripheral vision. Stomping on the breaks, I turn around, and sure enough, it's Alyssa. She's rushing out of the brightly lit house, her arms wrapped around her middle tightly.

I frown, looking at her more carefully.

Is she crying?

"Maddox?" Hayden calls, reminding me he's still on the line.

"What?" I ask absentmindedly, my eyes still on my best friend, who had just got to her car. She tries to unlock it, but her keys slip out of her fingers, so she crouches down to get them.

My stomach clenches with unease.

Something's wrong.

"Don't be late, or I'll leave..."

"I changed my mind," I rush out before he can finish. "Go on without me."

Not bothering to wait for his answer, I hang up and check my rearview mirrors. The road is empty. Turning on the hazard lights, I get out and jog between the parked cars until I get to Alyssa's white convertible. I have no idea why she thinks it's reasonable to drive that death trap.

"Aly?" I call out tentatively.

She looks up at the sound of her name. Those cornflower blue eyes meet mine, and it's like all the air is kicked out of my lungs. They're red-rimmed and stricken, her long lashes glued together as the tears run down her cheeks.

My fingers clench into fists at my sides. "What's wrong?"

Her lower lip trembles, and she sinks her teeth into it to stop it from wobbling. I crouch down next to her and slowly wrap my arms around her. "Did somebody hurt you?"

Aly relaxes into my touch, her arms slipping around my waist as she burrows her head into my chest. Her body molds to mine perfectly, and it's like I can finally breathe again. Every muscle in my body relaxes now that she's in my arms, knowing that she's safe, and I'll do anything to make this okay. Alyssa shakes her head no, a loud sob coming out of her.

My eyes fall closed as I hold onto her tighter, my Adam's apple bobbing as I swallow.

"Shhh..." I rub my hand over her back as I pull her closer. "It's going to be okay."

I don't remember the last time I've felt as helpless as I do at this very moment. Aly has always been the stronger of the two of us. When we were kids, and people used to bully me for being a scrawny geek, she'd be the one to step in and put them in their place. But this vulnerable and crying Aly? I've never seen her like that, and I don't know what to do about it.

"I-I-It's not." Her fingers grip my shirt. "I messed up, Maddox. I messed up badly."

Messed up? I pull my brows together, confused. *What the hell does she mean, messed up?*

I want to ask her so badly, get to the bottom of this so I can fix it somehow, but we're standing out in the cold January evening, and she's shaking in my arms.

"It doesn't matter," I run my hand up and down her back, hoping to reassure her. "Whatever it is, it doesn't matter. We'll find a way to fix it." At least I hope I'm telling the truth. "C'mon, let me drive you home. You're freezing."

I take a step back to help her to my car when I see the keys to hers are still on the ground, so I quickly pick them up and shove them into my pocket.

Aly looks around as if she's completely lost. "I can't leave my car here."

"I'll come and get it later," I promise, placing my hand on the small of her back. "Do you have something you need from your car?"

"My bag."

Nodding, I unlock her convertible, grab the bag out of her passenger seat, and close it again. I wrap my arm around her shoulders and steer her toward my car. "C'mon, let's get you home."

This time Alyssa lets me lead her to my car and help her

into the passenger side. I quickly walk around the hood and slip into the driver's seat. Aly's teeth chatter, so I crank up the heat to the max before starting the car.

The drive to her house is so short it barely takes a few minutes to pull into her driveway. My mind is filled with questions, but I keep them to myself. I'm not sure what has happened, or whose house that was, but if somebody hurt Aly...

Just the thought of it has my fingers squeezing tighter around the steering wheel.

She's fine. She's fine. She's fine.

I chant those words as a mantra, letting them be my anchor.

The driveway in front of her house is empty when I pull to a stop. Killing the engine, I jump out of the car and walk around just as Alyssa opens her door. I help her out, grabbing her bag out of her hand.

"Where's your key?"

"Inside."

I shuffle through her bag. Thankfully, it's one of those little ones, so it doesn't take me long to find the key and unlock the door.

The house is dark when we step inside. I flick on the light and look around. "Your roommates aren't here?"

Alyssa flinches slightly, but Coco, her three-year-old terrier, comes rushing from the living room and starts barking excitedly before she can answer. A small smile tugs at the corner of Alyssa's lips. The first smile on her face since I found her earlier.

She bends down and picks up the dog, lifting it in her arms.

"I missed you too, Coco," she whispers, burrowing her head into the dog's fur. I place my hands on her shoulders and guide her into the living room. Alyssa sits on the couch, pulling her legs underneath her, the puppy still safely clutched in her arms.

Anxious, I sit on the coffee table in front of her and just look at her. Usually, she'd chastise me for it but not today. The tears have dried on her face, but her eyes are still puffy and red-rimmed from crying.

"Will you tell me what happened now?"

Aly grazes her teeth over her lower lip, her gaze darting away as she shakes her head. "You'll never look at me the same way again."

"Hey..." I move closer, my hand slipping under her chin and turning her to face me. Her skin is soft and warm under my fingertips. "Do you seriously think I'd do that?"

"Okay, not really. You're too good to turn your back on your friends," Aly sniffles. "Doesn't mean I'm less scared to say it."

"Why?"

Once again, those big blue eyes fill with tears. Somehow, they seem larger than usual, more vulnerable. "Because things will change."

I struggle to swallow, the unease creeping under my skin. "Things are constantly changing."

Aly shakes her head. "Not with you and me. You're my best friend, Maddox. My constant." A tear slips down her cheek. "If you were to turn your back on me..."

My best friend.

Of course, she looks at me like a best friend. That's what we've been for as long as I can remember. The only difference is that, over time, she's become my everything, and she doesn't even see it. There isn't anything I wouldn't do for her if only she'd let me.

Some days I wish I could just shake her.

Look at me. Just look at me, Aly. I'm right here.

But I don't. Of course, I don't.

I would never forgive myself if I said it and things changed between us. If that doesn't make me a hypocrite, I don't know what does. I'm asking her to confide in me even when I don't divulge to her. Not about my feelings for her. Because there would be no taking those words back, and I'm too big of a chicken to even try. I'd rather have Aly, even if only as a friend, than not have her at all.

She shakes her head helplessly, more tears falling.

"I'm never going to turn my back on you, Aly. There is nothing you could tell me tha—"

"I'm pregnant."

Pregn— I blink and then blink once again, unsure if I heard her correctly. "What?"

She can't mean...

"Pregnant," she repeats, this time, her voice firmer.

"Are you..." *Pregnant. She's... pregnant. What do I even say to that?* "A-are..." I clear my suddenly dry throat. "Are you sure?"

"Do you really think I'd be telling you if I wasn't sure?"

"I—"

Pregnant. That one word keeps ringing in my mind. *Pregnant, pregnant, pregnant.*

Alyssa pushes off the couch and starts pacing. "It's true." She turns to me, those big eyes of hers filled with unshed tears fixing on mine. "I'm having a baby."

"H-how long have you known?"

Aly runs her hand through her hair, pushing her locks back. "I first suspected it before the Christmas gala. That's why I took the test, but I just had my first doctor's appointment today."

I think back to the charity gala. Seeing her dancing with her boyfriend and later on finding her standing outside. Alone. Cold.

"Why are you crying here?"

"I'm not crying," she protests.

My gaze darts toward the ballroom where I'm pretty sure I

saw her asshat of a boyfriend go just now. "Did I just see Chuck leave?"

She was crying that night too. And although she didn't say it outright, I'm pretty sure they fought that night. "Does Chuck know?"

"*Chad*," she corrects, an irritated undertone to her voice.

I shrug, not in the least bit interested in remembering his name.

He made Aly cry.

"Was that what you were fighting about?"

Alyssa's legs give out from under her, and she sits down on the couch. "Yes. I told him about the test. To say he was surprised..." Another shake of her head.

I grit my teeth, trying to keep my cool. *Aly. Concentrate on Aly. She's the only one that matters.* "Let me get this straight, you told him you were pregnant, and he left?"

There's a heartbeat of silence, and then...

"He wanted me to have a doctor's appointment to make sure the test was right." Aly looks away, shame and anger warring on her face. "I was just at his house to let him know the results, and he said he didn't sign up for this. He doesn't want the baby."

He didn't go with her to the appointment?

My hands curl into fists as the all-consuming rage squeezes my insides. I've never felt anything like it in my life.

Pure, blinding rage.

How could he have done that? How could he have just left her to do this alone? Who does that?

"Why didn't you say anything?" I croak out, the words barely audible.

Aly shrugs. "I guess a part of me hoped the test was wrong. No sense in worrying anybody for nothing."

"It's not nothing!" I yell.

Alyssa flinches at the sound of my voice. I don't think I've ever raised my voice to her, to anybody really, but I can't help myself. I'm so freaking angry, and if I don't get it out, I fear I might burst.

"I'm sorry." I pull her into my arms. Coco squirms between the two of us, clearly not happy I'm getting in her personal space, but I don't let go. "You didn't have to do this all alone," I whisper. My eyes fall shut as I try to relax my taut muscles.

"I don't know how I'm going to do this," Aly admits, her arm tightening around my neck, her body quivering. "What the hell do I know about being a *mom*?"

I pull back and run my fingers over her cheek, brushing her tears away. "You'll be an amazing mom, Aly."

She scoffs. "My life is a mess. How can I do it? I still don't know if the path I'm on is the right one, and I'm graduating soon. How the hell should I do all of this? Maybe Chad is right. Maybe I should just..."

She lets the words hang, not finishing the sentence. It takes me a moment to realize what she's talking about. What the fucker suggested to her.

"Is that what you want?" I ask slowly. It's hard to keep a neutral face, but I try anyway because this isn't about me. It's not about my wants and needs; it's about Aly.

If this is what she wants, I'll do everything I can to help her. If that's her choice...

"No. But maybe..."

"Then don't do it." I stop her before she can even finish. "This is your choice, Aly. You can do whatever the hell you want. If you want to keep the baby, you can do it. It'll be the luckiest baby ever, and I'll do everything I can to help you."

"P-promise?" she hiccups.

"I promise." More tears fall, so I brush them away. A lump forms in my throat, making it hard to breathe. I force my lungs to open and let the admission out. At least part of it. "I'd do anything for you, Aly."

"I don't deserve you," Aly chokes on a laugh. "God, I'm a mess. Is it too early to start blaming the hormones for my behavior?"

I use the excuse to observe her. She might look like a mess, her eyes puffy and red, cheeks pink, hair disheveled, but God, if she isn't the most beautiful woman I've ever met.

"You look gorgeous."

Another little truth.

Look at me, Aly. All you have to do is look.

But she doesn't. Instead, she gives me a playful shove to the shoulder. "Now I know you're lying."

I grab her hand and give her a squeeze. "I'd never lie to you. You're going to do great, Aly."

She turns serious, a longing smile curling the corner of her mouth. "I really hope so."

Chapter 5

ALYSSA

A light shuffling in the hallway draws my attention. I look through the crack in the doorway and see Jennifer gently closing her door.

I lean against the doorway and cross my arms over my chest. "Hey."

Jennifer's body freezes, and for a moment, I can see her debating if she should walk away or just turn around and face me. In the end, it's the latter.

"Hi, I didn't see you there," she says, her lips curling in a fake smile.

I quirk my brow at her. "I guess that's a new normal these days, huh?"

I've barely seen either of my roommates ever since school started, but even more so since I caught Jennifer with Chad the other day at his house. Coincidence? I think not.

Jennifer tucks a strand of her hair behind her ear. "I've just been too busy."

Too busy, my ass. The semester has barely started, and nobody's that dedicated—especially not Jennifer.

"Mhmm..." I take her in from head to toe. She's dressed in a dark blue dress that accentuates her pale complexion; her platinum hair falls down her back in one sleek line. "What are you up to anyway?"

"Oh, just going out."

"Going out?"

She shrugs, but I catch a flash of guilt on her face before she looks away. "Just hanging out with Miranda."

"Oh..."

Thank you so much for the invite. I bite the inside of my cheek, holding the words in.

Miranda is our other roommate. She's been the last part of our trio since freshman year, a friend. The image of Jennifer standing with Chad in his kitchen flashes before my eyes. At least I thought of them as friends, but the more I think about it, the less I'm sure of anything.

Is there something going on between Chad and Jennifer? And if so, for how long has it been going on? Was I simply too blind and too stuck in my head and missed it? Or am I just being paranoid?

It doesn't matter. You and Chad broke up; I chastise myself. *He's not worth it, and you have way bigger worries than who Chad is flirting with.*

I'm not even angry, okay, maybe a little, but mostly disappointed. Miranda, Jennifer, and I have been friends since day one at Blairwood, but we've grown more and more apart in the last year. This is just one example of the distance growing between us. I'm not sure exactly when it happened or what might have caused it. I just know it's there, the gap between us growing larger by the day.

Jennifer must see something on my face because she rushes to explain: "We were planning to invite you..."

Yeah, right, I can totally see that happening.

Not.

If they wanted to invite me, they would have done it hours if not days in advance. That's just the way we roll.

"It's fine, really." I force out a smile. "You girls have fun."

I turn my back to her and grab my lipstick, carefully applying the dark red color over my lips.

From the corner of my eyes, I can see her shift her weight from one leg to the other. "Do you have the rent? Mrs. Finley will be here on Friday."

I grab my clutch and drop the lipstick inside. "I should have it today."

Jennifer gives me a once over. "Dinner with the parents?"

"Yup."

I think I'm the only adult around here who has to have monthly dinners with her parents in order to get her allowance released from the trust fund my grandmother set up for me, but it is what it is. I keep reminding myself that it's just a few more months, and then I'll graduate.

If you don't have to take a step back because you're pregnant, the skeptical part of me reminds me.

As if I need the reminder. A lot of girls finish college while they're pregnant and even while they raise kids. If they can do it, I'm sure I can too.

But first, I have to survive this dinner. To say my parents and I don't see eye to eye would be an understatement. I'd usually take Chad with me as a buffer since my parents adore him, but that won't be possible any longer.

Since our conversation earlier this week, I've been checking my phone every now and then. I'm not even that upset that he broke up with me. If I'm being completely honest, a part of me felt relieved. However, the other part of me wanted him with me because being pregnant and alone is scary as fuck.

I'll do everything I can to help you. I promise. I'd do anything for you, Aly; Maddox's words ring in my mind. He's seriously the best friend a girl could ever ask for, and I know what he said is true. He'd do anything for me, but how could I ask that of him? This is my mess. No, not just a mess. This is another human being we're talking about here—*my baby*.

How can I expect him to help me with another man's baby? I can't, that's how.

And let's not forget the fact that I'll have to tell my parents what's going on sooner rather than later. If it's to believe all the mom sites I've been browsing since I saw that plus sign, I'll probably start showing soon, and since I can't avoid them until I give birth, 'cause monthly dinners, I'll have to tell them. Just the thought of it has my blood turning to ice.

Seriously, could this become an even bigger disaster than it already is?

"Aly, about the other day..." Jennifer's words snap me out of my thoughts.

"It doesn't matter." There's no way I'm opening this can of worms, not now. I run my hand through my hair, letting the locks settle more naturally around my shoulders. "I should probably get going. I don't want to be late."

"I..." Jennifer shakes her head. "Yeah, sure. I guess I'll see you later."

I turn my back to her. "Sure."

I fiddle with my bag as I listen to her footsteps disappear down the hallway. Only when I hear the front door close do I let out a sigh of relief.

Closing the clutch, I wrap my fingers around it tightly, so it doesn't fall out of my grasp since my palms are clammy with nerves.

One down, one more to go.

I've never liked dinners with my parents, but there's something incredibly nerve-wracking about tonight.

You don't have a choice.

KISS TO BELONG

I settle my hand over my stomach. At least I haven't thrown up the last three days. I'm not sure if it's the vitamins the doctor gave me or the fact that I'm in my second trimester, but whatever it is, I'm thankful.

I give myself one last glance in the mirror. I'm still a little pale, but at least I look and feel half-human. I'll take it because I'll need all the shields I can get in order to survive this dinner.

I look down at Coco, who's sleeping at the foot of my bed. As if she can feel me watching, she peeks through one eye and looks at me.

I give her a little scratch behind her ears. "It's now or never, Coco."

Why couldn't it have been never?

The thought echoes in my brain as I shove the food back and forth on my plate. I was hungry when I got to the restaurant, a surprise in itself, really. Since all I've been doing until now is throwing up everything that I put in my mouth, however, that changed as soon as I sat at the table with my parents.

"Stop fussing with your food," my mother hisses, giving me a stern glare across the table. "I'm not even sure why you ordered that; it's not like you need all the calories."

"Gee, thanks, Mom."

Keeping my gaze on my plate, I roll my eyes and stab a fork into a piece of chicken more forcefully than I probably should before pointedly bringing it to my mouth. My mother's red lips press in an even harder line, the wrinkles around her eyes growing deeper.

Even though she's in her early fifties, Lucinda Armstrong Martinez could probably pass for somebody ten years younger. Her platinum hair is cut in a short bob and touched up exactly every three weeks. Her makeup is neutral, with just a tad of eyeshadow and mascara, some foundation, and her signature red lipstick. Family pearls hang around her neck, shining brightly against the black Versace dress.

"I'm just saying it as I see it. You've gained weight."

No, I most certainly have not.

At least not based on what I saw when I went to my doctor's appointment. But if you asked my mother, I could always stand to lose some weight. From an early age, she's tried to make me a younger version of herself—a skinny debutant with a fake smile and a sharp wit. At least one of those things is true, although not the way she intended it to be.

Mom wraps her fingers around her glass of wine and takes a long sip, draining the rest of it. Thankfully, the waiter comes almost immediately, not that either of my parents notices, and refills our glasses. God forbid she actually slows down on the wine. "Where is Chad again?"

The question makes the chicken feel heavy in my stomach. So much for that. She asked me that same question when I got here, and I gave her some lame-ass excuse figuring it's going to be the end of it, but I wasn't that lucky.

"No idea, probably busy." Placing my utensils on the plate, I take the napkin and carefully wipe my mouth. I don't think I'll be finishing my dinner.

"No idea?" Mom shakes her head. "No idea? Did you hear that, Bryce?"

Dad hums non-committedly. He's been glued to his phone ever since they got here. From what I've gathered from him, he's been working on a big case. "I hear it."

"Chad is an amazing young man with a bright future in front of him. You should seriously be nicer to him, Alyssa. Do you really think guys like that come around every day?" Of course, she doesn't wait for me to answer. Who cares about my opinion when she has one of her own? "No, they don't."

Since Chad is a sleazeball. I sure hope not. The last thing I need is more guys like him.

"You should keep a close eye on him, so he doesn't slip through your fingers."

Tuning her out, I look longingly toward her wine glass.

No alcohol for you, missy. At least not anytime soon.

"I have to admit I was skeptical at first. God knows you only ever brought losers home, but Chad is actually a well-mannered boy. From a good family, too. You should be more considerate of him."

"Well, fat chance of that happening since we broke up," I snap. The words were out of my mouth before I could stop them.

Well, damn. I close my eyes shut for a moment. *That escalated quickly. So much for keeping my cool.*

"You... What?!"

Mom actually looks shocked by my revelation. Her lips are parted, blue eyes wide as they stare at me.

I let out a breath, leaning back in my chair. "We broke up." The words hang in the air making the silence stretch. Mom looks at Dad and then at me, seeming lost for a moment. Even Dad finally lets go of his phone to concentrate on the conversation for longer than two seconds.

But the quiet doesn't last long. Not that I expected it to.

"Are you insane?" Mom yells. "Why would you do that? Chad is such—"

If I hear her say *an amazing young man* one more time, I think I'm going to throw up right then and there.

"Because..." I interrupt her before she can finish, but then words betray me. I pull my hands down in my lap, intertwining my fingers tightly. So tightly, in fact, that my knuckles turn white.

It's going to be okay. You have to tell them sooner or later, so you might as well get it out of the way now, right? Right!

"Seriously, Alyssa, haven't I taught you anything?"

Oh, you have Mom, you most definitely have. But I'll be damned before I turn into you.

Swallowing the knot in my throat, I look up. "I have to tell you something."

My parents watch me expectantly. The restaurant is filled with chatter: clinking of utensils against the plates, conversation, laughter, but it's all just background noise. My heart is beating rapidly in my chest, the sound echoing in my eardrums as I'm trying to find the words.

"What's going on?"

My palms turn sweaty as my stomach clenches nervously. I force my fingers to unclasp and wipe them against the side of my legs, not that it's much use.

"Aly—"

Shutting my eyes, I blurt the admission out: "I'm pregnant."

The silence that follows is so long, for a moment, I think I might have said the words in my mind and not out loud. However, when I open my eyes and find my parents staring at me with matching shocked expressions on their faces, I know that's not the case.

My fingers grip the edge of my chair. "Mo—"

"P-p-p-pregnant?" Mom stutters, her eyes wide, voice high pitched. "What do you mean, you're pregnant?"

"Just like I said." I tuck a strand of my hair behind my ear, trying to stay composed. Or at least appear so. Fake it till you make it, right? "I'm pregnant. I'm three months along, which means I'll be giving birth…"

"I know what pregnant means!" She looks around as if she's

afraid somebody will hear her, but this isn't a small-town restaurant. No, I have to drive to the next town over to meet them every time they visit. Blackwell's is the fanciest restaurant in the county. With pristine white tablecloths, porcelain dishes, crystal glasses, and nothing on the menu that's under a hundred bucks.

Mom's eyes narrow on me, fury burning brightly in her blue eyes. She lowers her voice, each word coming slowly through her gritted teeth. "How did that happen?"

"... in June." I finish, my hand falling on the table. "I'd have thought you know how babies are made since you have one of your own."

Mom grabs my hand, her nails digging into my skin. "Don't be sassy with me, Alyssa."

"I'm not being sassy, Mom." I tug my hand out of hers, angry red half-moon marks appearing on my skin almost instantly. "I'm just saying it as it is."

"Who's the father?"

"Lucinda," Dad tries, but she just glares at him.

"Don't you, Lucinda-me! Did you hear what she just said?"

A pleasant smile is plastered on his face, but I can see the hard line of his mouth. He's boiling inside, but he won't let it show. Not in public anyway. "Yes, I heard what she said, but you're making a scene."

That gets her attention. God forbid people see the real Martinez family.

Taking a deep breath, Mom turns to me. "Is Chad the father?"

"Yes, Chad's the father." I grit my teeth. "Who else would it be?"

"Knowing about your past, and since you said he broke up with you, you can't blame me for asking." Her words are a punch to my gut, leaving a bitter taste in my mouth.

Although she might not think it, I'm aware of my past. I was all over the place when I was in my teens. Defiant and rebellious. I could never meet my parent's expectations so I stopped trying and, instead, decided to act out. Dating boys I knew my parents would hate, partying all night, drinking. You say it; I've most likely done it. I wasn't ashamed of it either, but I hated when she brought it up. "What does he think about all of this? I'm sure we can fix this. I mean, it's not ideal, but if you were to get married..."

Married? Is she crazy?

"Didn't you hear what I just said? Chad and I are over," I repeat, slower this time, in case it didn't register in her mind. "And *I* broke up with him, not the other way around. He doesn't think anything since he's not in the picture."

"You..." She sucks in air, her cheeks turning red in anger. "Why would you do that?!"

"Oh, I don't know, maybe because of the fact that he left me to my own devices when I told him I might be pregnant?" I ask bitterly. "He's not interested in having a baby."

"Seriously, Alyssa? You had one job." Mom lifts one finger as if I don't understand the concept of one. "*One job* going to college. And when you started dating Chad, I thought, finally! She's finally doing something right!"

"I thought the point of going to college was to get a degree," I comment dryly.

"A real degree, not some artsy bullshit," Dad says, picking up his glass.

Mom shakes her head. "There has to be something we can do to fix this, Bryce. He can't just walk away from this."

"Chad's a smart boy." Dad takes a sip of his scotch. "He's going to law school next year, and that's not a joke. He doesn't need unnecessary distractions."

Of course, they would worry about him. But what about

me? What about my school? My life being altered? Who cares about that, right? But God forbid Chad's life changes!

Mom nods in agreement. "Besides, you two are too young to have children. We can go to the doctor and..."

"I was at the doctor's already." *Not that either of you cared enough to ask.* "She assured me everything's okay and scheduled me to come back in a month."

"Not that kind of doctor, Alyssa," Mom snaps, clearly exasperated. "I'm sure we can find somebody to get rid of this little..." She waves her hand before picking up her wine glass. "Problem."

Little problem? She can't think... But looking at my mother, I know she can. *She does.*

"I'm not going to get rid of anything." I shift my attention between the two of them. "I'm keeping the baby."

"You're not," Mom says instantly.

"Yes, I am. I've already made up my mind."

Telling Maddox the other night was hard, but a part of me felt relief. Like a weight I hadn't even realized I'd been carrying since the moment I realized I might be pregnant has been lifted from my shoulders. Knowing that I'm not alone in all of this, that there is at least one person in my corner, made it easier for me to think about all the possibilities. No matter what, I couldn't imagine myself getting rid of this baby. Just the idea of it had bile rising up my throat.

"And what are you going to do?" Mom scoffs. "Keep it?"

The way she says it, you'd think I just suggested I'd join a circus or something equally as crazy.

I lift my chin, making sure to meet her gaze straight on. "As a matter of fact, I am."

Mom pulls her brows together, or as much as she can, thanks to all the Botox. "And how do you think you're going to do that?

You're twenty-one, alone and unmarried. You don't have a degree or a job, and nobody will hire you once they find out about your..." She looks down at my stomach, and I've never been more thankful that I'm sitting down. "Condition," she finishes bitterly. "You can barely take care of yourself, much less a child."

I grit my teeth. "I've been taking care of myself just fine. I have an apartment, and I'll get my degree before the baby is here."

I have to do it. There's no other way.

Dad traces his finger over the rim of his glass. "And with whose money are you doing that?" He lifts his gaze slowly to mine. "As far as I know, we're the ones paying for your rent, your insurance, your bills, your food, your school."

I suck in a breath, not expecting him to go there. I'm not sure why. I should have. They never fail to remind me that it's only thanks to *their* money that I have all the things I do.

"If you don't get rid of this..." Mom says carefully, weighing her words, the corner of her mouth tipping up in a satisfied smile. "Nuisance, you'll leave us no choice but to cut you off."

I bite the inside of my cheek so hard I can feel the coppery taste on my tongue.

Cut you off.

Cut you...

Her words ring in my mind, matching the frantic beat of my heart.

Forcing myself to unclench my teeth and inhale deeply, I push my chair back. It scratches against the floor, making heads turn in our direction. Not that I pay them any attention since it's focused on two people sitting across from me.

I never thought they'd be able to fall lower, but this shows exactly how wrong I've been.

"Fine." I've let my parents control a lot of aspects of my life. I'm not going to let them control this. "Do it."

Chapter 6

MADDOX

"Well, that was... something." I zip up my backpack and throw it over my shoulder, looking up at my classmate, Mia.

"It was, wasn't it?"

Mia moved to Blairwood at the beginning of the year for her master's, and both this and last semester, we've had a class together. She was the new girl on campus and, even in a class full of extremely smart people, I was the loner geek. Somehow, we hit it off.

"All this business stuff is giving me a headache. Why can't I just code, you know?" Mia pulls her brows together and gives me a side glance. "Not sure why I'm complaining to you since you're just as good in business as you're at coding and design."

I push the metal frames up the bridge of my nose. "Not *as* good. But I manage, I guess."

Mia rolls her eyes at me and checks me with her shoulder. "Always so humble."

Color creeps up my cheeks at her teasing, so I duck my head in embarrassment. Mia might be my friend, but she's still a girl. And I have no idea how to act around them. If one of my roommates were here now, they'd have a field day with me. I lost count of the number of times they tried to set me up with somebody and insisted I should go out more—not like I listened.

"What are you up to?" I ask, changing the subject.

"I've got some reading to catch up on and an essay to start. Why?"

"I was planning to grab something to eat before going back to the lab to work on my project. Do you want to join me?"

Mia checks her watch. "I've got some time."

I nod. "How is your project going?"

While I'm getting my master's in computer science and am more interested in the development part of business, Mia focuses on cyber security. With the assistance of one of her professors, she's been working on improving Blairwood's security system.

I'm listening to her talk about some problem she found last week that's been bugging her as we walk to the cafeteria and pick up our food.

"Are you seriously going to eat that?" Mia looks at my plate with a look of disgust on her face.

"What's wrong with it?" I glance at my tray and pull my brows together. Neatly piled on top of my plate are rice, steak, and some steamed veggies. "I always eat this."

"Exactly! It's boring," she draws out the last word and rolls her eyes. "Why don't you try something new every once in a while?" Mia elbows me playfully, a teasing smile on her lips. "You might even like it."

"Yeah, well..." I duck my head and shrug. "I think the only thing I can get is an allergic reaction."

"You're such a party pooper, Maddox."

Party pooper—that'd be me, all right.

I shrug once again, not knowing what to say. I know I'm boring, especially compared to my friends. They're all-star athletes, popular and outgoing—my complete contrasts. Even after three years of living with them, I still don't know how we ended up being friends.

But the thing is, I like boring. It's safe.

Looking up, I scan the room until my gaze falls on the loud table in the middle of the room where my friends are sitting. Just then, Hayden looks up. He recognizes me, a smile spreading over his face as he waves me over.

"Yo, Maddox!" Hayden yells loudly, all of my friends turning around to look at me—us really.

I shift my weight from foot to foot, looking down at Mia. "You wanna join us?"

She nibbles at the corner of her mouth. "I don't know..."

"They don't bite," I try to joke like I've heard Hayden and Nixon do, but it doesn't sound the same.

Mia watches the table for a moment as if contemplating what to do. Finally, she gives her head a shake. "Rain check?"

"Sure. I'll see you in class next week?"

She flashes me a small smile. "You know it."

Mia waves and turns around, joining a group of girls I don't know. Sighing, I walk to my friends' table to find them all openly gawking at me.

Placing the tray in front of one of the last open seats, I push my glasses up my nose and sit down. "Hey, guys."

"Hey, guys? That's all you've got? *Hey, guys?* Who is *that?*" Hayden asks, looking over his shoulder toward Mia's table.

"Did you finally get a girlfriend, Mad?" This comes from my other friend, Nixon.

"Mia is just a friend," I correct, pushing my glasses up my nose. "We have a few classes together."

"A hot friend," Hayden chimes in. "In that nerdy girl way. *Ouch!*" Hayden looks down at his girlfriend, Callie. "What was that for, Angel?"

"Stop checking out other girls."

"I'm not looking at her for me." *As if that makes any sense.* Hayden throws his arm around Callie's shoulder and pulls her closer, giving me a side glance. "I'm just surprised Maddox has found himself a girlfriend."

"Mia is a *friend*," I repeat, but it's not like any of them are actually listening to me. Hayden and Callie continue bickering, completely lost in their own world.

"Seriously, who'd have known there are such hot chicks in the IT department?" Nixon shakes his head.

"Not me, that's for damn sure," Prescott, one of Hayden and Nixon's teammates, chimes in from the other side of the table.

"Exactly!" Hayden claps his hands, turning his attention back to our friends. "Which makes her perfect for him!"

I look around the table. "Can we not talk about me like I'm not sitting right here?"

"We're just trying to help you..."

Yasmin elbows Nixon. "Stop making the poor guy uncomfortable."

"What?" Nixon rubs his nape. "I'm just helping him."

I cut my steak and put a piece into my mouth as they continued their discussion as if I wasn't even there.

"You're making him blush and enjoying it," Yasmin chastises. "If Maddox says she's a friend, then she's a friend. Now stop it."

"Fine," Nixon pouts exaggeratedly. "I'm just happy for him. We didn't even have to drag him out of the house to meet this girl."

I shove some broccoli around my plate. "Trust me, if I knew you'd make such a big deal out of it, I'd have gone home."

Yasmin turns to me, smiling softly. "Just ignore him, Maddox. You know your roommates can be assholes sometimes."

Nixon sucks in a breath and wraps his arms around Yasmin,

pulling her toward him. "Is that any way to talk about your boyfriend?"

"Oh, please," Yasmin rolls her eyes. "I know your virtues and faults better than anybody."

"You weren't talking about my faults this morning when I had..."

Yasmin covers Nixon's mouth with her hands, giving him a stern look. "You better stop now, hotshot, before I ban you from my room."

I tune out the rest of their discussion, not in the least bit interested in the details of *that* particular encounter.

In the past year, all three of my roommates have paired up, and things have changed yet again.

Hayden's girlfriend Callie moved in with us at the beginning of the year. These days Nixon spends more time at Yasmin's than in his own room, and Zane is dividing his time between his new girlfriend's place and our house.

I'm happy for them; I really am. Things are just.... Different, I guess. And I'm not good with change.

"Hey." Yasmin places her hand over mine, snapping me out of my thoughts. "Have you talked to Alyssa since the winter break?"

My best friend's tear-stained face flashes before my eyes.

I'm pregnant.

I still couldn't wrap my mind around what she told me the other day. After we talked, Alyssa fell asleep in my arms. I took her to her room and covered her before leaving to get her car. The walk did me good since I was still fuming from what she told me. I knew her boyfriend, *ex*-boyfriend, was an asshole, but leave your pregnant girlfriend to fend for herself? Who the hell does that?

Just thinking about it has my blood boiling all over again. I swear if I see the guy, I'm going to punch him in the face.

"A few days ago. Why?"

Yasmin lets her lip pop. "I haven't heard from her in a while, so I'm just worried. She wasn't feeling well, but you know Alyssa."

I guess pregnancy will do that to a person. Not that I know shit about pregnancy. Or sex, for that matter. Seriously, can I be more pathetic than I already am? How many nineteen-year-old virgins are out there? Okay, probably quite a few. But how many have been waiting for their best friend to notice them as something more for years? Not so many, I'd wager.

Not that it'll happen now when she's pregnant with another guy's baby. Guys and sex are probably the last things on her mind. And after having to deal with her, piece of shit ex, it's not like I can even blame her.

"Maddox?"

"Huh?" I shake my head, pushing those thoughts away. I look up, only to realize Yasmin's been telling me something while I've been feeling sorry for myself. "What did you ask?"

"If you see Alyssa tell her to answer one of my damn calls, will you?"

"Sure thing," I say absentmindedly.

"Thanks." Pressing her mouth against Nixon's, Yasmin pushes away from the table. "Gotta go. I have a class and then a shift at Cup It Up."

Nixon leans in his chair. "Meet you after practice?"

"Sure. Later, guys!"

Muttering goodbye, I return my attention to my plate, suddenly not hungry at all.

"So, what about the hotty?" Nixon turns to me and wiggles his brows. "You planning to do something about that?"

I don't bother hiding my scowl. "I'm not doing anything. Will you leave it alone already?"

"Why not? She clearly has a thing for you." Nixon wiggles

his brows playfully. "Besides, you two would be perfect together."

Mia? A thing for me? I almost laugh out loud at the idea.

"She's just a friend."

And not the friend I've been in love with for years.

ALYSSA

"I need a coffee." I slide on the high chair, leaning against the counter, and let out a long sigh.

"Oh, look who finally decided to show up!" Yasmin props her hands on her hips and gives me a stern look. "Where's your phone? I tried calling and texting, but I have yet to hear back."

"Sorry," I rub my hand over my face. "It's been a long day. Long week really."

Yasmin lifts her brow at me. "That bad?"

Since her freshman year of college, she's been working at Cup It Up, the local café and bakery, which is around the time we met at Maddox's. First, her friend Callie started dating Hayden, and then Yasmin fell for Nixon—who are both Maddox's roommates.

"Something like that."

Yasmin takes the cup. "Your usual?"

I remember the cup of coffee I drank this morning and regretfully shake my head no. "How about some mint tea instead?"

Tea should be good, right? I rub my hand over my face. Seriously, I'm already fucking this whole pregnancy thing royally, and the baby isn't even here. Maybe my parents were right after all. Maybe I'm not cut out for this. Maybe...

"One mint tea coming right up." She moves behind the

counter to grab one of the tea bags. "What's up with you? I haven't seen you around much."

"Same old, same old."

"Are you feeling any better?"

"A little."

I look down at my phone to try and avoid Yasmin's gaze. We've become really close in the last year, and she'll see right through me. The last thing I want to do is lie to her.

I should probably tell her about the baby. I know she won't judge me, not like Chad or my parents did, but I'm just not ready to talk about this whole thing. Not yet.

"I actually talked to Maddox earlier about the same thing."

"Oh, did you?"

My phone beeps with a message. The sound startles me, almost making the phone slip out of my hand.

Get a grip, I chastise myself, opening the message.

Jennifer: Just a reminder to bring home the rent.

I roll my eyes at the reminder. She's acting as if I've forgotten to pay the damn thing in the past.

Me: I'll bring it tonight.

"I'm seeing more of him lately than I do of you." Yas places a steaming cup in front of me. I look up just in time to see her give me a pointed look. "If that's not saying something, I don't know what is."

I run my fingers through my hair, pushing the unruly locks away from my face. "I'm sorry, it's been a crazy few days."

"More like weeks." She looks at me worriedly. "Seriously, are you doing better? Did you end up going to the doctor?"

"I'm..." My tongue slides over my lower lip. "I'm getting there."

"Aly..."

"I'm fine. Really. I went to the doctor and all," I smile, hoping it reassures her. "I'm just not ready to talk about it."

Yasmin nods, understanding shining in her brown irises. Not that long ago, she had her own secrets to protect. If anybody can understand it, it's her.

"Whenever you're ready, I'm one phone call away. You know that?"

"I do."

My phone vibrates once again, making me groan.

Yasmin quirks her brow and grabs a towel to wipe the counter. "What's with that reaction?"

"It's my roommates."

"Things not going right with you guys?"

I shrug, unsure of what exactly to tell her. "I think we drifted apart recently. Ring me up? I have to go to the ATM to withdraw the rent money."

I pull out my credit card and press it against the machine. The light flashes and I put the card back in my wallet, getting up.

"Umm, Aly?"

"Yeah?"

Yas looks at the machine and then back at me. She's chewing on her lower lip, clearly uncomfortable by what she's about to say. "Your card was rejected."

My whole body freezes, an icy-cold feeling is running down my spine.

You'll leave us no choice but to cut you off.

As calmly as possible, I open my wallet and pull out another card. "Let's try this one?"

I repeat the process, but the result is the same.

"Maybe you should call your bank?" Yasmin suggests, but I'm already shaking my head as I run my trembling fingers through my hair.

You'll leave us no choice but to cut you off.

"They actually did it." A nervous laugh escapes me. "They actually did it."

When I walked out of that restaurant, I didn't think they would go through with it. This wasn't the first time my parents threatened to disown me, so I figured it was just empty words. But I guess I was wrong.

My legs feel wobbly underneath me, so I sit down on the chair. My stomach clenches tightly, a queasy feeling spreading inside my belly. I place my hand over it, giving it a small rub.

They actually went and did it.

A frown appears between Yasmin's brows. "Who?"

"My parents." I glance up and meet my friend's worried eyes. "They cut me off."

Chapter 7

ALYSSA

"Wait, they did what?"

I lift my head to face my friends, two equally stupefied faces looking at me.

Shortly after my credit card debacle Callie came into Cup It Up. Yasmin was just about to clock out and wasn't about to let me go home without an explanation, despite my protests. So we ended up waiting for her. Callie ordered coffee while Yasmin grabbed her things, and then we came to my house, where I confessed everything.

And I mean *every-single-thing.*

"They said they'll disown me if I don't get rid of the baby." I lean back against the wall with a little more force than necessary. Coco looks at me worriedly. She nudges my hand with her snout and licks my fingers until I lift it and start scratching her behind her ears.

"They can't be serious," Callie shakes her head, eyes wide.

I want to laugh at her astonishment. She was lucky enough not to have met my parents. None of my friends have, except Maddox, for which I was grateful. If they did, they wouldn't be surprised by this at all. I know I wasn't.

"Umm... I think the credit card not working is a prime example of how serious they actually are."

"I seriously don't understand it." Yasmin shakes her head. "Do you think they'll change their mind?"

Knowing my parents?

"I don't think so."

It wasn't strange that they couldn't understand it. Yasmin has two parents who love her and would do anything for her. And although Callie lost her parents to an accident a few years ago, if they were alive, they'd do anything to make her happy.

"Can they even do that?" Callie asks. "Don't you have a trust fund or something?"

"The term of the trust my grandmother left me is that my parents are the handlers until I finish college."

At least, I think so. Those few weeks after Granny Edith died were a blur. Out of all my family, she was the only one who understood me. A wild spirit, just like me. She was strong, wicked smart, and with a mouth on her that would make a sailor blush. How she gave birth to my mother, I'll never know because those two were complete opposites.

But not me and Granny. She was the closest person I had in my life and losing her had wrecked me. She was old, sure, but she had so much energy, so much life left in her, it seemed impossible that one day I'd wake up and she'd just be gone. But death doesn't care about that. Now, years later, I could appreciate the fact that she went peacefully in her sleep instead of slowly dying from a disease, but it didn't mean I missed her any less. If she were alive, she would have known what to do. She would have supported me till the end, and you can bet your ass that she'd be the first to knock on Chad's door to give him a piece of her mind.

God, how I miss her.

"At least that's just a few more months." Yasmin's words snap me out of my thoughts.

"But somehow, I have to live for the next few months, and I currently have..." I pull my bag into my lap and fish out my wallet. "Three hundred twenty-two dollars and fifty cents." I close my eyes for a moment, the reality of my situation hitting me all at once. That familiar prickling behind my eyelids is back. I hate it. I hate feeling weak, vulnerable, and helpless as I do at this very moment.

This isn't me, dammit.

I bite the inside of my cheek hard, focusing on pain instead of this vulnerability. Because if I give in to it, I'll drown, and I don't have time for that. So I push it to the back of my mind, my heart, before facing my friends. "How the hell am I supposed to support myself with that until May?"

I'm screwed.

Quite literally.

Coco jumps into my lap and lays down, letting out a long sigh. I want to squeeze her to me, bury my head into her fur, and let her comfort me.

Yasmin places her hand on my knee and gives me a soft squeeze. "We'll figure something out."

"How?" Letting my hands drop, I look at my friends. "The only job that could potentially get me the money I need and fast is if I turn into a stripper, and I don't even think that'll hold on for very long."

My hand slides over my stomach. It's still flat, but for how long?

"You should calm down; this can't be good for the baby," Callie says, shifting on the bed next to me and wrapping her arms around my shoulders.

I know she's probably right, but I can't help myself. How the hell am I supposed to do this? I'm all alone, with no money and a baby on the way.

Shit like this shouldn't be happening in real life.

"What about Chad?"

I shake my head before Yasmin can even finish. "He doesn't want to be involved. And I'm not about to beg him to change his mind."

He doesn't want us? Fine, that's his prerogative. I don't need him. I'll find a way to make this work myself.

"He sure didn't seem to mind when he was making the baby," Yas says dryly, her lips pressed in a tight line.

No, he damn sure didn't.

"Can you believe he thought I did it on purpose?"

I still couldn't comprehend he thought I'd do that. That I'd want to trap him this way. We'd dated for almost a year. Did he really not know me at all?

Callie gasps at the revelation, but not Yasmin. Her voice turns dangerously cold, eyes narrowing into tiny slits. "He what?"

"He actually thought I did it on purpose." I chuckle half-heartedly. My friends give me wary glances, but seriously, I can either cry or laugh, and I'd much rather do the latter, thank you very much. "Like I'd choose to get pregnant just months before I'm due to graduate. Hell, I didn't even plan to stay with him after that!"

That gets my friends' attention.

"Seriously?" Callie's brows furrow. "I thought you guys were solid. You've been dating for what? A year now?"

"Chad's fine. He's safe. I don't know," I shrug helplessly. "You probably think I'm crazy."

I kind of feel a little bit crazy myself.

On paper, Chad was the perfect choice. He's well educated

and mannered. He comes from a good family and has high aspirations in life. My parents love him.

Maybe it's that last thing that's been bugging me silently this whole time. Not that I don't want my parents to love my boyfriend because I do. God knows it'd make things so much easier on so many levels, but Chad is somebody my mother would choose for me.

I want somebody who'll stand by my side no matter what—somebody who'll put me first and not run at the first sign of trouble. I want somebody...

"Does Maddox know?" Yasmin asks softly.

I let out a loud sigh. "He does. Well, he knows about the baby, not about the disowning." I give my friends a pointed look. "You can't tell him about that, promise me."

Yasmin and Callie exchange a silent look.

"Do you..." Yasmin starts, but I interrupt her. "Promise me."

Maddox can't know. I've already unloaded a crap ton on him—I can't tell him this too. If he knew what my parents did, he'd be angry at them for me, and he'd try to help me. And while I know financially he can do it, I can't rely on others to help me through this. I got myself in this mess, and I have to find a way out of it, hopefully, before this baby comes.

"We won't tell him anything, please, calm down, okay?" Callie rubs at my tense back.

"Yasmin?" I look at her, waiting for her answer.

"Fine," she huffs, clearly unhappy with the whole situation. "But he could help you."

I'd do anything for you, Aly.

I know he could help me. I know he *would* help me; no questions asked. But that's the exact point. I don't want to pull Maddox in my mess because he doesn't deserve it.

"I'll figure it out."

Somehow. Some way. I have to.

"What did he say about the pregnancy?" Yasmin asks.

"He was surprised."

Callie huffs. "Weren't we all?"

"I wouldn't have even told him, but he saw me the other day after I ran out of Chad's house. I was a mess because Chad had basically told me he doesn't want anything to do with the baby and that I should have an abortion."

Yasmin mutters curses in Spanish. "What a grade-A asshole."

"Screw him. His loss."

"Exactly," Callie agrees.

"It's better this way." I place my hand on Coco's back and give her a little rub. "At least I know from the beginning he's not interested in being a part of our lives."

I'm not about to spend another second thinking of Chad. He's not worth it. Besides, I have much more important things to worry about.

"Who needs asshole Chad anyway?" Yasmin sits down on my other side and wraps her arm around me. "This baby will have the coolest aunts and uncles on this planet."

A small smile tugs at the corner of my mouth. "It sure will."

Callie shakes her head as if she still can't believe it. "You're going to have a baby."

"Yeah." I press my palm more firmly against my belly. It still feels surreal, and I've known for a few weeks already. "Now I just have to figure out how to take care of this little one." I look at Yasmin. "Any chance your boss is hiring?"

Chapter 8

MADDOX

My fingers slow down as the last few characters appear on the screen until they finally stop. I blink and blink once more, thoughts slowly starting to swirl and creep back in my mind as I gradually become aware of my surroundings.

The darkness of my room contrasts with the bright light of the monitors flashing in my face. The blinking cursor pulsates on the screen at the end of lines and lines of code that would be gibberish to most people but are more familiar than English at this point. At any point, if I were being completely honest.

Removing my glasses, I rub my hands over my face and pinch the bridge of my nose. My eyes burn since I've been staring at the screen for the past... I narrow my eyes, fighting the blurriness and giving my eyes time to adjust so I can decipher the small numbers in the corner of my screen. Damn, five hours?

I didn't even realize how much time had passed. I was supposed to just fix a few things the guys mentioned while playing the game I'm working on, but as always, I got carried away. Not that it's anything unusual. It's so easy for me to get lost in my work for hours on end. I don't need to eat or drink or even go to the bathroom; in those moments, nothing else matters.

Making sure that my work is saved, I push from the table and get to my feet. I raise my arms in the air and feel my muscles protest the movement. My back is stiff from sitting in the same position for hours. Alyssa likes to joke that if I don't take better care of myself, I'll turn into a hunchback like that dude in the Disney movie she always liked to watch when we were little. I guess she wasn't that far off either.

Shit, Aly! I was planning to check in on her.

After my conversation with Yasmin in the cafeteria yesterday, I tried calling her, but she wasn't answering. Then I started working and totally spaced out.

Grabbing my glasses off the desk, I put them on and turn around in my room, searching for my phone, but it's nowhere in sight. Sighing, I check my backpack, and beneath all the books and papers scattered on my desk—still nothing. God knows where I put it.

I guess I'll just stop by her house.

Locking my computer, I grab my jacket and slide it on before leaving my room. Low noises come from the kitchen, and when I get down the stairs, I can see my roommates huddled around the island.

Hayden peeks through the doorway, a spatula in his hand. "Look who finally decided to grace us with his presence."

"What..." Callie lifts her head from whatever she's working on at the counter. "Hey, Maddox."

"Hey, what are you two up to?" I go straight for the coffee machine. Might as well get a caffeine kick while I'm at it, but when I put my cup under and press start, nothing happens.

"Sorry." Callie lifts her cup apologetically. If somebody has a coffee addiction that can rival mine, it's Callie. "I just had the last of it. We were planning on going grocery shopping later."

"It's fine. I'll just go to Cup It Up to grab some before going to Alyssa's to check in on her."

"What's wrong with Alyssa?" Hayden asks from the stove where he's stirring something in the pan.

"She..." I start but stop, not knowing how to finish.

...*is pregnant with her douche ex's baby.* I don't think that would cut it. Besides, I don't even know if she has told anybody else she's pregnant—if she even wants to. Although let's be real, apart from leaving Blairwood until she gives birth, it's not like she'll be able to hide it for much longer.

"Just broke up with Chad," Callie chimes in, saving me from having to come up with an excuse.

At that, Hayden looks up, brows raised. "When did that happen?"

"Not that long ago." I shrug. "She's been off, and I just want to make sure she's okay."

Hayden hums non-committedly. "Yeah, I'm sure you do."

"Anyway." I rub the back of my neck, for some reason feeling self-conscious about the whole situation. "I guess I'll see you guys later."

With one final nod, I turn around and walk into the hallway.

"Have fun!" Hayden calls after me.

I don't bother replying as I grab my jacket, making sure my wallet is in the pocket before I walk outside where my Tesla is parked in front of the house.

The drive to the campus is short. Since classes had started not that long ago, there aren't many people mingling around. Parking the car, I cross the road and enter the café, the warm air hitting me in the face. The smell of freshly baked muffins reaches my nostrils, and my stomach rumbles loudly in protest.

When was the last time I ate? The hell if I remember. Maybe I could get coffee and some baked goods and bring them to Aly.

"Wel— Maddox."

My head snaps up at the sound of a familiar voice. And not just any voice. Alyssa's voice. I blink, thinking I have it wrong, and then blink again, but she's still there—standing behind the counter in the peachy fitted t-shirt with the Cup It Up logo on it, a tentative smile on her lips. Her red hair is pulled in a high ponytail, a few strands curling around her face.

"Aly, hey." I look around, confused. "What are you doing here?"

She pushes the runaway strands behind her ear, shifting her weight from one foot to the other. "What do you mean?"

What do I mean?

I tip my chin toward her. "What are you doing behind the counter? Wearing that shirt?"

"I'm working."

I pull my brows together. *Working?*

"You don't work here," I point out, feeling stupid. Just like me, Alyssa comes from a well-situated family. Not only that, but her grandmother has left her a trust fund, so she would never have to work. Instead, she usually volunteers in a dog rescue center in town.

"I do now. I needed a change." She smiles, bouncing on the balls of her feet. "What can I get'cha?"

I keep staring at her blankly, waiting to hear the punchline, but it never comes. "Are you serious?"

Alyssa sighs. "Yes, Maddox. I'm serious. Now, will you tell me what you want, or will you just stand there and gawk at me?"

"I— Sorry." I rub the back of my neck. "I'll just have black."

"One black coming right up." Aly gives me one of those blinding smiles of hers. Her mouth spreads wide, a dimple popping in one cheek and making the blue of her eyes twinkle.

My stomach clenches like it always does. All these years

and the girl still has me unnerved, like the first time I saw her back when we were just two little kids.

Even then, she was devastatingly beautiful—all that gorgeous red hair, freckles scattered over her face, and a pair of blue eyes as clear as the sky on a summer day. I couldn't wrap my mind around the fact that somebody like her would like to hang out with a nerd like me. I still can't.

Aly grabs one of the tall cups and goes straight for the pot with black coffee. She turns over her shoulder. "You should consider yourself lucky. I've messed up every girly drink that has been ordered to—"

Abruptly, she shifts her attention back to the cup and mutters curses under her breath. I follow her line of sight and see the cup has somehow tipped over, the contents spilling over her hand and middle.

"Shit."

I slip under the counter and grab the pot out of her hand, putting it on the counter before taking her hand in mine to inspect it. Her pale skin is dusted in pink and all sticky from coffee. "Are you okay? Does it hurt?"

Not giving her time to answer, I look around until I spot the sink. My heart is galloping as I pull her toward it and turn the cold water on, pushing her hand under the spray.

Aly hisses softly at the first touch of cold water on her skin. She tries to pull her hand back, but I hold it firmly under the spray. "Keep it under the water."

"It's fine, really."

"It's not fine. You burned yourself."

I take her in, inspecting her from head to toe. Or I would, but my eyes stop at the stain on her stomach. "Shit. You should probably..."

The door to the kitchen opens. Yasmin comes out, a tray of

brownies in her hand, and stops in the doorway, looking between the two of us. "What's going on here?"

"Just a little..."

"She spilled hot coffee all over herself," I say, not giving Alyssa time to finish, knowing she'll try to downplay it. "I really think you should change that shirt given the fact—"

Aly shoots me a death stare and pulls her hand out of mine. "I'm fine." She grabs the towel and wipes her hands. "It was just an accident. I'll clean it up..."

Yasmin shakes her head. "It's fine, don't worry. I'll grab a mop." She gives her a lingering gaze. "Are you sure you're okay?"

"Yeah, nothing a clean shirt won't fix. My pride, on the other hand..." Alyssa rubs her hand over her face. "God, I'm such a mess. Did Monica tell you to fire me? I wouldn't blame her if she did."

"Of course not." Yas waves a hand dismissively. "Accidents happen all the time."

Alyssa purses her lips. "I've never seen you spill anything."

"That's 'cause I've been doing this for a while. You'll get the hang of it." Yasmin takes a towel and cleans the counter, throwing the cup into the garbage in the process before pulling a new one.

"Tell that to all the poor souls who came in today and got my mess."

"Nobody said this will be easy." Yasmin fills the cup with black coffee and puts a lid on it before handing it to me. "On the house."

"Don't be silly." I pull my wallet out and hand her a ten.

Yasmin rolls her eyes, but doesn't fight me, knowing she won't win. "Do me a favor and take her home?" She tips her chin at Aly. "She's had enough excitement for one day."

Aly nibbles at her finger. An old, nervous habit of hers. "You sure this isn't just a nice way of telling me I'm fired?"

"Nope, Monica expects you here tomorrow at the same time. Dan will be here. You two will work on some easier stuff tomorrow."

"Yas, I legit just spilled a plain black coffee all over the floor and myself. How much easier can we get?"

Yasmin places her hands on Alyssa's shoulders. "It will get easier. Trust me. Now go home and get some rest, okay?"

I watch as Aly lets out a long breath and nods. "Okay."

She turns to me, and for the first time, I notice the bags under her eyes. And not just that. There's a vulnerability shining in her gaze that I don't think I've ever seen before. She's trying to put on a strong front, but she's tired and scared. "Can you drop me off at home?"

"You know it."

"I'll be back in five." With another nod, she walks toward the back.

I watch her until she's behind the closed door before shifting my attention to Yasmin. "What is this all about?"

Anger flashes on Yasmin's face for a split second before she schools her features. Not anger at me, I realize, but at something else. "You'll have to ask Aly that."

I press my lips in a tight line, unhappy with her answer, and nod. I could respect Yasmin's need to protect her, although I'm the last person Alyssa needs protecting from.

"Now, although I think you'd look pretty cute in an apron, I need you to get out of here and let me work."

"Yeah, sorry." I turn around and find a few people standing in the line, waiting to get their coffees. Pushing my glasses up my nose, I feel my cheeks heat from their attention. Crouching down, I slip from underneath the counter, just as Yasmin calls my name.

"Take care of our girl, okay?"

She knows, I realized. *She knows that Aly is pregnant.*

Something must have happened, and she told the girls. But what? What are they hiding from me?

Wordlessly, I nod.

Yasmin gives me a small smile before shifting her attention to her next customers. My fingers tighten around the cup in my hand. I take a sip, my mind still whirling.

What had happened? Why did Alyssa suddenly decide to get a job? Not that there's anything wrong with working, but if she hasn't worked all this time, why get a job now that she's pregnant and should be taking it easy? And what does Yasmin, and possibly Callie, know that I don't? Did some—

"All done."

Startled out of my thoughts, I face Aly. She changed her shirt and put on her jacket.

"Want to grab something before we go?"

Aly shakes her head. "I just want to get home and rest."

"Okay, then let's get you home."

Waving at Yasmin, we exit the café and cross the road to get to my car.

"Will you tell me what is happening now?" I ask as I slide into the driver's seat and buckle my seatbelt.

"I'd rather not."

I turn my attention to her. "Why not?"

She tilts her head back, letting out a long sigh. "Because it's embarrassing?"

I frown, turning on the ignition. "That you work?"

"That I suck at said work, and the reason I had to get the job in the first place." Aly shakes her head and quickly continues before I can ask any questions. "Can you believe I actually messed up *all* of today's orders? You'd think I'm competing for the title of the most incompetent barista. Like seriously, it's just coffee. Why is it so hard? I even messed up your order, and you drink your coffee *black*."

The way she said black, you'd think I drink Satan's drink, not coffee.

Aly grabs my cup from the holder as she talks. She takes a sip, frowning at the bitter taste. "Why you don't add cream or sugar to this, I'll never understand."

"Because it's coffee. It's supposed to be drunk black."

"Only for those who have black souls. We both know you're not one of those people." She returns the cup back to the holder. "Maybe it's better this way. I probably shouldn't even be drinking coffee."

My fingers tighten around the steering wheel. "Because of the baby?"

"Yeah," she huffs. "I should probably get one of those cliché books. *What to Expect When You're Expecting* or *Pregnancy for Dummies*."

"You're not a dummy," I protest, keeping my eyes on the road.

Alyssa chuckles, but the sound is bitter. "These days, I feel like one."

"Yasmin was right, you know. You shouldn't be so hard on yourself. You just weren't expecting it. Give yourself time."

"But I don't have time! That's the problem," Aly yells just as I pull into her driveway only to find a shiny new Toyota is parked in the driveaway. "Oh, shit!"

Killing the engine, I turn to Alyssa. Her blue eyes are wide, the lines around her mouth harder.

"What's wrong?" I look around, expecting to see somebody. Is this Chad's car? Is the asshole here to try to pressure Alyssa into an abortion? Or maybe he wants to get back together? But there's nobody around, only the car. "Who's that?"

Seriously, if that's her douche of an ex, I swear I'll punch him for hurting Aly the way he did when she's so vulnerable.

"My landlady." Aly unbuckles her seatbelt. "I've gotta take care of this. Thanks for the ride, Maddox."

I open my mouth to call after her, but she's already outside and walking toward her house.

Chapter 9

ALYSSA

Shit. Shit. Shit.

Is there such a thing as a pregnancy brain? If so, I'm pretty sure I have the damn thing. I knew there was something I needed to get done this morning when I woke up, but I couldn't remember for the life of me what it was. Then I saw what time it was, so I hurried out of the house to get to my class on time, and as the day progressed, I completely pushed it out of my mind.

There's low murmuring coming from the back of the house. I slip out of my boots and follow the sound toward the living room.

I'm not sure if I make some kind of noise, but both women turn toward me as soon as I step through the doorway.

"Finally!" Jennifer crosses her arms over her chest and glares at me. "We've been waiting for you. It's not like I told you three times that Mrs. Finley would come today. *Per usual*, I might add."

I narrow my eyes on her. "Well, I had other things on my mind. You know, like classes and work?"

Jennifer pulls her brows together. "Work? Since when do you..."

Ignoring her, because seriously, I don't need to explain myself to her, I turn to the older woman. "Hi, Mrs. Finley. Sorry for being late. This week has been a lot."

Try the last month, but who's counting?

Mrs. Finley's mouth spreads in a tight smile. I was never too sure if it was because she doesn't like me, or maybe it's the fact that she uses too much Botox. "Alyssa, so glad you could join us."

"I'm so sorry to keep you waiting. I actually meant to call you." The older woman arches one of her brows at me, waiting for me to continue. "I, ummm..." The color creeps up my cheeks as I shift my weight from one foot to the other. God, this is so embarrassing. Why didn't I call her and explain the situation? But, no, of course, I had to space out, and now I have to do it with Jennifer listening behind me. "Do you think that maybe... Umm, could you give me an extension?"

Her smile, if that could even be considered a smile, disappears almost instantly, her dark eyes hardening, so I hurry up to explain. "I'm a little short on cash this month, but I'll pay you back next month, I promise."

Even before I can finish, Mrs. Finley's already shaking her head. "I'm sorry, Alyssa, but you know the terms of the lease. I need the rent by the fifteenth of the month. No exceptions."

My stomach sinks, and the panic slowly starts to rise inside of me. "I know, but maybe..."

"No maybes." The older woman shakes her head decisively. "I've had issues in the past with students not paying rent. That's why I set the rules. I know how you young ones can be careless with your money, spending it on partying and shopping. If you can't pay the rent, I'll have to kindly ask you to move out." Her hard dark eyes meet mine, no sympathy in them whatsoever. "Today."

Today?

As in right now?

I stagger a step back. My throat closes up, making it hard to breathe. I sway on my feet, my fingers clenching and unclenching by my sides.

She can't be serious, can she? Where should I go after she kicks me out to the curb? I can't even sleep in my car because there's just no...

"What's happening today?"

My back stiffens at the sound of my best friend's voice coming from behind me.

No. No. No.

"Aly." A gentle hand touches my shoulder.

This can't be happening. He was supposed to go home. Why does he have to choose today of all days not to listen?

When I don't budge, Maddox walks around me, stopping, so he's facing me. He looks at me for a moment, those deep, dark eyes that see everything observing me carefully. "Is everything okay?"

I force a smile out. "Y-yeah, just talking."

"About?"

The leather couch creaks as Mrs. Finley gets to her feet. "What will it be, Alyssa?"

My throat bobs as I swallow, the lump so thick I can barely get the words out. "I can't get it to you today. I'm sorry."

I look over her shoulder, unable to meet her gaze. I have never felt more mortified in my life. More alone than I do at this moment.

What the hell am I going to do?

Tears start to burn my eyes, so I duck my head, not wanting anybody to see my distress.

Just what am I going to do?

Heels *click* against the wooden floor, and the tips of Mrs. Finley's shoes come in my line of vision as she comes to a stop in front of me. "Then I'll have to ask you to pack your things, and I'll be back in an hour to pick up your key."

I force myself to face her. "Su—"

"Pick up your key?" Maddox looks between the two of us. "Why?"

I press my lips in a tight line, tears burning my eyelids. "Sure," I nod at Mrs. Finley. "An hour."

"I'll see myself out." With a curt goodbye, she turns around and leaves the room.

Maddox steps in front of me, his hands gripping my shoulders. "Aly, what's going on here? Why is she coming for the key?"

I just shake my head. *I can't do this. Not here. Not now.*

Compartmentalize, Aly.

Pack first, fall apart later.

I wait until I hear the door close behind Mrs. Finley, and only then do I run out of there.

Avoiding looking at Jennifer or Maddox, I dash out of the room and up the stairs.

"Aly!" Maddox yells after me, but I don't slow down. I take two steps at a time until I'm on the second floor.

How is this my life?

An hour.

I have a freaking hour to pack my things and figure out what I'm going to do with my life. Where the hell am I going to live? And how should I pay for the place when everybody is asking for a security deposit along with the first month's rent, and I can't pay for the rent?

I'm screwed.

Completely and utterly screwed.

I wipe my face, brushing away the tears that have finally spilled.

I push open the door to my room and come to a stop. Coco looks up from the bed where she was snoozing, her tail wiggling in excitement when she sees me. She jumps to her feet, shakes, and barks once in greeting.

Crossing the room, I pick her up in my arms. "Hey, Coco," I murmur, whispering into her soft fur. "I've gone and done it now."

What will happen to Coco?

Living here was ideal because Mrs. Finely didn't mind a dog as long as she didn't make a mess, but most landlords don't want pets inside their apartments, and there's no way I can give Coco up.

I tighten my grip on my puppy.

No freaking way. I'm not taking Coco to a shelter. I'd rather live with her in my car than do that.

My breaths are coming out in short, ragged pants, white spots flickering in my vision as the panic spreads through my belly like poison.

God, I think I'm going to be sick.

I try to force my lungs to open so that I can inhale deeply, but it's useless.

"Aly!" A hand falls on my shoulder, turning me around swiftly. "What the hell is going on here?"

Even Maddox's thick glasses can't hide the worry in his big brown eyes. He cups the side of my face, his finger sliding over my cheekbone. "Why are you crying?"

I open my mouth to protest, but the only thing I manage to do is suck in a sharp breath. The move is so sudden I start choking. I bend forward, holding onto Coco for dear life as I cough.

In the distance, I'm pretty sure I can hear Maddox swear. If

I didn't try to start breathing, I'd find it funny because my best friend never swears like ever.

"Hey." A hand runs down my back, and the next thing I know, Maddox is crouching in front of me. "Look at me." Soft fingers cup my cheek, coaxing me to lift my head. "*Look at me.*"

With his free hand, he grabs one of mine and helps me sit down on the floor. Coco uses that moment to wiggle out of my arms and jumps down.

"Breathe," Maddox says calmly, placing my palm over his chest.

I try to inhale, but I can't get enough air in. My fingers spread over his chest, feeling the warmth of his body creeping from under a plain cotton tee. I shake my head—I want to, but I can't—but Maddox's having none of it.

"Breathe," he repeats and takes one deep breath in.

Damn, he's bossy.

I try to do as he says. My fingers dig into his shirt as I will my lungs to open and let the fresh air in.

"Good, now out."

We exhale together. I hold his stare, trying to follow Maddox's lead.

"Again. In."

Calmer, if only slightly, I take another breath before I let it out. I'm not sure how long we keep breathing in tandem like that. My thoughts still swirl in my head, but I try to push them back and concentrate on breathing. Concentrate on Maddox. On the way, his chest lifts and falls, those hard lines between his brows that appear when something frustrates him, the warmth of his body.

"You're doing good, Aly." He swipes his thumb over my cheek, brushing away the last of my tears. My body shivers; tingles run under my skin where he touched me.

Closing my eyes, I take one final deep breath before pulling back. "I'm sorry, I'm such a mess."

"You're not a mess."

"I'm sitting on the floor after I just had a mental breakdown. If that's not the definition of a mess, I don't know what is." I sniff and push to my feet.

I need to start packing. Mrs. Finely will be back in less than an hour, and I already had one humiliating encounter with the woman today. I'm not going to let her kick me out of the house on my ass.

"Things will get better."

I pull open my closet and grab a handful of hangers, as many as I can, pulling them closer to my chest.

"When will they get better, huh?" I turn around and walk to my bed, throwing the hangers on the mattress before facing Maddox. My eyes mist with new tears as the rage at my helplessness begins boiling inside of me. "I'm falling, and when I think I can't sink further, something happens to show me how utterly wrong I am. In a matter of days, I've lost it all. I've lost my boyfriend. I've lost what little I had of my parent's support. And I've just lost my apartment. I'm pregnant, hormonal, and the only thing I have left is less than three hundred dollars in my name. My car can't fit any of my shit, and I have a job that I'm not capable of doing, and I'm pretty sure I'll be fired from before I can even get my first paycheck. So tell me, Maddox, when will things get better?"

By the time I've finished getting it all out, I'm panting hard. Maddox's watching me with huge eyes; his lips form a little O in surprise at my outburst—an outburst at the last person who deserves my anger.

I let out a shaky breath. "I'm sorry, Mad—"

"Shit, Alyssa."

Before I can say anything else, Maddox wraps me in his

arms, and although I know I shouldn't let him comfort me, I don't have it in me to resist him.

I'm tired.

So damn tired of pretending.

Tired of pretending all is fine. Tired of pretending I'm fine. Tired of pretending I'm not scared. Tired of pretending I'm not breaking by one little piece at a time.

Just... tired.

"Your parents cut you off?" Maddox slides his hand over the back of my head. "When? Why?"

I tighten my grip on his shirt, burrowing my head more into his chest. He's warm and steady. Familiar.

"I told them about the baby," I croak out, my voice raw. "They want me to..." I shake my head, unable to form the words. "They don't want me to keep the baby. Not on my own."

"Fuck, Aly." Maddox's arms tighten around me. "Why didn't you say something?"

"It just happened the other day. I didn't really think they'd go through with it, but then I went to grab a coffee, and when I tried using my card... Well, I guess we can say I was lucky Yasmin was the one serving me."

"That's so messed up."

"Welcome to the Martinez family. We're fifty shades of fucked up."

Maddox takes a step back, his hands still on my shoulders. "Why didn't you say something? You know I could..."

I press my finger against his lips, stopping him from finishing. "This isn't your problem, Maddox."

"The hell it isn't!" Maddox yells. I take a step back, completely thrown off guard. Maddox doesn't yell. Or swear, for that matter. But before I can say something, he continues. "We're best friends, Aly. You should have said something."

"We are, but that doesn't mean I'm going to take your

money. I don't want charity." I wrap my arms around myself, rubbing my upper arms.

"And you wouldn't have offered to help me if the situation was reversed?"

"You know I would."

"Then how is this any different?"

"I don't know, Maddox." I lift my arms in the air, exasperated with the turn this conversation has taken, and let them drop by my sides. The last thing I want is to fight with my best friend. "I need to do this the right way. On my own."

"I'm not saying you can't get a job. Just let me help you until you figure things out." His gaze darts to my stomach. "Should you even be working? You're..."

"Pregnant," I finish. "I'm not disabled. I'm just pregnant. Monica is aware of that, and she's fine with it. I'll just be pouring coffee, not lifting anything if I manage to learn how to make a damn latte. Now, if you'll excuse me, I have an hour to pack my stuff before Mrs. Finley comes to get her key."

An hour before I'll be left to my own devices.

Homeless.

An hour before I'm homeless.

I look over the clothes on my bed—all the designer stuff mocking me.

You can do this, Aly. You'll figure it out.

Taking a step back, I go back to my closet and get out my suitcases.

Maybe I could sell some of this stuff. God knows I won't be able to wear it anytime soon.

"What are you going to do about a place to live?"

I pull the suitcase by the bed and unzip it. "I guess I can sleep in my car until I figure it out or something," I shrug, putting all the bravado I can muster in my voice. I grab the first hanger and look over the Gucci dress. I guess I could at least get a couple of hundred bucks for it.

"Are you insane?" Maddox yells so loudly my head snaps up.

His cheeks are red, eyes blazing. I don't think I've ever seen Maddox angry like this.

"You heard her. I can't stay here. And since I don't have money to pay for my rent, where do you expect me to sleep?"

"Not in the damn car, that's for sure. Do you even know how dangerous that can be?"

"Well, if you have any better ideas, I'm all ears, but until then, I really need to pack."

I turn around to go over the pile of clothes and separate it into two sections, but Maddox's next words stop me in my tracks.

"Come home with me."

Chapter 10

MADDOX

"Come home with me." The words are out before I can overthink it.

I'm not the only one surprised. Aly turns around abruptly, her wide eyes meeting mine. "You can't be serious."

The way she says it, you'd think I suggested she goes running around campus naked, or something equally as crazy, instead of coming to live with me.

Aly. In my house.

My throat tightens as the suggestion settles in my mind. But seriously, the more I think about it, the clearer it is.

That's it, the perfect solution.

"Please tell me you're not serious, Maddox."

"But I am." *Why doesn't she see how perfect this is?* "You need a place to stay, and I have a house. If you don't want me to pay for your rent, and I'm not planning to let you sleep in your car, this is the only real solution we have."

Alyssa shakes her head. "Your house is already full."

I guess she has me there. The house has four bedrooms, one for me and one for each of my roommates.

"Nixon basically doesn't sleep in his room," I wave her off, but Aly is apparently having none of it.

She crosses her arms over her chest, her chin tilting upward defiantly. "That doesn't mean you can kick him out!"

I run my fingers through my hair, exasperated with her. "I'm not kicking anybody out. I'm just pointing out that he's barely home as it is."

Why is she making this so difficult? Aly can't really think that I'd let her sleep in the damn car or that any of our friends would allow it! Really, if they knew what was going on, I'm sure they'd agree with me wholeheartedly.

"Then where do you expect me to sleep? On the couch?" Her nose scrunches at the idea. "Because sorry to disappoint, but I'd rather sleep in my car than on that thing. God knows who all slept on it and if that's the only thing they did."

That she might be right about.

Although I'm not one for parties, I've been to a few the guys threw at our house, and sometimes things got pretty wild.

And if we want to be technical about it, all the bedrooms are occupied. Nixon might not sleep every night at the house, but he and Yasmin are around half the time. Callie moved in with Hayden at the beginning of the school year, and Zane is dividing his time between our house and his girlfriend's dorm. Still...

Aly puts her hand on my shoulder, snapping me out of my thoughts. "I really appreciate the gesture, but..."

I push my glasses up my nose. "You could take my room."

I mean, how bad can it be sleeping on the couch? It would be only for one night, and I could pay somebody to get it deep cleaned in the morning or something.

"I'm not throwing you out of your own bed!" Aly protests, stomping her foot.

"You're not throwing me out of anything." I let out a sigh.

"You can try to protest all you want, Aly, but you're *not* sleeping in your car. So either it'll be the couch or my bed, which one is it?"

Her lower lip wobbles, tears filling her eyes. No matter how much it hurts to see her this upset, I hold my ground. I'm not giving into this.

"There is always the option that you let me pay for your rent when the landlady comes back." I lift my brow in challenge, waiting.

That does the trick. Aly's eyes narrow at me. The tears are still glistening on her eyelids, but at least the sadness is replaced by anger. "I'm not taking your charity. I got myself into this mess, and I'll find a way out of it."

"It's not charity, and I don't doubt that for a second. I've known you my whole life, and I'm aware of how stubborn you can get when you set your mind to something. Remember that pageant show your mom wanted to force you into?" I shake my head as the image of a seven-year-old Aly pops into my mind. I was only five at the time, but I'll never forget that day.

"Oh my God!" Aly groans and buries her face in her palms. "Don't even remind me. That was awful."

"It wasn't that awful." Aly cut her own hair in protest of her mother forcing her to participate in one pageant or another. Alyssa cried all the while doing it, but she did it regardless. "I think I still have that picture of you somewhere," I tease.

Her hands fall down instantly, and she glares at me through narrowed eyes. "Maddox Anderson, you better not pull that awful picture out if you're not planning to burn it for eternity."

"And miss seeing that cute face? I don't think so."

"I looked hideous."

"I don't remember it like that." Even with her hair chopped unevenly, and tears staining her face, she was the most beautiful girl I'd ever encountered. Sometimes I think that particular moment was the one when I realized I loved Alyssa Martinez.

"You don't count."

"Maybe. However, I know what it looks like when you set your mind to something. I know you'll figure this out, but let me help you in the meantime. Just until you get your feet under you again."

"Maddox..." She sighs, her eyes taking in the mess that's her room. "Fine, but only until I get my shit figured out. I'll try and sell some of these. Get some fast cash. It's not like I'm going to wear them much longer anyway."

"Okay," I agree.

She narrows her eyes suspiciously. "That was fast."

I shrug, trying to play it off. "I'm just happy you've seen reason. C'mon, let's get your things."

ALYSSA

"You're seriously moving out?"

I turn around and find Jennifer standing in the doorway, looking at the half-empty space. I just packed the last suitcase, and Maddox took them downstairs to his car. In the end, to make this whole thing faster, I just shoved everything inside. Once I'm at Maddox's, I'll have to go over everything in peace and see what's worth selling. Even if Monica lets me stay at Cup It Up, it'll be a while until I get my paycheck, and what little I have of my money is slowly running out. I might have allowed Maddox to help with my accommodation *temporarily*, but I'm not about to accept any more charity than that.

I continue putting books into my backpack. "You were there when she told me to pack my bags."

"Well, I figured this is all a joke. Can't you like, I don't know, call your parents or something?"

I'd rather die, thank you very much. But instead of saying it, I opt for a more neutral answer. "We're not talking any longer."

Jennifer frowns. "Why?"

Pulling the zipper more forcefully than necessary, I drop the bag onto the bed. I might as well say it now. It's not like I'll be able to hide it much longer anyway. "Because I'm pregnant, and they don't want me to keep the baby."

Jennifer's eyes widen in surprise. "You're... what?"

Her gaze falls from my face down to my stomach, her mouth hanging open.

"Pregnant," I repeat, making sure to enunciate every single syllable.

Her head snaps up. "You're joking?"

I raise an eyebrow. "Do I look like I'm joking?"

"I..." She clears her throat, suddenly looking anywhere but at me. "W-what are you going to do about it?"

I grab my makeup bag from the bed where I left it and head toward the door. "What do you mean what am I going to do about it? I'm keeping the baby."

Jennifer moves out of my way, and I go across the hall toward the bathroom. Since she found this house the summer before our sophomore year of college, she was the one that got to keep the master, while Miranda and I shared the hall bathroom.

"But... What about the father?"

Slowly, I look up from the drawer I've started emptying. "What do you mean, what about the father?"

Color creeps up her cheeks. "Is it..." Her tongue darts out to wet her lips. "Is it Chad?"

"Of course, it's Chad!" I shove the drawer back with more force than necessary and glare at her. "We've been dating for almost a year. Who do you think would be the father?"

"I don't know. I'm just asking."

"You don't know? Or you don't *want* to know?" I cross my arms over my chest and actually look at her. "What was really happening that day I got to Chad's house and saw you together, Jennifer?"

"What do you mean? We were just talking, that's it."

But as she says those words, she looks away, not meeting my eyes, and that nagging feeling that didn't leave me since I saw them in his kitchen is back in full force.

"You seemed awfully cozy to be just chatting. Is there something going on between you two?"

"It's not like that. We're just friends."

I just look at her. I want to believe her—I do. Last year, the thought wouldn't even have crossed my mind. Jennifer and I had similar opinions on many things, clothes, makeup, movies... Never guys, though. But I can't escape that tingling feeling at the back of my neck. Doubt.

Before I can address it, she asks: "Did you tell him?"

I grit my teeth, irritated with her questioning. "Yes, I told him, not that he cares either way. He didn't sign up for this. And that would be an exact quote. Do you have any more questions, or can I pack?"

"You don't have to be such a bi—"

"Hey, Aly." Maddox appears in the doorway, startling us both. He looks from Jennifer to me, clearly noticing that he interrupted something. He pushes his glasses up his nose. "What else do you need me to take to the car?"

"I put my books and school stuff on the bed. And all of Coco's stuff is in the dog bed."

"Okay."

With that, he's gone. Jennifer looks after him while I turn my attention back to the cabinets, quickly emptying my shelves.

"Where are you going to go?"

"Maddox's." I rub the back of my neck. "Until I get on my feet."

Which I really hope is sooner rather than later. I have six months to get my shit in order before this baby comes; just six more months.

Even thinking about it has my stomach unsettling. Or maybe it's the baby.

I press my palms against my stomach and send up a silent prayer. *Please, please, please don't make me hurl.*

"Couldn't he have given you money so you can stay here?"

"And why would I do that, Jen?" I lean against the counter and look at her. The girl I've been best friends with since orientation week and who now feels like a stranger to me. "Why would I want to stay here? So I can watch you hook up with my ex?"

"We didn't hook up!" She protests. "Yes, we've talked more recently, I'll give you that. But he told me that you guys were having issues. He told me you two were broken up."

"Issues? The only issue we have is that he was fine having sex without wrapping it up, but not so fine when I told him I was pregnant. And no, we weren't '*broken up.*'" I draw the air quotes in case the sarcasm in my tone isn't clear enough. "Not that it matters. You were my friend, and he's my *ex!*"

Jennifer huffs. "Like you cared who you hooked up with."

My body stiffens. "What the hell does that mean?"

"Oh, please, Aly." Jennifer rolls her eyes. "Let's not play games. You were the biggest party girl on campus the last few years."

"I might have partied," I grit through my clenched teeth. "But I sure as hell haven't slept with unavailable guys." Making one last sweep of the room to ensure I packed all of my things, I grab my bag. "It doesn't matter. I'm leaving, and you can do whatever the hell you want." I stop just as we're toe to toe. "But if I were you, I'd be careful when it comes to Chad. He doesn't like to own up to his responsibilities."

Shoving past her, I get into the hallway just as Maddox comes back up the stairs, Coco running after him.

A soft smile spreads over his lips. "She didn't like it when I took her bed."

"She's possessive like that."

"I think she just might be worried you'll leave her behind."

I crouch down, let the bags drop on the floor, and wrap my arms around Coco. Pulling her to my chest, I bury my face into her soft fur. "Not a chance in hell."

"You done?"

Brushing a kiss against Coco's head, I put her on the ground and pick my makeup bags up. "Yeah, this is the last of it."

"Here, let..."

I clutch them closer to my chest, giving him a warning glare. "I'm quite capable of carrying this on my own. But thanks for taking care of the rest of the things."

"No problem." His gaze darts to my room. "Wanna go and check if you packed everything?"

Nodding, I go back inside. I give one last look to the room that's been my home for the past two and a half years. The knot in my stomach grows tighter, but it has nothing to do with all I'm leaving behind, but with the uncertainty of the upcoming months.

"You good?" Maddox wraps his arm around me, rubbing my upper arm. I lean into his touch, letting his familiar body hold me as I let out a long breath. "Yeah, I'm good."

"Okay, then. Ready to go?"

I nod. "C'mon, Coco. Let's get out of here."

Chapter 11

ALYSSA

Pulling my car in the driveway, I watch Maddox's Tesla disappear into the garage attached to the house.

I kill the engine, but my fingers stay glued to the steering wheel, my stomach rolling uncomfortably. If it's to be judged by the nerves, you'd think this is the first time I've been to Maddox's house, but something about this time feels different.

Maybe the fact that you're moving in with your best friend?

But it's not just that. It's telling everybody in there what has happened. And *everybody's* in there. I saw a glimpse of Nixon's BMW in the garage, Hayden's truck is parked in his usual place by the curb, and I'm pretty sure I spotted Yasmin's car down the street too. All the people that I've become close to in the last year are inside that house, and they have no idea what's happening. Sure, they're my friends, but I didn't want to disappoint them. Or even worse, have them *pity* me.

"You can do this, Aly," I mutter softly. Maybe it's better this way. If they're all here, it'll be like pulling off a band-aid. Fast, slightly painful, but at least I'll have to do it only once. Right? *Right?!*

As if she can hear my thoughts, Coco tips her head, her

tongue lolling out on the side. "Right, Coco?" I rub her ears. "It's going to be okay."

She barks once, her tail wiggling in excitement.

"If you say so."

Movement in front of me catches my attention. Maddox is coming toward us, the garage door closing behind him. I let out a shaky breath and force my clammy fingers to uncurl. Before my car door fully opens, Coco is already jumping out and running toward Maddox, who crouches down to pet her.

"Missed me already, Coconut? It's been just a few minutes." He laughs as she barks excitedly at him. She jumps up, leaning her front paws against the side of his leg, and starts licking his face like her life depends on it. "Okay, okay," Maddox laughs, pushing her away. "I get it. I missed you, too." Maddox lifts his head that smile still on his face as his eyes meet mine. "You good?"

"Yeah." I push a strand of hair behind my ear. "Are you sure you want..."

"I already told you, I'm sure." He scoops Coco in his arms and gets to his feet. "C'mon, let's get you two inside, and then I'll bring your things upstairs."

The need to protest is strong, but I bite the inside of my cheeks, holding the words inside. "Thanks, Maddox."

He smiles and wraps his arm around me. "What are friends for?"

At least that's one department I've lucked out in.

Maddox leads me toward the front door. At this point, I'm not even sure if he's holding onto me because he wants to or because he's scared I might bolt. Not that I have anywhere to run. What little I have left in my name is divided between his trunk and mine, and he has my dog, too.

The noises and laughter come from the kitchen as soon as we step through the threshold. Maddox lowers Coco to the ground, and she instantly dashes toward the kitchen, barking excitedly. Taking off my jacket, I put it on the hanger in the foyer, slowly counting.

One. Two. Thre—

The conversation comes to a halt.

"What the..." somebody mutters as Coco's barking grows louder.

"Is that a dog?"

"Who brought a dog?"

"That's Coco!" Even more questions from the group follow Yasmin's yell, but she ignores them all. Not even two seconds later, her curly head pops through the kitchen door. "Aly! I knew it was Coco." She looks from me to Maddox and back, her smile falling a little. "What's going on? Is everything okay?"

"Yeah..." Maddox nudges me forward. I glare at him but move toward the kitchen. As we step inside, all heads turn in our direction, a mild curiosity in their gazes.

Everybody's in the kitchen. Callie is sitting on Hayden's lap at the table. Zane and Spencer, one of his hockey buddies, are next to them, while Nixon stirs something on the stove.

"Hey, guys." I lift my hand and wave.

Yes, *wave*.

Shoot me now.

"Maddox, if you wanted to get a dog, couldn't you have gotten the real deal, not this stuffed animal?" Spencer jokes, looking down at Coco. As if she can understand exactly what he's saying, she goes straight for his shoes, biting into his laces, which only makes him laugh harder.

I shake my head. "Now you've offended her."

Spencer lifts his gaze. "I guess I have that effect on some women."

"More like all women," Zane mutters as he gets up and goes toward the fridge.

"Hey now!" Spencer protests. "Do I have to remind you that just a few days ago you were a sad sap because you thought Rei was too good for you?"

Zane looks over his shoulder at his friend. "She's still too good for me, but if she wants to believe the best in me, who am I to tell her no?"

"You guys are clueless," Callie shakes her head, pulling Coco up in her lap. The dog ignores her and goes straight for Hayden, licking his nose. "Girls don't need the best guy out there. We just need a guy who'll love us with all his heart and put us first."

"Exactly," Yasmin nods in agreement. "So, what brings you two here?" She gives me a pointed look. "I figured you'd go home and get some rest."

I rub the back of my neck, my muscles feeling stiff under my touch. "Well, about that..."

Before I can come up with a way to explain what's going on, Maddox does it for me. "Alyssa will be moving in with us."

So much for finding the right words.

You'd think he just threw a bomb because the silence that follows is almost deafening. Even Coco is quiet; her head tilted to the side as she looks at me.

Maddox's roommates exchange a silent look that makes me shift my weight from one foot to another.

"It's just for a little while," I say quickly to reassure them. "Until I find a new place to live."

Maddox steps in front of me, turning his back to his roommates. "It's going to be for as long as you need it. I mean it, Aly." He crosses his arms over his chest and gives me a pointed look. "I don't want you working yourself to the bone. It can't be good for the baby."

My eyes fall shut, and at this moment, I'm grateful to have

Maddox's tall frame in front of me, shielding me from the reaction of our friends at the bomb that he just dropped.

"Wait, what?" Nixon asks.

"A baby?" This comes from Spencer.

"I'm pretty sure I heard him say baby," Hayden mutters.

"When did Maddox become a baby daddy..."

The pressure at the back of my head grows along with the tones of their voices. I gulp down the lump in my throat. My mouth feels dry, but I force the words out. "Maddox is just helping me out."

Even though my voice is low, everybody stops talking.

I move around Maddox so I can face our friends. "I'm pregnant, yes, but Maddox is just trying to be a good friend. He's not the father."

"Forget about that." Callie waves me off and gets off Hayden's lap. "What happened to your place?"

I look down at my clasped hands. My fingers are intertwined so hard the knuckles have lost all the color.

"What do you mean, forget about it?" Hayden asks her. "Did you know about it?"

Nixon rolls his eyes. "Of course, they knew about it, you dumbass. They're best friends."

I guess I might as well get it all out in the open now and be done with it. "My parents cut me off," I shrug, trying to play it off. "When they found out about the pregnancy. And my landlady doesn't do extensions. Since I just started at Cup It Up, I won't be getting paid for a while. That's if I manage to keep the job in the first place."

If I thought the silence was deafening before, it has nothing on it now. It's so quiet you'd be able to hear a pin drop.

My head drops down.

God, I hate this.

I hate feeling this exposed—this vulnerable. I hate having to explain myself to people. Even the people I care about.

"What about your boyfriend?"

My head snaps up at the question, and I find Nixon's blue eyes fixed on me.

"He's out of the picture."

"Son of a bitch," somebody mutters quietly. Hayden, or maybe Spencer, I'm not sure.

"Anyhow, it doesn't matter. I'll get through this. I just need..." I shake my head. "Time, I guess."

Room to breathe wouldn't be bad either.

Yasmin wraps her arms around me and pulls me in for a hug. "It's going to be okay, Aly."

Tears burn my eyes. I blink them away, refusing to let them fall. "Yeah, I hope so."

The lie slips easily from my lips. Maybe if I say it enough times, I'll make it come true.

"Did you eat anything?"

I shake my head no. "I'm not that hungry."

"You have to eat. For the baby." Yasmin pushes me toward the table. "How about I make you some soup? Or maybe a sandwich?"

She doesn't wait for me to answer, just pushes me down in the first open chair and goes to the fridge.

All the guys are still watching me. "If you don't want me to stay here, I completely understand..."

"I'm fine with it," Hayden says quickly. "We were just surprised for a moment, that's all."

You and me both, buddy. You and me both.

Nixon puts a glass of orange juice on the table in front of me. "Me too."

Zane takes his seat next to Spencer. "Any friend of Maddox's is welcome."

Spencer nods. "I agree."

"Dude." Nixon slaps him on the shoulder with a rag. "You don't even live here."

"What?" He lifts his arms in defense. "I wanted to feel included."

New tears come. God, I hate these hormones. "Thanks, guys," I croak out, pushing back all the feelings that are swirling inside me.

"Don't worry about it." Callie wraps her arms around my neck. "We'll take good care of you two."

Coco barks from her spot on Hayden's lap, making Callie laugh. "Okay, you *three*. No need to get your tail all tangled up."

Seemingly content with that, Coco curls up on Hayden's lap.

"I really appreciate it. I'm not sure what I would have done if it weren't for you guys."

"Hey, what are friends for?" Yasmin nudges me in the side, putting a plate of soup on the table. "Now eat. You can't grow a baby on an empty stomach."

Chapter 12

MADDOX

"Let me get this straight. She told him she's pregnant, and he said he hadn't signed up for it?" Nixon asks, his voice growing darker by the second.

"That's what she said," I mutter, opening the trunk.

Once Aly was seated and finally started to eat with the girls fussing over her, I asked the guys to help me carry her stuff up to my room. Spencer had to leave to meet his tutor, but the rest of the guys jumped at the opportunity to help.

Or maybe they just wanted to gossip since as soon as we were out of earshot, they demanded more information.

"What an asshole," Hayden says, his face grim. "And she had signed up for it? Like what the fuck, dude? Grow a pair, and own up to it."

That's my thoughts exactly, but I don't bother to point it out. I'm still too riled up about the whole situation, and with everything that has happened today, my fingers are itching to slip into gloves.

Nixon just shakes his head. "I knew he was a tool, but this is the next level."

KISS TO BELONG

I guess I can sleep in my car until I figure it out or something.

Alyssa's earlier words still ring in my mind. If I hadn't stayed and intervened, she would have done it. She would have actually packed her things and slept in her car. God only knows where.

Just the thought of it makes my teeth clench.

What if somebody saw her? What if something happened to her, and there was nobody around to help?

All the possible worse-case scenarios start running through my head, one after another. If anything happened to her...

A hand lands on my shoulder, startling me out of my thoughts. I turn around to find Zane's concerned eyes watching me. "Hey, how are you doing?"

I rub my forehead feeling the headache building between my temples. "I'm fine."

"Are you sure?" Nixon crosses his arms over his chest. "This whole thing is messed up, dude. And we all know how you fe—"

"Aly is my friend," I interrupt, not wanting him to say it out loud. I might have never voiced my feeling for Alyssa, but my friends aren't stupid. Everybody can see how I feel about Alyssa. Well, everybody *but* Alyssa. "Yes, the whole thing is messed up, but it's ten times worse for Aly." I meet my friends' gazes. "Thanks for letting her stay."

"Hey, what are friends for?" Hayden slaps me on the shoulder; his eyes fall to my trunk. "Holy shit, how much stuff can one girl have?"

I give him a warning look that has him lifting his arms in defense. "I'm just asking."

"Just don't say it in front of Alyssa." I grab the first box out of my trunk. "She's already talking about selling some clothes, and God knows what else."

"Her parents really cut her off?" Zane asks, grabbing one of the suitcases.

I think about Alyssa's parents and how hard they've always been on her. "They're sure capable of it." I shake my head. "But for them to demand she get rid of the baby..."

"That's so messed up."

"Especially since they have the means to help her." Nixon shakes his head.

He's right about that. It's not like they couldn't afford it or something. But this wasn't about money. It was about appearances, and that mattered more in our world than anything else.

My fingers tighten around the box in my hand. "C'mon, let's get this over with."

Each of the guys grabs something from the car, and together we start toward the house.

"Where do you want us to put it?" Zane asks from the doorway.

"My room."

All the movement stops, the garage suddenly turning quiet. I continue walking toward the door, but Zane's not moving. His brows are raised so far up his forehead they almost touch his hair. "*Your* room?"

"Yes, my room." I look at my friends, bewilderment clearly written all over their faces. "Where did you expect her to sleep?"

"I don't know... It's just, do you think that's smart? The two of you in the same bed?"

I look over my shoulder and glare at my friend. "I'll take the couch until we figure something else out. Can we please get to work now? There's more stuff in her car."

"Of course, there is," Hayden mutters.

"I think I finally feel human again."

I look up from the book I've been reading and do a double-take. Alyssa's standing in the doorway of the ensuite bathroom, her hair pulled in a topknot, and her face clean of makeup. But that's not what's making my mouth go completely dry. No, that's due to the fact that she's wearing just an old, worn t-shirt. It reaches mid-thigh, leaving her long legs entirely bare.

I gulp down, the motion so hard, I wouldn't be surprised if I swallowed my tongue.

I'm not sure why I'm even surprised. Alyssa has always been beautiful, but seeing her like this—straight out of the shower, the hair at the nape of her neck curling from the steam in the air—is different.

Shifting in my seat, I close my book and put it in my lap, not even bothering to mark the page where I was.

Oblivious to the effect she has on me, Alyssa crosses the room and hops onto the bed, curling her feet underneath her. "Who would think that a little food and a shower is all a girl needs to feel decent?"

My eyes dart to her legs. The shirt has risen up even higher. So high, I can see freckles covering her thighs.

Get a grip, Anderson, I chastise myself, shifting in my seat.

I clear my throat, but the words still come out rough. "I'm glad you're feeling better."

"Thanks for letting me crash. I really mean it, Maddox, if it wasn't for you..." She shakes her head. "Thank you."

"You don't need to thank me. I already told you, you're my best friend. There isn't anything I wouldn't do for you."

"I'm going to pay you back, I promise." Aly places her hand over mine, the one on top of the book covering my hard-on, giving it a hard squeeze.

Seriously?

"I don't need you to..." I shut up when I see her glaring at me.

She tilts her chin upward in that stubborn way of hers. "I know I don't need to, but it's important to me."

"Okay," I finally give in. "But not before you're ready. I mean it, Aly."

"Not before I'm ready," she agrees.

I nod and gently pull my hand out of hers, getting to my feet.

Distance, I need distance.

"I think I'm going to take a shower."

Without waiting for an answer, I grab a pair of sweats and a shirt and go to the bathroom, not stopping until the door is firmly closed behind me. I lean my back against the hardwood and tilt my head back, slowly letting out a long breath.

My heart is beating a mile a minute, blood pounding in my eardrums. Every muscle in my body is stiff like a string.

Get a grip, dude. Aly needs a friend right now. A friend.

Pushing off the door, I drop my clothes on the counter and take off my glasses. My vision turns blurry instantly, but I barely notice it at this point. Methodically, I take off my clothes, turn on the water and get in the shower, bracing my hands against the wall as the cold water cascades over me.

It took us a few tries, but we got all of Aly's stuff into my room. Just in time for Aly and the girls to come upstairs accompanied by Coco. The dog instantly went to her bed, happy to see something familiar in the middle of all this madness.

I didn't even have to make some space in the room. More than half the closet sat empty, the same for the bathroom. The only thing where there was no space was my desk. I never spent money on trivial things. More times than not, I'll forget to buy shampoo, but you can be damn sure I'll get the newest hardware on the market to add to my computer. If there was something I didn't mind spending money on, it was my work, and I needed top-notch technology if I wanted to produce top-notch games for the market.

Shaking my head, I snap out of my thoughts and finish washing. I quickly dry off, put on my clothes, and brush my teeth.

The room is dim when I get out of the bathroom. Aly is sitting under the covers and scrolling through her phone.

Seeing Alyssa sitting in my bed is like a punch to my gut. All the air is kicked out of my lungs, and I can't breathe properly. Her hair is loose, copper strands falling in waves around her face.

She looks up when I close the bathroom door, a small smile on her lips. "Done?"

"Yeah." I scratch my nape, taking in the room.

Coco's bed is just next to my desk, the dog curled inside it with at least a dozen toys. Aly's books are next to mine on the bookshelf. A pale pink sweater is hanging off the back of my chair. It's not even been a few hours, and she's already all over this space.

The scariest part?

I like it. I like it a little too much for my comfort. Because Aly won't suddenly open her eyes and fall madly in love with me, no, she's here temporarily, needing a friend to have her back while she gets her life in order.

Nothing more, and nothing less.

Getting used to having her in my space would be a foolish thing to do.

"I guess I'll leave you to rest."

Turning on the balls of my feet, I go toward the door.

I need to get out of here before I do something stupid. Like, finally, tell her how I feel.

"Where are you going?"

I stop just at the doorway, my hand on the doorknob. I tighten my grip around it before looking over my shoulder. "I'll take the couch."

"What?" Aly sits upright. The blanket falls down to her lap, revealing that overly large shirt covering her body. "I'm not kicking you out of your bed." She slides her legs over the mattress, all that naked skin showing. Calling to me. Taunting me. "I'll take the couch."

I force myself to lift my gaze. "You're not sleeping on the couch, Aly."

If she can hear the strain in my voice, the rough edge in it, she doesn't comment.

"Well, you're not sleeping on the couch either," Alyssa huffs.

Letting go of the door, I turn to face her. "Where do you want me to sleep then?"

"You can sleep here."

My mouth falls open. "Here?"

She can't mean...

"Yeah, here," Aly rolls her eyes and chuckles. "It's your room, Maddox. Besides, this bed's huge." She pats the other side of the queen-size bed. Definitely, not huge. "I'm pretty sure it's big enough for both of us."

I shake my head. "I don't think this is a good idea."

As a matter of fact, I'm pretty sure this is a really, really bad idea.

"I'll keep to my side of the bed. Please?" She clasps her hands together. "I already feel like crap for barging into your life and turning everything upside down. If you let me take your bed..."

Tears shimmer in her eyes, making me feel like an asshole for making her cry. It's the last thing she needs on top of this day.

"Fine," I agree quickly. Too quickly. But I'd do anything, so she doesn't cry.

The tight knot in my stomach is totally worth the smile that spreads over those lush lips. It's so big; it's almost blinding. That grip is once again back around my heart, squeezing tightly. Seriously, will I ever be able to say no to her? Highly unlikely.

"You'll stay?"

"Yeah." God help me. "I'll stay."

Slowly, I cross the room to the other side of the bed and push away the covers. Aly slides underneath the blanket herself and lies back down against the headboard. Her red hair shimmers brightly against the plain white fabric.

How many times did I imagine her like this? Lying in my bed? Her hair spread over the pillowcase? Her beautiful face the last thing I see at night and the first thing in the morning?

Too many to count.

Having her here is everything I've ever wanted. The only problem is that she still sees me only as her best friend. Oh, and she's pregnant with another man's baby. Can't forget about that little detail.

"It's like when we were kids," Aly whispers as I lie down next to her, making sure to keep to my side of the bed. "Do you remember? You always wanted to keep the light on."

That's because I liked to look at her while she slept. Alyssa was always full of energy, but there was something peaceful about her when she slept. And it was the only time when I could look at her without worrying she might see how I was feeling written all over my face. Then again, if she hasn't noticed it in the last nineteen years, she probably won't now.

"That's because you got scared when you woke up in the middle of the night and needed to go to the bathroom."

Aly shoves me playfully. "Only because your house is scary."

I guess she's right about that. My parents own a huge Victorian mansion that's more fitting to be a museum than an actual home. The place had belonged to my great-great-grandfather and has been in my family for generations.

Aly yawns loudly and nuzzles her face more into the pillow.

"Sleepy?"

She nods and blinks a few times, fighting exhaustion. "It's been a long day, and apparently, growing a human requires energy."

"Go to sleep," I whisper softly.

"I think I will." She pulls the covers closer to her chin. "'Night, Maddox."

"Goodnight, Aly."

She nods, her eyes already closed. A strand of hair slips in her face, and my fingers itch to brush it away, but I hold that need back and just look at her.

Without her makeup on, I can clearly see the freckles scattered over her cheeks and the bridge of her nose. I'm not sure when was the last time I saw them. Alyssa always hated her freckles because people teased her about them when she was younger. But I loved the tiny brown dots covering her skin. They make her seem younger, more vulnerable.

I let myself watch her for a few minutes longer until her breathing evens out. It doesn't take but a few minutes. Only then do I turn to my back, letting out a sigh of relief.

My mind is restless to the point I'm not even sure I'll be able to fall asleep.

I turn off the light, but it's even worse in the darkness. All of my senses are suddenly in overdrive.

I can feel her body heat. Hear her soft breathing. Smell her shampoo. It's the same one she's been using for as long as I can remember, vanilla and orange.

The bed creaks as she shifts, snapping me out of my

thoughts. Before I can react, Aly turns toward me in her sleep. She's always been a restless sleeper, so it's nothing new. But this time, it's different. This time we're not kids, and the bed isn't that big.

The next thing I know, Aly's leg is between mine, her arm wrapping around my waist as she snuggles into my side.

I suck in a sharp breath as my body reacts to hers almost instantly. My muscles stiffen, the soft hairs on my hands rise as that sweet scent of hers surrounds me. She shifts a few times, and I have to bite the inside of my cheek to stop a groan from coming out as she adjusts her position.

Once she's done, or at least I pray to God she is, Aly lets out a soft sigh. As if she's finally content.

"Aly?" I rasp out, my throat tight, but there is no answer.

What will I even tell her if she wakes up? Can you please move so I can adjust the boner in my pants? Yeah, right. That's exactly what I need. My best friend finding out I got a boner when she snuggled into my side.

I try to shift softly so not to wake her, but the only thing it accomplishes is that her grip on me tightens.

Okay. No moving. Got it.

And if things couldn't get any worse, I hear shuffling on the side. Nails scrape against the floor, and the next thing I know is a little fluffy bundle is on the bed. Coco. She gets between my legs, circles a few times before she finally settles down, her head on my other foot.

It's official. I'm screwed.

Chapter 13

ALYSSA

The incessant buzzing wakes me up from a deep sleep. I groan, holding tightly onto my pillow.

No, no, no. I shake my head, refusing to believe it's time to wake up. It can't be. I just went to bed. It can't possibly be time to do this shit all over again.

I bury my face firmer into the pillow, hoping to tune out the alarm clock to no avail. I inhale deeply, smelling a strong citrusy scent. Not the usual vanilla sheet softener I use. Before I can even contemplate why that is, my stomach rolls uncomfortably as the wave of nausea hits me out of nowhere.

Oh shit.

My eyes pop open. I jump out of bed, barely registering the sleeping Maddox—definitely *not* a pillow—and run for the bathroom, hand covering my mouth as I try to hold it in long enough to make it. The door bangs against the wall as I fall to my knees in front of the toilet and start throwing up.

I hold onto the toilet seat as everything I ate last night comes rushing back in full force. Cold sweat coats my skin, my fingers clammy, knuckles white from trying to hold myself upright.

"Aly, shit." A warm hand touches my back, making shivers run down my spine. "Are you okay?"

I give my head a little shake, the best I can do until all of it is out.

"Hey, it's okay. It's going to be okay."

No, it's not, I want to protest, but I'm too busy throwing up.

In the background, I can hear the water running in the sink. The next thing I know, my hair is pulled away from my face, and a cool towel is pressed against the back of my neck. The goosebumps rise on my skin as a shiver runs through my body when the cold cloth touches my flushed flesh.

I'm not sure how long we stay like that—me kneeling on the tiles and holding onto the toilet as I throw up, Maddox standing behind me, his hand running up and down my back as he holds my hair away from my face. My rock through this madness. I might feel embarrassed, but I don't have it in me to care. For once, it feels good to have somebody to hold onto, somebody who cares.

Only when I'm sure that I'm done puking, I let out a shaky breath and press my forehead against my arm.

"Better?" Maddox asks, sitting down on the floor next to me. His brows pull together as he squints at me. Those warm brown eyes are filled with worry. There's something different about him, and it takes me a moment to realize what exactly.

"You're not wearing your glasses," I murmur, touching his face.

It's weird seeing him without those big black frames that cover half of his face. It makes him look more open. He has dark, long eyelashes I can only dream of. And his irises aren't some dull-brown color. No, they're like milk chocolate, with a thin circle of dark green just around the pupils, none of which you can see when he's hiding behind those frames.

Maddox had always had bad eyesight, so he started wearing

glasses when he was just a kid. I remember trying to convince him to switch to contacts when we were in high school, but he always said they make his eyes dry.

Maddox slides the towel from my neck and carefully wipes my forehead. "You scared me when you jumped out of bed like that."

Bed, right.

The same bed we shared last night.

I remember the pillow I thought I'd been holding onto—only it wasn't a pillow. It was Maddox.

My cheeks heat as I duck my head down. "Sorry, I didn't want to wake you."

"It's not a problem. My alarm was going off anyhow. I was just worried about you."

"Just your good ol' morning sickness. And since I've already caused you enough problems as it is, the last thing I wanted to do was throw up in your bed too."

Maddox brushes a strand of hair that's stuck to my sweaty cheek away from my face. "Does it happen often?"

"It did, in the beginning. That's why I thought I had a stomach bug or something, but no stomach bug lasts for weeks. I started to feel better recently. I really hoped I was done with throwing up." My nose scrunches when I remember the smell of the sheets. "I think it's your fabric softener."

Maddox frowns. "What's wrong with it?"

"Hey, don't look at me like that. I don't have a problem with it." I lower my hand to my stomach. "It's this little monster. I swear this baby hates me."

"She doesn't hate you."

"Of course, you'd say that," I roll my eyes at him. "It doesn't make you throw up at least once a day because it doesn't like the smell of something."

"She has a picky taste. I know a few other people who're the same," he gives me a pointed look.

"I'm not picky," I protest. "And we don't know if it's a she just yet."

"I think it's a girl. Only women can be opinionated like that from an early age. And don't worry about it. I can change the fabric softener. It's not a big deal."

I shake my head. "No matter how thankful I am, you can't change your whole life for this baby and me. We're not your responsibility."

Maddox presses his lips into a tight line; his brows pulled together. I know that look very well. He opens his mouth as if he's going to say something, but I stop him. The last thing I want is to get in another fight with the one person who's by my side.

"I should brush my teeth." I pull the shirt that's sticking to my body. "Probably take a shower too."

After a heartbeat, Maddox nods in acknowledgment. He gets to his feet and offers his hand to me. I slip my fingers into his warm touch and let him pull me up.

Startled by the swiftness of the motion, I collide with him.

"You good?"

I look up at Maddox.

My heart hammers wildly in my chest, the rushed beat echoing in my eardrums as I try to steady myself. *What the hell's wrong with me?*

I push my hair back. "Yeah, sorry."

He takes a step back, my hand falling down by my side. Maddox starts to push his glasses up his nose, only to remember he's not wearing them. "I'll leave you to it."

I watch him turn around and exit the bathroom, the door closing softly behind him.

I lean against the counter, letting out a shaky breath. When I look up, my pale reflection is staring back at me.

What the hell just happened?

When I get out of the bathroom some twenty minutes later, showered and dressed, the room is empty. Maddox and Coco are nowhere in sight. The dog was so used to my sudden jumping out of bed that she barely paid attention to it any longer.

I quickly check I have everything I'll need in my backpack before throwing it over my shoulder and descending the stairs.

A soft buzzing sound comes from the kitchen, the strong smell of coffee filling the air. I follow it and find Callie standing by the counter, still in her pajamas, a big coffee mug clasped in her hands.

"Good morning," I greet as I slide my backpack into a chair and go straight for the coffee machine.

It was funny, this whole pregnancy thing. First, I had to throw up, but as soon as I did, my appetite would show up.

"Mhmm... It's definitely a good morning now."

"How so?" I ask, opening a few cabinets. I was sure they were...

"Finally got my hands on coffee. Left cabinet," Callie says. "The one by the fridge."

I open it, and sure enough, different coffee mugs fill the cabinet. I grab a smaller one and put it under the coffee machine, put in a pod, and press start. Maddox has this fancy Keurig machine that he got recently, and I have to admit, the coffee is delicious.

"Not sure whose smart idea it was to put them there since the coffee machine is on the other side, but boys," she shrugs as if that one word explains it all.

I chuckle just as the machine beeps. I grab my cup and take

a sip from it, savoring the taste. My doctor said coffee was okay as long as I took it in small doses, and I planned to enjoy every drop of it. "Where's everybody?"

"The boys went to the gym or something. Hayden thought it would be funny to wake me up at the crack of dawn." She rolls her eyes. "Seriously, just because he loves to torture himself by waking up early doesn't mean the rest of us do."

"Girl, just be happy that you can drink coffee." I lift my cup. "One of these is all I can have these days."

Callie's eyes widen, mouth falling open. You'd think I just told her Santa Clause isn't real. Knowing her? This is way worse.

Before she can comment, the front door opens, and Coco comes rushing in. I crouch down to scratch her between her ears. "Hey, pretty girl. Where were you? I was looking for you."

"Took her out for a walk." Maddox walks into the room, his glasses fogged from the difference in temperature. "She was up, so I figured I might as well let her out to do her thing."

My heart does a little flip inside my chest.

Why am I even surprised? This is Maddox we're talking about.

"Thanks, Maddox." I go to him, lift on the tips of my toes and press a kiss to his cheek. "You're the best."

With a grateful smile, I pull back. I go toward the cabinet, pull out another mug, this one larger, and put it under the coffee machine.

"You feel better?" he asks as I hand it to him.

"I'm good, hungry actually."

"Better?" Callie looks between the two of us. "What's wrong? Is it the baby?"

"It's morning sickness." I let out an exasperated sigh. "I really hope my doctor was right, and the damn thing stops soon because I'm sick of being sick all the time."

"That bad?"

"Just annoying." I open my bag and find the bottle of vitamins. Popping the lid open, I take one pill and go toward the sink to grab a glass of water. "I never know if something will make me wanna hurl, which is inconvenient."

Maddox opens the fridge and starts pulling out different ingredients. "What do you want to eat?"

I give him a warning look. "You don't have to cook for me."

"I'm making myself an omelet." Maddox looks over his shoulder, brows raised. "How about that?"

My nose furrows at the idea. I guess that'd be a no to an omelet. Or any kind of eggs, for the matter.

"Hey, what about me? How come you never cook for us?" Callie asks, leaning against the counter.

"You never asked," Maddox shrugs as he starts to prepare breakfast. "If you want, I can make you some too?"

"Well, if you're making breakfast for yourself, you might as well make some for us too. Right, Alyssa?"

"Umm... I think I'll skip the eggs. Maybe just some cereal?"

Cereal and milk I can do.

I start toward the fridge, but Maddox stands in my way. "Sit down. I'll get it for you."

"Oh, you don't have to..."

Maddox gives me his no-nonsense, you better do as I say, look. "Sit."

Callie tugs me into the chair next to hers. "If the guy wants to make you breakfast, you do as he says. Trust me, it doesn't happen often. Might as well enjoy it while we can."

Sighing, I take the stool next to the one she was sitting on moments ago and pick up Coco in my arms. "You guys are going to spoil me."

"Somebody should after all the shitty things that have happened lately." Callie gives me a pointed look. "I don't remember you being so difficult when it comes to accepting help. That's always been Yasmin's thing."

I huff, "Like you were any better."

"Touché. But seriously, what gives?"

Coco licks my hand, demanding attention. I smile softly and nuzzle her under her chin.

"I guess it's this whole situation." I look up. Maddox's attention is on making breakfast, but I know he's listening. "It made me realize how much I've relied on my parents. On my trust fund, but now that it's taken away..." I slide my tongue over my dry lips. "What the hell am I going to do? I have no money. No work experience. No home. And a baby on the way. It's scary, and I don't know..."

"Hey, it's going to be okay." Callie wraps her arm around me, pulling me in a hug. "We'll figure it out."

For a moment, I let myself lean on my friend. Let her hold me because I know once I get up, I'll once again have to carry this weight on my own. "I know that. And I appreciate everything you guys are doing for me, I really do. But the clock's ticking, and I'm running out of time."

Maddox turns around and places a bowl of milk and a box of cheerios on the counter. My favorite.

He doesn't say anything, but there's a frown between his brows that says more than words ever could.

"How far along are you?" Callie asks, drawing my attention.

"Fifteen weeks."

"So, you have what?" She tilts her head to the side. "Some twenty-five weeks to go?"

"About."

"That's more than enough time." Callie lets go of me and grabs my hands. "You have a place to stay. You have a job."

"You have us," Maddox chimes in.

Callie nods. "You have us. We'll help you through it."

Tears fill my eyes, and I sniff loudly. God, I hate crying.

"Now, now, there's no need to cry. I know I'm awesome."

I chuckle, wiping my eyes with the back of my hand. "It's these damn hormones."

"See? You're already doing good."

"Because I'm crying?"

Callie tsks. "Can you imagine what we can accomplish if you only turn those big blue eyes on the guys? I'm pretty sure they'd do anything just to make you stop. And that's *before* the baby's even here."

I chuckle and shake my head. "You're crazy."

"We'll see about that. Now eat that cereal. You'll need energy to grow that baby."

I smile at Callie before turning my attention to Maddox. "Thank you, guys. I seriously don't know how I would have done it without you."

Chapter 14

MADDOX

"That'll be all for today. I'll see you all next week."

Before the professor can even finish, I'm already putting my things into my backpack and getting to my feet. I pull out my phone, expecting to find a message, but my screen is empty, and the anxiousness that I've been feeling ever since I woke up grows into a full-on panic.

This was the fourth morning in a row that Alyssa woke up and went straight to the bathroom to throw up. She tried to hide it, hating to wake me up. As if I could peacefully sleep knowing that she's feeling sick. Only today, she felt so bad she couldn't even eat breakfast.

Is she okay? Did something happen? Is that why she hasn't answered my messages? Did she need to go to the doctor?

I don't know anything about morning sickness, but I hated seeing Aly brought to her knees, struggling to get out everything she ate last night.

She tried to play it off as if nothing was wrong, but that's Aly for you.

I check my watch. Aly said she has two classes, and then she has to be at Cup It Up for her shift. And I have thirty minutes until I have to meet the guys at the gym. Just enough time to stop at Cup It Up and grab a cup of coffee since the café is on my way.

And if she's there by then, well...

"Maddox!"

I turn around at the sound of my name and see Mia jogging after me. I slow down, letting her catch up.

"What are you up to?" she asks, breathing hard as she stops by my side.

"I just finished with my class, so I'm going to grab a coffee."

Mia pulls the strap of her backpack higher on her shoulder and smiles at me. "Mind if I join you? I could use some coffee before I head to the library."

I shake my head and start walking. "That project of yours still giving you trouble?"

"Yeah, but I have to cram in some studying before my next class. Our ICT Technical Foundations professor likes to surprise us with pop quizzes, and since we haven't had one in a while, it's just a matter of time."

"Good luck with that."

"Thanks, I'll need it. I haven't picked up that textbook since classes started."

"If anybody can do it, it's you."

It's not even flattery. Mia is really intelligent and good at what she does.

"You have too much faith in me."

I look over my shoulder. "I've seen you in action."

I push the door open, and the bell chimes as we enter Cup It Up.

Turning around, my eyes land on her as soon as we're in the café. That grip around my heart loosens, if only slightly, making it easier to breathe.

She's okay. She was just throwing up. It's normal. She's pregnant. Pregnant women throw up all the time.

But this is Aly we're talking about, not some random woman. Seeing her like that, cheeks pale, eyes big and vulnerable, sitting on the bathroom floor does something to me I can't explain.

Aly bites into her lower lip as she carefully makes the drink. Her colleague says something to her as she finishes the beverage and puts a lid on the cup. When she looks up, she smiles up at him and nods to whatever he's been telling her before handing the drink to the customer.

Fingers curl around my bicep. "Earth to Maddox."

Shaking my head, I look down at Mia. "Sorry, what were you saying?"

Mia chuckles. "Where did you wander off to?"

Oh, I was just thinking about how beautiful my best friend looks—same old, same old.

"Just got lost in thought for a little bit." I scratch the back of my neck and take a step closer to the counter as the line moves. "Sorry."

"I could see that. It's like you were here one moment, and then you were gone. How is your game coming along?"

"Good. There were some issues I had to fix the other day."

"What kind of issues?"

"They found the item they were looking for, but instead of transporting them to the next level as it should have, it took them back to the beginning of the quest. I had to rewrite some code, but I think I finally figured it out. I'll have to tell my roommates so they can try it out."

"Maybe I could try it one day."

My brows shoot up. "You're a gamer?"

Mia shrugs. "I wouldn't say I'm a gamer, but I enjoy playing a game every now and then to destress. But if you'd rather..."

"No, it's fine. I'll let you know when the guys organize the next game day."

Mia smiles. "Sounds like a plan."

Just then, the person in front of us moves, and I come face to face with Aly. She raises her brow, a smile playing on her lips. "Maddox, what brings you here?"

"Coffee?"

Aly chuckles, but although there's that familiar spark in her irises, I can't help but notice how pale she is or those dark circles under her eyes. "Don't you usually get it at the cafeteria? I figured their muddy taste is more up your alley."

"I…" my voice trails off. I try to come up with a believable explanation, but no words come.

Aly rolls her eyes and gives me a knowing look. "Seriously?"

I'm so damn busted.

"I know you're working here, so I wanted to support you," I shrug, sticking with the half-truth. I wanted to support her, sure, but I also needed to make sure she was okay.

"Yas has been working here for a year, and that didn't sway you."

"You're not Yasmin." The admission is out before I can think better of it. Aly's lips part in surprise, and I can feel the heat creeping up my cheeks.

Too much.

I've said too much.

"You two know each other?" Mia's question snaps me out of my Aly-induced trance, reminding me we're not alone.

I push my glasses up my nose. "Yeah."

"We're childhood friends," Aly supplies. She moves her attention to Mia and extends her hand. "I don't think we've met. I'm Alyssa."

Mia glances at me before taking Aly's hand for a handshake. "Mia. It's nice to meet you."

Alyssa looks between the two of us. "How do you two know each other?"

Mia glances at me. "We have a few classes together."

"Do you now?" Aly shifts her attention from Mia to me and quirks a brow at me.

The silent question is clear with that simple move. I ignore it, instead changing the subject. "Mia is doing a Masters in Cybersecurity."

The look Aly gives me clearly says that she knows I'm evading, but she'll let me off the hook. For now.

"That sounds interesting." Aly takes the tall cup and starts pouring black coffee.

Mia shrugs. "It has its moments."

Aly puts the lid on my cup and hands it to me wordlessly. "What can I get you, Mia?"

"I'd like a grande iced vanilla macchiato, two shots of espresso."

"Iced vanilla, two shots." Aly nods. "Coming right up."

"You need help?" The guy comes from behind Aly. His hands brush against her shoulders.

Aly gives him a bright smile. "I think I'm good, but thanks."

"Okay, I'm off to the kitchen to bring up more baked goods, but if you need anything, just holler."

"You know it."

Aly brushes a strand that slipped out of her ponytail behind her ear, and grabs a new cup, putting it under the coffee machine. Although she's barely been here for a week, she's already moving with more ease. Her brows are pulled together, lips moving as she mutters something quietly to herself as she prepares Mia's order.

"So... You two are friends?"

Reluctantly, I shift my attention to Mia. "Yeah, we've been since we were kids."

"Was going to college together part of the plan?"

Depending on who you ask.

"I guess it just happened that way." I shrug, trying to play it off.

In reality, I always knew I'd end up wherever Aly went. She might not love me the way I love her, but she's my best friend, and being without her wasn't an option.

Although I was two years younger than her, I was always ahead in school. It wasn't until I started middle school that they decided to test me and put me two grades ahead. It was a compromise my parents agreed to since they didn't want to jeopardize my social and emotional well-being for the sake of school. I'd usually attend AP classes, and even those I'd find too simple and boring. By the time I graduated high school, I had so many college credits I practically didn't even need my bachelor's degree. I really didn't care much about which college I would go to as long as she was there. I could study anywhere, but there was only one Aly.

"Here you go." Alyssa puts Mia's drink on the counter, snapping me out of my run down memory lane.

"Thanks." I check on Mia. "Want anything else?"

"No, I'm good, but..."

Before she can protest, I put a twenty on the counter next to her drink. "It's my treat."

Mia shakes her head. "You didn't have to do that."

"I don't mind."

Alyssa laughs. "Don't even try. Maddox can be so stubborn about some things. At least now, I know I'm not the only one you like to boss around."

"I'm not bossing anyone around." I push my glasses up my nose. "It's just a drink."

Aly rolls her eyes and goes to the register. "Yeah, right."

"Keep the change."

She stops what she's doing and looks up, her eyes narrowing on me. With a shake of her head, she turns to Mia. "See what I mean?"

"It's a tip!" I protest. "I always leave a tip."

"I guess there's that."

There is no guessing. She knows it's true. Besides, it's *her*. She isn't just anybody, and she's the one insisting on working. The least I can do is leave her a good tip so she can save more money for when the baby comes.

"How long until your shift is done?"

Aly looks at the watch around her wrist. It's the one I got her as a high school graduation present. "It's another two hours."

"Want me to come and pick you up?"

"I can walk home. It's not a big deal."

"I don't mind."

Her gaze goes to Mia, who's texting somebody, and then returns to me. She does that little tilt of her head. I frown, trying to figure out what the hell she means by it, but come up empty.

"What?" I ask at the same time, Mia says, "I've gotta go. My friend just texted me to meet her for a study session before my class. Thanks for the coffee, Maddox."

"Not a problem. Good luck."

Mia shakes her head. "Let's hope I don't need it."

With a nod in Alyssa's direction, Mia leaves the café, one hand wrapped around the cup, the other typing on her phone.

Aly pinches my arm. "Seriously?"

"Ouch." I pull my arm out of her reach. "What?"

"Oh, Maddox, you're so clueless sometimes."

"What did I do?" I ask as the doorbell chimes, and a group of girls enters.

She shakes her head. "Later, I've got to take care of this. Seriously, go home. I'm fine."

"I..." I open my mouth to tell her I'll be on campus anyway, but then think better of it. "Okay. Call if you need anything."

"Do you ever rest?" I ask as I jump on the treadmill next to Hayden's. He's already running at full speed, sweat dripping down his forehead.

"No time to rest," Hayden pants.

"Hades is just trying to make the rest of us look bad," Nixon says as he stretches lazily, coming to a stop behind us. Zane, Spencer, and Emmett are a few feet behind him. They were debating whether it's better to have a protein shake before or after a workout.

Hayden glares at Nixon. "Well, some of us have to *run*. We don't just stay in one spot and throw the damn ball."

"That's damn true," Prescott mutters as he hops over, fingers wrapped around his crutches. "Somebody's gotta make this slacker look good."

Nixon crosses his arms over his chest as he turns to face his teammate. "Hey now, who do you think throws you those perfect passes?"

"Perfect, my ass," Prescott scoffs. "Hayden's grandma could do the same."

"What about Grams?" Zane looks between us as they finally join the group. His gaze stops on Prescott, and he gives him a once-over. "How's the leg?"

Back in November, Prescott broke his leg during a football game, and just recently, he got out of the cast, but he still has to wear a brace and lean on crutches, neither of which he likes.

"Fine," Prescott says through gritted teeth and takes a seat at the workout bench. Even if he tries to hide it, the relief at taking his weight off his leg is enormous. "Or it might be if

Snow didn't try to break it all over again every time I come to PT."

"Stop bitching about it. Doctor Snow is one of the best physical therapists in the state. If anybody can bring you to the playing level before the season starts, it's her."

"Yeah, well, tell that to my leg." Prescott drops the crutches and rubs the side of his leg, just above his knee. "Every time I leave her office, I have to lean on the crutches."

Zane's brows pull together disapprovingly. "Something you should be doing anyway. Healing takes time, Wentworth. If you don't listen, you'll reinjure yourself, and then there'll be no more football ever."

A shadow passes over Prescott's face. There one second, gone in the next.

"Yeah, yeah, Mom. I've heard all of it." Prescott rolls his eyes. "Are we here to work out or what?"

Zane just shakes his head and turns around. The guys scatter, taking different machines to warm up. I increase the speed of my treadmill, going into a moderate jog.

I never went into the gym until I became roommates with Hayden and Nixon during our freshmen year of college. It was the challenge of their football friends that got me started, but I actually ended up enjoying my time in the gym—the dedication, the repetitiveness, the thrive of executing an exercise to perfection. Exercising gave my body what writing code was for my mind—a challenge.

For a while, we work out in silence. I let my brain disconnect as I stare ahead and just run. My leg muscles flexing, my heartbeat steadily increasing, and my lungs pumping in air. I concentrate on breathing properly, which is always a challenge—forcing myself to breathe in through my nose and exhaling through my mouth.

I get lost in the beat of my feet against the machine, letting the soft hum pull me out of my head. I'm not sure how long I'm at it, but at some point, from the corner of my eye, I see Hayden slowing down, so I do the same, shifting to a walk until I come to a stop.

Getting off the machine, I grab my water bottle and my phone. I take a pull from the bottle as I check my phone in case Alyssa messaged me, but there's nothing.

Was she always so stubborn, or is this something new?

"What has you frowning like that?" Emmett drawls in that Texan accent of his as he nudges me.

"Nothing." I quickly lock my phone. When I look up, I find all of my friends' attention on me. "What?"

"That was unusually fast." Nixon slaps his hands over my shoulders. "Is it Alyssa? What's going on with you two, anyway?" He wiggles his brows. "We couldn't help but notice the couch has been empty this past week."

They couldn't help but notice.

Why am I not surprised? My roommates can be as nosy as a group of gossiping old ladies. Worse even if I'm being honest.

"Wait, Alyssa?" Emmett's head snaps toward me. "Did you finally tell her how you feel?"

"What? Of course, not."

The last thing I need is to tell my best friend that I've been in love with her my whole life. Talk about a disaster in the making.

"Seriously, Santiago?" Spencer shakes his head. "As if he'd ever admit it out loud. I don't think he ever said it out loud to himself. Besides, not all of us are romantic saps like you."

He's not wrong there. Emmett might be one of the biggest and scariest players on the defensive line, but he is the romantic of the group. He fell in love with his now-fiancée when he was in high school, and they've been together ever since. Now they're planning their wedding this summer once they graduate college.

"It's called being a *man*. Maybe you should try it sometime, playboy." Emmett shifts his attention back to me. "So, what the hell's going on with you and Alyssa?"

"Don't forget about the couch," Nixon chimes in as he goes to the shoulder press machine.

Emmet's gaze darts to Nixon and then back to me, clearly confused. "Did Alyssa move in with you or something?"

"Or something," I mutter, going for the leg extension machine, hoping they'll leave it alone.

"Oh, she moved in with him, all right," Spencer chuckles.

Zane takes a set of dumbbells and shoves them into Spencer. "If you're going to talk, you might as well get to work on your legs."

Spencer rolls his eyes but takes the dumbbells.

"How do you know that, anyway?" Prescott asks, sliding the towel from his shoulder and wiping his face. Although he can't do leg exercises, he usually joins us to work on his arms, core, and back.

Spencer wiggles his brows as he goes to the mats in front of the mirror. "I was there when Maddox moved her in; that's how."

"Damn, I miss all the good stuff," Prescott groans. "What gives? Didn't she live with those girlfriends of hers?"

"She did, but..."

I give Nixon a warning glare. "But it's none of anybody's business."

Seriously, why can't they just leave it be?

Nixon shrugs. "It's not like she'll be able to hide it for much longer."

"Hide what?" This comes from Emmett.

I let out an exasperated sigh and rub my hand over my face. My head is starting to hurt, and it's all my friends' fault.

I take a sweep of the room. There are a few people around us, but they're concentrating on working out—something we should be doing—and nobody is paying us any attention. Still, I make a point to keep my voice quiet. "Aly's pregnant."

Prescott's eyes bug out while Emmett's mouth falls open.

"She's... what?!"

"Can you keep it down?" I ask, once again making sure nobody's listening. "It wasn't even my secret to tell, but since they're being so nosy..." I shoot a glare at Nixon and Spencer. "So now you know. Can we leave it be?"

"That still doesn't explain the empty couch."

I turn to Nixon, seriously contemplating punching him if he doesn't shut up.

"I wasn't about to let her sleep on the couch. Not after all the parties and hookups that happened on that thing."

Nixon either doesn't see that he's pushing me too far, or he simply doesn't care. "Didn't you say *you'd* sleep on the couch?"

My jaw tightens. "I was planning to, but Aly didn't want to kick me out of my bed."

Prescott nods. "So you sacrificed one for the team and decided to sleep in your bed. With her. I mean, I get it, dude. She's hot."

I slowly turn my narrowed eyes from Nixon to Prescott. I swear, sometimes I think they're related or something.

"She's my best friend."

"Who you've had the hots for, how long again? Oh, yeah, *forever*." The sarcasm in Prescott's voice is evident. "Besides, isn't she in a relationship?"

"They broke up."

That gets his attention. "What? But isn't he..."

"He isn't interested in owning up to his mistakes," I stop him before he can finish. My fingers clench into fists.

You'd think every time I say it, it'd be easier, but the only thing I want is to punch him in the face even more.

Prescott swears silently.

"So, he what?" Emmett crosses his arms over his chest, his face grim. They don't call him Hulk for nothing. "Just walked away?"

I shrug because what is there to say? He did walk away, leaving Alyssa to deal with the fallout without any regard for her wellbeing or interest in the baby she's carrying.

How can somebody just walk away like that? I'll never understand.

"What an asshole," Emmett mutters.

"That's fucked up, man." Prescott nods in agreement. "So her boyfriend leaves her, and she moves in with you? Why?"

"Her boyfriend isn't the only one who left her to her own devices." In all honesty, I didn't expect better from Chad. The guy has always been a tool, but her parents? I hadn't seen that one coming. Yes, they haven't been the best parents to Alyssa growing up. They didn't understand her, didn't like her free spirit nor her stubbornness, but no matter what happened, they never turned their back on her—until now. "Her parents cut her off after she refused to give in and have an abortion."

Emmett pulls his brows together. "They cut her off because she got pregnant? Who the hell does that?"

I feel the vein in my forehead tick. "Rich people who care more about their appearances than about their daughter's needs and wishes. That's who."

"So basically, the girl you've been in love with your whole life is pregnant with another dude's baby. She's currently homeless and lives in your house, and sleeps in your bed every night.

Shouldn't you be happy about it?" Prescott says, counting each thing with a rise of his fingers.

More like constantly angry and sexually frustrated. Not like I'd admit either out loud. Especially not in front of my friends. They'll never let me live it down.

"The only thing I care about is that Aly is safe." I rub my fingers against my temples, feeling a headache rising. "Are we done with this?"

Prescott lifts his hands in defense. "Hey, I'm just saying, you should take advantage of it."

"For once, I have to agree with Prescott. You should use this opportunity to your advantage," Emmett nods. "Show her what she's missing. That a real man who loves his woman will do everything to make her happy."

"See? Even Romeo agrees with me," Prescott grins. "You, assholes, should listen to me more. Think about it. What's the worst thing that could happen?"

"Oh, I don't know? I'll lose my best friend?" I shake my head. "Aly needs a friend right now. Not some asshole who'll hurt her even more than she already has been."

Hayden tilts his head to the side. He's been quiet this whole time, working out, but now his sole focus is on me. "But, you're not an asshole. Are you?"

Chapter 15

ALYSSA

Coco's head snaps up as soon as I open the bedroom door. She wiggles her tail excitedly as I walk toward the bed and throw myself at it, my fingers digging into her fur. "Hey, pretty girl."

She moves closer and licks my face in greeting, making me laugh. "You're slobbering all over me, Coco. Stop!"

I try to wiggle out of her reach, but she's relentless once she sets her mind on something.

Wrapping my hands around her middle, I turn on my back and push her in the air. She keeps squirming, but I don't let go.

"Nope, no more licking, young lady. I mean it."

She whines, clearly not happy with my answer. I lower her down and press my nose against her snout. "I missed you, baby."

Today has been a crazy day at work. At first, there was barely anybody, but once two o'clock chimed, it was like all the campus finally awoke, and they all needed their coffee fix to help them deal with the rest of the day.

I yawn so loudly I can barely cover my mouth with my hand. I'm tired, my feet hurt, and all I want to do is curl up here and sleep.

I put Coco down on the mattress and place my hand on my

stomach. It still feels surreal that there's a baby growing inside me. A human being that I'm supposed to bring into this world; a human being I'm supposed to raise, take care of, love.

My fingers slip under the hem of my shirt. My stomach is still flat, but there's an unfamiliar tightness to it.

Coco nudges my hand with her snout.

"What?" I ask, but she just does it again until I finally remove it, and she places her head on my lower belly. "You wanna nap, too? Fine, but just for a little while."

I'm just about to pull the blanket over us and snuggle when the door to the bathroom opens. "Hey, do you mind…"

The words die on my lips when a very shirtless Maddox comes out of the bathroom.

Holy shit.

Maddox is towel drying his wet hair as he strides into the bedroom. I watch as a drop of water falls to his chest and slides down, down, down…

My tongue darts out, sliding over my dry lips as I blink and then blink some more. 'Cause holy hell, when did my nerdy best friend get *abs*?

And we're not talking about a flat stomach with barely visible lines; we're talking about a hard-core six-pack.

"Aly?"

My head snaps up, eyes meeting Maddox's narrowed ones. My cheeks heat, and I'm thanking God that he isn't wearing glasses, so he probably didn't catch me gawking. Because seriously, how weird would that be?

He's your best friend!

But he doesn't look like my cute, guy-next-door best friend— a best friend who tends to wear baggy clothes that are a little too big for his skinny frame. My kind, slightly shy friend with the biggest, most caring heart ever.

He's all that, okay, but he's also… hot?

When did that happen?

Get a grip, girl! I chastise myself.

"Y-yeah?" I squeak. So much for keeping my cool.

"You were saying something?"

I was, wasn't I? Not that I can remember what it was to save my life.

"I... I just hadn't realized you were home, that's all."

Maddox rubs the back of his neck, the movement making his bicep flex. Like I needed more reason to drool over him.

Best friend. Best friend. Best friend.

You shall not drool over your best friend.

No matter how sexy he is.

"We just got back from the gym."

I guess that explains all the muscles.

"Wait... Since when are you going to the gym?"

"Freshman year."

"What?"

Maddox shrugs as if it's not a big deal. "The guys were giving me shit, so I wanted to show them I could do it too. Turns out I like it."

My eyes slide down his body, and instantly, I feel bad for ogling my friend.

"I didn't know that."

Maddox pulls the towel down and just stares at me for a moment. "I guess it's good I can still surprise you after all this time, huh?"

"Yeah, I guess," I say softly, my stomach clenching as a feeling I don't know how to name spreads inside my belly. It's... unsettling.

"What are you up to?"

I let out a long sigh. "I should probably study, but my brain is fried. I think I'm going to rest for a little while. The shift was hard, and I'm just about ready to pass out."

"You mind if I stay here to work? I promise I'll be quiet."

I shake my head no. "That's fine. I told you a dozen times you don't have to change your life to accommodate me."

I sit up, upsetting Coco, as I reach for the blanket and pull it over us. As soon as I'm lying back down, Coco does her usual three circles before she settles next to my stomach. "Do you think she knows?" I ask, rubbing between her ears.

Maddox pulls his brows together. "What?"

"That I'm pregnant. Like can she smell it or something?"

"I have no idea." Maddox shakes his head. "Why?"

"I've noticed lately that she's been paying more attention to my stomach." I yawn. "Like earlier? She placed her head just over my stomach, and even now, she's sleeping in front of it. I guess it's crazy."

"It doesn't have to be," Maddox shrugs, and it takes all of me not to let my eyes fall under his chin. "Dogs have a great sense of smell, and she's really protective of you."

"Yeah, maybe." I pull the blanket higher, fighting another yawn. My eyelids feel heavy, and it takes everything in me to keep them open.

Maddox comes into my line of sight and tucks the blanket under my chin. "Try to get some rest."

I hum non-committedly, my eyes half-closed. But even as I fall asleep, I can't get the image of my shirtless best friend out of my head.

MADDOX

Aly murmurs something in her sleep. I turn around just as she shifts, tucking her arm under the pillow. Coco opens one eye and looks at her owner before she gets up and scooches, close to her middle once again.

Maybe there is something in what Aly was saying earlier.

Saving the essay I've been trying to work on, not very successfully, I get up. Coco's eyes snap open instantly, and she stares right at me.

"Just going to get some coffee, Coconut," I whisper softly as I leave the room.

The TV is on in the living room, but I bypass it and go straight for the coffee machine. I refill the water methodically and add a pod in before starting it.

While I wait, I pull my phone out of my pocket, and open a browser, typing in my question. A bunch of results pops up instantly. I click on the first link, scanning the page.

Dogs are highly sensitive and intimate in studying behavior. They can react in different ways, from being overly protective to clingy, fearful, or even indifferent. It's common for dogs to be more alert...

"What are you doing?"

I turn around at the sudden question and bump into Nixon, who's standing right behind me.

"Why are you sneaking up on people?"

"Sneaking up? I was literally yelling at Hayden as I was coming in the kitchen."

"Hadn't heard you." I shrug.

"I'd figured that out, Einstein." Nixon tilts his chin toward my phone. "What has you preoccupied?"

"I'm just looking into something."

"Like what?"

"Aly made a comment about Coco acting differently."

"Differently how?"

"Just more protective, I guess."

The coffee machine beeps, and I grab my cup, taking a sip of coffee.

"You think she knows?"

"Maybe," I shrug. "It says it's possible."

Nixon tilts his head to the side. "Maybe I should give her a sniff next time I see her."

"Not like that. But animals have a heightened sense of smell, and women's hormones are all over the place when they're pregnant. So, I guess it is possible."

Nixon just stares at me like I've just spoken in Chinese. "How do you know all that?"

I push my glasses up my nose, feeling the heat creep up my cheeks. "I've been reading some stuff online."

"Of course, you have." Nixon shakes his head. "Where's Alyssa, anyway? I haven't seen her today."

"She got home a little after us." I grip the back of my neck, remembering Aly's stupefied face when she saw me coming out of the bathroom.

Her blue eyes widened, lips slightly parted as a pretty pink color raised up her neck and spread into her cheeks. She thought I couldn't see it because I wasn't wearing my glasses, but I saw it all right. I saw the way her eyes lowered down my chest and stopped on my abs. The way her throat bobbed as she tried to swallow.

She saw me, alright.

Probably for the first time ever, but she saw me. And a part of me thinks she actually liked what she saw.

What does it all mean?

An elbow connects with my stomach, snapping me out of my thoughts. "What's with that face?"

"Huh?"

"That face." He tips his chin at me, eyes narrowing. "What's with it?"

"What's with what?" Hayden gives us a look as he enters the kitchen and goes for the fridge, grabbing a bottle of Gatorade.

"His face."

Hayden takes a sip from his bottle, carefully observing me as he drinks. "What's with his face? I don't see anything."

"How don't you see anything?" Nixon growls. "Just look at him."

Hayden shakes his head. "Still don't see it."

"You're seriously clueless, Hades." Nixon turns to me. "What happened with Alyssa when she got home?"

Heat spreads through me, and I know my cheeks are probably beet red by this point.

Hayden groans, "Will you leave it alone already? If he wants to tell Alyssa, he'll do it when he's good and rea—"

"Maybe there is something to what you said earlier," I say quietly.

Both my friends shut up and turn to look at me.

I can't believe I'm actually doing this.

"When Aly got home, I ugh—" My voice is raspy, so I clear my throat before continuing. "I was just getting out of the shower."

"Naked?" Nixon wiggles his brows.

"What?" I pull my brows together. "Of course not."

"Maybe you should have. 'Cause fun fact, pregnant women are extra horny. Did you look up that statistic? Way more useful than knowing about a dog's heightened senses to female hormones or whatnot."

"Shut up, Nixon," Hayden says, slapping him over the head.

Nixon rubs the back of his head. "What? I'm just telling the truth. And I don't think our friend here would mind giving her a hand, or you know, a *dick* when she needs it."

I shake my head. "Forget it."

Coffee mug in hand, I start for the door.

This was a bad idea. A really, really bad idea.

How the two of them have girlfriends is beyond my comprehension.

"See what you did?" Hayden hisses.

"What? I'm just joking. Maddox, wait."

"It doesn't matter, forget I said anything."

I get out into the hallway just as the front door opens, and Yasmin walks in. She smiles when she sees me. "Hey, Maddox."

"Yasmin."

"Where's Nixon?"

"Kitchen." With a smile in her direction, I climb the stairs until I'm on the second floor and make my way down the hallway.

Softly, I push the door open and enter the bedroom. Not missing a beat, Coco's eyes snap open and look at me with quiet intensity. Aly is still asleep on the bed, but since I left, the blanket slipped off of her.

I make my way quietly across the room and put the mug on the nightstand before sitting on my side of the bed. She's curled on her side, her legs pulled close to her chest, hands hugging the pillow as she murmurs something in her sleep.

Shaking my head, I pull the blanket up, so she isn't cold. A strand of hair falls in her face. Gently, I push the silky lock back. My fingers graze over her skin, silky and smooth under my fingertips, that familiar smell of oranges, vanilla, and something that's simply Aly filling my lungs.

Aly stirs. I'm not sure if it's because the mattress dipped when I sat down, or if it's my touch, but she shifts, her eyes blinking open sleepily.

"Maddox?" Aly asks softly, fighting the sleep. "What time is it?"

"Shhh. I'm here. Sleep."

"Mhmm..." Aly shifts closer, her hand landing on mine, our fingers twining together. "Will you stay with me?"

Her gentle words pierce my heart. Her hand is warm in mine, small and delicate.

"I..." My tongue darts out as those hazy blue eyes focus on me.

Just for a moment.

Until she falls back asleep.

What's the harm in that?

"Okay."

I lay down in bed, and Aly snuggles into my side.

For a moment, my body tenses, but then I can feel my muscles relax almost as quickly. I wrap my arm around her, smoothing it over her back. "Sleep, Alyssa."

But she doesn't hear me because she's already asleep, and soon after, so am I.

Chapter 16

ALYSSA

"Please read chapters ten through fifteen before our next class. I'll see you then."

Jotting down a note, so I don't forget because I've learned lately that pregnancy brain is an actual thing, I close the book. Sliding it into my backpack, I zip it and throw it over my shoulder.

This is my final class of the day, and I can't wait to get back home.

I shake my head at my own thoughts.

Home.

It's so easy to think of Maddox's place as my own. I constantly have to remind myself that it's not, and I shouldn't think of it as such. What I should do is start looking for my own place, so I can leave sooner rather than later. Maddox is too sweet for his own good. He won't throw me out, but I can't keep imposing on him.

In the last couple of weeks, I've gotten into a routine of sorts. I wake up, go to classes, work, and then go back to Maddox's place, where I crash on most days. Although lately, I've been feeling better. Less tired. And I've finally stopped throwing up, which is a huge plus. There was no more jumping out of bed first thing in the morning and rushing into the bathroom. No, now when I wake up, there's only Maddox sleeping in the bed next to me.

The memory of his hard body under mine flashes in my mind, making my cheeks feel warm.

What the hell? I don't blush, like ever. And this is *Maddox* we're talking about. My oldest and best friend. We slept in the same bed countless times when we were kids.

But you've never slept in the same bed since you became adults, a little voice reminds me.

My phone buzzes, startling me out of my thoughts. Grateful for the interruption, I answer before even checking who's calling. "Yeah?"

"Alyssa."

The voice on the other side of the line makes me stop in my tracks. "Mother."

My voice is cold, even. Not my body, though. My fingers curl around the device, gripping it tighter.

She's the last person I'd expected to call, especially after the way we left things and the whole credit card debacle. I still couldn't believe they cut me off.

Yeah, we've always had a rocky relationship. As the only daughter of the New York socialite Lucinda Armstrong-Martinez, and one of the most sought out lawyers in the state Bryce Martinez, there were certain expectations of me. Expectations I never met. It's not that I did it to spite them either, well, not all the time anyway. It's just that nothing I did was ever good enough, so at some point, I stopped trying. I was always too stubborn, too headstrong, too independent. My mother expected me to be her mini-me, and my dad wanted a quiet trophy daughter to go along with his trophy wife. However, I was never interested in pretty dresses, sitting still and smiling politely at people I secretly hated and gossiped about behind their back.

"How are you doing?"

I scoff. "Is that why you called? To ask me how I'm doing?"

"Can't a mother just want to talk to her child?" she asks defensively.

"The same mother that cut the said child out of her life a few weeks ago? I don't know, can she?" I roll my eyes, although I know she can't see me. "What do you need, Mom?"

"You don't have to be so cross, Alyssa."

Cross?

My fingers clench into a fist as red clouds my vision. "Cross? And you didn't think you were being cross when you set that ultimatum? You didn't think you were being cross when you actually went through with it, leaving me to fend for myself? You're my mother! I came to you asking for help, and you sent me away."

With each word, my voice grows louder, so loud I can see some people turning their heads to look at what the commotion is about. I turn my back to them, running my fingers through my hair.

"We gave you our support!"

Support? Is she freaking serious?

"By telling me to have an abortion?"

"We just want what's best for you!"

Best for me?

"I'm twenty-one years old!" I hiss into the phone, trying to keep my composure. "If I can't decide what's best for me, I don't know who can."

"Well, obviously you can't since you're making a mistake."

I grit my teeth. "This *mistake*, as you call it, is your grandchild."

"This *mistake* will ruin your future," She sighs exasperatedly. "What do you think people will say when they see you pregnant and without a husband?"

I let out a loud groan, rubbing my temples. "It's not the nineteen sixties. I don't need a husband to have a child."

"And you think just because it's not the sixties that people won't stare at you? Won't judge you?" Mom scoffs. "Please, Alyssa. If you really think that, then you're even more naive than I thought."

How can't she see it?

"I don't care what other people think. What I care about is this baby." I press my hand against my stomach as if that simple motion can protect it from the bad things coming from my mother's mouth. "Why did you even call, Mom? We're obviously never going to see eye to eye on this matter, so why bother?"

"I just wanted to see if you've gotten reasonable…"

I chuckle, but there's no humor in my voice. "You mean if I've decided to cave to your demands? Your ultimatums?"

"I didn't…" she starts, but I don't let her finish. I'm done. Done with this conversation. Done with my manipulative parents. Done with her. Just done.

"Well, I haven't," I cut her off. "Goodbye, Mom."

"Aly—"

I hit the end button before she can finish.

My hand falls to my side, the phone still clenched tightly in my grasp. My chest is rising and falling rapidly as my heart thunders inside my rib cage. I press my free hand against my chest, feeling the accelerated beat.

Breathe.

Forcing my lungs to open, I take in a deep breath and hold it for a few seconds before slowly letting it go. I repeat that a few times until I have my breathing under control.

This shit can't be good for the baby.

Which is the wrong thing to think about because it only

makes me more anxious. But she makes me so mad sometimes! Did she really think that just because they cut me off, I'd come running back home?

Well, they have a completely different thing coming.

I can do this. I *will* do this. Whatever it takes.

I rub my hand over my still flat stomach. "It's you and me, little one," I whisper softly. "Just you and me, and I promise I'll do my best not to let you down."

I check the time on my phone. I was planning to go home, maybe take a nap before catching up on some reading for my classes, but now I'm too agitated to do it. I need to go somewhere that will help me relax. Somewhere where I can just breathe for a while and not have to think about anything.

And I know just the place.

"Alyssa! I haven't seen you in a while."

"Hey, Angie." I pull the door closed behind me, a shiver running through me as the warm air hits my face. "Sorry, it's been a busy few weeks," I say apologetically as I make my way to the counter in the reception area.

"Nonsense." Angie waves me off. "I'm just happy to see you. How have you been?" She gives me a long, assessing look. "You look tired."

"It's been one hell of a day," I admit, not wanting to go into detail. "How have things been around here?"

"Same ol' same ol'." Angie shrugs, the movement rattling the long, dark brown braids falling over her shoulders. "We've got a few new dogs. Some got adopted. Holidays are usually a good season when it comes to pet adoptions. If only we didn't get more pets after the holidays are over."

"That sure sucks."

I couldn't imagine how people could just leave their pet somewhere and never look back. Or be so careless with them that they run away and get lost. Seriously, what's wrong with people?

"It sure is. But that's people for ya. I'm always saying animals are way better than we deserve." She shakes her head. "On that note, how is that little fluff ball of yours doing?"

I can't help but smile at the mention of my baby. "Coco is doing great."

Angie is a regular here and has been managing the dog shelter long before I even came to college. It was thanks to Coco we actually met.

I found Coco during my second year of college. She was dumped as a newborn puppy near the garbage in town, and when I saw her, I couldn't just leave her there, so I decided to take her to the shelter to get some help. Little did I know that I wouldn't be going home without her. Oh no, she would have none of it, even if I tried. Not that I could. It was love at first sight.

I always wanted a pet, begged my parents to get me one, but they never did. It's as if finding Coco was my destiny or something. She was mine the first moment our eyes met.

"That dog sure has you wrapped around her little paw." Angie's ebony skin glimmers under the fluorescent lights. She tilts her head, pulling her brows together as those gentle dark eyes take me in. "Are you sure you're okay?"

"Yeah, I just wanted to do something I love and forget about all the shitty things that have happened lately. That's all." I run my fingers through my hair.

"You know I can always use an extra set of hands around here."

A small smile spreads over my lips. "That's what I was counting on."

"C'mon, let's get you to work."

Putting the food in the bowl in the last crate, I gently pet the little chihuahua. The animal is visibly shaking every time I make a sudden move, probably due to previous abuse.

Poor baby.

"All done." I close the door and dust my hands against my jeans, rising to my full height. My back protests the movement, muscles aching. I've cleaned all the cages, taken the dogs out to the backyard, where I played with them for a while before getting back inside to feed them dinner and refill their bowls with fresh water.

"Now, just to put this thing back in its place."

I pull the bag of dog food back toward the pantry and almost trip over the old Maltese, who's been trailing after me since I got here.

"Shit, Gigi, I almost fell on you," I scold lightly, petting between the dog's ears.

The little thing is so old her hair has a grayish hue, and if it's true what Angie told me, she's both deaf and blind from her old age. Her owner died, and since her kids couldn't take care of the dog, they brought her here.

Noticing I've stopped, Rex, some kind of golden retriever mix, comes rushing toward me, demanding my attention. His tail waggles as he walks around me.

"What?" I ask, cocking my brow at him. Rex barks happily, his tail working even harder as he touches my palm with his snout. "You need something?"

Another bark, and then he repeats the motion, making me laugh.

"Wait a little bit. I have to tie my shoe." I crouch down and quickly work the laces when he barks again. I'm just reaching my hand to pat him, but apparently not fast enough because the next thing I know, he's tackling me to the ground.

The air is kicked out of my lungs, and I extend my hand back to soften my short fall. In the process, I knocked over the bag of dog food, making it scatter all over the floor. "Rex!" I chastise just before his slobbery tongue attacks me in full force. "Oh my..." His tongue swipes over my mouth, and I gently push him away. "Seriously, dude? I didn't realize..."

"What is going on here?"

It feels like all the movement stops at the stern question.

As one, Rex and I turn toward the door where Angie is standing; her hands propped on her hips, foot tapping.

"Do you two have anything to say about your behavior?"

"Hey, why are you looking at me? It's all his fault." I playfully poke Rex in his cheek, which is the wrong move because once again, his attention is on me. "Oh, no, you don't."

I push him away before he can assault my face with his tongue once again—the pup whines, clearly unhappy.

"He can be too much sometimes." Angie grabs his collar and pulls him away so I can get to my feet. She lowers her face to Rex's. "I guess his previous owners didn't teach him any manners, now did they?"

Rex looks away, the picture of innocence. Angie shakes her head. "It's always the same with this troublemaker."

"Who're you calling a troublemaker? The poor baby was just playing."

"Yeah, that's why you have to clean up the mess now."

I look around, but thankfully there isn't that much food on the floor since the bag was half empty already.

"Gizmo," Angie warns in her strict voice and points her finger toward the dog's cage. "Your bowl, mister."

Or maybe some of the dogs already ate it while I was fighting with Rex.

"I swear these dogs will be the end of me."

"And yet, you love them."

"To the bones." Once Gizmo is back in his cage, Angie turns to me. "You done soon? I'll be closing in fifteen."

Sighing, I pick up the spatula that fell out of the bag when it fell down. "I guess I'll clean this and head home."

"Sounds like a plan. Do you need help?"

I wave her off. "I'm good. Go take care of what you need. I'll finish up here."

Angie places her hand on my arm and gives me a short squeeze. "Thanks, Alyssa."

With her gone, I quickly clean up the mess we made and put the dogs back in their cages, petting them before I close the door.

The front desk is empty when I get back to the foyer.

"I'm done, Angie!" I yell, unsure of where she's at.

Her head pops out from the back office. "Going home?"

"Yeah, thanks for letting me hang out here. It's exactly what I needed."

"Thank you for the help today."

I grab my things from under the counter. "Don't even mention it."

"I'll see you soon?"

I give her a sad smile. "Maybe. Things are really messy right now, and my free time is pretty limited."

Angie gives me an understanding smile. "Well, if you want, you know where to find us. Kiss Coco for me, will ya?"

"You know it."

With a goodbye and wave, I'm out of the door and walking back to Maddox's house. Since I'm still pretty low on funds, I decided to walk instead of drive so that I could save some money on gas.

Maybe I should sell my car. That should bring me a few thousand. But then what'll I do once the baby comes? Although, I guess a convertible isn't the best solution when it comes to driving babies either. Aren't you supposed to put the baby in the back seat? There is no back seat in my car.

Irritated with myself, I run my hand through my hair.

Seriously, how did I get myself in such a mess?

I'm so lost in my thoughts I don't notice when a car pulls by the curb, window rolling down. "Hey, what are you doing?"

Startled, I turn around only to find Maddox looking at me from the inside. "Walking home? Ever tried it?" I quirk a brow, a smile playing on my lips. Maddox's brows pull together, clearly not amused.

"At night? Alone?"

I roll my eyes. "This is Blairwood, not New York."

"Still, anything could have happened." Maddox shakes his head. "C'mon, hop in."

Too tired to argue with him, I do as he asks.

"Where were you anyway?"

"Dog shelter." I secure the seat belt. "I was just going home."

Maddox pulls the car back on the road. "How is Angie doing?"

"Good. Busy as always. There's usually more work after the holidays. Seriously, I'll never understand people."

He gives me a wary look. "You didn't adopt any more pets, did you?"

If anybody understands my love for animals, especially dogs, it's Maddox.

"I wish. But I have too much on my plate now as it is. A dog back home, and a baby on the way."

"When you put it like that."

I lean my head against the window. "I just needed a moment to breathe after..." My words trail off as I look out the window as Maddox pulls onto our street.

His street.

His home.

I really need to remember that.

This is a temporary arrangement until I get back on my feet.

"After?" Maddox prompts, his worried gaze darting toward me. "What happened?"

Shit, I shouldn't have said anything.

"Nothing, really."

"It didn't sound like nothing." Maddox pulls the car into the garage and kills the engine before giving me his full attention. "What happened?"

I sigh, "My mother called."

Maddox's brows furrow. "I thought they cut you off."

His words shouldn't hurt, but for some reason, they do.

"Oh, they did," I say bitterly. "She just wanted to see if I suddenly had a change of heart given the recent circumstances."

Maddox's lips press in a thin line as the realization sets in.

"Aly, I..."

"It's fine, really." I force a smile, but my face feels tight. "Just another day in the fucked-up lives of the Martinez family." Unbuckling my seatbelt, I open the door and quickly change the subject. "Do you think they made something to eat? I'm hungry."

Chapter 17

ALYSSA

Callie: We're at the cafeteria. You coming?
Me: Be there in a bit. I just finished with my shift.

Locking my phone, I put it into my pocket and wrap my scarf tightly around my neck. Although days are just a tad longer now, and the sun is slowly starting to appear more often, it's still a far cry from spring. And knowing New England, just when you put away all your winter clothes and are ready for warmer weather, a storm will come out of nowhere and remind you that winter isn't over just yet.

I throw my backpack over my shoulder and look around to ensure I have all my things before heading out to the hallway.

"Oh, hey, Alyssa." My head snaps up at the mention of my name, and I see my boss, Monica, sitting behind her desk in the office. She looks up from whatever she's doing and smiles at me. "Can you come in for a minute?"

I tuck a runaway strand behind my ear and take a step inside. "Sure, what's up?"

She won't fire me, right? I know I'm not the best barista on the payroll, but I've gotten better since I started working at Cup It Up, and I haven't made any mistakes like I did in those first few days.

"I was just doing payroll." She hands me a check. "This is for you."

"Oh..." I take the piece of paper and glance down at it, my throat growing tight. The amount written on the check is nothing compared to my trust fund, but to me, it means everything. It's the first money I've actually had to work to earn. Something that's just mine. "Thank you," I rasp, looking up at Monica. "I really mean it. You gave me this job when I needed it the most even though I was terrible."

"You weren't terrible. You were just starting. There's a difference."

I shake my head. "I don't know about that."

"I know. You made it through the first two weeks. If you were really that terrible, I'd have fired you." Monica smiles softly. "How are you doing?"

"I'm doing good. I stopped throwing up, so that's a plus."

"How far along are you?"

"Seventeen weeks," I smile. "I should have my next doctor's appointment soon, but so far, I feel better."

"That's the most important part." Monica nods, her smile falling a little. "Make sure not to overwork yourself. I mean it. If you need help around the café, don't hesitate to ask."

"I will. Thank you."

"Great. I'll see you tomorrow?"

"You know it." With a wave and a goodbye, I'm out of her office and on my way to meet the girls.

I carefully fold the check and slip it into my wallet, so I don't lose it. It was just in time, too, since I've been running low on cash. The tips I've been getting have definitely come in handy, and I've cut down on some of my expenses, but that'll take me only so far.

I should probably get around to sorting through my things and finally put them up for sale. Between classes, work, studying, and plain tiredness, I've been putting it off. But no more. Having a job is going to be a lifesaver, but I need to *save* some money. And for that, I need to sell some of my things.

Soon.

I'll do it soon.

The cafeteria is buzzing with activity as I enter. I quickly pick my lunch: mac and cheese, salad, and a bottle of water. Thankfully my tuition has already been paid, including my meal card for the rest of the year, so at least I'm not going to starve.

I look around, trying to find the girls, but our usual table is already occupied, so I walk around, searching for them.

Why didn't I ask where they were sitting?

I'm ready to turn around and check the other section when I notice a familiar group of people sitting at a table: the table and the group of people that were my usual go-to crowd. Until recently, that is.

Chad laughs at something one of his friends said. He throws his arm over the chair of the girl sitting next to him. Not just any girl but Jennifer. His gaze darts over his shoulder, and just when he starts to look away, he does a double-take.

My fingers grip the tray in my hand tighter. I lift my jaw up, refusing to look away. Chad's eyes are wide as he realizes it's actually me. He gives me a long look, his gaze staying on my midsection a few seconds longer than necessary.

So much for nothing happening between him and Jennifer. They sure seem cozy.

Assholes.

Even from a distance I can see his throat bob.

What the hell does he think? That I'll march over there and make a scene? No chances of that happening. I'm done with both of them. So, freaking done.

With a shake of my head, I turn on the balls of my feet and walk away.

I haven't seen him since I confirmed I was pregnant, and I was fine with that. I'd actually prefer things to stay that way, but the campus is too small, and our paths are bound to cross eventually. I guess I should consider myself lucky I managed to avoid him this long.

Thankfully it doesn't take me long until I spot the girls sitting at one of the tables by the window.

"Hey, guys. Sorry, I'm late." I put the tray on the table and let my backpack drop to the floor before I start to take off my puffy jacket. "I stayed late at Cup It Up, and then…"

"Turn."

I pull my brows together at her request, completely thrown off guard. "What?"

"Turn," Yasmin repeats, but when I don't do it fast enough, she takes my hand and turns me to the side. "Is that a bump?"

"You think?" I look at her and then down to my stomach. Placing my tray on the table, I glide my hand over my shirt, making it plaster against my belly.

Every morning after I shower, I look at myself in the mirror, waiting to see… something. Some kind of change that's obvious to the eye, but there's nothing yet. My doctor told me it usually takes longer for the first pregnancy to show, but still. The only thing that doesn't have a problem in showing is my boobs. I swear they grow every second of the day. I'm already a whole cup-size bigger than I used to be. None of my bras fit any longer, and I wear a sports bra since I can't be bothered with getting new ones. It's not like anybody will see me in them anyway, so what would be the point? If that's not bad enough, they hurt like a bitch most of the time.

Callie leans her head to the side. "Maybe. Just a little."

"Or maybe that's a muffin I ate during my break." With a sigh, I sit down next to Yasmin.

"You should consider yourself lucky." Yasmin gives me a side glance. "You're almost at the halfway mark and have gained barely any weight."

"I guess there's that." I stab a piece of pasta and throw it into my mouth, my eyes closing for a second as I chew. *The best thing ever.* "My doctor said I'm right on track and shouldn't worry about it."

"You had another doctor's appointment?" Callie asks.

"Oh, no. I have another one in a couple of weeks."

Yasmin frowns. "I still can't believe you went alone to your first doctor's appointment!"

I shrug and tuck a strand of my hair behind my ear. "I mean, yeah. I told Chad, but he just wanted me to confirm it was actually real. You'd think he'd want to be there to make sure, but we all know his stance on the topic one way or the other."

"Screw the dickhead." Yasmin turns in her chair. "Why didn't you say something? One of us could have gone with you."

I look between the two of them. Are they really upset about this?

"I just wasn't ready to tell anybody. That's it."

It might have been my first solo appointment, but it won't be my last. First, solo anything, really, because there's only going to be this baby and me.

Yasmin places her hand over mine. "It is a big deal. We already told you. You don't have to do this on your own. Let us help you."

"Yasmin is right. You just have to say the word, and we'll

rearrange schedules, so you're not alone. You might be a single mom, but you don't have to do it all by yourself."

"I know, but..."

"Yeah, yeah, yeah..." Yasmin rolls her eyes at me. "You don't want to rely on others. I get it. I really do. But let us fight for the best aunt status, okay?" She turns to Callie and pokes her tongue out at her. "A status that I'll totally win."

There's a low *thump* as Callie kicks Yasmin under the table. "We'll see about that, chica."

I chuckle, but the tears prickle my eyes. "Thank you, guys," I sniffle softly. "God, I hate these hormones."

Yasmin chuckles. "I don't see why. It's funny to see you all mushy like that."

I shove her away. "I'll give you funny."

"When did you say your next appointment is?" Callie asks. "We're not letting you get out of this."

"February 15th, I think."

"Great." Callie pulls out her phone. "Morning or afternoon?"

"Morning." That one, I'm pretty sure of. I've tried to squeeze it in between my classes, so I can take an afternoon shift if there's one available.

Callie pouts. "Shit, I have classes until two in the afternoon."

"But I'm free as a bird," Yasmin grins. "See, Cals? I'm *the* best aunt, after all."

Callie glares at her. "Don't get your hopes up; there's still a long way to go."

I shake my head at their antics. "Can't you just share?"

They both turn their heads toward me as one and yell: "No!"

"Oh-kay." I lift my hands in the air in surrender. "I was just asking. No need to bite my head off."

"But seriously, see how easy it was? We'll work it out."

"I really appreciate it. You guys have done so much for me..."

Yasmin waves me off. "Hey, what are friends for?"

"I know, I know. But I still have to repay you." Which reminds me... "In other news, look at what I got." I pull the check out of my pocket and show it to them. "My very first paycheck!"

"That's amazing, Aly!" Callie smiles.

"Congrats!" Yasmin pulls me in for a hug. "I knew you could do it."

"Thank you. It feels surreal."

Still, I can't help the grin that spreads over my face. By how big my smile is, you'd think I won a lottery or something, but damn. I'm proud of myself. Sue me.

"I know it's not that much, but I can finally give Maddox rent money and hopefully put something in savings for when the baby comes."

Callie and Yasmin exchange a look and then burst into laughter.

"What?"

I look between the two of them. I know it's not *that* much, but even a little bit is something. And I'll take something over nothing any day of the week.

"You want to give Maddox rent money?" Callie shakes her head, still chuckling. "Do *you* even know Maddox?"

"Umm... considering we've been friends for the better part of my life. I'd say I do."

"Then you should know he won't accept rent money. None of us pay rent for the place. We just pay the utilities, split the grocery bill, and make sure everything is stocked at all times. If we didn't, Maddox would probably do it himself, too."

"Seriously? I didn't know that."

"I didn't know it either until I moved in and asked him about it, and he just waved me off. Apparently, buying a house there was a good future investment, and he doesn't want his friends to pay," Callie shrugs.

Yasmin just shakes her head. "The problems of being rich."

"I guess so."

I mean, I know Maddox comes from money. Our families have been friends for generations. Between that and the fact that he sold some of his video games in the last few years, he doesn't even have to rely on his family's money to get by since he has money of his own.

He made something out of himself. Not like you, a little voice reminds me.

But is that even surprising? Maddox was always extremely bright, even as a child. He skipped a couple of grades in middle school, and even though he was the youngest, he was the smartest person in our class. More often than not, it seemed like he didn't even have to try, and he'd get an A+, but I knew better than that. I've seen his mind work, and I've seen the toll it took on him socially and emotionally. He always had difficulty making friends, even just interacting with other people. He was quiet and shy, and often people would only approach him when they needed something from him. I've seen it too many times to count, and I never wanted to be *that* person.

Yasmin nudges me with her elbow. "What are you thinking about so hard over there?"

"I still want to do something as a thank you. Maddox has done so much for me. If it weren't for him, I'd probably end up homeless and sleeping in my car."

"I mean, you could go to the store and get some groceries?" Callie suggests. "Hayden and I were planning to do it this weekend."

I think about it. It's not a bad idea, but it's so... impersonal?

"Or you could cook him dinner?" Yasmin shrugs. "That boy doesn't eat nearly as much as he should."

I chuckle. "If somebody asks you, nobody's eating enough."

"Hey, don't blame me; it's all thanks to my Mexican side of the family. We love to feed people."

Ain't that the truth.

"I don't know." I look down at my plate of half-eaten pasta. "I'm not that good of a cook."

"It doesn't have to be anything fancy. I'm pretty sure everybody can do pasta. Do you want me to send you the link to one of my favorite recipes? It's really easy to make."

I give Yasmin a skeptical look. "Easy for you or easy for us normal non-cooking people?"

She opens her mouth, but Callie interrupts her. "It's *easy*. I made it the last time we were at Grams' place. Granted, it wasn't as good as when Yasmin made it, but it was edible."

Even the fact that Callie made it doesn't inspire confidence in me.

"If the queen of takeout can cook it, you'll be fine," Yasmin tries to reassure me.

"Yeah, I guess we'll see. How much should I make for all of us?"

"Oh, we're not going to be home." Yasmin pulls out her phone, presumably to find the recipe.

That gets my attention. "How so?"

"The hockey team has a home game tonight, so we've decided to go and watch Zane play. So, it's going to be just you and Maddox."

Just Maddox and me.

For some reason, my heart does a little flip, and my stomach tightens. I shift in my seat. "Oh... Okay."

Callie must see something on my face because she asks: "Did you want to go?"

"No," I shake my head. "If I can choose between a hockey game, party, or sleep, I'll choose sleep."

Just then, my phone vibrates.

"That's the recipe," Yasmin says, putting her phone away.

Unlocking my phone, I opened the link she sent me and scanned the instructions.

"It's for six servings," Yasmin explains. "But if there's any extra left, somebody will probably eat it later. I swear those guys could eat an entire fridge in a day."

"Welcome to life with athletes," Callie smiles sweetly. "Where fighting for the last sandwich will make *The Hunger Games* seem like child's play."

At that, we all burst into laughter.

An hour later, I'm greeted by Coco's excited bark when I enter the quiet house. Letting the grocery bags drop on the floor, I crouch down to pet her. "Hey, pretty girl. What have you been up to?"

As if she can understand my question, she barks excitedly as I get to my feet and take the grocery bags into the kitchen.

Since I was walking, I'd decided to just get the essentials, so I didn't have to carry too many things, but I've also got everything I'll need for that recipe Yasmin sent me.

I put the bags on the counter and look over my shoulder at Coco, who's fallen in step with me. "Just let me put this away, get that pasta cooking, and we'll go out. Okay, Coco?"

It takes me a while to find a pot, but when I do, I fill it with water and put it on the stove to heat as I pull out the groceries. When the water starts to boil, I grab the bag of spaghetti I got and check my phone for the recipe.

"A pound of spaghetti?" I pull my brows together.

Coco barks again. When I look up, I see her standing by the door, watching me expectantly.

"Just a second, Coco."

I glance at the recipe and then at the bag in my hand.

"What the hell." I open the bag and pour it all into the pot. "Somebody will eat it later."

Tossing the bag in the garbage, I turn around. "C'mon, Coco, let's get you outside for a few minutes until this is done."

Chapter 18

MADDOX

As I push open the garage door, I open my mouth to yell hello to anybody who might be downstairs when I smell something burning in the air. And then I see smoke.

What the...

Coco starts barking from somewhere in the distance.

"Shit, shit, shit!"

Aly?

My stomach sinks as I imagine Aly stuck in a burning house. Aly trying to get out but not being able to find a way. Aly trying to breathe but only inhaling smoke.

My heartbeat jumps, my hands turn clammy. I let my bag drop to the floor and rush down the hallway, following the sound of barking.

"Aly?" I call out, my voice filled with panic.

She has to be okay. She *has* to. I'll get to her, and I'll get her out, and everything's going to be oka—

"How did this happen? They said it was *easy!*" I can hear her grumble, and then something clatters loudly.

"Aly!" I yell as I enter the kitchen, only to come to a stop.

It takes me a moment to register that while the space is filled with smoke, so much smoke I'm surprised the smoke detector didn't go off; there's no fire.

Thank fuck.

Aly turns around abruptly when she hears me, her blue eyes wide as they land on mine. They're red-rimmed, her hair is a mess, and she's biting the inside of her cheek, but even so, one lone tear slides down her face.

"Maddox."

She's fine.

The relief that slams into me almost knocks me on my ass.

I give myself a few more seconds just to look at her, to convince myself she's really okay. Then, I get into action. Crossing the room, I make sure the stove is turned off before I go and open every single window in the kitchen. Then, I go back out in the hallway and open the front door to let the smoke out.

Only when that's done do I return to the kitchen to find Aly holding onto Coco, her face burrowed into the dog's fur as she leans against the counter.

"How come I always make a mess of things?"

I run my hand over my face. "What happened?"

"I put the pasta on to cook." Aly shakes her head, more tears gathering in her eyes. "The girls convinced me it was going to be easy; it's just pasta, after all. Ha! There's no "just" anything when it comes to cooking. Me cooking? I guess I should have known it had bad idea written all over it, but no, I had to do it. I wanted to surprise you. Do something nice as a thank you for letting me stay here, but then the damn thing got *burned*. Seriously, how does one *burn* pasta?"

With each word, she gets more agitated until the tears finally start to fall.

"Shit, Aly." I go to her, wrapping her into my arms and pulling her closer. I lean down, burrowing my nose into her hair and inhaling deeply. She smells of smoke, but there's that familiar smell of vanilla and orange hiding amongst it. "I don't care about the pasta. I'm just glad that you're okay."

"I figured I had time. I swear I left it for not even ten minutes, just to let Coco out since she's been in the house all alone and needed to do her business. But when I got here, the smoke was everywhere."

I look over her shoulder at the pot she dropped in the sink. The spaghetti is overflowing the small pot. All the water has evaporated, and I'm pretty sure I will find the pasta burned if I look at the bottom.

I tighten my arms around her. "It's okay."

"It's not okay!" She stomps her foot and pulls back. Good, I'd rather see her angry than have her crying because if there's one thing I can't take, it's Aly's tears. "I almost burned your house down."

"You didn't burn my house down. It was just an accident." I wipe away the tears staining her cheeks. "C'mon. I'll clean up, and we can order something in."

"You don't have to..."

She tries to turn around, but I don't let her budge. "I'll do it. You go and take a shower."

"You're saying I stink?" she asks, that adorable furrow appearing between her brows.

"I didn't say that. I just want you to relax."

"You just don't want me to see the extent of the damage."

That too. She is too hard on herself as it is.

"It's just a pot, Aly. I don't give a damn about it. I'm glad that you're okay. You scared me to death." I shake my head, refusing to go back to that moment when I just entered the house and realized she might be inside—the almost paralyzing fear of something happening to her. "You're what matters. Now go take a shower and pick a movie. I'll clean this up and order something. How does pizza sound?"

"Pizza sounds amazing. But," she jabs me in the chest, "I'm paying."

I lift my arms in the air. The corner of my mouth twitches, but I try to keep a serious face. "As you wish."

She gives me a doubtful look, for a good reason too. "I mean it, Maddox. It's my treat."

"Didn't I just agree to it?"

Aly rolls her eyes. "As if I don't know you."

She has me there.

"Maybe I should see if anybody else wants to eat pizza before I order."

Aly stops at the doorway and looks over her shoulder. "They're not home. Zane has a game, so they went to watch."

I scratch the back of my neck. "So, it's just the two of us?" Hello Mr. Obvious.

"It's just the two of us," Aly confirms. "So, pizza?"

"Pizza," I nod. "Sure thing."

With a smile, Aly walks out of the kitchen. I stare into the hallway, listening to her soft steps climb to the second floor before letting out an audible sigh and wipe my palms against my legs.

It's just like any other day.

Just like any other day.

Maybe if I repeat it enough times, I'll actually believe it.

After placing our order, I go to the sink and look at the damage. Just like I suspected, the pasta is completely burned to the bottom, so I don't even bother cleaning it up; just throw it all into the garbage and take the bag out for good measure.

The last thing I want is for Alyssa to see it. Knowing her, she'll probably insist on buying a new pot or something.

Then I quickly put away some of the groceries left on the counter before going back into the hallway. I pick up my bag and take it upstairs just as Aly is getting out of the shower.

My throat tightens when I see her. She's wearing one of those oversized shirts she likes to sleep in; only this one isn't hers. It's mine.

"I hope you don't mind." She stops in the doorway, her fingers curling around the edge of the shirt, tugging it this way and that. "Mine was dirty, but I didn't do laundry, so I'm a little short on clothes."

She's not wrong. The shirt falls short, barely reaching her mid-thigh.

And now, I'm having all kinds of thoughts, and none of them are exactly clean.

Fuck. Me.

My throat tightens as I try to swallow a groan. I need to get myself in check and fast because if I don't...

"Maddox?"

"It's fine," I croak. "Maybe put on some pants? Or do you want me to go and get that pizza when it arrives?"

"What's wrong with this?"

Besides the fact that it's too freaking short?

Nope, nothing wrong with it at all.

I open my mouth, still trying to come up with an answer that doesn't include: I don't want the delivery dude to see your panties—*Which you shouldn't be looking at either because she's your* best friend—but she's already rolling her eyes and walking away.

"Doesn't matter."

She pulls open the closet and bends down to get a pair of pants from a lower shelf.

Not looking, I remind myself, turning my back to her. *Definitely, not looking.*

"I think I'm going to take a quick shower." I clear my throat. "You good?"

"Go, I've got it. I'll pick a movie while I wait."

I look over my shoulder to find her grinning. "You would *cheat?*"

Aly throws the damn pants on the bed and turns to me, her arms crossed over her chest. "Who're you calling a cheat?"

"You." I lift my brow, which earns me an eye roll. "Fine."

We extend our hands at the exact same time. "Rock, paper, scissors."

The motion is flawless, the result of countless times we've performed it in the past just because of this exact reason.

"Damn, how do you do that?" Aly groans when my paper beats her rock.

"Luck?"

Aly plops down on the bed, disturbing Coco's sleep. "Why do I find it highly unlikely? You leave nothing to luck."

I guess she has me there.

"Which one will it be, Mr. Lucky?" Alyssa grabs her pants, it's one of those tight ones, and I watch her slowly pull them up her long legs.

"How about you choose out of my favorites while I take a shower?"

A cold, cold shower.

"You're letting me choose?" Aly mock gasps, but I can see the corner of her mouth twitch.

"Out of my favorites," I remind her, grabbing a quick change of clothes.

"Yeah, yeah. *Captain America,* it is. I don't have the patience to watch *Star Wars* all over again."

I look over my shoulder. "What's wrong with *Star Wars?*"

"Besides the fact that it's boring? Absolutely nothing."

"It's a classic!"

"Exactly! Boring."

I pull my brows together, trying to give her my most serious look. "If I were you, I'd be really careful what you say."

"Why?" Aly bats her eyelashes innocently. "What are you gonna do?"

Dozens of different scenarios of what I could do pop in my head, but none of them are exactly friendly. Like tackling her to the bed and pulling those leggings off, letting my hands feel that smooth skin and trace the freckles covering her body. Or even better yet, lowering my head and finally, *finally* kissing her like I wanted to for years.

Get out of here. Now!

I take a step toward the bathroom, a pair of sweats and a t-shirt in hand. "I might change my mind about letting you pick the movie. I haven't watched *Star Wars* in quite some time. Maybe it's time for a marathon."

Aly lets out a soft gasp, "You wouldn't."

No, I wouldn't, but I don't need her to know that.

"Don't say I didn't warn you." I knock against the doorway and slip inside the bathroom, pulling my shirt off and tossing it into the bin.

"When did you say the pizza is coming?" Aly calls from the bedroom.

"Should be here in fifteen minutes or so," I yell back.

"Sounds good."

Taking the rest of my clothes off, I turn on the shower. Without bothering to wait for it to warm up, I step under the spray, hissing softly when the cold water touches my skin.

"Fucking hell."

The water is icy, but even that doesn't help extinguish this need rising inside of me.

This is bad. So, so bad.

Stability. Friendship. That's what Aly needs right now. Not for her best friend to suddenly turn into a horny teenager.

I press my palms against the tiles, my head falling down as I close my eyes. Which is a bad idea because the image of Aly standing out in my bedroom, wearing nothing but my shirt that barely covers anything, pops back into my head. Her bright hair falling around her in wild curls. Those silky-smooth legs going on for miles...

My dick throbs painfully, reminding me that after all, I'm just a man—a weak one at that.

I let my hand fall down, wrapping my fingers around my dick. I give it a firm squeeze, but even the pressure at the base doesn't help with the raging hard-on.

"Jesus."

I give my head a little shake.

It's not like I can go back like this. There's no way she won't notice.

At least, I use it as an excuse as my hand slowly slides up my hard length, my grip firm. A low groan rumbles at the back of my throat. I bite the inside of my cheek as I work my length slowly.

An image of Aly laying on my bed, her hair spread over the white pillow as those blue eyes look at me, twinkling with amusement, pops in my mind.

My hand tightens around my dick, movements growing faster. I slide my thumb over the sensitive head, and a shudder runs down my spine. I inhale deeply; a faint smell of Aly's shampoo still lingers in the air, making it almost seem like she's here. Like my hand is hers. It's her, not me, who's working my cock with a vice grip. I can see it. Hear her softly whisper in my ear as her hand slides up and down my dick. See her drop to her knees and then...

My release is so sudden I barely manage to hold back my groan as my muscles tighten, and I come all over my hand and tiles. My breaths come out in ragged pants as my muscles relax, and I take a few steps back, leaning my back against the wall.

I listen, praying to God that Aly didn't hear me, but I can

barely hear anything over the running water and roaring in my ears.

It takes me a whole minute to gather myself enough to finish washing up. The whole bathroom is foggy when I get out of the shower. I quickly dry myself and put on my clothes, grateful that I can't see my reflection in the mirror, see the guilt written all over my face.

What the hell was that? What is wrong with me? Imagining Aly like that...

I shake my head. Now is not the time. If I stay in the bathroom much longer, Aly will start wondering what the hell I'm doing, and there is no way I can explain it.

Taking in one long breath, I open the door and enter the room, just when Aly does.

She smiles at me, a pizza box in hand. "Just in time!"

The smell of pizza fills the room almost instantly. She walks to the bed, Coco in tow, and sits down, putting the box on the bed. She opens the lid, grabs one slice in hand, and takes a big bite.

Her eyes fall closed as she chews and moans softly. "This is so good."

I close my eyes, fighting the reaction of my body.

So much for my cold shower.

This is real torture; having something you want desperately so close but so far away.

"Are you coming?"

"W-what?!" My eyes pop open, and I swear I can feel the heat rise up my neck.

Aly smiles, but I can see she's confused by my reaction. "Are you coming to bed, or do you plan to stand there all night? If you don't hurry up, I won't be responsible when there's no pizza left, just sayin'."

"Bed," My throat feels tight, the word sounding more like a

croak. "Right."

Get a grip, Maddox.

Slowly I make my way to the bed and sit down, making sure to leave some distance between us as Aly starts the movie.

The screen of my laptop lights up with the intro. "*The First Avenger?* I thought we were watching my favorite."

"You love Marvel."

She's right, but I can't help but tease her. "Not like *Star Wars.*"

"I got you pizza. You can't have both pizza and *Star Wars.*" She pokes her tongue out at me. "Can we now watch in peace?"

"Fine." I grab a slice of pizza. "But just for the record, I know what you're doing."

"Having my fill of Chris Evans? What's the harm in that?"

I tilt my head to the side. "Nothing, I guess."

Is that what she wants? A real-life Chris Evans? Is this why she was dating Chuck? Because he looks similar?

"God knows I don't have luck with real men. I can at least enjoy some fictional eye candy."

"Chuck's an asshole," I mutter. My eyes are on the screen, following the geeky actor. That's me, while Aly usually goes for the Chris Evanses of the world.

Aly gives me a look. "Chad," she corrects and turns her attention back to the movie. "And I picked him, so I'm also at fault here. But all that's done. I need to concentrate on my future."

Her palm brushes over her lower stomach, the gesture soft and loving. "Our future."

My throat grows tight. I push my glasses up my nose and turn my head to the side. Aly's eyes are fixed on the screen, but her hand is still on her stomach. "You're going to do great," I whisper, needing her to know that.

No matter how much she tries to hide it, Aly worries about

the future, the uncertainty of it all. I can't even imagine what she must be going through, but what I know is that if anybody can do it, she can. Besides, she's going to be an amazing mother. I just know it.

Aly turns toward me, one lone curl falling in her face. "Thank you."

"For what?" Unable to resist it, I lean closer and gently push it back.

"For believing in me even when I don't."

I let my hand drop and cover hers. Intertwining our fingers together, I give her hand a squeeze. "Always."

Aly smiles, and shifts in her seat, moving closer to me. She leans against me, resting her head against my shoulder. I try to let her sit like that for a bit, but the pose is uncomfortable, so instead, I wrap my arm around her shoulders.

For a while, we watch the movie in silence. We've seen it so many times in the past since it's her favorite out of all the Marvel movies that I know it by heart now. Still, every time she suggests it, I can't help myself but agree.

I'm probably a sucker for punishment. There are so many similarities between Steve Rogers and me; it's not even surprising. He also had a thing for a pretty girl that was way out of his league. Maybe it's a nerd thing. I push my glasses up my nose. Maybe...

"Oh my God, will you stop already?"

Aly tilts her head back, her blue eyes meeting mine.

"What?"

"The glasses. Seriously, when was the last time you changed the frames?"

Aly's hand reaches for my face. I try to pull back, but it's useless since I'm leaning against the headboard, and her body is plastered to mine.

"What are you doing?" I ask just as Aly pulls the glasses off my nose, instantly making my vision blurry.

"Maybe if I break them..."

Before she can finish, I grab her arm and flip her on her back.

Aly sucks in a breath, her eyes growing wide as I loom over her.

It takes me a moment to register our position. The feel of her soft curves under me. The way her chest rises and falls rapidly, making her breasts brush against my chest with each inhale.

A wave of heat spreads through my body. My muscles tighten in response, electricity coursing under my skin from every point of contact. It's like I've been burned.

It's too much—her smell, her nearness, her touch. It's all too damn much.

"I-I... Shit, I'm sorry."

I pull back quickly and casually, or at least I hoped so, grabbing one of the dozen pillows Aly brought with her and pulling it over my lap to hide my hard-on.

Fuck, fuck, fuck.

Did she see? Does she...

Aly turns on her belly, those blue eyes dancing with mischief. "It's fine."

"It's not fine," I protest.

Did I really have to flip her over and brush myself against her like that? Seriously, what's wrong with me? Now I wouldn't even be surprised if she once again starts talking about leaving...

Aly rolls her eyes. "Just because I'm pregnant doesn't mean I'm made of porcelain."

Wait... "What?"

"I know it might be strange to you, but women have been pregnant for millennia now. Carrying another being inside of us doesn't mean we're suddenly fragile."

She thinks I'm worried about hurting the baby?

That thought didn't even cross my mind until now. I was too busy going over all the scenarios of what might have happened if Aly realized that I got a freaking hard-on for her.

I rub my neck, trying to avoid her gaze. "Yeah, sure. Sorry. I didn't think."

"We're fine." Aly turns to her back and raises her shirt.

My throat bobs as the smooth skin of her belly appears in my line of vision.

Not helping, Aly. Not helping.

She slides her hand over her stomach.

"Do you think it got bigger?" Aly asks, her focus on her belly. "Yasmin said she saw a bump earlier, so I tried looking at it from different angles before I took a shower, but it looks the same."

"S-should..." My voice comes out rough, so I clear my throat before continuing. "Should it be by now?"

"Maybe? I'm in my second trimester, but even so, I feel like something *should* have changed, you know?" Alyssa turns her head toward me. "I'm pregnant. Shouldn't it be different? It feels different, yet the same."

I guess she's right on that. I can feel it too, but it doesn't have anything to do with her being pregnant—this strange place where all is the same, yet different. She's still my best friend, but now she lives in my house. I'm still in love with her but can't tell her because of the fear of losing her. We're sleeping in the same bed, yet she's carrying another man's baby.

"It's going to get better."

"I really hope so."

Finally, she pulls her shirt down, her gaze moving back to the screen. "Damn, so much for watching the movie."

"It's not like it's the first time we're watching it."

"I guess you have that right." Aly turns to her side. She

slides her hand under her head, but apparently, she's not comfortable enough because she keeps shifting trying to find a better position. "Do you mind..."

Before I can even react, she lays her head on the pillow in my lap—the same pillow covering my bulge.

Great. Just great.

Aly lets out a satisfied sigh, "Better." She looks over her shoulder, those blue eyes staring right at me. "You mind?"

How could I say yes when she's looking at me like that? With those bright blue eyes that see to my very core?

I can't, that's how.

"It's fine."

Finally, content, she lies back down.

"I love this scene," Aly murmurs, her eyes fixed on the screen.

I hum non-committedly, my attention not on the movie but on her. The way her eyelashes cast a shadow over her cheekbones. The dusting of freckles covering her cheek and the bridge of her nose. The way her hair spreads over the pillow.

"They are the ultimate relationship goals. Every girl deserves a guy who looks at her the way Steve does Peggy."

I look at you that way, I want to say, but the words are stuck in my throat like they always are. *I've always looked at you that way.*

Not that she ever noticed it.

My chest squeezes, that familiar phantom pain spreading through me as we watch the movie in silence. At some point, Aly falls asleep, but I don't stop the movie. I don't move. I barely even breathe.

I just hold her, watching over her as I always do and hoping one day, she might see how I really feel.

Hoping that one day she might see *me*.

Chapter 19

MADDOX

Something tickles me just under my nose. I frown, trying to pull back, but it's there again. I raise my hand, rubbing my finger under my nose as I open my eyes, and my gaze falls on the red hair that's spread over my torso.

My chest tightens like it does every time I wake up and find Alyssa sleeping next to me. I guess after three weeks, I shouldn't even be surprised by it, but I am. It's like a part of me is waiting for the other shoe to drop.

Slowly, so as not to wake her, I slide my hand over her hair, smoothing the unruly curls away from her freckled face. Aly snuggles closer to me, clinging to me like a koala. Her arm is thrown over my stomach, leg slipping between mine as she sleeps soundly.

I shift slowly, trying to move, so her knee isn't pressed against my dick, but it's no use. The only thing it does is wake up Coco from her sleep at the bottom of the bed. Her large brown eyes fixed on me with such intensity I stop moving because I'm wondering if she's contemplating biting my foot off for disturbing her beauty sleep.

Just then, Aly's alarm starts to ring, and she stirs. A frown appears between her brows, her body tensing as if she's protesting the wake-up call before she blinks her eyes open. The big blue irises focus on me, and for a heartbeat, we just stare at one another.

There's always this moment, a split second, every time she opens her eyes when my heart waits for her to finally see me.

It waits and waits and waits...

"I swear I don't do this on purpose," Aly says, rubbing her hand over her sleepy face.

... but it never comes.

"I know. It's not a big deal."

Just big, freaking torture.

"It should be. You didn't sign up to be my own personal pregnancy pillow."

I pull my brows together. "Pregnancy pillow?" What the hell is a pregnancy pillow? "Do I even want to know?"

Aly opens her mouth but then seems to think better of it. "You know what? I don't think so." Before I can say anything more, Aly gives me a tight squeeze. "If I'm being completely honest, you're even better than a pregnancy pillow."

My eyes fall shut, and it takes all of me to hold back a groan. "Thanks?"

"You're welcome." Aly pushes upright and smiles at me. "I better get up. I want to do some studying before my shift at the café."

Her shirt slides down, giving me a good view of her cleavage as she gets up and out of bed. I listen to her coo to Coco before she slips into the bathroom. Only when she's out of sight do I turn around and bury my head into the pillow, letting out a groan.

Not that it helps, because it's her pillow, and although she barely sleeps on it, it smells like her.

It all does. It's like she's imprinted on this room, and I won't ever be able to get her out of it.

I clench my fingers tighter and make a few quick jabs at the bag. A drop of sweat falls in my eyes as I take a step back, readjusting my position and going back into a two-three combination.

My breaths come out in ragged pants, but I don't let it slow me down. There is so much restless energy buzzing under my skin that I fear I won't be able to get it out of me anytime soon.

"What did the bag do to you?"

I throw another jab at the bag and mutter: "I'm not sure what you mean."

My eyes fixed on the bag, my motions not wavering for a second. One-two. Three-two. One-two.

Zane walks by me and stands behind the bag, fixing it for me. "Let's not pretend like we don't know what this is about."

A left jab. "No idea what you're talking about. I'm just practicing."

"What you're doing is trying to beat this bag into submission," Zane grunts, his muscles flexing as he tries to keep the bag in place at the quick succession of punches I deliver. "This doesn't have anything to do with the fact that you haven't been sleeping on the couch?"

A right hook. "Did they send you to check in on me?"

"No, I figured I might check in on you since you rushed by the kitchen without stopping to grab your morning coffee, and you haven't come out of the gym in close to two hours."

Two hours? I didn't even realize that much time had passed.

Time moves differently down here, slower. Or maybe that's all just in my head.

"I'm still alive, as you can see," I pant, each word accompanied by a jab.

"I can see that." His eyes narrow as he follows my movements. "Lift that left arm higher. You're leaving yourself too open."

I do as he says before going into another set of well-practiced jabs.

Zane corrects a few more things. The guy's a perfectionist when it comes to coaching athletes, and he's still in college. One day he'll lead a gym or a team of his own, and he'll produce some top-notch athletes. I readjust my stance, letting him take over. My mind empties of all the distractions, and it's just me, the bag, and Zane's steady voice leading me through the motions.

By the time he calls it quits, my shirt is drenched in sweat, and my whole body feels like jelly.

I fall on the mat. Zane walks to the fridge on one side of the room and grabs a couple of water bottles, tossing one at me. "Ready to talk about what's eating at you?"

I open the bottle and chug down the contents. "Not particularly."

Zane just lifts his brow and leans against the wall. Slowly he opens his own water bottle and takes a pull, waiting.

I run my hand through my sweaty hair. "It's this whole situation."

"With Alyssa?"

"Of course, with Alyssa. Do you know of another girl that's sleeping in my bed?"

"Well, no. That would be awkward."

"It's awkward enough as it is." I shake my head, the image of a sleeping Alyssa popping in my mind. Her arms wrapped around me, her scent clinging to my sheets. "I'm serious. It's driving me crazy. She's driving me crazy, and she can't even see it. She's etched into every single aspect of my life, and it's messing with my mind. But I can't have her see it because I don't want to upset her when things are so fucked up in her life. But I don't think I can go on much longer like this. It's not fair to me..."

The step creaks, stopping me mid-sentence. Zane's eyes widen, and I'm pretty sure mine match his expression as we both turn around just to catch a flash of red hair as Aly climbs upstairs.

"Shit." I start pulling my glove off, but the damn thing doesn't budge. "Shit, shit, shit. I have..."

Zane stops in front of me, his palm pressing against my chest and pushing me back. "I don't think this is a good idea."

Not a good idea? I shake my head in protest as panic spreads through my body. "I have to catch up to her and explain."

How much did she hear? Probably enough since she decided running away was a better option than staying here and confronting me about it.

"You both are upset. The last thing you need is to go after her right this moment. It'll only complicate things further."

"But..."

"You can explain later. You need to get your head on straight now if you don't want to make an even bigger mess out of it. That is if you're not willing to tell her how you really feel."

My gaze darts over Zane's shoulder. I know he's right. I know if I go after her, the only thing I'll do is make everything even worse than it is. How can I explain what I just said without telling her the real reason behind my frustration? I can't. And if I try to give her some bullshit excuse, she'll see right through me.

"C'mon, let's get this all out in the open on the mat, and then you can call the guys over, and we can have a game night." Zane slaps my cheek to draw my attention. "You straight?"

I let out a breath, turning my attention to him. "I'm straight."

"Good," Zane nods. He goes to the wall and grabs the second pair of gloves. "Let's see what you've got."

He pulls me toward the mat, but once again, my attention turns back to the stairs and the ghost of Aly running away.

Fuck this.

"I can't," I say, rushing toward the stairs. I take two at a time, and I'm panting by the time I make my way upstairs. Hayden peeks his head through the kitchen doorway.

"Have you seen Aly?"

"No, I just got home. Why?"

"Just asking." After checking the living room, I continue up toward our bedroom, only to find it also empty.

I curl my fingers into a fist and slam it against the doorway. "Shit."

Coco lifts her head at the sudden noise.

"Sorry, Coconut," I say, going for my desk to grab my phone. *Where the hell is she?*

Ignoring the messages, I dial the number I know by heart and wait. The phone rings and rings, but nobody answers. When the voice mail picks up, I swear once again, running my fingers though my sweaty hair.

She heard. She must have heard something. That's the only explanation.

I open my inbox, my fingers hovering over the keyboard.

But what do I even tell her when I don't know how much she actually heard?

No, I'll have to talk to Aly once she gets back home.

Exiting the draft, I catch the sight of the message on top of my inbox. Mia. I open it to find a meme attached inside along with laughing emojis.

The corner of my mouth twitches.

Me: We're having a game night tonight. If you wanna join.
Mia: I should be working on an essay.
I'm about to tell her it's okay when three little dots appear on the screen.
Mia: Which means I'll definitely come.

Chapter 20

ALYSSA

She's etched into every single aspect of my life, and it's messing with my mind.

Maddox's words still ring in my head, loud and clear. The look of despair I saw on his face is still engraved into my memory. The way his eyes were blazing, brows pulled together in frustration, the jitteriness... It's been the only thing I could think about during my shift.

I was so lost in my own mind. It was like my first day at the job all over again. In the end, Monica sent me home since there weren't that many people anyway.

I can't have her see it because I don't want to upset her when things are so fucked up in her life. But I don't think I can go on much longer like this. It's not fair to me...

I swallow the lump in my throat, my hands shaking as I pull the last of my clothes out of the closet and drop them on the bed.

Coco gives me an annoyed glance, huffs like the drama queen she is, and jumps down, going to her own bed as I start to go through my clothes.

It shouldn't hurt. I knew this was only temporary. I knew I

shouldn't get used to being here and that sooner or later, Maddox, would have enough of me and want to get his life back.

Tears burn my eyes.

Then why does it hurt so much?

I bite the inside of my cheek to hold them at bay.

Because this is Maddox we're talking about.

My Maddox. My best friend. And I didn't expect it'd happen so soon. Not when my life was slowly going back to normal.

"Hey, Aly..." Yasmin stops abruptly in the doorway of my room—Maddox's room, I remind myself, it's Maddox's room—and takes in the space. "Did the closet explode or something?"

Blinking a few times to clear my vision, I look around to avoid her gaze. "Or something. What's up? When did you get here?"

I managed to sneak into the house without anybody noticing since Maddox and the guys were occupied playing video games. I figured I could use the time and go over my clothes to figure out what's worth selling. I planned to do it the day I moved here, but then I kept pushing it off for different reasons. Not anymore.

It's not fair to me...

Maddox is right. It's not fair that I use him like this. I have to get my shit in order and to do that, I have to sort through this mess and sell the majority of this, so I may be able to scrap enough for one months' rent.

Yasmin walks into the room and picks up one of the dresses I put on the bed. "What are you doing?"

"Seeing what I'm going to sell."

She lets the dress go and shifts through a few more. "Is this the keep pile?"

"This is the sell pile." I point to the almost empty closet. "That is the keep pile."

Yasmin's mouth falls open. "You're selling all of this? Why?"

I was actually pretty surprised with the amount of stuff I've bought over the years. Most of those dresses I've worn barely a time or two, meaning they were in pretty good condition. Considering each piece cost at least five hundred bucks, I had a small fortune in fabric just laying around.

"That's the idea. At least I'll try." I take the dress from her and toss it back on the bed, giving her a pointed look. "And you know why."

"Alyssa..."

"What?" I lift my hands defensively. "It's not like I'm going to wear it, anyway."

"You could wear it after you give birth. You shouldn't sell it all."

I roll my eyes. "Because Gucci goes so well with baby's puke. No way. Besides, I need the money now."

"I could lend you..."

"No, I'm not taking your money. You already helped me find a job. Maddox and the guys gave me a place to stay. I'm not taking any more. I just need to figure out where to sell it. I don't expect to get the money I paid for it, but I don't want to give it for cheap either."

I don't have the luxury to just give it away to the first person offering any amount of money.

"eBay?" Yasmin suggests.

"I guess I could try that. Not that I ever sold anything online."

"I'm sure if you asked Maddox, he'd help you."

"I..."

She's etched into every single aspect of my life, and it's messing with my mind.

I blink, pushing Maddox's harsh words out of my head. "I guess I could ask him," I say, careful not to give anything away.

The last thing I need is my best friends asking what's with this sudden need to sell my stuff and find another place to live.

"If he can create something out of nothing, I'm pretty sure he can help you set up a seller's profile on eBay." Yasmin starts folding the dresses. "How is that going, anyway?"

I turn to my closet, trying to avoid her gaze. "Oh, you know…"

"No, I don't. I just heard the guys gossiping."

I frown. "Gossiping about what?"

"How Maddox said he'll sleep on the couch, but the living room has been empty so far."

"I'm not about to throw him out of his own room!" I protest. He hates me enough as it is. Okay, maybe hate is too strong of a word, but I'm definitely messing with his life, and he was loud and clear about not appreciating it.

For a moment, I thought they heard me come down to the gym. I was hoping to ask Maddox to give me a lift to work; instead, I found him pounding at the bag and telling Zane all about how I was disturbing his life.

Yas lifts her arms in surrender. "Hey, don't shoot the messenger. I mean," her gaze darts toward the bed. "It's a big bed."

Did they seriously think I'd do something like that? This is his house—his space. And as somebody who has recently lost both, I'm not about to do the same to another person.

My best friend, no less.

"That's exactly what I said. Besides, we're best friends. Have been since we were kids. I don't even remember the number of times we've slept together. It's not like it's a big deal."

"So, it's working okay?"

The image of Maddox's strong hands wrapped around me, his warmth surrounding me, crosses my mind. My cheeks heat.

What the hell?

"Alyssa?"

"Hmm?" I look up, shaking myself out of my thoughts. "Oh, yeah, everything's perfect."

Not fair. Not fair. Not fair.

Yas's eyes narrow. "Are you okay? You seem a bit flushed."

"F-fine," I croak and quickly busy myself with folding the clothes. "I just feel hot from all the shuffling around."

And thinking about my best friend sleeping under me. Like seriously, what the hell's with that? The bed *is* big. I'm not sure how I find myself always on his side, curled around him. It's like I've turned into Coco. I love my dog, but that puppy is a real bed hog.

And apparently, so are you.

Only I'm not just a bed hog; I'm a life hog, too.

"I think I'll crack open a window."

The cool late afternoon air hits me right in the face, but the only thing it does is accentuate even more how hot I feel. Maybe it's the pregnancy hormones?

I shake my head at myself. I can't believe I've become one of *those* women so quickly.

"What are you going to do about all these clothes?"

I look at the mass rising from the bed. "I guess I should put it in the suitcase until I figure out how to set up the eBay profile to sell it."

"Or just ask Maddox to help you."

"Or that."

Yasmin grabs the suitcase I left by the dresser and pulls it to the bed. Coco looks up, curious about what's going on. Not that I can blame her, the number of changes we've been through in the last few weeks just keeps rising.

Yas picks up the first dress and folds it before dropping it into the suitcase. I cross the room and take the next one from the batch.

"I seriously don't understand how you do it."

I grabbed another one, the dress I wore to the Christmas gala with Chad just a few weeks ago. I let the soft fabric slip between my fingers.

How is it possible that somebody's life can change so drastically in a matter of weeks? How's that fair? One day you're just a regular college student doing your thing, and the next, you're homeless and pregnant.

How is this my life?

"Because I was left with no other options," I murmur softly, lifting my gaze to look at my friend. "And I'll do anything I need to in order to do right by this baby."

Yasmin just observes me quietly for a moment before nodding her head. "And we'll be here. *I'll* be here, every step of the way." She places her hand over mine. "You're not alone in this, Aly. We'll get through this."

I don't think I can go on much longer like this.

Tears prickle my eyes, but I blink them away. I'm so grateful to have the friends that I do. If it weren't for them, especially Yasmin and Maddox, I'm not sure what would have become of me. I'd probably be sleeping in my tiny-ass car and contemplating giving in to my parents.

How messed up is that?

But now Maddox is already tired of me disrupting his life. What if Yas is next? How am I supposed to go forward then?

"Thanks," I sniff. "C'mon, let's get this sorted out. I'm starting to get hungry."

Together, it takes us some fifteen minutes to fold every piece of clothing and put it in the suitcase. I also pulled out some of my bags and shoes. All in all, it makes a nice batch that I hope secures my deposit for my own place.

"Damn, that's a lot of stuff."

I prop my hands against my hips and stare at the pile. She's right. Even neatly folded and put in the suitcase, it takes up a lot of space. "Let's hope they find a good home."

Yasmin wraps her arm around me. "Come on, let's feed you."

I look over my shoulder at Coco, but she's happily snoozing on her bed, so I don't bother calling her.

"Okay," I nod, letting Yasmin pull me out in the hallway. "How is it that you aren't with Nixon?"

"He's playing with the guys." Yasmin rolls her eyes. "When he texted me, I figured we'd get some alone time, but Maddox invited the guys for a game night. Apparently, he made some improvements to his game and wants them to test it out."

"You decided to come and check in on a crazy pregnant lady?"

"I decided to check in on my friend," Yas corrects, giving me a side glance. "The crazy part, well, that's debatable."

I narrow my eyes at her. "Debatable?"

"Hey, you said it first!"

"I did, but you didn't have to agree!" I protest.

The noise level rises when we descend the stairs. I glance toward the living room where all the shouting is coming from. Emmett rises to his feet, shouting loudly at something on the screen, which earns him snickers from the rest of the group.

I shake my head at them.

"What do you want to eat? I was thinking..."

I stop mid-step, Yasmin's words drifting away when I see her. It's the same girl that came to Cup It Up with Maddox recently. May? Martha? No, that's not it... Mia. Her name's Mia.

She's sitting on the couch next to Maddox, a controller in one hand. Their lips move, smiles on their faces as they discuss something.

An uneasy feeling spreads through me at the sight of them,

at the sight of that smile on Maddox's face—because it's usually the smile that's directed at me.

I don't think I've ever noticed it up until this moment, but it's true. Maddox is always so serious, even reserved in a way, but when he smiles, it lights up his whole face.

Is this what he meant when he said it's not fair to him? Because he's interested in this girl and doesn't want to explain our situation to her? Not that there's anything to explain, we're just friends, and he's giving me a hand. But I could see how Maddox would be conflicted about it. After all, he's one of the good guys, and explaining about another girl in your bed to the girl you like can't be easy.

"Aly?" A hand lands on my shoulder snapping me out of my thoughts.

I turn my back to the living room. "Yeah?"

Her gaze darts over my shoulder, before meeting mine. "Are you okay?"

"Of course," I tuck my hair behind my ear, forcing out a smile. "Everything's fine."

Maddox is sitting out there with a girl—smiling at her. A girl who's the female version of him. How much more perfect could things be?

"Let's go find something to eat."

MADDOX

"Seriously, how is it possible that you're this good?" Emmett asks, shaking his head.

Mia shrugs, an innocent smile on her lips. "Beginner's luck?"

Prescott scoffs, "Nobody has that much beginner's luck."

"My thoughts exactly!" Emmett turns to me. "Did you bring a hustler to play with us, Anderson?"

Before I get to say anything, a pillow flies and hits Emmett in the head.

"Don't be a sore loser, Santiago. It's not her problem you're a lousy player," Hayden grumbles.

Emmett turns to him and throws the pillow back, which Hayden catches easily. "That's not what you said the last time I made you eat grass at practice, Hades."

"Made me eat grass? You'd have to catch me first, old man."

"Old man?" Emmett cracks his fingers. "I'll give you an old man."

Mia's eyes grow wide as they get into it in full force, Nixon and Prescott joining in on the discussion too. She looks at them for a moment before shifting her attention to me.

"You're hanging out with an interesting bunch," Mia says softly. Not like they can hear her considering they're preoccupied with discussing who's the best player on the field. By the amount of trash talking being thrown around, you'd think they're rivals instead of playing for the same team.

"They're something, all right."

She shifts on the couch, pulling her legs under her. "It's interesting, really."

I pull my attention from the guys and look at her. Her head is tilted to the side, her arm leaning against the back of the couch. "What is?"

"Seeing you hang out with your roommates."

I let out a short chuckle, "Not how you imagined them?"

"Well..." Mia gives a little shrug, her cheeks turning pink. "I don't..."

"It's fine. Nobody does, really. Nerds and jocks don't really move in the same circles."

Mia leans her hand on the back of the couch. "Then how did you end up becoming friends?"

"Hayden and Nixon were my roommates their first year of college," I explain, thinking back to those early weeks we lived together. My roommates the year before were also jocks, and they were pretty horrible, so I expected more of the same, but I was wrong.

"Their first year of college?"

"Yeah, it was my second year on campus, but because I was underage, I had to stay in the dorms until I was eighteen."

Mia laughs, "The problems of being a genius."

I rub the back of my neck, feeling self-conscious. "Something like that."

"But it turned out well in the end? You guys seem to be tight."

"Yeah," I turn around, looking at the guys fighting over the remote controls to see who'll play next when I catch a glimpse of red, but before I can say anything, it's gone.

Aly?

My heart does that little flip it always does when I first see her. I didn't even realize she got home. I was waiting for her, but she never showed up. Then everybody came and...

"Maddox?"

A hand lands on my knee, startling me out of my thoughts.

I give my head a little shake before shifting my attention back to Mia. "What?"

"I said you have great friends."

"They're okay." My friends' fighting gets louder, making me regret inviting Mia over. "When they're not acting like five-year-old kids. They're usually more civilized than this."

"They're fun. Besides, you should be proud. They're fighting over who's going to play your game. Not that I can blame them."

"It's just a game," I shrug, looking over my shoulder.

Maybe I just imagined it, and Aly wasn't there at all.

"Only you'd say it's just a game. I honestly have to admit I'm impressed. The design is insane, and it didn't feel like a work in progress version at all."

"Thanks," I push my glasses up my nose, feeling uncomfortable as always talking about my work. "And that's because I'm in the final stages. There shouldn't be any big issues, just some minor polishing."

"Are you planning to sell it once it's done?"

"Yeah. I actually had a meeting with the company who bought my last game, and they seem interested in buying this one, too."

Mia shakes her head, her smile growing into a big grin.

"What?"

"Only you can be so chill about something like selling your video game to one of the biggest video game companies in the world."

"It's a good deal." I shrug. "Besides, what should I do with it once it's done?"

"I guess there's that. Do you have any idea what you want to do next?"

"I've been playing around with a few ideas, but nothing concrete."

It was hard to think about the future with everything that's going on right now. And on that note...

"I'm going to get some coffee." I push to my feet. "Do you want something else?"

"I..." Mia tucks a strand of her hair behind her ear. "A Coke would be good, thanks."

I nod. "I'll be back in a bit."

"No need to rush, Maddox. We'll keep the lady company." Prescott winks at me before turning his attention to Mia. "Play me? We'll see if you're really that good or if Santiago here just likes to bitch."

I look at the door and then back at my friends. The need to go and see if Alyssa is back is strong, but I don't feel good about just leaving Mia to her own devices. In the end, propriety wins over.

"You good?" I ask Mia, unsure if I should leave her with them or not.

"I'm fine." Mia waves me away and grabs the controller Prescott offers her. "Go. I've got this."

There are some catcalls as I leave the living room and walk down the hallway to the kitchen but stop before entering when I hear voices inside.

"Are you sure you're okay? You seemed off there for a little bit?" Yasmin asks.

"I'm fine, just got lost in my thoughts for a second. There's just so much I need to do, and there's never enough hours in the day."

"I feel you," Yasmin agrees.

"At least you finished going through your things, so there's that," Callie chimes in.

Going through her things?

"Yeah," Aly lets out a sigh. "I still have to sell them, though."

"I really think you should keep at least some of them. You don't know if you might need them later."

"I highly doubt that, Yas. I don't see myself going to any galas or high-class events in the near future, which works just fine for me. They're boring anyway, and the last thing I need is to stumble into my parents. Talk about awkward."

"Have you talked to them at all?" Callie asks softly.

"My mom called recently," Aly scoffs.

I lean closer to the door, so I can hear better. I remember the day Aly's mom called. She was visibly upset, but when I asked her what that was about, she didn't want to tell me the details.

"She wanted to see if I changed my mind after figuring out they cut me off."

What the hell?

I tighten my hands into fists. The guys yell something, but I can't decipher the words from the buzzing in my ears.

I knew her parents could be crappy, but to taunt her like that? Ask her to get rid of her baby? Their grandchild? Who the hell does that?

A stream of Spanish curses follows her statement.

"That's seriously messed up."

"Yeah, well, it is what it is. I'm..."

Just then, the front door opens, startling me. I turn around as Zane and his girlfriend, Rei, enter the house. His brows shoot up when he sees me standing by the kitchen.

Zane tips his chin at me. "What's up?"

Shit, I'm so busted. My fingers tighten around the cup in my hand. I lift it in the air, so he can see it. "Just going to grab some coffee." The look he gives me is clearly skeptical, but before he can comment further, I say, "You're late."

"Hey, Maddox." Rei smiles at me, letting her duffle drop on the floor. The bag is almost bigger than her, not like that's difficult since the girl is tiny. But I guess one has to be in order to be a professional figure skater. "Sorry, that's my fault. The practice ran late since I insisted on landing one more quad before calling it a night, and we all know how that goes."

More shouting draws their attention.

Zane frowns. "What's going on?"

"They've probably started another discussion of who's the manliest football player of them all." I shake my head. "I'm going to grab some coffee. You want anything?"

"I'm good. You want something, Pix?" Zane throws his hand

over Rei's shoulder and looks down just as she shakes her head. "We're good."

With a nod, I enter the kitchen, all three girls staring at the doorway. "Hey, what's up?"

"Did we just hear Zane?" Callie asks.

"Yeah, he and Rei just got here," I say absentmindedly. My gaze goes straight for Aly as she gets up, a plate in hand, and goes for the sink, ignoring me. "They joined the guys. Maybe you should go and check in on Hayden and Nixon. They were in the middle of another discussion just now."

"Aren't they always?" Callie rolls her eyes and jumps from her chair. "C'mon, Yas. Let's see what's going on." She hooks her arm through Yas's. "You coming, Aly?"

"I'm not..."

Yasmin must see the uncertainty on Aly's face because she stops. "C'mon, just for a little bit. Please?"

"We can google all the baby stuff you'll need," Callie suggests with a smile. "Make a wishlist on Amazon for later?"

"Yeah, maybe. Although I worry seeing how much it all costs is going to frustrate me and not help me relax."

"I don't see why." Yasmin shakes her head. "That's what a baby shower is for."

"Yas..." Aly starts to protest, but they're already walking out of the kitchen.

"Not listening," Yas calls over her shoulder. "Get your skinny ass into the living room in five, or I'm coming to get you."

With that, they're gone, and it's just the two of us.

"Aly..." I start, taking a step closer to her. "About earlier..."

Slowly, she turns to me, those big blue eyes just staring at me for a few heartbeats. For a moment, I think I see something flash in her gaze, but then she smiles. "What earlier?"

My brows pull together. "Gym?"

Can it be that I saw it wrong? That it wasn't actually her?

But it can't be. Zane was there, and he saw her too. And why is she starting the whole talk about selling her things again? It can't be a coincidence.

"Wha—"

"Alyssa Martinez, get your ass in here!" Yasmin yells from the living room.

"I'm coming!" Aly yells back and shakes her head. "I love them, but God, sometimes they make me crazy."

"I feel you." I make my way to the coffee machine and put my cup under, pressing the button to start the machine before turning around to face Aly. She opens the dishwasher and puts her plate away before doing the same with the dishes in the sink.

"You don't have to do that."

"It's just a few glasses. I don't mind." Once she's done, she wipes her hands on the towel.

"Aly..." I start, not even sure where to begin, just knowing I have to say *something*.

Something like why? Why are you pretending like you weren't down in the gym and heard me talk shit when I know you did? Why didn't you tell me the reason your mother called and upset you? Why don't you want to come hang out with everybody? Why do you keep insisting on being so stubborn and don't let me help you? Why don't you see me? Why don't you see how much you mean to me? "I think we sho—"

But Aly is faster; she leans against the counter, her eyes meeting mine. That fake smile I hate from the bottom of my heart, still on her mouth. Because that's not my Aly.

"I see you've invited your friend."

"Friend?" I repeat, confused by the change in subject.

"Mia? It was Mia, right?"

Mia, right.

I was so concentrated on Aly I completely forgot about Mia. I grip the back of my neck. "Yeah, it's Mia."

Which reminds me, I promised I'd bring her a drink. Picking up my coffee, I go to the fridge. "You want something?"

"I'm good, but thanks."

I pick up a can of Coke and close the fridge only to find Alyssa looking at me. There's a distant look on her face like she's here, but at the same time, she's lost in her own thoughts.

I clear my throat, "You coming?"

Her head snaps up, "Do I have a choice?"

"I could always come up with something if you really want me to."

"No, it's fine," she waves me off. "I don't mind hanging with everybody for a little bit, but then I should really go up and figure out how to set a seller's account on eBay."

"A seller's account?"

"Yeah, I finally went through my things, separated what I'm going to sell from what I'm keeping. I figured I might as well set up the profile now, get the ball rolling. The sooner I do this, the sooner I can get out of your hair."

"I can help you with that later if you want, but Aly, you don't need..."

Aly stops a few steps away from the living room and turns to me, giving her head a little shake. "I have to do this."

I hold her gaze. There's resolve in every line of her face, and I know that no matter what I say or do, she won't back down. Not on this. "Okay. We can do this later. I've set it up in the past, so I know how to do it."

"Thanks, Maddox." A small smile curls her lips. "You're the best."

She steps closer, her arms wrapping around my middle. I want to hug her back, but with both my hands occupied, the best I can do is lean my chin against the top of her head.

"Anytime," I whisper, a shudder running through my body at her nearness.

The living room turns into a cacophony of noises as everybody cheers and yells, startling us. We turn toward the room where Yasmin and Mia are doing a happy dance after their victory.

Aly takes a step back, turning toward the living room. "You should ask her."

"What?"

Aly gives me a little shove and smiles. "You should ask her out on a date, silly."

"Who?" I look toward the living room, the realization dawning on me. "Mia?"

"Of course, Mia." Aly rolls her eyes. "Or is there another girl you brought home, but I haven't seen?"

Her words are light, almost playful, but there's something...

"Isn't that why you invited her over?"

I push my glasses up my nose. "I invited her over because she's a friend, and she likes to play video games."

"See? She's pretty *and* smart. You should ask her out." Aly's attention shifts back to the living room. "Besides, I can't believe you haven't seen how she looks at you."

How she looks at me?

As if Mia can feel us watching her, she turns her attention to the door and smiles when she sees us.

Aly turns to me, her eyebrow raised as if she wants to say, *see what I mean?*

Then she turns on the balls of her feet and joins the girls, leaving me speechless.

What the hell just happened?

Chapter 21

ALYSSA

"What do you think about this one?" Callie asks.

"It looks nice," I say absentmindedly, my attention definitely not on the phone. No, it's on Maddox and Mia. They're sitting on the other couch, so close their shoulders are brushing together, controllers in their hands as they play the video game. It's the two of them against Nixon and Emmett, and so far, they're winning.

Do they really have to sit that close? Like seriously, I saw that couch sit four *football* players at one point.

So what if they are? a little voice in my head challenges me. *Didn't you just tell him to ask her out on a date?*

I swallow the lump in my throat, but even that doesn't help remove the bitter taste from my mouth.

What's wrong with me?

Maddox is my friend! I should be happy he found somebody he likes enough to introduce to his friends. Somebody who understands him in a way even I, his closest friend, can't. Somebody—

A finger jabs into my arm. "You aren't even watching."

"Sorry," I let out a sigh and shift my attention back to

Callie's phone and strollers. They all look pretty, but maybe I should wait and get something once I find out the sex of the baby? Although maybe something black or gray would be be—

Holy shit! I choke on my own saliva, and I'm pretty sure my eyes bug out as my gaze falls on the price. *Why are they so expensive?*

"What's on your mind, anyway?"

"How much of this is really necessary since I can't spend over six hundred bucks on a stroller."

Callie gives me a knowing look. "That's not what I was talking about." She clicks on a stroller and scrolls down to the reviews. "I already told you, this is just a wishlist. You're allowed to have one of those. You don't have to get the most expensive one, but I guess it would be good to check the reviews and see what other people think. Like here, easy to navigate."

"Shouldn't that kind of be a given?"

It's a freaking stroller!

Callie pulls her brows together. "Apparently not." With a sigh, she lets her hand drop. "So, what's with that frown?"

"Nothing," The words come out in a rush. So not suspicious.

Callie raises her brow. "Mhmm... I'm totally buying it."

Thankfully before I can come up with an answer, Coco comes rushing into the living room. She makes a sweep of the space, barking excitedly before stopping in front of me and rising on her back paws.

"Who let you out?" I ask as I scoop her up into my arms and put her into my lap.

"Look what I found!" Yasmin yells when she comes back into the living room, a bottle of tequila in one hand, and... is that Pictionary in the other? Her eyes fall on Coco. "She heard me when I was walking through the hallway and started scratching the door, so I let her out. I hope that's okay."

"It's fine. She was probably bored and heard us downstairs." I tilt my chin at the box she's carrying. "Where did you find that?"

"In Nixon's closet." Yasmin turns to her boyfriend. "Do you mind explaining this?"

Nixon's gaze darts to Yasmin before returning to the screen since they're still playing. "Hey, don't look at me like that! Jade brought it that one time she was here because she thought it would be fun to play."

"Yeah, yeah. Blame your sister now that she's not here." Yasmin sits down on my other side. "What did I miss? Did you find something pretty?"

"Apparently, not all the strollers are easy to navigate, and they cost so much I'll have to sell a kidney to get one. Would it be so bad if I just carry the baby in my arms?"

"Give me that." Yas takes the phone from Callie.

The room erupts, startling me. Emmett groans while the others laugh, the words "game over" flashing on the screen. Mia and Maddox high-five each other, matching smiles on their faces.

That flash of jealousy is back, strong and unyielding. Never have I been a selfish person, so feeling like this is weird. But I also never had to share Maddox before either. Is that it? It has to be because...

"Six hundred bucks?" Yas yells, drawing my attention to her. Her eyes widen when she looks at the screen. "Are you shitting me?"

"I told you, it's crazy. I'm definitely rethinking this whole thing. Like, do I really need it at all?"

"What are you looking at?"

My eyes fall closed for a second at the sound of the new voice joining our conversation. Mia. She even has to sound nice.

"Baby stuff," Yasmin explains before I can stop her. "Like seriously, why is it so expensive? They're *tiny-ass* humans."

"Then better not look at clothes. It's the cutest thing ever, but damn, some of those things are more expensive than adult clothes!"

Mia looks between the three of us, searching for any signs of pregnancy, most likely. "Oh, one of you is expecting?"

There's a tense beat of silence.

"That would be me," I admit finally, meeting her gaze. A part of me braces for an ugly comment, but of course, it doesn't come. She just smiles at me.

"That's exciting. Do you know what you're having?"

I shrug. "It's still too early to know."

"It's a girl," Maddox stops by Mia's side.

I roll my eyes at him. "You can't know that."

"Maybe, but it's a gut feeling."

"I guess we'll see about that." I look away because it's too hard to watch him. And it's not just the fact that he's standing so close to her. It's his smile. Like he's genuinely excited about the baby. But how could he be?

I don't think I can go on much longer like this. It's not fair to me...

My gaze falls on the game Yas brought. I take the box from Yasmin's lap, grateful for a distraction. "I haven't played one of these in... Gosh, I don't even remember."

"We could play it now," Yasmin suggests, wiggling her brows. "What'cha say?" She looks at the guys still sitting on the couches. "You guys up for a game?"

Prescott groans, "Do we have to?"

"Will you be more inclined if we turn it into a drinking game?" Yasmin asks, lifting the bottle of tequila in the air so he can see it. "If the couple guesses the word on the card, the group drinks; if the couple doesn't guess correctly, they drink."

"I can't really drink," I point out the obvious.

"Then you can be my pair, Red." Prescott gets up and walks to the table where we're sitting. He throws his arm over my shoulder and pulls me into his side. "I can drink for both of us."

"Okay, so Prescott and Aly, Nixon and me, Callie and Hayden, Zane and Rei..."

"Sorry guys, but I'm out," Emmett says, typing something on his phone. "Kate just texted me to come and pick her and Penny up, but y'all have fun. See you assholes in the gym tomorrow?"

Hayden nods. "You know it."

"So that leaves Mia and Maddox?"

The two of them exchange a look.

"I'm game if you are," Mia says, smiling up at him.

I look down, biting into my lower lip.

This is for the best. He's happy. That's the only thing you've ever wanted. For your best friend to be happy.

"Great!" Yasmin clasps her hands. "Let me just grab some pens and paper. Aly, get the game out. The couple with the biggest number of losses treats the rest to pizza."

"Balls?" Nixon asks as he frowns at the paper where Yas is furiously drawing.

"It's not all about balls, Nixon," she groans. "Focus!"

"No talking!" Zane warns. "Also, you have thirty seconds left."

"Okay, okay. How about basketball? Or scoring a point?" Yasmin glares at him. "What? There's a basket, and these are balls. Don't you all see it?"

"Over."

"It's garbage!" Yasmin slams her hand against the desk. "Not basketball or any kind of ball."

Nixon shakes his head. "It looked like a basketball." He glances around the table. "Don't you all see it? Hayden?"

"Dude, I'm not getting in the middle of this."

"This would be your..." Zane looks down at the score sheet. "Fifth loss, which still keeps you in last place."

Yasmin groans, "You're so bad at this."

"Hey, I can't be good at everything. I'm already too perfect as it is," Nixon winks at his girlfriend.

"Yes," Yas snorts. "A perfect pain in the ass who got me drunk."

Prescott grabs a bottle of tequila and pours their two shot glasses. "Bottoms up, love birds."

"C'mon, it's not that bad. You love tequila." Nixon clinks his glass against Yas's, and they down it in one go.

Yasmin makes a face. "Even I have my limits."

"Well, then I guess it's good that the bed is just up these stairs."

"If I can make it up the stairs once we're done."

Her tongue is twisting as she speaks, and she's not the only one. All of my friends are at some level of buzzed, if not drunk. Callie and Rei are giggling about something, Prescott is overly cheery, and Hayden is lazily leaning in his chair, his eyes glazed. It's seriously hilarious watching them like this while I'm the only one sober. Okay, and maybe a tiny bit depressing too.

I clasp my hands to get their attention. "How about we do another round and call it quits while we're ahead? I really don't want any of you to puke tonight."

"Can't make any promises about that, Red," Prescott shakes his head, chuckling. "After all, this is all your fault."

"Maybe you'll think twice next time before volunteering to drink for the pregnant chick."

For some reason, he finds it extremely funny because he bursts into laughter. "Hopefully, you're the closest I'll get to a pregnant chick in like forever, so no worries about that."

"We'll see about that. But maybe you should sleep here tonight and not drive home."

Prescott raises his brows. "Are you inviting me to your bed?"

My eyes meet Maddox's across the table. "My bed is already full."

Prescott tsks. "All this, and she won't even share a bed with me."

"You have too many ladies waiting to share their bed with you, so I think you'll be fine." I look at Zane, who's the only one who still seems down to earth. "Who's playing next?"

"It's Mia's turn."

"Already?" Mia picks up a card out of the box and looks down at the word. She nibbles at her lower lip as she thinks. "Okay, let's do this."

Zane picks up the sand timer. "And go."

Mia's hand slides over the paper easily, a car appearing on the page. For a quick sketch, it's actually pretty good and quite detailed.

Maddox watches her work. Compared to the others, he doesn't just throw out words off the top of his head but actually gives her time to work and thinks his answer through. Maddox lifts his hand, pushing his glasses up his nose just as Mia starts drawing little details.

What is she...

"Dashboard," Maddox says.

Mia drops her pen, a smile forming on her lips as she shows us the card.

"How did..." Nixon leans over the table and snatches it from her hands, bringing the card all the way to his nose as he squints at the word. "How the fuck did you know?"

"It's right there," Maddox points at the paper.

"There is a *car*."

"No, you see..." Maddox pulls the paper closer, but Nixon is already shaking his head.

"Nope, I don't believe this shit. There was also a freaking basketball when Yasmin was drawing, and the freaking card said garbage. This thing isn't right."

Hayden just laughs. "Don't even try, dude. They beat our asses."

Mia turns to Maddox, that smile of hers even bigger than before. "We do make a pretty good team."

The corner of Maddox's lips tugs upward. "We do."

I just stare at them, unblinking. The pressure builds in my throat, making it hard to breathe. My throat bobs as I try to swallow the knot that's formed, but it's like the damn thing is stuck there.

Of course, they make a good team. They're both ultra-smart, and have this weird connection. It's like they're on the same wavelength and can read each other's minds or something.

"It's your turn, Aly," Zane says, offering me a box with cards. I pull one out of the stack and look at the term.

Seriously?

I shake my head and grab my pen, looking up at Prescott. "Ready?"

He just nods, and Zane flips the clock.

I start drawing, not nearly as good as Mia, but it's a decent drawing if I do say so myself.

"Waves? Sea? Beach? Sunbathing?" Prescott leans his elbows on the table, moving closer. "Hot chicks on the beach? Seriously, Red, what did you have written on the damn card, a freaking novel?"

"Twenty seconds to go," Hayden reminds him.

"Damn. Coast? Summer? Summer v—"

"Time," Zane says.

"Damn, you were so close. It's vacation."

"Oh well," Prescott shrugs and pours tequila in his two glasses, downing one after the other. "Since I haven't been on a freaking vacation in for-fucking-ever it's not even strange I didn't recognize the word."

Hayden stretches his arms in the air. "Damn, I wouldn't mind a vacation right now."

"Me neither. Although the season is over, because of a certain somebody," Nixon gives a pointed look at Hayden, "we've been working harder than ever. I swear my body aches all the time."

"Poor baby," Yas coos.

"We should go."

The whole room seems to go still, heads turning in Callie's direction.

"What?" she shrugs. "We should all go on vacation together. Spring break is just around the corner, and this is the last time we'll have together before…" her voice trails off. She lets her hair slip from behind her ear. "This is the last year we'll all have together before some of you graduate."

Yasmin purses her lips. "I mean, we could. But where would we go?"

"I don't know. Florida? California? Hawaii? Somewhere warm and sunny." She closes her eyes and tilts her head back. "Just think about it. Beach. Sun. Partying all the time for a week straight. How fun would that be?"

She was right; it did sound nice. And a year ago, hell, a few months ago, I'd be the first to jump at the opportunity.

"You guys should go," I say, starting to clean up the game. "Those kinds of trips are the best."

Callie turns to me. "What about you?"

"Well, even if I had extra cash to spend, I'm not sure I'd be able to go. I don't think pregnancy and flying mix that well together."

"Damn, I didn't think about that. Maybe we could go somewhere we could drive?"

I shake my head. "You shouldn't spend half of your spring break on the road. But seriously, you should go. It'll be so much fun."

Callie nibbles at her lips clearly conflicted.

"I mean it," I chuckle. "You should go. I still remember when I went to Hawaii a few years back. We had an amazing time."

Callie looks at Hayden, who just shrugs. "If you guys are down, I'm down."

"I'm always down for a good party," Nixon turns to his girlfriend. "What do you say, Yas?"

"I mean, why the hell not? Callie is right. This might be our last chance to do it together."

"Zane?" Hayden asks.

"Sorry, but Rei is going to Boston to practice, so I'll go with her."

Rei tilts her head back to look at her boyfriend. "You don't need..."

"I see these assholes every day, Pix. Going with you will be a vacation for me." He pushes his chair back. "On that note, I think it's time for bed."

Rei joins him, and the two of them say their goodnights before leaving while the rest of the group continues discussing their trip.

"I guess I should get going," Mia says, getting to her feet.

Maddox looks up at her. "Are you sure?"

"Yeah, it's getting late."

Maddox nods. "Let me walk you out."

I watch as Mia says goodbye to the whole group, and I can

see that they're genuinely sorry to see her leave. She slid so easily into our little group, and I can't help but feel jealous of that.

"Aly?" Yasmin turns around when I abruptly push the chair back and stand to my feet. Coco, who was sleeping all this time in my lap, is now in my hands. "You, okay?"

"Yeah, kind of tired. I think I'll go lie down."

"You sure?" Yasmin gives me a worried look.

"Yes, I'm just tired. But you guys have fun planning your spring break. If I can help in any way, let me know."

"Okay, if you're sure."

With a soft goodnight, I head into the hallway just as the front door closes behind Maddox and Mia. My gaze lingers on the door for a moment, the ache in my chest growing.

"Get a grip, Aly," I mutter to myself, shutting it all down. Then I climb the stairs.

MADDOX

"I know I said this before, but your friends are really nice," Mia says as we step out on the front porch.

"They have their moments." I look at her as we descend the stairs and cross the short distance to her Honda that's parked by the curb. "You could have stayed a little while longer."

Mia stops in front of the car and turns around. "I know, but I wasn't joking. I really have work to do. This was supposed to be my two-hour break, but I ended up staying way longer than anticipated. Now, I'm so not in the mood to go back home and get to work, but I have to finish an essay for my International Cyber Security class that I have to turn in on Thursday and prepare a presentation, too. So, yeah..." Mia smiles. "But this was exactly what I needed. Thanks for inviting me."

"Anytime." I return her smile. "I still can't believe you're that good at playing video games. I think Emmett will be traumatized for a while."

Mia chuckles. "It was just beginner's luck."

"No beginner is that lucky."

Mia looks down to the ground shyly. "I don't know about that."

You should ask her out on a date, silly.

Alyssa's earlier words choose right this moment to pop up in my head. My palms turn sweaty, and I can feel my heartbeat race.

Mia glances at me. She's chewing on her lower lip, but even that doesn't help diminish her smile.

Besides, I can't believe you haven't seen how she looks at you.

Mia shifts her weight from one foot to the other. "I should..."

"Maybe we..."

We both start and stop at the same time. I chuckle nervously, rubbing at the back of my neck. "You should..."

Mia shakes her head. "You go first."

"Maybe..." My voice breaks as I struggle to find the right words. I clear my throat and start again, "Maybe we could do it again?"

Mia's lip pops, the color spreading through the flesh as a smile curls her lips. "That would be nice."

"Or go out?" I add as an afterthought.

"Go out?"

"Yeah, to eat or something?" I let my hand drop, feeling awkward as hell. "If you want, I mean. If not, that's completely..."

I should have thought this through, made a game plan, not just blurted it out of the blue like this. But maybe that's not the issue. Does she not want to go? Maybe Aly had it all wrong. Maybe Mia isn't—

"No, I'd love to." Mia's smile widens. "Maybe this weekend? Once I'm done with my presentation?"

"Yeah, this weekend..." Once again, I clear my throat. "That sounds okay."

"Okay. It's a date then." Then Mia rises on the tips of her toes. I suck in a breath, my whole body still as she leans closer and presses her mouth against my cheek. "See you in class?"

"Yeah," I nod as she pulls back. "See you in class."

With a nod, she takes a step back and slides into her car. I watch her turn it on, and with one final wave, she drives off.

Once her car lights are too far for me to see, I turn around and make my way inside. I can hear voices in the living room as they discuss spring break. I listen for a moment, but when I don't hear Aly, I slowly make my way upstairs. Although I've tried to push back what had happened earlier, now that there aren't other distractions, it's back, front and center.

My steps falter as I come closer to my room. The door is closed, so I give myself a few seconds to collect my thoughts.

Why did she say she wasn't in the gym when I saw her? And what was that look on her face downstairs?

You're not going to get those answers if you keep standing here and staring at the wall, now, will you?

Taking one deep breath, I push the door open. I'm not sure what I was expecting, but Aly sitting on the bed, a laptop in her lap, and Coco curled beside her wasn't it.

"Still up?" I ask, slowly closing the door behind me.

I give a quick glance at the room, and my whole body relaxes slightly when I still find little tidbits that Aly left behind. The candle and a few books still sit on her nightstand. Some of her makeup and perfumes still stand on the dresser, and a shoe is peeking from under the bed.

She's not leaving. Not yet, at least.

Aly looks up at me. "Yeah, I figured I might as well try and set up that profile to get the ball rolling."

"I told you I'd help." I cross the room toward her. "What's the sudden rush?"

"There's no rush."

She looks down at the screen, avoiding my gaze. But this time, it's just the two of us. No friends waiting for us. No distractions. Just her and me, and this time, I'm not going to let it go so easily.

"You haven't done it in the last few weeks, so what's one more day?"

Aly stubbornly keeps her eyes on the screen. "Well, I didn't have time before, but I do now so..." She shrugs, trying to play it off.

I sit down on the bed next to her. The mattress dips causing Aly to move closer to me. "What's this really about, Aly?" I ask softly, looking down at her.

This close I can smell her sweet scent—oranges, vanilla, and just plain Aly. I can feel the heat of her body, her forearm brushing against mine as she shifts in her seat.

"Nothing."

"It doesn't look like nothing. If—"

"I just want to sell those things so I can get enough money for a deposit on a new apartment, and you can go back to your life, okay?" Aly snaps before I can even finish, the hurt evident in her tone.

She's etched into every single aspect of my life, and it's messing with my mind.

My eyes fall closed as my earlier words ring in my mind. So much for her not hearing what I said.

"Aly, I didn't mean it like that," I rasp.

She turns to me, those blue eyes wide and vulnerable as

they stare into mine. "Then how did you mean it?" she asks softly. It's as if all the fight has left her, and all she wants to do is understand.

I open my mouth, but no words come out. I wish I could say it. I wish I could tell her exactly what this is about. Tell her exactly how I feel, so she'd get how utterly wrong she is, but I can't, so I close my mouth like the coward that I am.

Aly smiles sadly. "That's what I thought."

She turns her attention back to her laptop. My hand jolts out, covering hers. "At least let me help you."

"Fine."

She lets me transfer her laptop into my lap, so I can open her a profile on eBay. I explain everything as I work, grateful for the distraction, showing her how to add new items and how to delete the sold ones, but when she yawns for the third time, I decide it's time to call it a night.

"You should go to sleep."

She rubs at her eyes, the exhaustion clear on her face. "Yeah, I guess so."

Turning off the laptop, I get off the bed. I can hear the sheets rustle as Aly lays down. I put her laptop on my desk, and I'm about to grab my things to shower when Aly's words stop me in my tracks.

"You're my best friend, Maddox. I never wanted to pull you into my mess."

"You didn't."

"I did, and I'm sorry for that. You deserve better."

But I just want you.

That's all I've ever wanted. You. Nothing and nobody else.

I turn around, my mouth open, but whatever I wanted to say dies on my lips because Aly is already sleeping soundly.

I stay there for a moment and just watch her. There are dark circles under her eyes, not that it's strange considering how busy she's been lately, always pushing herself to do more instead of leaning on the people surrounding her.

And she'll only be harder on herself now that she thinks she's a burden when it couldn't be further from the truth.

That vice grip tightens around my throat, making it hard to breathe.

How do I make this right?

Shaking my head, I go to her and pull the cover over her sleeping body. Unable to resist it, I trace my finger over her cheek.

"You'll never look at me as anything more than a friend, will you?"

But the answer doesn't come, not that I expect it to. After all, that's the only reason why I dared to utter those words out loud.

Chapter 22

ALYSSA

Me: Just got home. I need to change and will be ready to go.

Hitting send, I rush up the stairs and into the room. Coco looks up, happy to see me as always.

"Hey, Coco." Dropping the backpack to the floor, I give her a quick pat before pulling my shirt off and throwing it into the basket. Of course, today was the day I had to spill my coffee all over myself.

I just hope this isn't the indication of how the rest of my day will go because then, I'm really screwed.

Coco watches me with rapt attention as I move around the room. Opening the closet, I grab the first shirt I can get my hands on and throw it on before quickly switching what I need from my backpack into a smaller bag.

"I'm going to the doctor now, but I'll see you in a little bit, okay?" I say, giving Coco one final rub between her ears before dashing out.

I check my messages as I descend the stairs, but there's no reply from Yasmin just yet.

Did she forget?

No, she wouldn't have. She and Callie have been talking about it ever since I told them about the appointment, and they seemed excited to go.

Just when I reach the bottom step, the door to the basement opens, and Maddox comes out. My heart does that little flip as I lay my eyes on him. His sweaty shirt is plastered to his chest, and he's checking something on his smart watch.

"Hey."

Maddox looks up, a small smile appearing on his lips. "Hey, I didn't realize you were home."

"I just came back for a minute because I needed to change."

He takes me in from head to toe, his assessing gaze not missing anything. "Did something happen?"

I wave him off, going toward the kitchen. "I managed to spill coffee all over myself. At least this time it was cold, but still." I hop onto the stool. "What were you up to?"

"Working out." Maddox opens the fridge and grabs a bottle of water. "You want something?"

"I'm good, thanks."

Closing the fridge, he leans against the counter and rubs his towel over his face, wiping the sweat away. "I was working through the glitch in my code for well over an hour without any luck, so I'd decided to just let it be and went downstairs to the gym to work the frustration out of my system. Sometimes it helps me figure out what I've been missing."

Apparently, that's his go-to these days.

Just thinking those words leaves a bitter taste in my mouth. It's not Maddox's fault that I've turned his life upside down, and I shouldn't blame him for voicing it out loud. But couldn't he have said it to me? I thought we were close enough to share things like that and be open with each other. Not talk about it behind the other person's back.

"And did you figure it out?"

Maddox chuckles, "Not really, but at least I got some exercise in."

"I guess there is that."

"Yup." Maddox tips his chin at me. "What are you up to? Going back to class?"

"No." I pull the phone out of my bag. "I'm actually waiting for Yasmin. I have my doctor's appointment today, and she said she'd go with me."

Unlocking the phone, I look at the messages, but still nothing.

Maybe she's driving?

"Is everything okay?"

I give him a reassuring smile. "Just a regular checkup."

The phone buzzes in my hand. *Finally!* I quickly open the message.

Yasmin: I'm so sorry. My advisor asked me to stay late, so I can't make it.

The message is accompanied by half a dozen crying emojis.

I just stare at the message for a heartbeat, fighting the disappointment. I didn't realize how much I was looking forward to having her with me until this very moment.

"What?"

I look up to find Maddox watching me; his brows pulled together.

"Yas can't make it," I say, just as the phone buzzes once again.

Yasmin: Are you angry?

Me: Of course, I'm not angry!

Me: Don't stress about it. You can come the next time.

Yasmin: But I wanted to be there today!

Yasmin: I'll come later, and you can tell me all about it?
Me: You've got yourself a deal.

"Yasmin was supposed to go with you?"

"Yeah." Locking the phone, I slide it into my bag. "She and Callie didn't want me to do it by myself, but Yasmin's internship is running late, and she won't make it in time. I'd call Callie, but she already told me she has a class today."

I give my head a shake. You're not getting sappy; you've got places to be.

"I guess I should get going." Jumping off the chair, I grab my bag. "I don't want to be late."

"I can go with you," Maddox says, stopping me in my tracks.

Go with me?

I look over my shoulder, unsure if I heard him correctly. "What?"

"I can go to the doctor with you," Maddox repeats, rubbing the back of his neck. "I mean if you want. Instead of Yasmin."

Is he serious?

"You don't have to." I shift from one foot to the other. "I'm sure you have more important things to do."

"Like what?" he lets out a chuckle. "Stare at the screen and try to find a solution to a glitch in my code that made me go down to the gym earlier? Seriously, I'd rather go with you than do that, so you're basically doing me a favor."

I roll my eyes at him. Typical Maddox behavior. "Well, we can't have that, can we?"

"Of course not. But if you want me to..."

"I..." my throat bobs as I swallow. "If you're sure."

The corner of Maddox's mouth lifts in a smile. "I'm sure. Give me ten to shower and change, and we can go."

This was such a bad idea.

I shouldn't have given in, but Maddox caught me in a weak moment. I didn't want to be that lone girl sitting in the waiting room while other people gave me curious, or even worse, *pity* looks. I didn't want to worry all on my own about if everything was going okay, or what I'd do if I heard bad news. Because no matter how well you think you might be doing, there can always be bad news.

Yes, I was reluctant to accept my friend's help initially, but since then, I was actually excited about it. To say I was disappointed when Yasmin texted me to cancel would be an understatement. I was looking forward to having her with me. Knowing I wasn't alone in this pushed the fear away temporarily.

"Your blood pressure looks good." The nurse loosens the strap around my arm. "You're all good to go to the back. Lie down on the table and pull your shirt up. The doctor will be with you shortly."

I smile at her and get to my feet. "Thank you."

Maddox's wide eyes meet mine. He seems like a fish out of water, has since the moment we stepped into the room. It's like all eyes have turned to us. Thankfully, nobody commented about anything because that would be a new level of awkwardness.

I tilt my head toward the back room. "Coming?"

I'm out of sorts. If he changes his mind, I won't force him to do this. I can do it myself.

You and me, baby, I rub my hand over my bump. *Just like it's always going to be. You and me.*

"Sure."

With a nod, I lead the way into the examination room.

Leaving my bag on the chair, I go straight for the exam table and hoist myself up.

Puffing my hair out of my face, I look up only to catch Maddox still standing by the door. He slowly takes in the room before stepping inside and closing the door.

"What now?" he asks, pushing his glasses up his nose.

I frown at the offensive object.

God, I seriously can't stand it. The damn pair is at least a decade old and way too big. You'd think he doesn't have the money to get new glasses. I swear I'll buy him a new pair myself if he doesn't change them soon.

Seeing his glasses slide, yet again, down his nose, takes me back to our last movie night. The way Maddox flipped me over like it was nothing. The feel of his body over mine. His warmth. How if only I leaned a little bit closer, I could have buried my head into his neck to inhale his scent, that familiar mix of cologne and something that's all Maddox.

"Aly?" I blink, coming back to the present. Color rises in my cheeks when I see Maddox observing me carefully.

What the hell, Aly?

I give my head a little shake, pushing those thoughts away.

"Now we wait until my doctor comes." I tilt my head to the side. "You know, you can move closer. Maybe sit on that chair? I won't bite. I promise."

Maddox shakes his head but does as I ask. "Okay, and then?"

"Then we'll see the baby."

Just saying it out loud has butterflies roaming inside my stomach. Regardless of the fear that always seems to creep in every time I come here, there's also a part of me that's excited to see my baby. The feeling of seeing it, of hearing its heartbeat... It's mesmerizing, and unlike anything I've ever experienced before.

There's this little being that I helped create that depends solely on me. It was hard for me to wrap my head around it at the beginning, but hearing that whooshing heartbeat made me realize I'm not imagining it.

Maddox opens his mouth, but before he can say anything, Doctor Jeremy enters the room. "Hey, Alyssa. It's so nice to see you again." Her astute brown eyes shift from me to Maddox. "And you brought company."

"Hey, Doc. Yes, I hope that's not a problem."

"Of course not," Doctor Jeremy smiles at Maddox and takes her seat in front of the ultrasound machine. "How have you been feeling, Alyssa?"

"Okay." I pull my shirt up just under my breasts, revealing my slowly growing bump. It was just big enough for my jeans not to fit but not big enough to be overly noticeable. "Still a little tired."

She chuckles, "You're growing a baby. It's normal to feel tired. If it becomes too much, it's okay to slow down and give your body time to adjust."

Maddox gives me a pointed look. "That's what I keep telling her. Not that she's listening."

"I know that, but I figured now that I'm in my second trimester, things will get easier. At least, that's what that pregnancy for dummies book says."

Doctor's brows shoot up. "Pregnancy for dummies?"

"It's *What To Expect When You're Expecting*," Maddox explains.

I wave him off. "Same thing."

"Well, every pregnancy is different and unique from woman to woman. You have to listen to your body." The machine flickers to life, and Dr. Jeremy turns to me, a gel bottle in hand. I push the hem of my leggings—the only thing that fits me any longer—down a little. "This will be a bit cold," she warns, squeezing a generous amount on my stomach.

I bite the inside of my cheek and hold onto the edge of the table as a shiver runs through me.

This feeling never gets any easier, no matter how many times I've done it.

A hand covers mine.

I shift my gaze to Maddox's serious face. His fingers gently unwrap mine from the table, and he intertwines them with mine, giving me a reassuring squeeze.

A lump forms in my throat. I try to swallow it, but it doesn't budge. Warmth spreads through my chest as a mix of feelings swells inside me—fear and excitement, anxiety and longing, but above all, love and gratefulness.

This is how it feels.

This is what it means not to be alone.

"Ready?" The doc asks, snapping me out of my thoughts.

I shift my attention to her and nod in confirmation. She presses her wand against the goo, spreading it over the bump.

Maddox's hand tightens around mine, warm and reassuring. My gaze darts to his, holding it for a moment, before shifting it to the screen and the black and white image on it.

My heart kicks up a notch as the doctor observes the screen carefully, her hand slowly moving the wand over my belly.

"How about we listen to the heartbeat?"

I nod my head. "Yes, please."

She presses a few buttons, and that familiar *whooshing* sound fills the room.

I let out a slow breath as the relief washes over me at the fast beat of my baby's heart, making my own heart race.

The grip on my fingers tightens. Slowly, I turn my attention to Maddox. Those big brown eyes look huge behind his glasses as he listens to the baby's heartbeat, his gaze fixed on the screen too. His mouth opens and closes a few times, tongue sliding out to wet his lower lip before he finally manages to get the words out, "Is that..."

"The baby's heartbeat, yes."

He looks at the doctor and then at me, panic flaring in his irises. "Why is it so fast? Is everything okay?"

The doctor returns her attention to the screen. "The baby looks perfect. And the heartbeat is completely normal. The average fetal heart rate is between 110 and 160 beats per minute."

Maddox still looks unsure, so I slide my finger over the back of his hand. He turns to me, and I give him a small smile. I can still remember the first time I heard it and the overwhelming feeling that accompanied the moment.

"The baby is fine." I give his hand a squeeze. "It's amazing, isn't it?"

Maddox nods, a smile slowly working its way on his mouth. "She's amazing, just like her mom."

I roll my eyes. "I already told you, we don't know the sex. For all we know, I could be having a boy."

Maddox shakes his head stubbornly. "It's a girl."

"You can't..." I try to protest, but the doctor interrupts me.

"Would you like to find out the sex of the baby?"

The sex of the baby.

My heart does a little flip in anticipation. I didn't think too much about it so far. It's always been just a baby in my head. But hearing her say it makes this whole thing real. If she tells me, it won't be just some baby. It'll be my daughter or my son.

"You can see that already?" Maddox asks since I can't seem to do so myself.

He leans closer to the screen as if he can read it himself. There's a look of complete and utter wonder on his face that makes my heart ache.

This. This is what my baby is missing. A dad who's excited about the prospect of meeting his child. A dad who'll go with me to the appointments and look at that screen with stars in his eyes. A dad who'll love him or her even before they're here.

"The baby is in a good position, but if you'd rather wa—"

"I want to know," Maddox bursts out, making me laugh. He turns to me, his cheeks heating. "I-I mean, if you..."

I shake my head, smiling. "I want to know too."

My heart starts racing in tune with the *whooshing* sound filling the room.

"Okay." Doctor Jeremy turns her attention back to the ultrasound machine and presses a few buttons. "You're having a girl."

My head snaps to the machine as if suddenly all the black and white images on the screen will start making sense.

A girl.

"I'm having a baby girl," I breathe, a smile slowly working its way to my lips.

The grip on my hand tightens. I turn my attention to Maddox, but his gaze is fixed on the screen. I return his grip, and his attention shifts on me.

"A girl," he echoes. His brown eyes are huge as he stares at me, a grin on his face, so big it's like a kick to my gut. "I told you so."

"Yeah," I chuckle. "Yeah, you did."

We just stare at one another, probably smiling like a pair of lunatics. But I don't care. Because I'm so happy, I feel like I might burst. I'm having a baby girl.

Doctor Jeremy looks at us over her shoulder. "Yes, a baby girl. Congratulations, Mommy and Daddy."

"Oh, I... we..." My cheeks flush at the assumption. Never before did we talk about the father, and now Maddox's here, so I guess she just thought he's the dad.

My mouth is open, but no words come out.

I expect Maddox to say something, but he doesn't even try to correct her.

Doctor Jeremy, completely oblivious to my turmoil, goes back to work, clicking something on that machine of hers. "As I said, everything else looks okay. Your baby girl is growing just as she should, and everything seems to be developing correctly."

Beeping fills the room, and the next thing I know, we're handed two identical sets of photos. "Once again, congratulations on your baby girl. I'll see you in a month for your next checkup."

With trembling fingers, I take the photos and look at the black and white image of my little girl.

My little girl.

Chapter 23

MADDOX

Daddy.

That one word rings in my head as we get back to my car, the photo the doctor gave me weighing heavy in the pocket of my jacket.

Daddy.

How is it possible that one word, just one mere word, can bring you peace and unsettle you in every way possible?

I should have probably corrected her, but I was as much at a loss for words as Alyssa seemed to be.

No matter where we went, nobody ever assumed we were a couple. Alyssa is Alyssa. She's gorgeous, smart, and funny. And I'm... Well, me. Her geeky best friend. A good guy who's the perfect best friend, but nobody ever looks at guys like me as something more.

Nobody would ever think of us as a couple. I can't even count the number of times people were surprised we were even friends, much less anything more.

"I can't believe you were right."

I glance toward Aly, but she's still staring at the photo of her daughter.

Her daughter.

Somehow, finding it out makes this whole situation seem more real. Alyssa is going to be a mother. In a few short months, she's going to have a baby girl, and nothing will ever be the same afterward.

What's even more strange is that although I've never seen her, I can imagine exactly how she'll look. A patch of fluffy ginger hair and the biggest, bluest eyes possible. She'll be a beauty, just like her mother.

My heart squeezes tightly as the image becomes so vivid in my mind, I swear I could touch her. All the feelings that have been building inside of me since the moment Aly told me she's pregnant hit me like a tsunami, making it hard to breathe.

This is real.

Why does it suddenly feel so real?

And how is it possible that I'm already in love with her? I recognize this warm feeling in my chest all too well. I've felt it for Aly for so long, I'd know it in my sleep. This mix of warmth and sweet ache, happiness and longing. But how can I already love her daughter just as much? She hasn't even been born yet. I've never seen her. Never touched her. But she already owns a piece of my heart.

"Lucky guess." Absent-mindedly, I rub at the spot in the middle of my chest. "Did you want a boy?"

Did she want a little boy that would look like that douche of her ex? So she can keep a part of him with herself forever?

"I didn't really have a preference. The only thing I want is for the baby to be healthy." She gives me a side glance. A smile plays on her lips, her blue eyes shining brighter ever since we left the doctor's office. "But I won't lie, I'm excited about having a little girl."

I hold her gaze for a moment. "She'll be your mini-me."

"God, no. I hope she's nothing like me." Alyssa shakes her head, a nervous chuckle escaping her. "Can you imagine that?"

Yes, yes, I can. I can see it in vivid detail, and that's the whole problem.

"She'll be beautiful and amazing, just like you."

Alyssa sniffs, "You're going to make me cry."

"No crying," I warn. The last thing I need is for her to start crying.

"I can't help it!" She wipes under her eyes. "It's these damn hormones."

I start the car. "How about we stop by the mall on our way home? I know how much you like those milkshakes from there."

Aly groans, "Not playing fair, Maddox. You know how much I love those. And now that you said it, I won't be able to think about anything else."

"Hey, it was just a suggestion. We don't have to go."

"Oh, no, you don't." Aly jabs her finger into my side. "Now you're taking me to get my milkshake. You better not get between a pregnant girl and a craving."

I bite the inside of my cheek, trying to hold my laughter in. "I wouldn't dream of it."

Aly lets out a long, happy sigh. "Damn, I didn't even realize how much I needed this."

"Good?"

"Mhmm..." She takes another pull from the cup before offering it to me. "Want some?"

I shake my head. "Yeah, I think not."

Aly pokes her tongue out at me. "You're no fun."

"You should be happy, more for you."

"Yeah, yeah." Aly rolls her eyes. "Oh, look at this."

Maybe I would if only I could take my eyes off her.

Aly claps her hands excitedly, happiness radiating off her. Watching her is intoxicating. Her eyes get all big and shiny like a kid on Christmas morning. Her smile is radiant, with just a trace of mischief.

Reluctantly, I force myself to look away from her and focus on what got her all excited. I blink, thinking I have it wrong, but no. We're standing in front of optometrist's office. Before I can react, Aly grabs my hand and pulls me toward the shop.

"C'mon."

"Aly, you know I don't like contacts..."

She looks at me over her shoulder. "Who said anything about contacts?"

"You always tell me I should wear contacts."

"That's because..." She stops abruptly, making me crash into her back. My hands land on her shoulders to steady her from falling. Just the idea of Alyssa falling down and hurting herself has my heart going into overdrive. But before I can say anything, she's already facing me.

"See?" Her hand is in my face as she pushes my glasses up my nose, completely ignorant to the fact that she almost landed on her ass; that she could have gotten hurt and given me a heart attack in the process. I open my mouth, but she just shakes her head. "They're too big. You need a new pair."

"But I like these," I protest even as they slip down my nose once again.

"Well, they don't fit. How long have you had these?"

"I'm not sure," I shrug. "Since freshman year?"

"Freshman year of college?" Aly's mouth falls open.

No, freshman year of high school, but I don't bother correcting her since I don't think it'll go over well.

Aly shakes her head and tsks. "If you're insisting on wearing glasses, the least you could do is wear ones that fit you and are fashionable."

"I'm not one for fashion."

"Well, I guess then you're in luck, 'cause I am." Aly laces her fingers through mine and pulls me toward the store.

Of course, I let her drag me inside. I try on every pair of glasses she gives me without any protest until she finds the perfect pair that "opens up" my face. I'm not sure what that means, but Aly seems happy, and they're not *that* bad, so I don't bother protesting since I know there's no way I can win this round.

"Are you done?" I ask as we walk out of the store, Aly still sipping her milkshake. "Or do you plan to give me a complete makeover?"

Aly grins. "Well, now that you've mentioned it..."

I shake my head. "Nope, not happening."

Aly jabs her finger into my side. "You mentioned it!"

"As a *joke*!"

"Well, joke all you want, but I'm serious. You could use a new shirt or even a sweater. They'd look so good with the new glasses."

"Aly..." I give her a warning look.

I love her, but I'm drawing a line when it comes to letting her drag me shopping.

"What?" She bats her eyelashes innocently. "I'm just saying."

"I'm not getting a new shirt." I shake my head. "Or a sweater. Or anything else for that matter."

I know if I give her an inch, there won't be any stopping her. That girl loves to shop.

"C'mon, let's go home." I start to walk toward the door only to realize she's not following me. "Aly? What are you..."

I turn around and see what has her attention.

A baby store.

The front window is full of all the baby stuff, half of which I don't even know the names for. Tiny clothes. Colorful stuffed toys. Cribs. Strollers.

"I haven't bought her anything yet," Aly whispers, her hand falling down on her bump and giving it a soft rub.

I'm not even sure if she realizes that she's doing it half the time. How much she loves and cares for her baby.

"Do you want to go in?" I offer, happy to get her mind off shopping for me and to the baby, instead. "See what they have?"

Aly gives a longing look to the store. "Didn't you want to go home?"

"I'm fine with staying a few minutes longer."

Aly turns to me and gives me a pointed look that says she knows exactly what I'm trying to do, and I'm not fooling her one bit, but then a smile spreads over her serious face.

"Okay, but just a few minutes."

"Sure thing."

I follow after her as she enters the store. Her eyes light up as she moves down the row. Silently, I follow after her and watch as she takes in different things, checking them out. The amount of items and options they have is overwhelming. Like seriously, how can one tiny human need all of that?

A shelf with stuffed animals draws my attention. I walk toward it and grab a pink bunny with floppy ears and a big white and pink bow on its head. It looks cute and girly.

What the hell.

I put the bunny under my arm and turn around, but Aly is nowhere in sight. I continue down the row until I find her standing in front of a wall filled with the tiniest clothes I've ever seen in my life. They're so small. I'm pretty sure my hand would barely fit inside.

Alyssa is holding a pale pink dress that barely covers both of her palms.

"Is she going to be that small?" I ask, stopping just next to her and looking at the row of different onesies. They're mostly pink, although there are some reds, oranges, yellows, and teals mixed in between.

"It could go either way, really. We won't know until closer to the due date."

A pale pink onesie draws my attention. I pull it out, the corner of my mouth lifting. "You should get this one."

"*Mommy's mini-me?*" Aly tilts her head to the side and looks at me.

"What? I told you, she's gonna be just like you. You know I'm right." I scan the clothes. "Or this one."

And though she be but little, she's fierce.

Aly smiles. "I like this one better."

I chuckle. "I thought you might."

"I think I'm gonna get that one, and..." She looks over the clothes and stops when her eyes set on one. She gently touches the letters printed on the onesie. *Daddy's little princess.* "I guess she won't be needing this one."

The sad look on her face, the yearning in her voice, they're my undoing. My throat turns dry as an unsettling feeling spreads through my stomach.

"Do you want it?" I ask, my voice hoarse; when I really want to ask something completely different.

Do you want Chad to change his mind?

"No." Aly shakes her head, and there isn't a trace of uncertainty on her face. "The last thing I want is to force anyone into anything. It's just..." She bites the inside of her cheek as she measures her words carefully. "I just don't want her to miss anything in life, you know?"

I wrap my arm around her and pull her in for a hug. "She

won't be missing anything. She'll have you, and she'll have all of us to love you two."

Alyssa leans her head on my shoulder. "Thanks, Maddox."

Her arms sneak around my waist, and I can't help myself—she feels so right next to me, her body molding to mine almost perfectly.

"Anytime." I rub her arm.

We stay like that for a while longer until Aly finally pulls back. Her eyes scan the shelf one more time, and a grin slowly appears on her lips once again.

"How about this one? It'll be like a gender reveal, but for our friends?"

Alyssa looks over her shoulder at me. "Can you hold the bag?"

"Sure thing."

She hands it over to take her jacket and shoes off just as the loud barking comes from upstairs, and Coco comes rushing down. She's so fast, Aly barely has enough time to catch her.

"Are you crazy?" she chastises, lifting her so they're at the same eye level. "One day, you're going to fall and break your paw, silly dog."

Of course, Coco doesn't take her seriously at all. Instead, she just starts licking Aly's nose, making her giggle.

"You're here!" Yasmin says, coming out of the kitchen. "I'm so sorry about ditching you today."

"It's fine," Aly smiles, pulling Coco to her chest. "Things happen."

"Doesn't make me feel any less shitty. My advisor wanted to talk to me, and then there was some issue..." Yas shakes her head. "You know how that goes."

Aly takes the bag out of my hands and mouths thanks before

the two of them go into the living room where everybody is watching tv.

"There's always a next time. Don't stress about it."

"So, how was it?" Yasmin asks, pulling Alyssa to sit on the couch next to her.

"All is good." Aly places Coco into her lap before her eyes dart to me, mischief twinkling in the blue depths of her irises. "Maddox offered to go with me." She shifts her attention to our friends, "We found out the sex of the baby."

We.

My fingers curl around the edge of the couch as that word rings in my mind.

It's a small word, only two letters. Why does it mean so much, then?

"What?!" Yasmin yells. "And I missed it? How's that fair?"

Callie elbows her. "That's because you wanted to take *my* best aunt spot."

Yasmin huffs and crosses her arms over her chest. "We'll see about that."

Callie rolls her eyes at Yasmin before turning her attention to Aly. "What are you having? Tell us!"

Even the guys are listening intently. Hayden is trying to hold onto Callie, who's practically jumping in her seat, which is technically his lap. Nixon takes his seat on the armrest next to Yas and tugs at her curls.

Zane's eyes meet mine. He raises his brow at me in a silent question, but I just shrug.

This is Aly's moment, not mine.

Aly's eyes dart to mine once again. She grazes her teeth over her lower lip to hide the smile, but it's useless.

"The answer is in..." Her words hang in the air as she grabs the bag from the floor where she put it and gives it to the girls. "Here."

Callie and Yas throw themselves at the bag. I kid you not. By their enthusiasm, you'd think the bag held a million bucks.

"Holy shit," Hayden yells, letting go of Callie.

They're in such a hurry the bag falls to the ground, the little onesie slipping out.

There is a moment of utter silence, and then both Yasmin and Callie cheer loudly and jump at Aly, pulling her in a group hug.

"*Díos mío!*"

"A girl! You're having a little girl."

"Can you believe it?" Yasmin gives her head a little shake. "This little girl will be like a princess!"

Callie nods. "We're going to spoil her rotten. Oh my God, all the little dresses and dolls. I can't even..."

The girls continue talking, completely stuck in their own little world as they plan everything they'll do to the poor baby once she comes.

Hayden and Nixon exchange a worried look, and then they turn to Zane and me.

"Is that normal?" Nixon asks warily.

"I think I'm a little afraid." Hayden's throat bobs. "Okay, scratch that. I'm scared shitless."

Nixon looks toward the girls who have taken the couch and have pulled out their phones, making a wishlist of the things they need to get for the baby.

"You don't think Callie and Yas will suddenly get baby fever, do you?"

Hayden's eyes bug out. "Please tell me you're joking. I love Callie, but I don't think I'm ready for..." He tips his chin toward the girls. "All that craziness."

"I think you're good," I say, my eyes still locked on the girls. "They'll get it out of their system with Aly's baby."

"Well, let's hope that's true." Hayden shakes his head. "A girl."

Glasses and a bottle of Jack appear on the table. Zane uncaps the bottle and starts pouring the whiskey into each glass.

"Well, that's a plot twist if I've ever seen one." He turns to me and hands me one. "How do you feel?"

I shrug, still unable to form the right words.

How do you express something as big as this in mere words? It's like I've been on a rollercoaster ever since we left for the doctor's office, and I still haven't gotten off of it. There's excitement, happiness, love, but also fear and self-doubt. And if this is how I feel, I can't even begin to imagine how it must be for Aly.

Aly hears him because she turns to us and rolls her eyes. "All smug. He's been telling me from the start that it's going to be a girl."

"When you know it, you know it."

I get to my feet and go to get my jacket. I carefully pull out the photos, my thumb swiping over the little form on the image before handing them to the guys.

Zane's brows shoot up when he realizes what he's looking at. "You got the photos? What did they think that you're the baby daddy?"

My muscles turn stiff at his words. I know he meant it as a joke, but it brings back the words of Aly's doctor.

Daddy.

Aly's blue eyes widen. We hold each other's gaze across the room, and I know she thinks it too—the fact that neither of us corrected her.

It was easy to ignore it since there were other things to concentrate on, but now that Zane said it, it's back front and center.

Bowing my head, I rub the nape of my neck. "I'm going to be her favorite uncle, so I get to keep the photos."

My words break the tension in the room.

Thank God.

"Can you imagine it?" Nixon leans back into the couch. "There'll be *two* of them. Do you think you're ready for it?"

No, I don't think I'll ever be ready for it. But she's coming, and I already know she'll tilt my whole world on its axis.

We stay downstairs for the next two hours, Aly and the girls making the lists while the guys have switched to ESPN. I've sat there, my eyes on the screen, but my mind still stuck on everything that has happened today.

"That was quite the day," Aly yawns softly when I get out of the bathroom.

I walk to my side of the bed and sit down. "I figured you'd be asleep by now."

Aly tucks her hand under her chin. "In a moment. I was catching up on some school stuff."

"How's that going?"

"Good, I think. I guess I'm lucky that the baby will come after I've graduated."

"Just take it one day at a time, and you'll be fine." I lie down on the bed and turn on my side to look at her. "Do you know what you're gonna call her?"

"I do, actually." Aly smiles softly.

I wait for her to continue, but she doesn't. She just looks at me, that teasing smile playing on her lips. I let out a small chuckle. "Are you going to tell me?"

"I didn't want to jinx it, but... Her name is Edie Mae. After my..."

"Grandmother, right?"

Alyssa's grandmother was a force of nature. I still remember how devastated Aly was when she found out she had died.

"Yeah." Aly tucks a strand of hair behind her ear. "It's in honor of the two most important people in my life."

"*Edie Mae*," I whisper, tasting the name on my tongue.
Edie for Edith, and Mae...
My heart speeds up, my throat growing tight.
It can't be...
Aly places her hand over mine, snapping my attention back to her. "Edie for my granny, and Mae for you, Maddox."
"Aly..." I shake my head, not knowing what to say. "Are you sure?"
"You are the other most important person in my life. You mean the world to me, Maddox. You're my best friend. And if it weren't for you, I wouldn't be here. She..." Aly looks away, her throat bobbing as she collects herself. "You were there when we needed you the most, and I'll never forget that. There aren't two better people I could name her after."
My best friend.
I close my eyes for a moment, her words sinking in.
It shouldn't hurt, not after all this time, but somehow, after today, I thought... It doesn't even matter.
Maybe it's better this way. Maybe I should let go of Aly and concentrate on somebody else. Somebody like Mia.
You two are perfect for each other.
If only my heart would get the memo.
"Hey, if you'd rather I don't..."
"No." My eyes snap open, and I find her nibbling at her lower lip. "It's perfect. I'd be honored, Aly. Really."
Aly holds my gaze. "You sure?"
"Positive. I love it." I turn to my back and look up at the ceiling. "Edie Mae."
"Edie Mae," Aly agrees softly.

Chapter 24

ALYSSA

"Which one do you think I should wear?"

Maddox's question breaks me out of my thoughts. I slowly lift my gaze from my laptop and find a shirtless Maddox standing in front of me.

My stomach quivers, mouth going dry as I stare at him. His skin is pale, muscles firm, a fine line of hair leading from his belly button all the way down... My throat bobs as I swallow. Warmth pools at the bottom of my belly, making me squirm in my seat.

How is this fair? On the outside, he looks like your regular boy next door, but the moment he takes his shirt off...

God, why is it suddenly so hot in here?

"Aly?"

I blink, feeling the heat rise to my cheeks. Shifting in my seat, I sit upright, which earns me a glare from Coco.

"Yeah?"

"Which one do you think looks better?" he repeats, lifting two button-down shirts in the air; one is baby blue, the other plain white.

"The blue one."

"The blue one it is." Maddox drops the white shirt on the bed and slips the blue one on. He slowly starts to button the shirt, but his long fingers fidget with the tiny buttons.

Putting my laptop to the side, I scoot closer to the edge of the bed.

"Let me." I quickly work the tiny buttons into the holes, forcing my eyes to stay on the task and not gawk at my best friend. "For somebody who has really agile fingers when it comes to the keyboard, you suck at this."

He rubs the back of his neck. "Yeah, well..."

"What's up with the shirt, anyway?"

"I'm going out on a date."

My whole body goes still at his words. Since my gaze is fixed on his neck as I am just about to do the last button, I can see his Adam's apple bob.

Get a grip, Aly, I chastise myself, slipping the final button in place before moving back.

"You're going on a d-date?" I ask, my voice breaking a little at the last word. My tongue darts out, sliding over my lower lip before I force myself to look up and meet his gaze.

Maddox nods. "With Mia."

Mia.

Of course, it's Mia, his uber-smart, uber-single, uber-interested friend; a friend that's everything that I'm not.

"When did you ask her out?"

Maddox takes a step back, and my hands fall down by my sides. "That day when she came over to play video games."

The day when you pushed him in her direction.

It was the first time I ever noticed a gap between Maddox and me. We've always been such good friends. I knew he had other friends besides me, but now there was this girl, a female version of Maddox, and they were perfect for each other.

It's better this way. He wants to lead a normal life, and you can't hold him back.

"Jacket or no jacket?"

A knot forms in my throat, and I barely manage to swallow it down. I tuck a strand of hair behind my ear. "Where are you going?"

"Anthony's."

The fancy Italian restaurant in the next town over. Of course.

I force a smile out. The motion feels foreign on my face, tight and unnatural. "Definitely a jacket."

Maddox flashes me one of his easy smiles. "Thanks, Aly."

I watch him put on the jacket, his muscles flexing as he does it.

I'm not sure if it's that smile or the whole situation, but that pressure in my throat keeps rising and rising and rising until I think I'll suffocate.

"I think I'm going to go grab something to eat," I say to nobody in particular. I scoot off the bed and slide my feet into my flip flops. "C'mon, Coco." The dog opens one eye and gives me a judging look; still, I don't budge. "Let's get you out too."

With a sigh worthy of a queen, Coco finally gets to her feet and shakes before jumping down and joining me.

Almost in a daze, I descend the stairs and walk into an empty kitchen.

This is good. Maddox should be dating. He's nineteen, for chrissake! He's smart, cute, and single. That's what guys his age should be doing. They should be taking girls on dates, kissing them goodnight, having se—

"Aly?" My head snaps up at the sound of my name. Yasmin is standing in the doorway looking at me funny. "Are you planning to actually take something out of that fridge, or did you just come to cool off for a bit?"

It's then that I notice the cool air touching my skin and making the goosebumps rise on my flesh. "I just spaced out for a moment there."

I look over the selection; some leftover mac and cheese, a few slices of pizza, salami, cream cheese. My nose scrunches the longer I stare at the fridge. Maybe I should just order something?

Yasmin whistles softly. "Where are you going all dressed up like that?"

My stomach twists, but it has nothing to do with the food and everything to do with these feelings that have been slowly building inside of me that I'm not sure how to name, or even less, how to express appropriately.

"Date," Maddox answers, and my heart clenches.

He's actually doing it.

What did you think, silly? That he'll suddenly change his mind?

"A date?" The surprise in her voice is as clear as day. I can feel Yasmin's gaze dart to me, but I keep my attention solely focused on the fridge, although the last thing I want to do now is eat. "With whom?"

There's a slight pause, or maybe it's all just in my head.

"Mia."

"Oh." How can one small word hide so much meaning? "I didn't realize you guys were more than friends."

"We're not. It's just a date. I should really get going; I don't want to be late."

"Sure thing. Have fun, Maddox."

"Thanks."

There's a beat of silence. I sink my teeth into my lower lip, waiting to hear his footsteps as he walks away, the sound of his engine purring, but there's nothing until... "Aly?"

The question is soft, and is there a trace of uncertainty in his voice? It can't be.

Still holding onto the fridge door, I turn to face him. He stares at me from the doorway, a flash of something passing over his face.

You've been selfish enough! I remind myself.

"Go." I bite the inside of my cheek, forcing out a smile and pushing out the words he needs to hear. "Have fun."

Ever since he found out about my situation, Maddox has been nothing but supportive, a true best friend. Now I have to do the same, no matter how much I want to ask him to stay.

Maddox holds my gaze for a moment longer, but then he finally nods. "I'll see you guys later."

My fingers grip the fridge door tighter as I listen to him put on his jacket. Coco goes after him. I call out to her, but she doesn't listen. The front door opens and closes softly, and I can hear Coco whine after Maddox.

Is it wrong that I want to join her? At least she can express her feelings, and nobody will think twice about it, but me...

Yasmin puts her hand on my shoulder, snapping me out of my thoughts. "Are you okay?"

"Peachy."

"Aly..."

I shake my head. "I should eat something."

Not that I'm actually sure I'll be able to swallow anything down, but I have to at least try.

"Do you want me to make you something?"

I shake my head. No matter how much I love her, right now, I need to be alone. "Nah, I'm sure you have better things to do. I'll probably make myself a sandwich or something."

"We were planning to go to Moore's for a bit, wanna come with? We could wait until you're done with your dinner, or you could..."

"I'm not really up for Moore's, Yas," I stop her before she can finish. "I'm tired, and I still have to finish studying. The last thing I need is for my grades to slip."

"If you're sure."

"I'm sure. You guys have fun."

Yasmin nods in understanding. "If you change your mind, you know where to find us."

"Yeah, sure." Yasmin raps her fingers against the counter and starts to leave. "Yas?" She meets my gaze over her shoulder. "Thanks."

She gives me a small smile. "Anytime."

I wait until she's out of earshot to close the fridge and lean against the counter. I can hear the faint voices of my roommates in the hallway, and in a matter of minutes, they're leaving the house. The door closes behind them, leaving only silence.

Coco tilts her head to the side.

"And then, there were two."

MADDOX

Go. Have fun.
   Go. Have fun.
   Go. Have fun.

Those three little words roll on repeat in my head, and no matter how hard I try to push them away, they always come back, louder than before.

But that's not even the worst part.

I can't get Alyssa's face out of my mind either. The shadow that fell over her eyes when she realized where I was going. The flicker of sadness she tried to hide under the facade of that fake smile. As if I didn't know her better than that.

Still, that familiar uneasiness wraps around me, making my lungs tighten and my heart race.

"You don't like your food?"

My head snaps up at the question to find Mia watching me carefully from across the table.

"Sorry, I spaced out for a moment there."

Mia chuckles lightly, "No worries. It happens to me all the time. Sometimes I get so engrossed into something, not even a bomb could get me out of my own head."

Although that isn't what had my attention, I take the out she offers me.

"Exactly, especially if I'm working. The other day I was in the middle of coding when apparently Hayden walked into my room. I guess he wanted me to go with him to the gym to spot him, but I didn't react at all. He ended up sending all the other guys into my room until I finally snapped out of it."

"Who was the one who got a reaction out of you?"

"Aly." The word is out before I can stop it. Is it really surprising, though? A tornado could be raging outside, and I wouldn't notice it, but have Aly enter a room, and that's all it takes to get my attention.

"You and Aly seem close," Mia comments, taking a sip of her red wine. If she finds it annoying that I brought another girl up, she doesn't mention it. "How long have you been friends?"

"Our whole lives. Our families are friends, so we hung out a lot when we were younger, attended the same schools..."

"How come you both ended up at Blairwood?"

I shrug and look down at my plate, pushing a piece of chicken onto my fork. "I guess it just happened that way."

Mia lets out a soft hmm. I lift my gaze and find her observing me carefully. I push my glasses up the bridge of my nose.

"What about you? Do you miss any of your friends from college? You got your bachelor's at Dakota State University?"

"Yes, and a little. I got pretty close with a few people, but most of all Tracy. We were roommates our junior and senior year. Then again, she found a job after college, so it's not like it would have been the same even if I stayed there, you know?"

No, it wouldn't have been the same. That's why I never even entertained the idea of going somewhere else. I knew I'd pick whatever college would keep me closest to Aly. I just couldn't imagine a universe where our two worlds wouldn't collide.

And here I am again, thinking about another girl while I'm on a date with Mia.

This was such a bad idea.

Get a grip, Anderson. You have a nice girl sitting across from you; regardless of your feelings, you can at least listen to her.

"So why did you choose cybersecurity?"

Mia comes to a stop at the front door of her building and turns around to face me, a smile playing on her lips. "I had a really fun time, Maddox. Thank you."

"You're welcome. I had fun, too."

I'm not even lying. We ended up chatting about everything and nothing. And once I actually invested myself in our conversation and stopped letting my thoughts wander, I was reminded once again of why I like Mia so much. Not only is she brilliant, but I love the fact that we can talk about software and coding, and she's also funny and kind. I loved listening to her stories from her days at DSU and hearing her tell me about her friends and family.

"I'm happy to hear that." Mia shifts nervously, her teeth grazing over her lip. "Do you want to come in?"

I blink, completely thrown off guard by her question.

"I..." I open my mouth, but no more words come out. I try to swallow, but the lump stays firmly in place. What the hell is wrong with me? I have this beautiful, smart, funny woman in front of me, inviting me into her room. Why is it that all I want to do, is run away?

But I know the reason for it.

Better yet, *who's* the reason for it.

Mia's head falls down, and she lets out a soft chuckle.

"Why did you ask me to go out with you, Maddox?" Mia asks, looking up at me. There's no reproach in her gaze, only curiosity. "I mean, I think you had fun, but..."

"I did. That's not the issue," I hurry up to reassure her. The last thing I want is for her to think that she's to blame for this when it's not even remotely true. "I really like you, Mia. I do, it's just..."

"I see." Mia nods, understanding dawning on her face. "It's her, isn't it? Alyssa?"

"I..." I rub the back of my neck, suddenly feeling self-conscious. I want to tell her it's not true, but I can't lie to her, and I don't want to. The least she deserves is the truth. "Yeah, it's her."

"I guess I should have known? There's something about you when you two are in the same room. It's like..." She shakes her head. "It's like she's the sun, and you can't help but gravitate toward her whenever you're close. I saw it, and yet, I thought... It doesn't matter what I thought." Mia takes a step closer, placing her hand on my chest. "She's lucky to have you."

"I don't know about that."

"I mean it, Maddox. If she can't see it, then she's a fool and doesn't deserve you."

Or maybe I'm the foolish one for wanting more than I can have.

"Aly has had a lot going on lately," I say instead, not wanting her to think badly of Alyssa.

Mia is quiet for a moment, just observing me, as if she's trying to figure me out. "How long have you been in love with her?"

All my life, I think but manage to keep my mouth shut. Apparently, in itself, that's answer enough.

"I figured as much." The corner of Mia's mouth lifts, but the smile doesn't reach her eyes. "You deserve so much better than her."

Mia's fingers tighten around my shirt. She lifts on the tips of her toes and starts leaning closer.

It takes me a moment to realize what she's about to do.

Kiss.

She's going to kiss me.

The thought registers in the last moment, giving me just enough time to turn my head to the side before her mouth touches mine. Instead, her lips brush against my cheek. I suck in a breath, and it feels like everything comes to a stop for a few heartbeats before the world resets again.

"So. Damn. Lucky," Mia whispers, a trace of longing clinging to her tone. With a long sigh, she pulls back.

"I'm sorry," I grip my neck, taking another step back for good measure. "This is the last thing I wanted."

"It's okay. I really hope she knows what she's missing out on because you, Maddox, have the biggest heart I've ever seen, and you deserve somebody to love you just as fiercely as you love them."

Aly's sad face flashes in my mind. Maybe she doesn't love me like I want her to, but she loves me in her own way. For now, that'll have to be enough.

I clear my throat and look around. "I should get going."

Mia nods. "I'll see you in class next week?"

"Sure. Goodnight, Mia."

"'Night, Maddox."

Although I want to leave, I watch her until she's safely in her dorm. Letting out a breath, I turn around and walk back to my car.

I don't bother turning on the music as I make the ten-minute drive home. I've always liked the quiet. It helps ground me. It gives me room to think. But tonight, the only thing it does is let my mind swirl where it has no right to go, Mia's words ringing in my mind.

If she can't see it, then she's a fool and doesn't deserve you.

That's where she's wrong.

How could Aly have known? I've never said anything, never even hinted at wanting something more between the two of us because of the fear that I'll mess up our friendship. Also, I've seen the guys that she's dated in the past. They were primarily douches that weren't worthy of her, sure. But they were all outgoing, sporty, and popular. All the things that I never was—never would be. Not that I wanted it. I just wanted her.

It's like she's the sun, and you can't help but gravitate toward her whenever you're close.

That's because she is my sun.

The center of my whole world.

And no matter how hard I try to fight it, try to resist it, it'll never happen. Tonight was the perfect example of it.

Pulling into the driveway, I open the garage and park inside. I kill the engine and let my head drop against the headrest.

How am I supposed to go inside and get in bed with Alyssa one more night in a row? Have her curl against my side, her sweet scent surrounding me as she sleeps soundly, her bump pressing against me? Have her so close to me, yet at the same time know she doesn't belong to me? Not really. But the scariest part? Maybe she never will.

"Man up already, Anderson."

Pushing open the door, I slide out and quietly enter the kitchen. The room is empty, but when I get into the hallway, I see a low light coming from the TV in the living room.

For a second, I just stand there, but there is nothing except the low hum of the voices coming from the screen.

Quietly, I make my way to the living room, only to come to a stop in the doorway.

Alyssa is sleeping soundly on the couch in a half-seated position, hugging a pillow to her chest. Her pink lips are slightly parted, long lashes casting a shadow over her cheeks.

I notice Coco curled up next to her, eyes wide open, tail wagging, as I move closer.

"Hey, Coconut." I rub between her ears, earning a happy sigh from the dog. "Keeping an eye on Aly? Of course, you are. C'mon, let's get her to bed."

I walk around and crouch down, wrapping my arms around her slowly so I don't wake her before picking her up.

"M-Maddox?" Aly murmurs, her eyes fluttering open.

"Shh... It's me." I pull her closer to my chest and start walking. "I'm just going to take you to bed. Your back will hurt if you sleep through the night like this."

Aly looks around, clearly disoriented. "You're home."

"Of course, I'm home," I chuckle. "Where would I be?"

She burrows her head in the crook of my neck. "I thought you'd stay with her."

I'm not sure if it's her words or the soft, almost vulnerable tone to her voice, but I can feel that familiar grip tightening around my heart.

"Aly, I..." I start but don't know what to say to make this right, how to explain what happened tonight. Before I can think of something, we're in front of our bedroom. "Can you open the door?"

She turns the handle, and I walk us into the room, letting Coco slip inside before closing the door with my foot and taking Aly to the bed.

Turning on the bedside lamp, I run my fingers through my hair and look down at her. "What's that all about?"

Why were you up and watching TV in the living room? Why would it matter if I came home or stayed? Why is there that shadow falling over your face every time Mia is mentioned?

"Nothing," Aly says quickly, looking away.

I press my fingers against the side of my head, rubbing at my temples. "It's obviously *something*."

I sit down in front of her and slide my fingers under her chin, turning her to look at me.

If only she could see me.

See the real me.

I'm here.

I've been here all along.

"You've been acting off all evening," I say, not wanting to let this slide. "What's going on? Are you okay?"

"I'm fine. It's just..." She shakes her head. "I should probably start looking for a new place to live. I've been imposing on you long enough."

"What? Why?"

Didn't we just have this discussion recently and agree that it's in her best interest to stay here for now?

She can't leave.

I don't want her to leave.

"What do you mean, why?" Aly pushes my hand away and sits upright. "You're dating Mia now. I'm sure she won't be happy that her boyfriend has another girl sleeping in his bed every night." Once again, she tries to turn around, but I grab her hand and don't let go. "I think I'll just go to sle—"

I'm shaking my head before she can even finish. "I'm not dating Mia."

Aly's mouth hangs open, her big eyes staring at me like I just told her I'd run a marathon naked.

"W-what?" She pulls her brows together. "But you..."

"I went on *a date* with Mia," I say slowly, in case she has a hard time comprehending the words in that thick skull of hers. "A date *you* insisted I should take her on if I remember correctly."

"That's because she's perfect for you!" Aly shakes her head as if she can't believe we're even having this discussion. "Maddox, seriously, I'm tired..."

"Perfect?" I push to my feet and run my fingers through my hair. Seriously, this woman is going to be the death of me. "Why are you so convinced that she's perfect for me?"

"Because she's not only gorgeous but also smart." Aly starts lifting her fingers as if she's counting off all the things. "You both study similar things, and she actually knows what the hell you're talking about while I'm clueless like ninety percent of the time, and I've known you my whole life."

"So you think I could only be with a girl who's into the same stuff I'm into?"

"I don't know!" Aly lifts her arms and lets them fall by her side, her voice rising. "I don't think I've ever seen you interested in another girl like you are with her."

"That's because I've been interested in you!" I yell, the words coming out before I can stop them. My breathing is ragged, breaths coming out in hard pants. My eyes fall shut, the sound of my heart galloping in my chest echoing in my eardrums. For a second there, I think I might be having a heart attack. Maybe I am because I'm pretty sure I just admitted to my best friend that I've been in love with her my whole life.

"W-what?"

Slowly, I open my eyes. Aly's mouth is open, lips forming a perfect little O. Her blue eyes seem even wider than usual as she stares at me like a deer caught in headlights.

I move closer. Each step takes forever, but then I'm standing in front of the bed, in front of *her*.

I raise my hand, willing my fingers to calm before I slide them over her cheek. Those little freckles teasing me as she just stares at me.

That's because I've been interested in you!

The words are out now, and there is no taking them back, so for the first time in my life I tell her the truth.

The real truth.

And I pray to God that it doesn't destroy us.

"I'm not dating Mia or any other girl for that matter because I've been in love with you for as long as I can remember."

Chapter 25

ALYSSA

I'm not dating Mia or any other girl for that matter because I've been in love with you for as long as I can remember.

I've been in love with you...

In love...

Maddox's words ring in my head on repeat. I try to make sense of it, of what he's saying, but I can't. How can that be possible? How could Maddox have loved me this whole time without me realizing it? How...

"Aly?"

Maddox cups my cheeks and lifts my head, so my eyes meet his. Those chocolate brown eyes look at me with such worry, such love I'd have staggered back if he weren't holding onto me.

"How? When?"

It just makes no sense. How did I not notice it before? And why am I so relieved to find out about it?

"I don't know exactly when," Maddox shrugs. "One day, you were my best friend, and the next day I noticed the way my heart would start beating harder whenever you were around. And then, there was this constant need to be together, to see your face, to see you happy. It's just different from the way I feel about other people."

My throat wobbles as I struggle to push the words out, "Why didn't you say anything before?"

Maddox chuckles, but there's nothing amusing in his tone. "You are my best friend, Aly. For a while, you were my only friend. I didn't want to put that in jeopardy, not for a slim chance of having you as something more. Besides, I've seen the guys you've dated in the past. I'm not one of those preppy, popular boys you always go for."

Tears burn my eyes at the realization of what it must have been like to be Maddox. Is that what he thought this whole time? That he's not good enough?

"No, you're not," I sniffle, trying to hold my emotions at bay, but it's useless. "You're way better than any of them."

I cover his hand with mine and lean into his touch, relishing in it. His brown eyes hold my gaze, gentle and caring and filled with so much love it's almost hard to look at him.

"I don't know about that," he rasps.

"I do."

I've known it all along. There might have been a lot of uncertainties in my life, a lot of people passing through, but I knew that no matter what, I could always count on my best friend.

I blink, one lone tear sliding down my cheek.

Maddox slides his thumbs under my eyes, an almost pained expression on his face. "Don't cry."

"I'm not crying," I sniffle, leaning my palms against his chest. "There is just something in my eye."

"I know you, Alyssa." Maddox presses his forehead against mine. "You don't have to lie to me."

"I'm not..." I suck in a shaky breath as his lips touch the tip of my nose. My fingers tighten on his shirt as he moves and presses his mouth against my right cheek, then left. "M-Maddox."

"Aly?"

His voice is rough as he whispers my name. He brushes a runaway strand behind my ear as he presses his lips against my forehead, my neck, the side of my mouth...

"Maddox," I breathe. This time my voice is steadier. My fingers curl tighter around his shirt. "We can't."

He's my best friend. He doesn't deserve this mess I'm in. He deserves a girl who will put him first. A girl without all this baggage. A girl that's not me.

If we do this, it'll change everything, and knowing my track record, something will happen, and I'll lose him. And I can't lose him. Not my best friend. Not the person who's been by my side through it all.

"Yes, we can."

"No, we can't." I shake my head. "You don't deserve all this mess I got myself into. I'm pregnant with..."

"I don't care."

Doesn't care? What does he mean he doesn't care?

My eyes snap open at the fierceness in his voice. The hard edge that I'm not accustomed to hearing.

"Maddox..." I start to pull back, but his hold on me is unrelenting.

"No." He shakes his head. "If that's the best excuse you have, then forget it. I've loved you my whole life, Alyssa. My whole. Damn. Life. And you being pregnant doesn't change anything. It certainly doesn't change the way I feel about you."

"How can it not?" I voice out the question that's been on my mind since his admission. "This isn't some silly shit I got myself into. This time I've fallen so deep I don't see a way out. I'm pregnant, Maddox. Pregnant with another man's baby," I repeat, hoping that if I say it loud enough, he'll register my words. He'll realize what he's getting himself into if we pursue this thing between us.

This thing between us.

Just thinking the words has my knees shaking, and if I weren't holding onto Maddox, I'm pretty sure they'd have given out on me.

"See? That's where you're wrong."

"Wrong?" I chuckle, but there is no amusement in my voice.

"Yes, wrong. There isn't another man. He's just a sperm donor barely worth mentioning. If he were a man, he'd have manned up when you told him and done the right thing by you. This is your baby. *Yours*, Alyssa. It's a part of you, and I could never hate a part of you even if I tried."

"Oh, Maddox." My eyes fall shut, more tears spilling down. If I didn't love him before, I'd have fallen a little for him right this second. "I don't deserve you."

"Then the feeling is mutual." Once again, he kisses my cheeks, stopping the tears from falling. "Just let me love you, Aly. Let me love you like you deserve it."

I want to protest. I want to tell him he deserves so much better than what I can give him, but I can't bring myself to utter the words out loud.

So selfish. I've always been so selfish when it came to Maddox Anderson.

There was just something about the nice guy with big, brown eyes that stole my heart since the first moment I met him. He might have fallen in love with me first, but I loved him before, when he was just a baby—my companion. My partner, albeit reluctant, in crime. My best friend.

When his mouth brushes against mine, almost tentatively, I don't pull back; instead, I slide my lips against his. Slowly, gently.

But there is nothing gentle about my body's reaction to him.

It's like a jolt of energy courses through my body at the first contact making every nerve ending come alive.

God, how is this even real?

My whole body trembles in his arms as his kiss turns firmer. I slide my fingers over his chest and onto his neck, pulling him closer. He grazes his teeth over my lower lip, sucking it into his mouth. My lips part as I let out a soft moan, and his tongue slips inside, tangling with mine expertly.

My friends have told me about their earth-shattering kisses, but I've never believed them until now. Until Maddox. Because kissing Maddox makes the world stop. It's like I'm flying and being pulled down by gravity all at once.

Maddox lets out a low groan as our tongues tangle together. His fingers dig into my hair and pull my head back as his tongue dives deeper, each measured stroke making the ache in my belly grow stronger.

I slide my hand down his chest, unbuttoning his shirt, but I only get a couple of buttons free because my fingers are too unsteady.

Breaking the kiss, Maddox draws back. He grabs the back of his shirt and pulls it over his head in one swift movement, and then his mouth is on mine once again.

I wrap my arms around his neck, letting my fingers slide over the strong muscles of his back, feeling his soft skin.

God, he's magnificent.

How some girl didn't see it until now, I'll never understand.

Because Maddox Anderson is everything a girl could ever ask for, everything a girl could ever want.

And he's mine.

Heat radiates off of him in waves, and no matter how hard we're pressed against one another, it's not enough.

"You feel so good," Maddox murmurs, slowly working his

way over my chin and down my neck. Every place he kisses, tingles in his wake. "Even better than I imagined."

"Did you do it often?" I slide my hands up his back, letting my nails graze over his back and neck until my fingers tangle in his hair, pulling his head so I can look him in the eyes. Those same brown eyes that have been watching me silently from a distance all this time without me even noticing. "Did you imagine me, *us*, like this?"

"Y-yeah..." He lets out a shaky breath as I run my fingers through his hair.

The corner of my lips tilts as color creeps up his neck.

His admission does something to me. I feel almost... giddy with the knowledge that he's thought about this.

About us.

About *me*.

The nice boy next door having dirty thoughts about his friend.

I trace my nose over his neck, smelling a faint scent of his cologne. That same scent I gave him for the first time years ago, when he was more boy than a man, overwhelming my senses.

"Did you come thinking of me?" I ask softly, my lips brushing against the shell of his ear, making goosebumps appear on his skin.

"Fuck, Aly." His head jerks back, those dark, dark eyes of his staring at me. They're filled with so much passion, so much need, they almost feel bottomless.

"Tell me, Maddox," I demand, needing to know, needing to discover this new, different side of my best friend.

"Y-yes," he breathes. "Yes, I did."

"Good." I slide my thumb over his lower lip. "But this time, it's a reality."

With those words, I kiss him once again.

There is nothing slow about this kiss, not any longer.

Maddox pulls me into his lap. The move is so fast it kicks the air out of my lungs, leaving me breathless. Or maybe that's just the way he kisses me. Like he can't get enough of me. Like any moment, the world will shatter under us, and he wants to make the most out of it before it does.

A shudder runs through me as I feel his hard bulge nestle between my legs. I rub against him, hoping to appease the ache inside me, this need to have him that I've been fighting for weeks now.

Maddox's hand slips under my shirt, slow and unsure. His fingers glide over my bump and up to my chest, cupping one full breast into his hand and giving it a tentative squeeze.

I hiss softly as pain and pleasure fight inside me. Ever since I've become pregnant, my boobs have grown bigger and more sensitive than ever before, so having Maddox touch them now is the sweetest of tortures.

I start to fumble with my shirt, trying to pull it over my head, but it's like the damn thing is stuck. Maddox helps me pull the shirt over my head, letting it join his on the floor, leaving me only in a tiny pair of lace panties.

"Tell me how to make this good for you," Maddox whispers softly, his dark eyes burning with desire.

"You're doing just fine."

Still, I place my hand over his and bring it back to my breast, loving the feeling of his rough fingertips on my skin.

"I've never..."

His thumb slides over one nipple, turning it into a hard peak. My head falls back as I moan softly at the touch, and it takes me a moment to register his words. But once I do, my whole body goes still. "Wait, what?"

"Nothing." Maddox looks away, his cheeks burning even brighter than before.

He can't mean...

"You've never what?" I ask once again, my finger sliding under his chin and turning him to face me.

"It's embarrassing."

"I don't care. Tell me."

"I've never done this." His Adam's apple bobs. "I've never had sex... with somebody before."

I blink, unsure if I've heard him correctly because it can't possibly be true.

"You've never..."

Maddox groans, his head falling back. He pulls his hand away, rubbing his palms over his face. "I'm not repeating it. Saying it once was embarrassing enough."

"Wait, you're serious?" My throat tightens as the realization dawns on me. "You're a vi—"

He gives me a warning glare. "Don't say it like that. There's no need to make a big deal out of it."

But there is. It should be a big deal.

Maddox's expression softens as he cups my cheek. "I just want to make sure if we're doing this that we're doing it right. I want to make you feel good, Aly."

Even now, he's putting me first.

Stubborn, stubborn man.

I give him a little push. Surprised, he falls down on the mattress.

"What are you do—"

"Let me." I lean down and press my mouth against his quickly. "I want to make you feel good first."

He shakes his head. "Aly, you don't have to..."

"But I want to." My tongue darts out, wetting my lower lip. "I really want to."

I straddle his legs and slowly remove his glasses, putting them on the nightstand. Only then do I slide my hands down his sculpted chest, over the valleys on his stomach. "The first time I saw these..." I shake my head, still unable to form the right words.

Maddox smirks, "Hadn't expected those?"

"Not in the slightest," I admit, leaning down and pressing my mouth against his chest, peppering him with kisses as I work my way down.

"I'm not that scrawny little boy I was before."

"I know that." My hands trail down his sides as I kiss his hard stomach to the slight V leading to his pants. "I can see that."

Maddox sucks in a breath as the tips of my fingers reach the band of his boxer briefs and slowly work my way down until I reach the button on his jeans. I quickly slip my finger underneath it, the button coming undone, easily followed by the zipper.

"Up."

Maddox lifts his hips, and I slide his jeans down his legs, throwing them on the floor.

Sucking on my lower lip, I look up at him before my fingers find their way under the band and pull them down, removing them just enough so I can wrap my fingers around his hot, hard length.

And oh my...

My mouth goes dry at the sight of him.

Who would have thought that's what's been hiding beneath those jeans all this time?

Maddox sucks in a sharp breath. "Fuck, Aly..."

"What?" I ask innocently, tightening my grip on him and giving his dick a few slow pulls. "I didn't do anything."

Maddox's fingers tighten around the bedsheets. "The only thing you have to do is look at me like that, and I'm a goner."

There's something about his words that undoes me. Nobody has ever said anything like that to me. Sure, I've had some good times in bed with other guys, but there was something about being with Maddox that was just different. And that's saying something since we have yet to get to the good part. He's a living contradiction. The way he looks at me makes me feel raw and vulnerable. His words... His words make me feel powerful.

Embracing that feeling, I grin at him. "Good thing I'm not going to just look?"

With that, I lower down and wrap my lips around his dick.

"Shit..."

His hips buck at the first touch of my mouth on him. Letting that empowering feeling lead me, I pull him deeper into my mouth. I want to make this good for him. I want him to remember this time and think of me, of how good it can feel.

How good *we* can feel.

With each up and down motion of my head, I pull more of his length into my mouth. One hand curled around his base; I let the other go to his sack, gently massaging his balls. I slowly pull back, letting my tongue slide over the underside of his dick.

Maddox lets go of the sheets he's been gripping, his hands tangling in my hair instead.

I look up and find his hazy gaze on me. Holding his eyes, I lower once more, taking inch after inch of him, until I feel him at the back of my throat before slowly releasing his length.

His jaw is set tight, his muscles bulging as he tries to hold back.

"Aly, if you keep doing that, I'm going to come."

I cock a brow at him as I release him, the tip of my tongue circling his head and tasting the salty precum. "That's the whole point."

Not waiting for him to answer, I go back to work. Speeding up my movements with each suck until I can feel him throb in my mouth.

"Aly..." Maddox warns, his fingers tightening in my hair to

the point of pain. As if he's trying to hold onto something. Like I'm his only lifeline.

I murmur softly against his length, my free hand sliding over the side of his leg, letting him know it's okay to let go. I want to feel it, to taste his release on my tongue.

Wrapping my lips around him tighter, I flick my tongue over his sensitive tip and lower down, humming softly. My hand slides higher, nails grazing over his abs.

That's what finally does it.

Maddox's body goes taut under me as he spills his release with a low groan, his body falling down on the mattress completely spent.

Chapter 26

MADDOX

I'm in heaven. Or maybe it's hell. Although it feels too good for it to be hell so...

The mattress dips, snapping me out of my thoughts. Aly slowly moves closer. I shift my head to the side, watching her curl into my side with a happy sigh.

"You'd think I made you come, not the other way around," I murmur softly, pushing a strand of hair behind her ear.

Maybe I should feel self-conscious. After all, I'm lying in bed naked with my almost naked best friend, but I'm not. On the contrary, being like this with her feels... *right*. There is no better way to explain it.

It's like this is exactly where I need to be, where I've belonged all along.

Aly pushes sweaty locks of my hair out of my face, a lazy smile on her lips. "I loved doing that. I loved watching you let go." There's a slight pause. Aly watches me, her teeth grazing over her lower lip. "Did you like it?"

"Like it?" I can't help myself; I laugh.

Aly bites the inside of her cheek and starts to pull away, but I wrap my arm around her and hold her in place.

"It was the best, earth-shattering experience of my life. It was everything I've ever wanted. I don't think 'like it' covers it."

Aly zeroes in on my chest, pink rising up her chest and neck. "Well, I wanted you to like it."

I press a kiss in the hollow of her neck, loving how the soft skin feels under my touch. "I already told you, there's nothing about you that I won't love." I slide my hand over the side, feeling the delicate curves of her body as I shift on the bed. "But I think you owe me a demonstration."

My fingers trace the underside of her breasts, the weight of it heavy in my palm. Aly has always been gifted in the chest department, but since she got pregnant, they have only grown larger, fuller.

"Oh, r-really?"

A slow tremor runs through her as I cup her breast more firmly. I massage the soft flesh, my thumb making circles over the hard nipple.

"Yes, really." I nibble at her neck before moving lower. "It's my turn to make you feel good, Alyssa. Show me how."

Her fingers tangle in my hair as she pulls me closer, so close my lips brush against those little hard peaks. The blue of her irises grows darker as she watches me. "Just be careful. They have been super sensitive."

I nod my acknowledgment, pressing a kiss between her breasts before I capture one hard nipple into my mouth and suck.

"Shit..." Aly arches her back off the bed, her grip on my hair tightening. "Maddox, I..."

I look up at her. Her eyes are closed, her long lashes casting shadows over her freckled cheeks, her teeth sinking into her lower lip.

I tentatively flick my tongue over the pebbled nipple before sucking it deeper into my mouth. Her lip pops out, a low moan parting her lips, making my dick jolt to life.

Down boy.

Aly's eyes pop open as I switch from one nipple to the other, repeating the process. Her irises are dilated, cheeks flushed. "Already?"

I press my hard dick against her thigh, hoping it'll alleviate some of the ache, but the result is the complete opposite. The nipple pops out of my mouth. "I have a lot of time to make up for."

"Then we better get to work." Aly's hand wraps around my cock, but I push it away.

"Oh, no, you first. I've waited years. I can wait a few more minutes." I press my mouth against hers, our fingers intertwining. "Show me how to make you come."

Holding my gaze, she presses her palm over the back of my hand and places our joined hands on her breast. I give it a slow caress before we make our way down.

Her belly is firm, the bump still small, but it's there. I give it a gentle rub before our hands dip lower over her silky mound, my fingers sinking between her lips, brushing against her clit.

"Yes," Aly whispers, her teeth sinking into her lower lip.

She's beautiful and so freaking wet already. I let my fingers slide down her slit, teasing her opening. Aly sucks in a sharp breath, her hand falling down to the mattress as the palm of my hand presses against her clitoris.

"Tell me what you like," I repeat, rubbing the small bundle of nerves.

"Y-you're doing so good…"

Hearing the praise from her lips feels good, too damn good.

"You think?" I whisper, nuzzling my face into the crook of her neck, pressing small kisses against her skin. My fingers lazily go up and down. A quick flick to the clit, before I slide back down, my fingers teasing her opening but never entering.

Aly shudders, her fingers gripping the sheets, and just nods.

"What about this?" I ask, dipping my finger inside her just a little bit.

Her eyes fall shut. "M-more."

"More?" I pull back, which earns me an unamused groan.

"Maddox!"

Her eyes pop open, the blue of her irises is darker, filled with passion, want, need.

Need for me.

"Not really patient, are you?"

She huffs, her lips twisting into a pout. "Don't tease me."

I slide my mouth against hers, slipping my tongue between her lips, twining my tongue with hers as I work my fingers back inside. Aly's irises grow wider as my finger sinks in, her wetness making it so easy for me to slide to the hilt.

Her pussy squeezes around my finger, trying to hold onto it as I slowly pull them out, creating a steady rhythm.

Aly's eyes start to close, so I break the kiss, slowing my movement. "Open those pretty eyes, Aly."

Her eyes blink open, although barely just enough so I can see those baby blues.

"It feels so good," she murmurs, half protest, half plea. "How is it so good?"

Because it's you and me, and you've always belonged with me.

My chest squeezes as the words ring in my mind, the enormity of this whole situation slamming into me.

This isn't just any girl.

It's Aly.

My best friend and the girl I've loved my whole life.

Whatever happens after this, nothing will ever be the same.

Maybe it should worry me. There's no going back, no erasing what's happening. But that's okay because I don't want to go back, not after having her like this.

"Good," I whisper, the corner of my mouth tilting upward. I continue the steady thrusts with my fingers. My free hand glides over her skin, my fingers wrapping around her breast and tweaking her nipple.

Aly's back jolts off the mattress. "Shit…"

Once again, her eyes start to shut. "Eyes," I grit, making myself slow down. "I want you to look at me as you come."

A frown appears between her brows, but she does as I say. "You're awfully bossy. Aren't you supposed to be inexperienced?"

"That doesn't mean I don't know what I want." I nibble her hard nipple before I'm facing her, our mouths brushing together as my fingers sink into her. I press my thumb over her clit, making little circles around the small bud, and then over it.

"And what do you want?" Aly sinks her fingers in my hair, gripping the strands tightly as she pulls me closer.

"You," I let the admission out. "It's always been that simple. I want you."

Our mouths brush together, and I slip my tongue into her mouth, each thrust matching the one of my fingers sinking into her molten heat. Over and over again, until her body is shaking with want.

"Maddox, I need…"

"What?"

"Harder."

So I give her what she needs. I add another finger, stretching her pussy wider. I can feel the tight grip she has on me as I sink them deeper. Once, twice, then I tweak her clit.

Aly lets out a loud moan, so loud I have to press my mouth against hers to muffle the sound. Her back arches off the mattress as her body shudders as she comes, her pussy gripping my fingers tightly, and it's the most beautiful thing I've ever seen.

We pull apart, both of us breathing hard. Aly's holding onto me and presses her forehead against my chest.

With my free hand, I brush her hair out of her face and slowly pull my fingers out of her. "You okay?"

Maybe I went too hard. Maybe I hurt her. Maybe…

"I'm perfect…" She grazes her teeth over her lower lip. Her mouth is swollen from our kisses, but she still pulls me in for another one. Her body brushes against mine, our skin slick with sweat rubbing together.

My dick rubs against her soft skin, and I can't hold back the groan.

"Now, I need you inside me."

Her legs fall open, and I settle between them when the realization hits me.

"C-condom." I press my head against her shoulder. *Shit, shit, shit.* "I don't have a condom."

Talk about a rookie mistake.

Aly gently caresses my cheek, nudging me to lift my head and look at her, so I do. "We don't need one."

"B-but…"

"I'm already pregnant, so it's not like that can happen again." She chuckles, but the sound dies quickly. Her throat bobs. "I'm clean if that's what's worrying you. I got checked after…" She shakes her head. "Well…"

"I'm clean too…" Dumbass, she knows. You're a freaking virgin. "Are you sure?"

I smooth her hair away from her face, staring into those bright blue eyes of hers.

"Yes, I'm sure." Aly nods once. "I don't want anything between us."

She spreads her legs wider in a silent invitation. I move closer, but apparently not enough because Aly's fingers wrap around my hard length, and she pulls me to her. She gives me a few slow pumps as my tip brushes against her entrance feeling her slick heat.

Holding her gaze, I kiss her and slowly push inside.

Holy shit.

She's like velvet, soft and warm, slowly wrapping around me as I slide into her.

"Fuck, Aly," I grit, breaking the kiss as the pressure around me becomes too much.

Aly sucks in a breath as I pull back and thrust inside her once again, slowly testing the motions. This time, I slide even deeper.

Aly's thighs grip mine tighter as I thrust inside her. My arms tremble as I brace them against the sides of her head. Aly wraps her arms around me and brushes her mouth against mine. Her fingers dig into my back as I slide deeper and deeper, barely holding onto my sanity.

The pressure at the base of my spine builds. I break the kiss, my muscles tightening. "I don't think I…"

Aly presses her forehead against mine. "Let go."

Her pussy tightens around me, holding onto me. The pressure builds inside of me, and before I can think about it, before I can do anything to stop it I erupt inside of her. My body tenses with the release, every muscle taut, and then I fall slack on top of her.

Aly swipes my sweaty hair out of my face. Her lips brush against my cheek. I turn around, capturing her mouth with mine. I don't think I'll ever get enough of it. Enough of kissing her. Enough of holding her. Enough of *her*.

"Fuck, Aly… I'm squishing you." I try to pull back, so I'm not lying on top of her, but she doesn't let go.

"It's fine. I don't mind being squished."

"But the baby..." I try to protest, but Aly just shakes her head.

"She's fine. Relax."

I do as I'm told, relaxing if only slightly. I trace my fingers over the side of her body, enjoying the feel of her soft skin.

"I'm sorry you didn't come." I look up at her. "Talk about a lousy lay."

"You're not a lousy lay." She tugs at one of my locks. "And I did come."

"Not just now you didn't."

"Maybe not," there's a wicked glint in her eyes, "but there's always the next time."

The next time.

"I sure hope there is." I press my mouth against her forehead, tightening my grip around her. "I'm going to clean up. I'll be back in a few."

Reluctantly, I let go of Alyssa and duck into the bathroom. I quickly clean up and then grab a towel, dampening it before I return to the bedroom.

Aly is lying on the bed, curled on her side, hand under her chin. Her eyelids fall closed every so often, like she's fighting sleep.

I kneel on the bed next to her, slowly push her to lie on her back and pry her legs apart.

"Wha—"

I place the towel between her legs and gently rub the cum away. "Good?"

Aly's face softens. "Y-yeah," she croaks. "Now come back to bed."

Nodding, I throw the towel toward the basket before I slide in next to Aly, pulling the blanket over us. She scoots closer, her legs slipping between mine, head resting on my chest, and everything finally feels right.

"'Night, Maddox," she whispers, her arms tightening around me.

I brush my lips over the top of her head. "Night, Aly."

Chapter 27

ALYSSA

I come to my senses slowly, clinging to the remnants of sleep, clinging to the warmth surrounding me. I don't remember when the last time I slept so well was, not in a while, that's for sure, and I don't want this moment to end just yet.

I shift, moving closer to the source of the heat. My leg slides over another leg. This one is harder, with soft hair...

My eyes fly open instantly, zeroing in on the man lying beside me. And not just any man—Maddox.

I suck in a breath as all the memories of last night come rushing back. Maddox going out on a date. The unsettling feeling brewing in my stomach as I watched him leave. Watching TV until I finally succumbed to sleep. Waking up in Maddox's arms.

I'm not dating Mia or any other girl for that matter because I've been in love with you for as long as I can remember.

Just remembering those words, the way he said them, has goosebumps rising on my skin.

It's real.

Last night... It actually happened.

I had slept with Maddox.

I had sex with my best friend, and it was amazing.

"I can hear you thinking from over here," Maddox groans, his arms wrapping around me tighter.

Slowly, he blinks his eyes open, the sleepiness clinging to his dark brown irises. He looks adorable, so much like the little boy I spent my childhood with.

"I was just thinking about last night."

Maddox narrows his eyes at me as if he's trying to focus. He reaches for my face, brushing my hair behind my ear. "Do you regret it?"

I pull back, surprised by his question. "What?"

Is he for real?

"Last night? Do you regret it?"

"No, of course not. I was just... surprised."

His brows rise, doubt flashing over his face.

"I thought it was just a dream." I run my fingers through his wild locks. The same locks I ruffled last night. The locks I clung to as he brought me to orgasm. "One really hot dream."

Maddox just watches me for a while, completely silent. "If you want to change your mind..."

I press my hand over his mouth to stop him from finishing. "I'm not changing my mind. I..." I look to the side, suddenly feeling self-conscious.

I've been in love with you for as long as I can remember.

He admitted he loves you. You should at least give him this back.

I clear my throat and turn to him.

"I didn't want you to go out with her," I whisper softly. "Yesterday. I didn't want you to go."

Maddox wraps his fingers around my wrist and pulls it back. "What do you mean? You were the one who told me to ask Mia out in the first place."

I did, didn't I?

"That was before."

"Before?" Maddox places my hand on his chest and slides his fingers under my chin, tilting it so our eyes meet.

"Yes, before."

Before I really saw you. Before I started to feel all these things, I was not even sure I should be feeling.

"You're confusing me."

Well, that makes two of us.

"It's you who should be running in the other direction. Not me."

Maddox shakes his head even before I've finished. "Never."

There's assurance in his voice, a silent intensity I'm not used to seeing in my sweet, kind best friend. My Maddox.

"I want this. I want you, Alyssa. I'm not going away."

Tears prickle my eyes. "I come as a package deal," I remind him. Just then, Coco jumps up on the bed, her tail whipping happily. I chuckle, "Quite literally."

"I know that." Maddox presses his forehead against mine, his thumb sliding over my cheekbone. "I want that. I want you. Both of you." Coco squeezes her way between us. "Okay, all *three* of you."

Coco lays down between us, turning on her back and lifting her legs in the air, offering Maddox her belly for rubs. Of course, he obliges.

"You're lucky I think you're cute, Coconut."

Maddox's eyes meet mine. I sink my teeth into my lower lip as the energy sizzles between the two of us. Vibrant and alive. I'm not sure how I've been able to ignore it so far because now that it's out in the open, I can't push it back any longer.

Maddox starts to lean closer, but just before his lips touch mine, my stomach rumbles loudly, breaking the moment.

Maddox lets out a soft groan and falls back on the mattress.

I feel my cheeks heat in embarrassment. "Sorry."

"There's nothing to be sorry about." He shakes his head as if to clear his mind. "Breakfast?"

"Yeah, breakfast sounds good."

"Breakfast it is."

He sits upright, his back turned to me. I slide my hand under my cheek and watch him cross the room to the dresser and pull a clean pair of dark gray boxer briefs out and pull them over his muscular ass.

Maddox peeks over his shoulder at me. "What?"

"Nothing, just looking."

And there's something to look at, all right. Who'd have thought beneath all these baggy hoodies and button-downs hid lean, defined muscles?

As if I've called it, he grabs a tee out of the drawer and pulls it on. Then he picks up a hoodie from the chair. I expect him to slide it on, but instead, Maddox stops by the bed.

"I thought you were hungry," he says as his eyes slide over my naked back, his eyes growing darker.

"Maybe I changed my mind. Maybe I'm hungry for something different."

Maddox blushes. Like legit blushes. Pink slowly rises up his neck and into his cheeks.

"Well, I…" He starts to push glasses up his nose, only to remember he isn't wearing them.

I sit up, the sheet falling into my lap and grab them from his nightstand. "Looking for these?"

His Adam's apple bobs as he swallows.

Holding his gaze, I slowly make my way across the bed and slip the frames in place. "Better?"

"Y-yeah. Thanks."

A smile curls the corner of my mouth. "I guess I should go and put some clothes on."

"Here." Maddox extends his hand, hoodie dangling from his

fingers. He slips it over my head, and for a moment, I'm enveloped in all things Maddox. The soft cotton smells like him, like sandalwood and home. "Arms."

I do as he asked, slipping my arms in the sleeves. When the hoodie falls in place, I get off the bed. Even with my bump, the material falls to mid-thigh and covers all the important bits. Still, I go to the dresser and grab a pair of panties, slipping them on, followed by a pair of shorts.

"C'mon, Coco," I call to her as we get out in the hallway, where the sun is shining brightly through the windows, blinding me. "What time is it, anyway?"

Between the surprise of waking up next to Maddox, *naked*, and our conversation, I totally spaced out as to what time it was. It felt good for a change not to have to worry about the next place I'm rushing toward and just be.

"After ten." Maddox looks at me. "Why? Did you have to work?"

After ten?

God, I don't remember the last time I slept in so long. It's been a while, that's for sure.

"No," I shake my head. "It's actually my day off."

Maddox's brows shoot up. "You took a day off?"

"I know, shocker." A soft murmuring comes from the kitchen. Maddox's hand brushes against the small of my back as we enter the kitchen.

As one, all the heads turn toward us, giving us curious glances.

A sly grin spreads over Yasmin's face. "Oh, look who the cat dragged in."

"Morning," I murmur, tucking a strand of my hair behind my ear, suddenly feeling self-conscious. I'm not sure why. They're my friends.

Act normal! I chastise myself. *It's not like you have it written all over your face that you two had sex.*

"We were about to send out a search party." Callie sets the last of the utensils next to the plates before grabbing her cup of coffee. She takes a sip, leaning against the table.

I look between my friends. "What for?"

"Umm, to see if you were alive?"

Maddox, completely unfazed, gives me a little push toward the table. "Sit. Do you want coffee or that ginger stuff?"

"Ginger tea," I say automatically. I've been drinking that stuff like water since it's been helping with my nausea, which is good since I might start to feel nauseous again right about now. "But I should probably let Coco out first."

Maddox turns on the coffee machine and kettle before looking at me. He gives me a pointed once-over before his eyes settle on mine. "Not in that. It's cold outside."

I look out the window at the sunny day. "It doesn't look that cold."

"It's not even March." He walks past me, his hand grazing over my back. "I'll let her out; you sit tight." He whistles softly. "C'mon, Coconut."

The little traitor doesn't even bother to look at me. She just sashays by following after Maddox like I don't exist.

Letting out a sigh, I turn around to find my two best friends watching me with matching suspicious looks.

"What's going on here?" Yasmin asks as soon as the door closes behind Maddox.

"What do you mean?" I ask, trying to appear as inconspicuous as possible.

Yasmin narrows her eyes at me. "What do I mean? You've been acting off since yesterday." Her gaze darts toward the door behind which Maddox just disappeared to. "And then there's him."

"I was just tired, that's all."

Seriously, why didn't we talk about this before coming down?

Like are we going to tell our friends? *What* are we going to tell them? That we've had sex? What are we really? Friends with benefits? Something more?

My stomach sinks.

God, this is a mess.

Yasmin shakes her head. "That's not it."

"I don't know what to tell you," I shrug and walk around her when the coffee machine beeps, grateful for the distraction. "It's been a long week, and I had a morning off, so I slept in."

I pour Maddox a cup of coffee just when the kettle whistles. Rising on my tiptoes, I grab a cup for myself and a bag of ginger tea, pouring the hot water over it.

"Still doesn't explain why Maddox slept in. That guy barely sleeps."

"Maddox sleeps," I protest.

I should know. I've been the one sleeping next to him for the past few weeks.

"Yasmin's right." Callie takes the high chair by the counter. "I've been living here for close to a year now, and I don't remember Maddox ever sleeping in. He's like one of those vampires. But he isn't shiny, nor does he drink blood."

Tingles run down my spine.

Maybe not, but he does give seriously good neck kisses.

My teeth sink into my lower lip as more memories from last night come rushing back. The hair at my nape starts to rise, and I can feel my nipples hardening.

Thank God for the hoodie.

Yasmin looks over her shoulder at Callie. "Right? One night when I was sleeping over, I went to the bathroom and almost screamed when I saw him coming up the stairs at like three in the morning. Scared me shitless."

Callie waves a hand dismissively. "He does that all the time. You'll get used to it."

"No way. He's lucky he's cute." Yasmin shakes her head and flips the pancake. "Maybe he was tired? He did go out on that date last night." She shifts her attention to me. "Did you see him come back?"

"Ummm..."

Thankfully, Callie interrupts me before I can answer. "Maddox went out on a date? With who?"

"Mia."

"Oh." Callie looks at me, her mouth forming a little o. "I didn't know that."

"It's fine," I shrug. "She's a nice girl."

A nice girl he's not interested in, I remind myself.

I've been in love with you for as long as I can remember.

"I'm not saying she's not, just that she's not right for Maddox." Yasmin shakes her head and slides the pancake onto the plate.

My brows furrow. "What do you mean she's not right for Maddox?"

Do I want Maddox to be with Mia? Hell, no. But is she practically his female version? Yes, yes, she is. She's all the things I'll never be—most importantly: single, unattached, and without any additional baggage.

Yasmin rolls her eyes. "I mean exactly what I said. She's not what Maddox needs."

I open my mouth, but just then, the back door opens. Maddox and Coco come inside, followed by a sweaty Nixon and Hayden.

"Damn, this smells so good!" Nixon groans, going straight for the stove and stealing one pancake off the plate.

"Hey!" Yasmin protests. She tries to smack him with the spatula, but he's faster. "No eating."

Nixon takes a bite off the pancake and continues talking with his mouth full. "Isn't it the whole point of making breakfast is so people can eat?"

"Yes, but like decent human beings. Meaning you should go take a shower, so you don't stink and sit down at the table."

"Oh, baby, you didn't complain about me being stinky last night…"

Yasmin crosses her arms over her chest and glares at him. "You were saying?"

Thankful that the attention is finally away from Maddox and me, I turn around when I feel him near and hand him the cup of coffee.

"Thanks, you didn't have to."

"You took Coco out." I glance at our friends, but they still seem to be occupied. Still, I lower my voice. "Besides, I had to do something since you left me all alone with the two of them."

Maddox pulls his brows together. "What's wrong with that?"

"Oh, Maddox," I sigh and shake my head. My stomach chooses that exact moment to announce itself once again, making Maddox frown.

"C'mon, let's get you something to eat." He tilts his head and looks at the stove. "Pancakes, or do you want something else?"

"Pancakes, please."

Maddox pushes a strand of my hair behind my ear. "Pancakes coming right up." He gives me a little push in the direction of the table. "Sit."

"What am I? Coco?" I roll my eyes at him but do as he asked.

Coco barks from under the table, her tail wagging as she attacks her bone toy.

"If only you listened as easily as her."

"Thanks," I mutter dryly. "There's nothing a girl likes more than being compared to a dog."

With a shake of my head, I take a sip from my cup, but as soon as I lower it, I see our friends watching us. Again.

"Am I missing something?" Yasmin narrows her eyes, her gaze shifting from Maddox to me and back. "I am. I know I am."

I look down at my cup, suddenly finding the contents quite interesting.

"Callie, please tell me I'm not the only one."

"Nope, definitely not."

The chair creaks as she shifts, and I can feel her probing gaze on the side of my face. So much about them forgetting about our earlier conversation.

What are the chances they'll let it go?

Yasmin taps her chin. "I'm just not sure what exactly I'm missing."

"Missing what?" Nixon tries to steal another pancake, but Maddox has already taken the plate and is carrying it to the table. "Aww, have you been missing me? I've been go—"

"Not you." Yasmin shoves him away and points her finger at us. "Them."

Maddox lowers the plate with pancakes on the table and takes a seat next to me. Not bothering to ask, he puts a few pancakes on my plate before getting some for himself and hands me the syrup.

"Thanks." I give him a grateful smile and put a generous amount over the fluffy pancakes before picking up my cup and taking a sip.

"Now that you mentioned it..." Nixon tilts his head to the

side, his eyes narrowing. "Did you two sleep together or some shit?"

The sip of the tea I just drank comes rushing back, and I start coughing uncontrollably.

"Holy shit! You did."

A hand falls on my back, and somebody, Maddox, I realize, gives me a few soft pats. "Are you okay?"

His head pops in my line of vision, his face blurry from the tears stinging my eyes.

I shake my head, or at least try to, because I'm still coughing and struggling to breathe.

"Dammit, Nixon."

"What? I just asked. I didn't actually think it was true. Not after all this time, anyway."

"Are you okay?" Callie asks, rubbing my back. "C'mon, inhale deeply."

I want to snap at her, but for that, I'd need to actually be able to inhale.

"She looks kind of blue."

Callie turns around and slaps Hayden over the head. "You're not helping."

Definitely not.

Maddox pulls out my chair and steps in front of me, his serious brown eyes staring into mine. His hands grab my shoulders. "Breathe, Aly."

I cough and force myself to take a shaky breath in.

"Good. Another one."

I nod, doing as he says.

Maddox has always been my steady place. He's like a mountain, strong and unmoving. Reliable.

I wrap my fingers around his wrists, holding onto him. I can barely feel the beat of his heart from the furious thumping of my own echoing in my eardrums. Still, I do my best, taking in one shaky breath at a time, until my coughing slowly stops, and my throat feels raspy from the exertion, but I'm not coughing anymore, so I'll take it.

"Want some water?" Yasmin offers.

I glance toward my friends. "I think not." The last thing I want is to suffocate all over again. "But thanks."

"It was supposed to be a joke," Nixon says.

"Never say that joking didn't kill anybody," Hayden mutters.

Nixon shakes his head. He comes to me and wraps his arm around my shoulders. "You okay?"

"Getting there." I tilt my head back to look at him. "But please, no more joking."

"No more jokes." Nixon nods. "Got it."

"Can we get back to breakfast now?" Maddox asks, looking around the table. "Or do we have to continue discussing our sex life?"

"You have a sex life?"

As one, we all turn toward the entrance where Zane is standing and looking at us. With all the commotion, we didn't even hear him enter.

"Not that that's any of your business."

"But didn't you go out on a date with Mia?" Callie asks, a frown between her brows. "'Cause I'm pretty sure Yasmin said you went out with Mia last night."

Maddox tilts his head back and pinches the bridge of his nose. "Mia is a friend."

"I thought Aly was a friend too," Yasmin comments.

"She is." His eyes turn to me, the brown of his irises growing darker just like it did... "Only now she knows I've been in love with her."

There are those words again.

I'm not dating Mia or any other girl for that matter because I've been in love with you for as long as I can remember.

They fall off his lips almost effortlessly. Like there's not a smidge of doubt inside of him.

"It was about damn time," Nixon mutters. Maddox gives him a stern look that has Nixon lifting his hands in the air in defense. "What? It's true. You've been moping after her since freshman year."

"I haven't been moping." Maddox pushes his glasses up his nose. "Can we let this go? It's not like it changes anything."

"Oh, buddy," Hayden slaps him over the shoulder as he makes his way to his seat. "This changes *everything*."

"I really don't see how. Aly and I have been friends."

"Only now, you're friends that kiss," Nixon lifts his brow. "And sleep together. No, wait, you've already been doing that, too."

Maddox elbows him. "Will you stop it? You're making a way bigger deal out of this than it has to be." He turns to me, his eyes narrowing at my still full plate. "Why are you not eating? You should eat."

"Oh, I'm just trying to make sure nobody will throw more jokes around," I huff, cutting a piece of pancake. "Seriously, you all are too bossy for your own good."

"C'mon, let the man feed you." Nixon takes a seat opposite me, next to Yasmin. "We're only trying to take care of you."

There's a light flutter in my stomach. I rub my hand over the bump. It's like butterflies. Or maybe it's just gas?

Of course, Maddox notices. His eyes narrow on my hand before he looks up. "What's wrong? Are you not feeling okay?"

"I'm fine."

"If you need, we can go to the doct—"

"Chill, dude." Nixon puts his hands on Maddox's shoulders and pushes him back into his chair. "Aly says she's fine. It's not like sex can damage the baby." He looks around the room. "It can't, right?"

"No, dumbass." Yas rolls her eyes at her boyfriend. "Sex can't hurt babies."

"What if a guy has a monster cock? I'm sure—"

"I wasn't talking about sex," Maddox interrupts him. "And can we not joke about this? In the last few years, the percentage of women who had some kind of complication during pregnancy or even childbirth has risen, which is stupid, considering how much technology has advanced, but still. If something's wrong, I need you to tell me."

"I'm fine. Really. If something's wrong, I'd tell you." I place my hand over his, giving it a soft squeeze. "I'm not risking her."

Anything but her.

I might have done a lot of stupid and reckless things in my life, but I'll do this right.

Maddox lets out a long breath. "Okay."

"But seriously, a monster... *Ouch*." Nixon glares at Hayden across the table. "Why did you kick me?"

"'Cause you're not funny," Hayden mutters. "Besides, it's not like you have to worry about it."

"You checking my equipment, Hades?"

"Not like there's anything to check."

A leg touches mine under the table. I look to the side to find Maddox watching me. "Eat."

"Fine." I roll my eyes at him and make a show of cutting a piece of pancake and putting it in my mouth. "Happy?" I ask, still chewing.

Maddox leans down and kisses the corner of my mouth. "Extremely."

Chapter 28

MADDOX

"So..."

The word hangs in the air between us. I push my arms up, my muscles quaking under the weight of the bar in my hands. I keep my gaze fixed forward and ignore Hayden's noisy gaze.

"So," I grit through my clenched teeth as I slowly lower my arms down before extending them up, trying to keep a steady rhythm and count my reps. Not that Hayden's helping. At this point, I wonder if he'd even be able to catch the damn weight if it slipped before it crashed on me.

"You and Alyssa, huh?"

"Me and Alyssa."

His eyes narrow. "Are you going to repeat everything I'm saying?"

"Are you actually going to ask a question?"

"You guys together or what?"

Isn't that the million-dollar question.

What were we? Friends? Friends with benefits? Dating?

The hell if I know. Our friends swamped us at breakfast, and then the guys dragged me out of the house for a workout, which in hindsight, I should have seen right through.

I knew this conversation was going to go there. My friends are too nosy for their own good. Now that they've settled down, they have even more time on their hands to get all up in my business.

The bar clanks against the rack as my hand wobbles a little, lost in my thoughts. I pull my brows together, my fingers gripping the bar tighter as I lift it in the air.

"They're having sex," Nixon points out helpfully.

"I'm having sex too, and I'm damn sure not in a relationship," this comes from sweaty Prescott. His face is beet red, his breathing labored. He's been on the leg press machine for a while now. Just recently, he got out of his cast, and he's been working on strengthening his muscles, but at this point, he only looks like he's in pain.

"I called it. I think I was the closest to how long it would take them to hook up in the first place. So you assholes owe me money." Zane grabs a towel and tosses it at Prescott. "And I really hope you're taking it easy with your sexcapades Wentworth. You don't want to re-injure your leg."

"Don't worry." Prescott tries to grin, but it comes out more like a grimace. "I make them put all the work in."

"Selfish asshole," Nixon chuckles and shakes his head. "Why am I not surprised?"

"Hey, I'm an injured man."

"Only you'd have pulled that card," Hayden grunts from above me.

"As if you wouldn't use the injured card if you could."

"As if you're better on any other day," Nixon snorts.

Prescott's grin widens. "What can I say? I'm charming like that."

"All I have to say is it was about damn time," Emmett drawls. "You've been in love with her for as long as *I* can remember."

Longer.

Way, way longer.

Prescott wiggles his brows. "So how was it? I've heard..."

I let the bar fall into the rack with a loud *bang* and sit upright to face the group. "Can we not talk about Alyssa like that? She's not one of your groupies."

"Dude, I was just..." Prescott starts to apologize, but I shake my head

"I mean it. She's going through enough as it is, and this isn't helping. You don't talk about Callie or Yasmin or Kate that way."

"So are you guys, like dating?" Nixon asks.

"I don't know what we are, but maybe if you weren't so nosy, we'd have had time to actually figure it out."

I grab my towel and throw it over my shoulder, pushing to my feet. "I'm out of here."

"Maddox!" Hayden calls after me, but I'm done listening. I need to get out of here before I'm tempted to punch one of my friends.

Not bothering to shower or change, I just grab my stuff from the locker room and get out of the gym. Thankfully, I came here in my car, so I slide inside and drive.

My fingers curl around the steering wheel to the point my knuckles turn white, mind still reeling from the earlier conversation with my friends.

I overreacted, but I didn't want to listen to them talk about Aly that way, not in front of me. She wasn't just a one-and-done kind of girl. Not before and definitely not now. I might not know where we stand, but, first and foremost, she'll always be my best friend.

I pull to a stop, noticing that I'm home.

Shaking my head, I get out of the car and enter the house. Taking two steps at a time, I climb to the second floor.

When I enter the room, Aly looks up from her laptop. She has showered and changed since I left. Her hair is still piled on top of her head, a few runaway curls clinging to her neck.

"Hey, didn't you say you were gonna go work out?"

"I did, but there was a change of plans." I let my backpack drop on the floor by the door and turn around toward the bed.

Aly is sitting cross-legged, her laptop opened in front of her. She observes me quietly, a frown between her brows. "Did something happen?"

"Nothing you have to worry about." I run my fingers through my hair. "Wanna get out of here?"

Aly blinks. "Like now?"

"Yes, now."

Because if I don't get out of here, I'll go nuts.

She looks down at herself, and then at me. "But I'm not dressed."

I slowly cross the room until I'm standing at the edge of the bed. "You look perfect."

And she does. She's in one of those tight-fitting knit dresses that hugs her every curve, the light blue color making her eyes seem brighter.

Aly sniffs, her nose furrowing. "And you could use a shower."

"Did you just sniff me?"

"What?" She jabs her finger into my abs. "You're standing right in my face. It's hard not to smell your stank."

"I was at the gym."

"Didn't you just say there was a change of plans?"

"I left early." I extend my hand toward her. "What do you say, Aly?"

She lets out a sigh. "Fine, but you better shower first."

ALYSSA

"Arcade?" I turn around, taking in all the old-fashion machines and then some, before making a full circle and facing Maddox. "You brought me to the arcade? I didn't even know these existed any longer! In Blairwood of all places too."

"There aren't that many left. They're not nearly as popular as they used to be. I figured we could play for a little bit, but if you'd rather do something else..."

I shake my head. "This is fine."

I'm not sure what happened with the guys to have him storming back home and wanting to leave almost immediately, but I didn't need an additional reason to push back writing the essay for my philosophy class.

"It'll be like the good old days."

Good old days.

His words ring in my mind, making me feel unsettled for whatever reason.

"Is that what you want?"

For things to be as they used to be before?

Maddox takes a step closer, the tips of our sneakers touching. His eyes hold mine hostage as he just stares at me. Raising one hand, he brushes a strand of hair behind my ear, his voice low, "I want you, Aly. In every way I can have you."

A knot forms in my throat. I want to tell him the feeling is mutual, tell him that he has me, but it's like the words are stuck in my throat, so instead, I settle for: "I'm not sure I remember how to play."

Maddox lets his hand drop. I expect to see a look of disappointment on his face, but instead, his fingers lace with mine, and he pulls me toward the nearest machine. "I'll show you."

"Is that..."

"Pinball? Yes."

I rest my hands tentatively against the machine. "It looks ancient."

"It's a classic."

"If you say so." I look over my shoulder only to find Maddox standing right there behind me. I let out a shaky breath, surprised by his nearness. He ended up taking that shower, and now, he smells fresh, like sandalwood and citrus and all Maddox. "I never did get the point of this game."

His brows pull together in a confused frown. "How could you not? It's simple."

His hands land on my hips as he maneuvers me closer. I can feel the heat of his body pressed against my spine as he leans over me. Maddox grabs my hands in his and puts them on the commands.

His chin brushes against my shoulder, and I can feel a jolt of energy run down my spine as he whispers in my ear. "You just have to..."

Maddox's warm breath tickles the skin of my neck as he explains how to play, but I can barely hear his words over the loud thumping of my heart. He puts in a coin, and the game comes to life; Maddox covers my hands with his.

"Ready?"

No, I don't think I am.

The words run through my mind, but I don't voice them out loud.

Because I'm fairly certain I'm not talking just about the game here. I'm not ready for... this. Whatever *this* thing that's happening between us might exactly be.

Still, I nod because what is there to say?

The little ball comes out of nowhere and starts jumping around. It startles me so much I take a step back, or I would have if Maddox wasn't standing right there behind me.

Maddox chuckles, the sound rumbling deep in his chest. "You have to push the buttons."

He presses his palms against the back of my hands. Together we manage to get the ball to bounce off a few times, but it's not enough to salvage the situation because the ball falls down, the screen proclaiming me one big loser.

I tilt my head back, leaning against Maddox's chest and groan. "I'm so bad at this."

"You're not that bad."

"Maybe I'd believe you if you didn't laugh at me!" I protest.

This time he doesn't even try to hide it. "You'll get the hang of it. C'mon, let's play again."

So we do; not that I'm any better the second or the fifth time. So after that last failed attempt, I gave up and let Maddox have his fun. Of course, he gets the best score on the damn thing on the first try, show-off. But I draw the line when he wants to do it again. Instead, I pull him toward the other games. I may suck at navigating a tiny ball over the screen, but I sure know how to play air hockey and foosball.

I'm not sure how long we stay playing different games, but with each one, the worry lines between Maddox's brows disappear more, and his smile grows bigger.

"C'mon, Aly. Try this one. It's not that hard."

I shake my head. "Nope, that's what you said for the last three games. I'm not falling for it. Because your easy and mine are two completely different things."

"It's not that hard."

"Nope, you can play it, or we can go play air ho..." I turn around and catch the sight of the booth tucked against the wall. "Oh my God!" I clasp my hands excitedly. "I haven't seen one of these in forever."

Maddox turns to me, and when he sees the source of my excitement, lets out a loud groan. "Photobooth? Seriously?"

"Yes! We have to take a photo." I wrap my fingers around his wrist and pull him to the booth. Putting a few coins in, I push away the curtain and pull Maddox inside.

The space is small and tight, way smaller than I remember.

"I'll never understand why you love these things so much," Maddox protests as he tries to find a good spot, but we can barely fit inside. Our shoulders are brushing together, and half of my butt is hanging off the bench.

"Because they're fun?" I lift his arm. "Move a little."

I slip beneath his arm, feeling the familiar weight settle over my shoulder. I look up and smile just as a timer goes off, and a flash fills the booth.

"Oh, come on!" I turn around and poke him in the cheek. "Smile."

Flash.

Maddox forces the corners of his mouth to rise. "Better?"

Flash.

I give my head a little shake. "I think I'm actually scared. Be serious about this."

"I'm always serious."

"Then goof around." I nudge him with my elbow. "Pretty please?"

Maddox rolls his eyes but smiles diligently just as the flash goes off.

"Did you have fun today?" Maddox asks softly.

I tilt my head back to look up at him. I'm not sure how to read the expression on his face. He's serious, which isn't that unusual, but there's something in the way that he watches me, a silent intensity, that has a shudder running down my spine.

"Yeah, I did." I smile just as another flash goes off. "You were right. It's just like the good old days. I missed it if I'm being completely honest."

Maddox nods, one unruly curl falling in his face. "Is that what you want? For things to be how they used to?"

"You're cheating." I lift my hand, pushing it away. "I asked you that question first."

His hand covers mine, stopping me from pulling it back.

"No, I don't think I can go back to how things were."

My heartbeat speeds up at his words. Fear, trepidation, uncertainty, mixing altogether in the pit of my belly, but beneath it all... happiness.

The corner of my mouth starts to lift, so I bite into my lip.

"Good," I raise my other hand, sliding the tip of my finger just over the underside of his lower lip. "Because I don't want that. It's completely selfish and unfa—"

Flash.

"Fuck fair." Our joined hands fall down, fingers disentangling. His hand slips under my tights, and he turns me, so I'm sitting across his lap. "I don't care if you're selfish. Then I'm selfish too because I don't care one bit as long as I get to have you."

Then Maddox's mouth is on mine. I suck in a sharp breath, surprised by the intensity of the kiss. My fingers grip his cheeks as he slides his mouth over mine, hard and fast. His tongue slips in between my lips, dipping into my mouth. The grip on my thigh tightens, fingers slipping under the hem of my dress, digging into my flesh.

The flash goes off, but neither of us cares. We're too lost in our kiss, too lost in one another to pay attention to anything else.

I tilt my head to the side, deepening the kiss and run my fingers through his hair, a low moan coming from my chest.

I shift slightly, and I can feel his hard dick pressed against my ass. Warmth spreads through my belly, and my pussy clenches in anticipation of what's to come.

"Maddox..." I breathe, holding onto him tighter.

I want this man to the point it's unbearable.

How did I survive all these years without having him? How did—

The loud ringing of my phone snaps us out of the frenzy as the first notes of *Best Friend* by Saweetie fill the small booth.

With one soft, lingering kiss, Maddox pulls back. For a while, we just stare at one another, panting hard. Maddox's glasses are askew, lips red and puffy from our kiss.

I correct his glasses and slide my fingers over his lips, removing any remnants of my lip gloss.

"I meant what I said, Aly," Maddox says, his voice hoarse. "I want you; I want to give this thing between us a try."

I want to give this thing between us a try.

Hearing him say it out loud has butterflies running through my stomach.

But...

"Even though I'm pregnant?"

Just then, my phone stops ringing, making my question seem even louder in the suddenly quiet space.

But I couldn't not ask. I couldn't not remind him of the reality of my situation. I'd never forgive myself otherwise. My situation is different. I'm not just a woman falling for her best friend. I'm a woman with a baby on the way.

Another man's baby.

Maddox presses his forehead into mine, his hand falling down to my belly. "I already told you, you belong with me. This baby, she's a part of you, and I could never hate a part of you. I want you—both of you."

You belong with me—both of you.

Tears prickle my eyes, making my vision blurry.

"Seriously? If you don't want to be with me, you can just say it. There is no need to cry."

I sniffle and rub my hand under my eyes. "I'm not crying

because I don't want to be with you. I'm just an emotional mess." I point at my eyes. "See? This is what you're signing up for. Sudden mood swings. Unexpected bursts of tears. Swollen ankles and expanding belly. Is this really what you want, Maddox Anderson?"

Am I what you want?

He doesn't even miss a beat. "All of it." His thumb slides over my cheekbone, wiping away the tears. "I want it all, and nothing you say or do will chase me away."

My throat thickens making it difficult to swallow.

Is this man real? And how did I get so lucky to have him by my side? Because I'm pretty sure I don't deserve him.

My phone starts to ring again.

"You better answer that," Maddox says, his arms tightening around me to pull me closer. "We don't want the girls to worry."

I turn around and grab my bag that fell on the floor, pulling my phone out of it. I barely hit Accept when Yasmin's voice rings from the other end of the line.

"Where are you?"

"Out with Maddox," I say calmly as I stare at the man in question.

I can hear Yas's sudden intake of breath, but then there's only silence for a couple of heartbeats followed by a faint, "Oh."

"Did something happen?"

"No. I didn't find you in your room, so I wanted to check in, that's all."

"Mhmm... Well, I'm fine. We just went out."

"Like on a date?"

"A date?" I lift my brow at Maddox in a silent question. His cheeks get that rosy color that makes him look all cute. "Something like that."

Yasmin squeals on the other side, the sound so loud I have to pull the phone away from my ear, so I don't go deaf.

"I knew it! Well, if you guys feel up to it, we'll be at Moore's so you can join us."

"Maybe. I'll ask him."

"Okay. Have fun on your *date*."

"Bye, Yasmin," I say, chuckling softly.

Not waiting for her answer, I hang up.

"You up for meeting the crew?" I lift my brow at Maddox. "Or are you still angry at whatever happened earlier?"

"I wasn't angry, just annoyed. And we can go if you want. Maybe have dinner."

I roll my eyes at him. "If you keep feeding me, I'll really turn into a whale."

"You won't turn into a whale," Maddox protests.

I start to get up, but it's harder than it looks. In the end, Maddox gives me a little push.

"No? I'm barely halfway through my pregnancy, and I can't get to my feet on my own! God knows what'll happen when I'm nine months pregnant."

"You'll be fine, and even if you won't, I'll be there to help you up."

I turn around to face him and lift my pinky. "Promise?"

"Promise." He links his pinky with mine. "Is this the moment I should ask you to be my girlfriend?"

I push him away and start to walk away. "Be serious."

"I am serious." His fingers wrap around my wrist, and he twirls me around, my body bumping into his. "Will you be my girlfriend, Alyssa Martinez, or am I going to be friend-zoned forever?"

I shake my head at the absurdity of it all. It's like we're pre-teens once again, and he's asking me to go steady.

The funny part?

I actually like it.

"I'll be your girlfriend."

Chapter 29

MADDOX

"You're here!" Yasmin smiles as she sees us. "You didn't have to cut your *date* short for us."

The rest of the group turn their heads toward us. Emmett and Kate in their one-designated chair with an unfamiliar blond girl next to them, sharing a booth with Hayden and Callie. Across from them are Yasmin, Nixon, and Prescott.

Aly waves her off. "I was done having my ass beaten by another ancient game."

She takes her jacket off just as I pull an available chair from the table close to ours. I scan the place, looking for another one, but the place is packed.

"Ancient game?"

"He took me to an arcade." Aly shakes her head at Callie. "Can you believe those still exist?"

"You were pretty good at some of the games." Giving up, I sit down and pull Aly onto my lap. "What do you want to eat?"

Aly purses her lips, thinking. "Mac and cheese? No," she shakes her head, her whole face lighting up. "Fries. With cheese. And bacon. And now, I'm hungry."

Her hand falls, and she rubs her belly.

I laugh, covering her hand with mine. "How about some meat with it? That chicken sandwich you like?"

Her nose furrows, "Do I have to?"

"You can't live on fries with cheese."

"Don't forget about the bacon. That counts as protein."

"Caesar salad?" I offer. Because seriously, that baby is going to come out covered in cheese otherwise.

Aly pouts unhappily. "Fine. Salad too."

"Good choice." I look around until I spot a server. She gives me a one-minute sign as she writes down the order from another table.

I wrap my arm tighter around Aly and pull her closer, only to catch Emmett watching me, his brows raised. "You stealing my moves, Anderson?"

I push my glasses up my nose. "Well, if you had saved us a place..."

"You try saving a place in this pandemonium," Prescott shakes his head. "You should feel lucky you found one chair at all. It's like everybody's here for one last round before the campus clears for spring break."

Just then, the server comes. I place an order for Aly, a burger for myself, and a round of drinks for the table.

Aly shifts on my lap, and I have to bite the inside of my cheek to stop myself from groaning. "Are you guys ready for the trip?"

Yasmin nods. "Just about packed."

Callie groans, "Maybe you organized people. I'll just throw something in my suitcase the day before."

Hayden gives his girlfriend a pointed look. "Or more like the morning of."

Callie jabs him in the side. "Like you're one to talk, Mr. I-Just-Need-Two-Shirts-and-a-Pair-Of-Pants."

"What more do you need? It's Hawaii. We'll be on the

beach half of the time anyway." He leans closer, his mouth brushing against the side of her face as he murmurs something in her ear. Whatever it is, it makes Callie blush.

Yasmin leans across the table. "Are you sure you can't come with us?"

Aly shakes her head. "Yeah. Even if I had the money, I'm not sure it's safe to fly because of the baby."

Yasmin pouts. "I guess there's that. You've gotta keep that bun safely in the oven."

Aly laughs. "There's so much wrong with that statement on so many levels it's not even funny."

"Hey, I'm not the one who invented the saying. Blame them."

"Wait, you're not coming?" Kate looks from Yasmin to Aly.

"Not this time."

"What about you, Maddox?"

Prescott snorts, "As if that's even a question."

My jaw ticks as I glare at Prescott. I'm not sure what his issue is. He's always been crude, sure, but lately, it's like he's been just plain rude. It's like he's testing how far he can push before people start pushing him away.

Aly grabs my hand and gives it a soft squeeze. I slowly move my gaze to her, giving her a reassuring smile, before shifting my attention to the rest of the table. "No, I'll be staying at Blairwood with Aly. Maybe if we get some alone time without all of you meddling, she won't change her mind and dump me."

"I'm not changing my mind. You, on the other hand..."

I wrap my arms around her middle tighter, my chin resting on her shoulder, and whisper so only she can hear me, "I told you, no way, no how."

Goosebumps rise on her skin, making her squirm in my arms. She looks over her shoulder at me. "Promises, promises."

But that's the thing; I would give this girl the world, just to have her with me.

"And who do we have here?" Aly asks, shifting her attention to our friends and thankfully changing the subject. "I don't think we've met."

The girl—who looks so young I'm not sure how they even let her in—tilts her head to the side.

Kate smiles, "That's my sister, Penelope. She's bli—"

"Blind," Penelope finishes turning toward the sound of her sister's voice. "I can speak for myself, Kate. I've been meeting people for a while now."

"Sorry, old habits."

"I know." Penelope places her hand over her sister's before turning her attention to the table, not actually looking at anybody in particular. "She keeps forgetting that I was doing quite fine for the last four years that she's been away."

"I just worry."

"We'd have never guessed," Emmett chuckles. "Right, Little Adams?"

"Right." Penelope rolls her eyes. "Not like you're any better."

Everybody bursts into laughter.

"Hey, now..." Emmett starts to protest.

"You've been burned, Santiago," Hayden chuckles.

Penelope turns to Emmett and Kate, brows raised. "Did you or did you not warn everybody who I've met to be helpful but otherwise stay away from me? Especially your teammates."

"Because you're a pretty girl, and I know how those assholes think! I was one of them."

Prescott laughs, "You still are, Santiago. There's no "was" there."

The guys continue bickering over who's right just as the server comes back, plates in hands. As soon as our food is on the table, Aly goes for the fries and puts one into her mouth, letting out a low moan.

"So good." She turns to me, plate in hand. "Want one?"

Her constant wiggling definitely doesn't help with the ever-growing problem in my pants. That girl's going to be the death of me.

I shake my head. "You eat."

Aly grins. "Oh, I will. These are seriously the best fries ever."

Callie laughs, "Look at how happy she is."

"Because these are delicious, and I'm hungry." With that, she pops another fry into her mouth, her eyes closing as she chews. The expression of pure bliss makes my stomach tighten.

Seriously, would it be so bad just to throw her over my shoulder and...

"Are you having cravings? Is this it?" Yas asks, snapping me out of my thoughts.

"Maybe? I don't know." Aly grabs another fry and dips it into the cheese. "Aren't cravings supposed to be weird? Like pickles with chocolate or something like that."

"Eww..."

"That sounds disgusting."

"Some best aunts you are." Aly tilts her head back and looks at me. "Would you satisfy my weird cravings if I had them?"

"As long as I don't have to eat them."

"What about fries?"

I let out a sigh, "If you really want them, I'll get you all the fries in the world."

Aly beams. "And that's why you're the best."

Then she presses her mouth against mine. The kiss is barely a brush of her lips against mine, but it's like I was struck by lightning. Because Alyssa Martinez, my best friend and girlfriend as of an hour ago, just kissed me in front of all our friends.

She grabs another fry. "You sure you don't want any?"

"No, I'm all good."

She shrugs and pops the fry into her mouth. Before she can go for another one, I grab her wrist and bring her fingers to my lips, sucking one into my mouth. The cheese melts on my tongue, and I let her finger pop out. "You were right. They are tasty."

"Are you sure you don't want to go?" I pull my stuff out of my pockets and line them up on the desk, glancing over my shoulder at her. "I could get us the tickets. You know that."

I wasn't sure if what she said earlier was true, or if it was just an excuse, so she wouldn't have to spend the hard-working money she's been saving for when the baby comes.

Knowing Alyssa, it could have been either of those things.

"I don't want you to get me the tickets, but if you'd like to go..."

I shake my head. "I've been to Hawaii before, so it's not like I'll be missing something."

Aly tilts her head to the side. "Besides having fun with your friends during spring break?"

Unhooking my watch, I place it next to the rest of my things before crossing the room to Aly. I wrap my arms around her waist and pull her to me.

"I'd rather be with you." I brush my lips against the corner of her mouth. "It doesn't matter where or how, as long as we're together."

"I don't want to drag you down. Just because I'm not going..."

I kiss her, stopping her from finishing that sentence. My mouth slides over hers easily. I trace the line of her spine, my fingers cupping the back of her neck. I tilt her head to the side and deepen the kiss.

With one final nip at her bottom lip, I pull back. Aly lets out a low sigh and leans against me.

"You don't play fair."

"I told you, Aly. It doesn't matter. I'd rather spend spring break with you right here than travel somewhere else and then think about you the whole time. I've spent too much time thinking about you. I want to be with you." My finger slides under her chin as I lift her head to face me. "Besides, didn't you hear? I'm a vampire." I wiggle my brows as Aly's mouth hangs open. "What? Am I not shiny enough?"

"You were listening in that day?!"

"Maybe, but it's not like you were being quiet."

"Oh my God! Stop it." She pushes me away. "It's not funny."

"You're laughing," I point out, tightening my hold on her.

"That's 'cause you're making weird faces."

"I'll give you weird faces…"

Before she can react, I pull her flat against my chest and lift her into the air.

"Maddox!" Aly squeals. "What are you doing? Put me down. I'm heavy."

"You? Heavy? In what world?"

"In this world. Seriously, you'll get hurt."

The bed squeaks when I kneel on it and gently put her on the mattress. "Maybe we can talk about it later when you're in your eighth month of pregnancy or something. Until then…"

I lean down and press my mouth against her neck, peppering small kisses over the column of her neck and collarbone.

Aly wraps her arms around my shoulders, her fingers sliding

into my curls as she pulls me closer. "You know what's the best part about staying home for spring break?"

"Mhhmmm?"

I nip at the hollow of her neck as my hands slide under the hem of her dress.

"We get the house all to ourselves."

I pull back to find her blue eyes staring at me. "That does have its perks."

A wicked glint shimmers from her baby blues as she looks at me. "It does, doesn't it?"

Chapter 30

MADDOX

"How about I drop you off on campus for class?" My fingers trail over Aly's lower back as I put my cup in the sink where she's rinsing her plate.

The fine hair at the back of her neck rises at my nearness, and a shudder runs down her body. She pulled her curls into a high ponytail earlier, but since then, a few strands have slipped out of the confines of the tie and are curling around her face.

Aly turns off the water and grabs a towel to dry her hands before she turns around to face me. "Isn't your class later?"

"Maybe," I admit, looking away.

I'm so busted.

Aly cups my cheek and forces me to meet her gaze. "You don't have to drive me around. I'm quite capable of walking."

"I know that, but I don't mind." I shrug. "I can grab a coffee or something before my class."

"You just had coffee."

"That was my morning coffee." A smile slowly spreads over my lips. "This one will be a breakfast coffee."

"Stop," Aly rolls her eyes, her hand connecting with my

chest to push me away. A smile curls the corner of her mouth, and although she tries to school her face, it's useless.

I place my hand over hers, holding her hostage. "What?"

"Worrying so much."

Her blue eyes shine brightly. Aly turns her hand around, her fingers intertwining with mine. Her teeth sink into her lower lip as she looks up at me.

And I just stare, completely transfixed.

It's still hard to believe that this girl I've been crushing on is here.

She finally sees me.

She's mine.

"I'm not worrying. I just want to be a good boyfriend and drive you to campus, that's all."

"Ugh, you two are just so cute."

At the sound of Callie's voice, we break apart—Aly's hand falls out of mine, and I miss her touch, almost instantly.

Callie rolls her eyes as she makes her way into the kitchen. "You'll have to get used to having people around, you know." Callie puts the cup under the coffee machine and leans against the counter. "Give a guy some slack? He's been in love with you for so long; he can't help himself."

"Thanks, Callie," I say dryly.

"Hey, I'm just telling the truth."

I turn to Aly to find her looking at me with a serious face. For a moment, I think she might say no, but she just gives her head a little shake. "I'll go grab my stuff."

She walks out of the kitchen with a smile, Coco at her feet.

I just stare after her, unable to look away.

Callie nudges me with her hip as she makes her way to the table. "You have it bad for her."

"Don't I know it."

Callie stops in front of me and playfully pokes my cheek.

"All joking aside, it's good to see you two together. You're good for her, Maddox."

I shake my head. "She's good for me."

"You're good for each other." Callie takes a step back. "I know we can be annoying, but we're just happy for both of you."

"Thanks, Cals."

Hurried footsteps echo, and Aly pops her head into the kitchen. "Ready when you are."

I push off the counter. "Let's go then."

Aly looks over my shoulder at Callie. "Bye, Cals!"

"You kids be careful with what you're doing. You hear me?"

Aly rolls her eyes at her. "Yes, Mom!"

I grab my jacket and backpack in the hallway before slipping into the garage. We slide into the car, and as I pull out on the road, I take Aly's hand in mine.

"What class do you have anyway?"

Aly groans, "Philosophy."

"You sound almost as excited about it as you're about going to the dentist."

"Can't say it's one of my favorite classes, that's for sure. Honestly, the more I think about it all, the more I worry."

I quickly glance at her before returning my attention on the road. "Worry?"

"About what comes after. I'll get this fancy degree, and then what?"

"Then you'll find a job in a career that makes you happy."

"That's the point!" Aly shifts in her seat, so she's facing me, a flicker of fear dancing across her face. "What kind of job? I've been listening to you all, and you're all so passionate about the career you chose. Emmett and Kate are going back to Texas, where Emmett will work on his father's ranch, while Kate plans to open a center to help kids with disabilities. Hayden enters the draft in a few short weeks, and Nixon will do the same next year. Zane will work as a physical therapist, Callie loves art and graphic design, and Yasmin teaches. You'll keep on creating apps and games. But what about me? It feels like everybody has their life figured out, except me."

The words come out in a stream. It's like once she opened her mouth, there was no stopping them from all spilling out. Never before have I heard her so worried about it, worried about what the future might bring. Is this all because of the pregnancy? The need to support herself and her baby? Or does it go deeper than that?

"That's not true."

"Isn't it?" Aly asks before I can even finish. "Because it feels that way most days. Maybe my mom was right when she said this whole thing was a sham, so I could find a guy and get married."

The mention of her mother has the muscle in my jaw ticking. Seriously, the next time I see her, I might just be tempted to give the woman a piece of my mind. "She wasn't right."

I look around until I spot an open space and park the car. Killing the engine, I turn to Aly and take her hands in mine.

"She wasn't right," I repeat, needing her to know it. "A lot has been going on, and it's normal that you're scared and uncertain. It's normal to question things, but you'll find your way. That's what college is all about—finding your path in life. Finding your passion. Finding the people to share that life with."

Aly lets out a shaky breath. "How can you have so much faith in me?"

"Because I know you." I gently caress her cheek. "C'mon, let's get you to class."

Before she can protest, I get out of the car and grab our backpacks, throwing them over my shoulder. Aly waits for me at the front of the car. She reaches for my hand and pulls me to her, her palm resting against my chest. "If you keep up with this, I might get used to it."

"I don't mind."

She shakes her head and takes a step back. Her ponytail swings with every step we make. Between the sun and motion, golden strands play peek-a-boo in her reddish hair, making it almost seem like liquid fire.

"So you'll walk me to class every day from now on?"

"I just might. For the right price, of course."

Aly presses her lips together and nods. "Of course. And what might that be?"

My gaze falls to her pursed lips. "I guess I'll have to think of an adequate payment."

Aly turns around and comes to a stop, her brow quirking. "An adequate payment?"

"Yes, something that'll make up for all the effort I've put into it."

Aly nods and takes a step closer. "That seems reasonable."

She wraps her arms around my neck, her fingers running through my hair and her nails grazing the sensitive skin at the back of my neck.

I shift my weight from one leg to the other. "Does it?" I croak out, my voice low and raspy.

"Yes. How about a kiss? Would that be enough?"

She pulls me down. Our mouths brush together, breaths tangling as we just stare at one another, the pressure building between us.

Unable to resist it any longer, I cross the distance and press my mouth against hers, a low rumble coming out of my chest as our kiss deepens.

It seems like no matter how many times we kiss, it's not enough—like it'll never be enough.

Aly slowly nibbles at my lower lip. My lips part, and our

tongues tangle together. Her fingers dig into my neck, pulling me closer. Her body brushes against mine, her bump pressing against my stomach, and I can't help but pull her closer, so there's not even an inch of space between us.

"So?" Aly whispers, breaking the kiss. "Will that be enough?"

"Yeah." I brush a strand of her hair behind her ear. "It'll be more than enough."

"Good." A smile spreads over her lips. "I'll see you later?"

Aly takes a step back, but I wrap my fingers around her wrist and pull her back to me.

"I'll see you later," I whisper into her ear.

Unable to resist it, I press my mouth against her forehead before pulling back completely.

Aly sucks in a breath, her eyes flaring slightly as if in a daze. She takes a shaky step back and then another one, her eyes holding onto mine.

"Aly?" I call out, trying to hold in my laughter.

"Y-yeah?"

I pull her backpack off my shoulder and hold it up. "You might need your bag."

Her mouth falls open, eyes moving from me to her bag and back. Aly shakes her head and snatches her backpack before turning on the balls of her feet and climbing the stairs that lead to her building.

The smile on my face stays long after she's gone.

It's good to know I'm not the only one unnerved by the whole situation.

"Hey."

My head snaps up as Mia slides into the seat next to mine. I was totally spacing out; my mind still on Alyssa, so I didn't even realize class was about to start.

Mia smiles at me as she shrugs out of her jacket. "What has you scowling like that?"

"I'm not scowling," I say automatically as my brows pull together.

She chuckles, "How about you try saying that again?"

I take off my glasses and pinch the bridge of my nose. "Just tired, I guess."

She looks at her phone and then at me. "It's barely four in the afternoon."

"It's been a long weekend."

Mia observes me for a moment. "Did something happen?"

"I..." I open my mouth but then think better of it.

Mia has been keeping her distance since we went out on our date. She still says hi when she sees me, and we still sit together in class, but she mostly comes just before class starts and leaves as soon as it's finished, so we haven't talked about what happened.

It might not be fair, but it worked well for me. I didn't know how to act around Mia or what to tell her so I wouldn't hurt her feelings any more than I already had, but I'll have to tell her about Alyssa, eventually.

A hand covers mine, snapping me out of my thoughts.

"I know I've been acting off these last couple of weeks, but this doesn't have to be weird, you know," Mia says softly. "We went on a date. It didn't work out. Can we just stay friends?"

"Of course, we can. It's just..." I shake my head, trying to clear my thoughts. "It'll take some getting used to, that's all."

If Alyssa didn't point it out, I wouldn't have given Mia much thought. Yes, she's my classmate, my friend even, but that's as far as it got. Even when I asked her out, I did it more because I was pushed in that direction than because I wanted to. It wasn't the same for

Mia. I'd seen it, probably for the first time, the night we went on a date. Mia wants something more. Something I can't give her.

"Please? I really don't have that many friends, and I'd hate to lose you because we went out on a date, and things didn't work out."

"I get that, but..." I hold my breath for a moment before letting the words out. "I'm with Alyssa."

Mia blinks, her lips parting slightly. "Oh."

Before she can say anything more, our professor enters the classroom, stopping any possible conversation.

For the next two hours, I try to concentrate on our class, but it's hard. I can feel Mia's eyes on me every now and then. I can almost hear her thoughts whirling inside her mind, trying to put everything in place, so when our professor wraps up the class, I don't waste any time closing my books and getting up.

I should have known better, though.

Mia turns to me, her voice soft as she asks: "So you and Alyssa?"

"Yeah." I rub the back of my neck. "Alyssa and me. I just... I didn't want you to find out from somebody else. Not after..."

"Right." She nods, forcing out a smile. "That's great, Maddox."

"Is it?" There is no hiding skepticism in my voice.

Mia slides her books into her backpack and pulls the zipper. "Are you happy?"

"I..." For a split second, I contemplate lying, but what would be the point? She knows how I feel about Alyssa and has known it from the very beginning. "Yes, I'm happy."

"Then, of course, it's great." Her tone is chipper, but she avoids looking at me. She pulls her backpack over her shoulder. "First and foremost, you're my friend. I want you to be happy."

Together, we make our way out of the classroom.

"I am. Aly..." I look down, the corner of my mouth lifting. "She's always been it for me."

"Why ask me on a date then?"

The slight note of irritation in her voice has me looking up at her. Mia's face is serious as she observes me carefully as if she's searching for something.

"It was actually Aly's idea," I admit. "Something about us having a lot in common and you being perfect for me."

Looking back, I know I shouldn't have asked Mia out. It wasn't fair to her to give her the wrong impression of what I wanted out of it.

"So much for her being right." Mia shakes her head. "I should have seen it from the get-go."

"Seen what?"

I pull open the door, and Mia exits first. I follow after her and look up, my eyes clashing with the ones the color of the bright summer sky.

Aly.

"The way you look at her," Mia lets out a self-deprecating laugh. I force my gaze away from Aly.

"And how is that?"

A little bit of sadness and a whole lot of longing flashes on Mia's face. "It's the way every woman dreams of being looked at. Alyssa is one really lucky woman."

She might think Alyssa is the lucky one, but she's wrong.

I am the lucky one.

More people come out of the building, forcing us to descend the stairs. Right, where Aly is waiting.

"Hey, you two," Aly greets, her attention shifting from me to Mia and back. "Did you see the messages?"

"What messages?"

"Everybody's coming to our house. Kind of like a goodbye

party before spring break. They asked if we can bring pizzas because delivery will take forever."

"Yeah, sure."

Before I can say anything else, Aly turns to Mia and smiles. "What about you, Mia? Wanna join?"

Mia shakes her head. "Nah, I'll skip this one. You guys have fun."

With one last glance in my direction and a smile, Mia walks away. We watch her disappear in the opposite direction, getting lost in the sea of students.

"What was that about?"

I look down to find Aly still watching in the direction Mia disappeared. "I told her." She turns to me, eyes wide. "About us."

"Oh." Aly shifts nervously. "She didn't take it well, I presume?"

"I guess she just needs time to get used to the idea." I put my hand around her and pull her to my side. "I shouldn't have taken her out on that date."

"It's not your fault. It was one date."

"Maybe, but it gave her the wrong impression. But the worst part? I can't even feel sorry about it because I got you out of it. How selfish is that?"

Aly leans her head against my chest, her hand snaking around my waist. "It's not selfish; it's human."

"I guess so." I brush my mouth against the top of her head. "So, pizzas?"

Chapter 31

MADDOX

I brush a strand of Aly's hair away from her face. She murmurs something and shifts in her sleep.

I don't think I'll ever get enough of waking up next to her, never get enough of watching her sleep next to me, knowing that she's mine.

Gently, I glide my fingers over her cheek so as not to wake her.

Although it's spring break, Aly decided to take shifts at Cup It Up. At least, she's not working in the morning, so there is that. And I don't want to wake her since we stayed up late last night watching movies.

Coco's eyes snap open, staring right at me, big and unblinking. Every night the dog falls asleep in the dog bed, and every morning I find her snuggled on the bed between us.

I give her a knowing look, but like everything else that doesn't hold her interest, she ignores it.

"Wanna go out?" I whisper softly.

That gets her attention. Coco blinks, her tail rising and waving excitedly from side to side.

"C'mon, Coconut. We'll let Aly sleep for a little while longer."

I slowly disentangle myself from Aly's sleeping body and slip out of bed. Coco follows suit, jumping down and shaking.

Unable to resist it, I lean down and press a kiss on top of Aly's head, pulling the covers higher before I grab my glasses off the nightstand and quietly exit the room.

The house is unusually quiet since all of our roommates have left for the week off. Hayden, Nixon, Yasmin, and Callie texted when they landed in Hawaii, but we haven't heard anything since. A day later, Zane left with Rei to go to Boston to spend some time with her dad while still getting enough ice time to be ready for the Winter Games next year. That left only Aly and me—and Coconut, of course.

Once in the kitchen, I go straight for the coffee machine. I take a cup and turn on the device. There isn't anything like the strong smell of brewed coffee. As soon as the machine beeps, I grab the cup and take one long pull.

Pure heaven.

Coco barks in protest.

"I'm coming," I groan. "So bossy, just like your owner."

Rubbing the back of my neck, I cross the kitchen and unlock the door. I barely start to open it when Coco slips through the crack and dashes outside in the backyard.

"Impatient dog," I mutter, leaning against the railing to keep an eye on her. The yard is fenced, but with the little daredevil, you can never be sure she won't slip through one of the cracks.

I take a sip from the cup and watch Coco run around the backyard.

It's strange to think that in a few short weeks, some of us will be graduating and going our separate ways. Nobody is talking about it yet. Well, except Emmett and Kate. But those two are different. They've known their path even before they came to college, and they stuck to it.

What will Aly want to do once she graduates from college? Will she want to stay here until she gives birth? But what about after? I still have one year left on my Master's, so like it or not, I'm staying here.

Just don't think about it, I chastise myself. *There's still time.*

"C'mon, Coco. Let's go make some breakfast."

At the last word, the dog stops in her tracks, her head snapping up, then she runs toward me.

Leaving my mug on the counter, I clean her feet and fill her bowl with fresh water and food before I start on breakfast.

I'm mixing together the batter for waffles when I hear footsteps coming down the stairs.

"Morning," Aly murmurs.

I turn around and find Aly rubbing her eyes. She's wearing one of my shirts that hangs on her to mid-thigh, her free hand pressed against her belly.

She looks beautiful, all messy hair and sleepy eyes. And despite it all, she somehow still manages to look radiant. I'm not sure if it's the pregnancy or if she's just happy.

"Morning. Sleep well?"

"Mhmm..." She wraps her arms around me from behind, leaning her head against my back. "Sleepy."

I chuckle, putting the batter into the waffle toaster. "Then why did you get up?"

"I woke up, and you weren't there."

My heart does a little flip inside my chest, knowing that she misses me if I'm not there when she wakes up. I'm trying to be patient; give her time to adjust to this new normal. It can't be easy having to readjust your life like Aly has had to in the last few months, and it's moments like this that put me at ease. She might not tell me she loves me, but she misses me, and it's enough.

"Sorry, I figured I'd let you sleep for a little bit longer while I let Coco out and made some breakfast." I close the waffle maker and turn around in her arms. "How do you feel about waffles?"

"Hungry?"

I tilt my head to the side. "Is that a question or an answer?"

"It's I-need-coffee-to-function kind of answer."

Aly tries to pop herself onto the counter, but when she slips for the second time, I put my hands on her hips and help hoist her up.

"That's what you get for forcing me to watch shiny vampires with you until three in the morning." I take a coffee cup and place it under the coffee machine.

Aly's eyes narrow, "What's wrong with shiny vampires?"

"The better question would be, what's not wrong with them?" I pull the creamer out of the fridge just as the machine beeps. "Vampires should be scary. The scariest thing about those vampires is that they could blind you on a sunny day."

"That's scary."

Grabbing the coffee cup, I add the creamer before handing it to Aly. "Not to me, since I'm already half-blind. You really need to start watching better movies."

"I don't want to watch better movies. I want to watch movies with cheesy lines that'll make me laugh, romance stories that'll make my heart flutter, and you won't hear me complain if, on top of that, they also have sexy actors that walk around shirtless."

I shake my head at her. "That's basically reality TV."

"It's entertainment," Aly counters as I pull back and put the waffles on the plate. "And you can say what you want, I saw you laugh last night."

"At the absurdity of it all, maybe." I look over my shoulder. "Chocolate or maple syrup?"

Her eyes gleam. "How is that even a question?"

"Chocolate it is." I grab the bottle and close the cupboard before going back to Aly.

Since her hands are holding onto the cup, I take a piece of waffle and dip it into the chocolate syrup before offering it to Aly. Her blue eyes connect with mine as her teeth sink into the waffle.

"Mhmmm... So good."

"Yeah?" I grab another piece and pop it into my mouth.

"Yeah. You're spoiling me, you know that?"

"I can't have you going around hungry. What kind of boyfriend would that make me?"

"Well, considering how I can get hangry these days in a matter of minutes. Probably not alive."

Putting her cup on the counter, Aly grabs a piece of waffle and pours some syrup over it. "Shit."

"What?"

I follow her gaze and see a line of chocolate decorating her thigh just as a few more drops fall from the waffle.

"Why did I think this would go over well?" She shakes her head. "Where's the towe—"

Aly sucks in a sharp breath as I lean down and press my mouth against her bare thigh. My tongue darts out, licking away the chocolate.

"M-Maddox," she stutters softly. Her hand falls down on the counter, the bottle of chocolate syrup dropping out of her fingers. "What are you doing?"

I look up to find her watching me with wide eyes, her cheeks flushed. I slide my fingers over the outside of her leg, feeling her soft skin under my fingertips. "Finish that waffle, or you'll make an even bigger mess."

"You expect me to eat? Now?" she asks, her voice unnaturally high.

"Why not?" I turn to the side, pressing my mouth against her knee. "I'm about to have dessert."

I glance at her as I keep kissing my way up her leg. Waiting to see if she'll tell me to stop, but she doesn't. So I keep kissing and nibbling at the exposed skin.

"M-Maddox..."

My name comes out on a stutter as her legs fall open. I slide my hands under her knees, pulling her closer to the edge of the counter. I brush my nose over the juncture of her thighs, inhaling her musky scent. Her heat. The silkiness of her skin.

Propping her legs over my shoulder, I move closer and press my mouth against her center. The lace of her panties clings to her pussy. I trace my tongue over her center, feeling the roughness of the material on my tongue. Her whole body shudders at my touch, her knees tightening around my head, holding me hostage—not that I want to run away.

God, she's all hot and wet already.

I pull her panties to the side with my teeth and put my mouth on her. Aly sucks in a breath, her hands sliding into my hair and pulling me closer to her center.

I slide my tongue between her folds, tasting her sweetness. I suck and swirl, making sure not to miss an inch of her. My fingers dig into her thighs as I tease her opening before dipping my tongue inside her.

Aly lets out a soft moan as I switch between strong and soft licks. Pulling back just enough to tease her and then sliding inside when she least expects it.

"God, I need..."

I pull back, pressing my tongue against her clit and rubbing the hard bud. Aly's body shudders in my arms. I suck it into my mouth and slide my hand from under her leg. I glide my finger through her folds before sliding it inside her. She's so wet; there's practically no resistance.

"More."

I pull it out and add another finger, nibbling at her clit as I thrust inside her. Her hips lift off the counter as her walls tighten around me, and she comes on my fingers, my name echoing in an otherwise quiet room.

I slowly lick her as she comes down from the high, only pulling back once her muscles are relaxed.

Licking at my lips, I stand up and look at Aly's content face. Her face is flushed, eyes glassy from her orgasm.

I shift from one leg to the other, readjusting my throbbing dick. At least I'm not wearing jeans because that would be another level of torture.

Aly wraps her arms around my neck and brushes her lips against mine. "Talk about a way to wake up."

I cradle her face, pushing her hair back, so I can see her face. "You look like you're ready for bed."

"Maybe later." Her fingers slip under the waistband of my sweatpants, tugging them down. "Now I want you to fuck me. Right here, right now."

My eyes fall closed as her fingers curl around my length, and she gives me a few firm pumps. I let out a shuddered breath as I try to hold onto the little bit of control I have left, but that's impossible when she's close to me.

"Shit, Aly," I hiss as her thumb slides over my head, smearing the precum over my tip. "You drive me crazy."

"The feeling is mutual."

I press my mouth against hers, my hands going to her hips. "Up."

Aly lifts her hips just enough so I can tug her panties down and throw them over my shoulder.

I slide my hands under her knees and settle between her

legs, pulling her to the edge of the counter as I slowly enter her. The counter is the perfect height for us to align, and she's so wet I slide inside her effortlessly.

"Fuck, you feel so good." I lean down, pressing my forehead against hers. "So tight."

Aly's fingers dig into my hair, pulling me closer. "I need you deeper."

I pull back before rocking back inside her. "Like this?"

"More." Her hands slide down my back, lips brushing against mine. "I need more."

Her heels dig into my ass as she holds onto me, her hips meeting mine for each thrust. I kiss her, hard and deep. My tongue slides into her mouth. Sucking and swirling with hers.

"I need..."

I slide my hand under her shirt, spreading my fingers over her naked body. I squeeze one of the breasts, tweaking a nipple as I thrust harder.

This time, when she comes, it's with me buried inside her.

I press my mouth against hers, swallowing her loud moan as I slide inside her, the pressure at the base of my spine erupts, and I empty inside her, my body going slack over hers.

"This was the best breakfast ever," Aly pants, puffing a strand of hair out of her face.

"Oh yeah?"

"Yes," she runs her fingers through my hair and brushes her lips against my mouth. "I might even be tempted to go for seconds. But first... can I have some of those waffles?"

I can't help myself... I laugh. "Waffles coming right up."

Chapter 32

ALYSSA

Maddox: It's our last night together.

I sink my teeth into my lower lip as I read Maddox's message to stop myself from smiling like a fool.

Me: Oh, is it?

Me: You finally got enough of me and are kicking me out?

Me: I mean, I knew it was too good to be true.

Maddox: I'm not kicking you out.

Me: No?

Maddox: Aly...

I chuckle, feeling all his frustration in those three little dots.

Me: Yeah?

Maddox: You know what I mean.

Me: So you're not kicking me out?

Me: Just to be sure.

Maddox: You're not going anywhere.

Maddox: But our nosy roommates are coming back.

Maddox: So how about I take you out for dinner tonight?

My heart does that little flip in my chest, and I swear I can feel the butterflies in my belly. This past week, when it was just Maddox and I, has been amazing, and a part of me is sad it's coming to an end. There will be no more sleeping in, late breakfasts on the counter, Maddox and I having sex all over the house without a care in the world.

But the other part of me missed my friends—no matter how nosy they might be.

My phone vibrates in my hand.

Maddox: Aly? You there?

Me: Yes, just got sidetracked.

Me: Go out… like on a date?

Except for that time we went to the arcade, we tend to stay indoors, which is completely fine by me. I'd rather stay home, snuggled with Maddox, and watch movies than have to dress up and go out somewhere.

Maddox: Yes, like a date.

Me: As long as I don't have to cook.

Maddox: No way. We're not going down that road again.

Me: Hey, it wasn't that bad!

Maddox: You set the kitchen on fire.

Me: It was just a little bit of smoke.

Maddox: Tell that to the fire department.

Me: There was no fire department involved!

I look up from my phone as the chairs scrape over the hardwood. The older couple stands up and gives me warm smiles as they say goodbye.

"Bye," I say, grabbing a tray and a towel as I go to their table to clean up. As was expected, work is slow, but I don't mind.

I quickly pile everything on the tray and wipe the table. I throw the towel on the tray, but it slips on the floor.

"Dammit."

I crouch down to grab the towel from the floor. Then, with one hand on the table to steady myself and the other on the small of my back, I slowly get to my feet.

My back has been killing me lately. I'm not sure if it's the fact that now I have an actual bump or because I've been working hard. Seriously, I'd kill for a good masseuse right about now, but a massage is a luxury I can't afford. Not when I still have to buy so many things for the baby.

The bell over the door rings as a new customer comes in.

"Welc—"

The words die on my lips as I slowly turn around and find none other than Chad standing at the entrance, looking at me, or more precisely, my belly.

I prop the tray on my hip and protectively put my hand over my bump. "What are you doing here, Chad?"

I assumed he wouldn't be here yet. Last year we went to his family's house in the Hamptons for the week, and we didn't come back until the day classes started, but I guess I was wrong.

"I heard you're working here."

"I don't see how that's any of your business." I turn my back to him and make my way behind the counter. But before I can escape, his hand is wrapped around my wrist, tugging me back.

I glare at him over my shoulder, my fingers tightening around the tray, so it doesn't fall. "What are you doing?"

"We have to talk."

"Now?" I huff. "You wanna talk, now?"

He gives me a once-over. "Yes, now. You can't walk around campus like that."

I tug my hand out of his grasp. "And how is that exactly?"

"How..." He blinks, confused. It would be funny if he didn't annoy the crap out of me.

I lift my chin higher. "Yes?" I ask impatiently.

"Like t-that!" Chad points at my stomach. "It's like you're rubbing it in my face."

"In your face? I'm *pregnant,* Chad. Your stomach tends to grow when you're expecting a baby. Seriously, didn't they teach you anything in that fancy-ass school of yours?"

"You know what I mean," he grits, his cheeks flushing.

"No, I don't know what you mean. And I'm really not interested in finding out."

"Well, I don't care!" His voice rises, color seeping into his cheeks. "Did you know my friends have been asking me if I knew my girlfriend was pregnant?"

"Did they?" I ask innocently. "At least some people have good observation skills around here."

I start to leave, but once again, he grabs my hand. I look down to where his fingers are digging into my skin. He better not leave a mark because I'm going to be pissed. "Get your hands off of me."

"Not until you listen," Chad hisses, leaning into my face. "What the hell should I tell them?"

What the hell should he *tell them?*

Is he for real? I never saw Chad as unreasonable, but maybe I was wrong.

"Tell them whatever you want. It's not like it's any of my business. It was your choice not to be involved in this from the start."

"So I should tell them my girlfriend is a slut who cheated on me?"

I suck in a breath as his harsh words slam into me. If he slapped me, it wouldn't hurt as much as those words did.

Gritting my teeth together, I tug my hand out of his. The

force of the movement has me stumbling back, my whole body shaking with rage.

"*Ex*," I lean closer, jabbing my finger into his chest. "I'm your *ex*-girlfriend. And if it makes you feel better about yourself and your decision, do it. I don't care what you or your friends think about me."

"You stu—"

"Aly?" Monica comes from the kitchen, her gaze shifting from me to Chad. "Is everything okay here?"

"Yes," I force a smile out. "Chad was just leaving."

He presses his lips in a tight line but doesn't protest. With another glare in my direction, he turns and marches out of the café.

Only when the door is closed behind him do I let myself relax. Monica ducks from behind the counter and takes the tray out of my hand.

"You okay?"

"Yeah," I tuck a strand of hair behind my ear. "Sorry about that."

"No need to be sorry. Who was that, anyway? Was a customer bothering you?"

"No, that's Chad. My ex." Just admitting it out loud leaves a bitter taste in my mouth. How could I have been so wrong about him? So blind about the type of person he really is?

Monica's mouth forms a little o. "As in..." she points to my belly.

"Yup."

"What did he want?"

"To complain." I roll my eyes. "Apparently, people have been giving him grief about the fact that I'm pregnant."

Monica blinks a few times, completely bewildered. Not that I can blame her. "What an asshole!"

"Tell me about it." I shake my head. "I'm honestly glad that he doesn't want anything to do with us. It's better that way."

The last thing I need is for Chad to destroy what little I've managed to rebuild of my life with his meddling.

I grab the tray from the counter. "I better get this cleaned up."

"If he comes again, let me know, and I'll deal with it."

My throat tightens from the gratitude. "Thanks, Monica."

"Let's hope it won't be necessary, but if it is, I've got your back." She pats me on the shoulder as she makes her way back into the kitchen.

I quickly put the dirty dishes away before grabbing my phone. My wrist hurts where Chad grabbed me, and the skin is slightly reddish, but it doesn't appear like it'll leave a bruise.

Thank God.

Me: You know what? How about we order in instead?

Maddox: Are you okay?

Me: Yeah, just tired. I'd rather stay home and watch movies instead.

Me: Do you mind?

Maddox: Not at all. I'll see you later.

Me: :* :*

I pull my keys out of my bag and unlock the door. Although the rest of my shift was slow and uneventful, I couldn't push everything that had happened with Chad out of my head. Add to that that my back has been killing me for the better part of it; the only thing I wanted to do was lay down and lift my legs up in the air with Maddox by my side.

Slipping out of my shoes, I yell, "I'm home."

I take off my jacket and turn around, but there is no answer. "Maddox?" I ask tentatively.

Did he mention he had to go somewhere?

I don't think so, especially not since he wanted to go out tonight.

Slowly I make my way down the hallway and stop in my tracks when I get to the living room, my mouth falling open when I see what he's done.

The light is turned off, but the soft glow comes from the dozens of candles around the room—vanilla scent permeates the air; my favorite.

Maddox was busy when I was at work because the furniture was rearranged, so there's an open space in the middle of the room where he put a blanket and pillows on the floor. The coffee table is pushed to the side, set for dinner, with more candles casting light over the plates and glasses.

Hands wrap around my waist, pulling me into a firm chest.

"Maddox," I sigh just as his mouth connects with my neck.

"You like?" he whispers, his warm breath tickling my skin and making goosebumps appear.

"I love it," I breathe as warmth spreads through my belly. This. This is exactly what I needed to feel better. "You didn't have to go through all this trouble."

"Well, you said you didn't feel like going out for a date, so I brought the date to you."

I turn around, wrapping my arms around his neck. "You're the best. You know that?"

"I don't know about the best." That familiar redness spreads over his cheeks. "I wanted to surprise you."

It was cute the way Maddox still gets embarrassed by doing nice things for others, for me, when it's the complete opposite.

"You did." I rise on the tips of my toes and press my mouth against his.

The kiss is supposed to be short, just a peck on the lips, but one swipe of my mouth turns into two, and then we're making out.

Maddox's arms tighten around me as his tongue slides over my lower lip, teasing me. My lips part, our tongues tangling together as a moan rises from my chest. My fingers dig into his neck as our kiss deepens. We're pressed so tightly together, and I can feel his hardness against me. My tummy clenches, heat pooling inside me.

It's insane. The way my body reacts to his when we're together. It's nothing I could have imagined in my wildest dreams, but now just thinking about not having it makes my heart ache.

With one final nibble at my lower lip, Maddox pulls back. "C'mon, let's feed you."

"You cooked too?"

Twining our fingers together, Maddox pulls me into the living room and looks over his shoulder. "That would be a no. I'm not testing our luck when it comes to cooking. But since I had a reservation at Alfredo's, I just called and told them I'll take it to-go."

"Alfredo's?" My stomach rumbles loudly at the mention of Italian food.

When we come to the picnic area, Maddox holds onto my hand while I sit down on the blanket. "You realize you'll probably need a crane to get me off this floor, right?"

Maddox shakes his head, lowering down to the floor far more gracefully than I did. "I think I can manage."

I lean back into the pillows. My muscles stretch, making me groan.

"You good?" Maddox asks, opening one of the containers.

"Yeah, just tired, that's all." I sniff the air. "Oh my God, is that..."

The smell of cheese and mushrooms fills the air, saliva filling my mouth.

"Chicken alfredo." Maddox smiles, showing me the insides of the container. "Your favorite."

I press my hand against my chest. "You know a way to a woman's heart."

Those serious eyes fix on mine. "I just need to know the way to your heart."

Shivers run down my spine as his words settle in my mind.

How did I miss it? How did I not notice the way he's looked at me all these years? Was I really that blind? Because now that I've seen it, I can't unsee it. The way Maddox feels about me is written all over his face—it's been right in front of my nose all this time—and I want to curse the old Aly for being so blind. Curse her for ever making this man feel like he didn't matter.

Before I can say anything else, Maddox moves the dish onto my plate. "C'mon, eat before it gets too cold."

"You can be so bossy sometimes." Still, I take the plate and stab my fork into the pasta. I moan loudly at the first taste of it on my tongue; the rich, creamy sauce with the best homemade pasta I've ever eaten. "So good."

"They do have the best food in the area."

"More like in the state," I say, eating more. I hadn't even realized how hungry I was until this very moment. For a while, we just eat in companionable silence until...

"How was work?"

The image of Chad coming to the café pops in my mind, making my back stiffen. I place my fork down on the plate and take a sip of water, giving myself time to collect my thoughts. "It was okay. Just the usual," I shrug and quickly change the subject. The last thing I want is to ruin tonight by mentioning Chad. "What were you up to is a better question?"

"Took Coconut out to the dog park. Then I did some work

on that new game I'm working on."

I smirk at him because that answer is so Maddox. "You know that the point of spring break is to relax, right?"

"Was it? I might have missed that part back in school."

I shake my head. "You work too hard."

"Since somebody decided to pick up extra shifts during the *break*," Maddox gives me a pointed look, "I was feeling bored. Might as well get some work done since I'm alone."

"You know I need all the extra money. And no," I point my fork at him and give him my sternest look, "don't even start. Now that we know the sex of the baby, I should probably start ordering stuff. I looked at the price of some of these things, and they're insane. Who spends over six hundred bucks on a stroller? And that's just the beginning. Although I think I found the perfect crib."

I pull out my phone and open my Amazon wishlist, scrolling until I find the one I like the best, before turning my phone toward Maddox so he can see it. "What do you think?"

Maddox takes the phone from me, pushing his glasses up his nose. I'm not sure why he keeps on doing it since he's wearing the new frames we picked together a few weeks ago, and they fit perfectly. Habit, I guess.

"Is this safe?"

I blink, thrown off by his question. "What?"

"This kind of railing? Don't you worry that she'll try to push her hand between the railing and get stuck?"

"It's a baby," I let out a laugh. "I highly doubt she'll try to push her arm through anything when she's that small."

Maddox frowns at the screen, his thumb swiping down presumably to get to the reviews.

"I guess I could always buy some kind of protection to put on the inside, just in case. What I'm not sure is if I should get a crib with a changing table or not."

"Will you need a changing table? I mean, it's a baby; how much changing will there be?"

This time, I can't hold it in; I burst into full-on laughter.

Maddox pulls his brows together. "What did I say?"

"Oh, Maddox. You're so smart about some things, but about others..." I shake my head, still laughing.

"What?"

"Babies need a lot of changing. And I do mean *a lot*. They spit up, they burp, and if you're really unlucky, they'll pee and even poop on you. Plus, she's a girl, so she'll probably be changed more times in a day than all the people living in this house combined."

Maddox's eyes turn into saucers as he just stares at me, unblinking. "You're kidding."

He looks petrified. If I didn't feel sorry for him, I'd probably laugh.

"I'm afraid not. Babies might be cute, but they're messy." I place my hand over his, sliding my thumb over his knuckles. "You still sure you want to do this?"

He doesn't miss a beat. "Always. I don't mind messy."

"Maddox, you're probably the tidiest guy I know."

"Yeah, but I don't mind this kind of mess." Maddox puts my phone on the table and turns his hand, lacing our fingers together. "What will it take for you to get it in that thick skull of yours? I love you, Aly."

My heart does that little flip it always does when he says those three little words. My tongue darts out to wet my suddenly dry lips.

"I-I..." I start, but once again, it's like the words are stuck in my throat. Which is silly because I've told Maddox I loved him since we were kids. Why is it so difficult to say those words now?

Maddox's hand squeezes around mine, his thumb sliding

over my knuckles. "I don't need you to say it back, but I want you to know how I feel. I've been holding it back for so long, it feels liberating just to admit it out loud."

He shifts, so he's sitting by my side, his hand falling over the couch as he pulls me closer to him. His warmth surrounds me, that familiar smell of sandalwood and citrus wrapping around me like a blanket.

Maddox cups my cheek with his free hand, his eyes taking in the lines of my face. "I love you, Alyssa. Every single part of you, even the ones you think aren't worthy of my love."

Warmth spreads through me like a wave, spreading through my whole body.

This boy… This boy will be my undoing, and he doesn't even realize it.

"That's because you deserve the best."

Something which I'm not.

I don't say it out loud, but I don't have to. Not to Maddox, at least. He knows me way better than sometimes I know myself.

"And I have it. Right here in my arms. I have what I've always wanted." His fingers slide under my chin, nudging my head back. "I have you."

His mouth brushes against mine, slow and sweet.

That's what I love about kissing Maddox. There's no rush, no sloppiness. He kisses me like I matter. Like there isn't anything else he'd rather do.

I meet every swipe of his mouth with one of my own. Shifting so we're closer, I slide my hand up his chest and behind his neck. My fingers tangle in his hair, nails softly grazing the sensitive skin.

Maddox sucks in a breath, his pupils dilating. The brown of his irises grows darker with passion, and I can feel my tummy clench in anticipation.

"It's insane how much I want you," he whispers, his voice

rough.

I push him back and straddle his lap. "You're not the only one."

Then my mouth is on his, our kiss growing stronger, hungrier with every second.

Maddox runs his hands under my shirt, his fingers playing over my naked skin before he helps me pull my shirt over my head and lets it fall by our side, my bra following soon after.

I let out a sigh of relief, but it doesn't last long because Maddox cups my breast, teasing the sensitive nipple.

My head falls back as a shudder runs down my spine all the way to my core.

"So pretty," Maddox whispers, dipping his head down, so his warm breath teases my skin.

I tighten my grip on his hair as he sucks one hard bud deep into his mouth. My hips buckle, and I rock against him, feeling his hard length press against my pussy.

"Maddox," I moan, my hands sliding down his back. I curl my fingers around his shirt and tug it upward. "I want to feel you."

Maddox lets my nipple pop out of his mouth and pulls his shirt off. I fumble with the button of his jeans and zipper and then work on getting rid of the rest of my clothes.

"Are you in a hurry?" Maddox chuckles, his eyes taking me in as I sit back down on his lap.

"Yes."

"Why?" Maddox runs his palms over my legs, his rough fingertips making goosebumps rise on my skin. "I'm not going anywhere."

"Because it's been a shitty day, and there's nothing like sex to make me feel better." My glance darts toward the dinner. "Okay, dinner and sex."

Maddox's hands tighten around my waist as he pulls me

closer. "We can't have that."

"No, we can't."

I hold his gaze as I lift my hips. Maddox wraps his hand around his base. I sink my teeth into my lower lip as I slowly lower myself on him.

Maddox's eyes grow so dark they almost seem black as he sinks inside me to the hilt. His muscles are taut under my palms like he's doing his best to hold back, his fingers digging into my hips.

Letting my lip pop, I lean down and press my forehead against his. "You feel so good inside me." I roll my hips, loving the feel of him. The way we fit together so perfectly, unlike anything I've ever felt before. "So, so good."

Maddox's hips buck underneath mine. His hands slide up my back, lips pressing against mine. "Take what you need."

My eyes fly open at his words, at the way he said it.

My tummy clenches, the delicious heat building inside me.

Cupping his cheeks, I kiss him more fiercely and do as he says, slowly starting to move. Every time I lower over him, it feels like he slides deeper inside me, stretching me to the point where pleasure and pain mix together just right.

It's like he's made for me—our bodies, our minds, our souls. They all fit so perfectly together. We fit perfectly together, and I'll never get enough of it.

Enough of him.

"Maddox, I..." I suck in a shaky breath, my pussy tightening around him.

My movements become hurried, jerky as I chase my release. The pressure builds inside of me.

So close.

So, so close.

He tugs my head back, his lips brushing against mine as he thrusts into me from below. "Come for me."

I'm not sure if it's the demanding tone of his voice, or the way that he hits just the right spot, but I come. My entire body shudders, my walls tightening around him and sucking him deeper as he thrusts a few more times and comes with me.

I sag against him, my breathing ragged, my heart racing.

"That was..." I let out a shaky breath, unable to form a coherent sentence.

"Amazing," Maddox gently pushes my hair away from my face, pressing a soft kiss against my forehead. "And so not what I had planned."

"Oh no?" I pull back so I can look at him. "What did you plan then?"

Maddox brushes my hair behind my ears. "A nice dinner, and then I wanted to show you something."

"Well, you won't hear me complain about the change in plans." I shift, and I can still feel his dick inside me. "I should probably clean up first, and then you can show me whatever it is that you wanted."

Maddox's mouth brushes against mine. "How about we clean up together?" His fingers grip my thighs as he pushes to his feet.

I wrap my arms around his neck tighter. "Maddox! What are you doing?"

"Going to the bathroom."

"No, you're not."

He can't seriously think he's carrying me all the way upstairs to his room.

"Yes, I am. And you're coming with me."

I protest all the way upstairs, but my words are muffled once he has me in the shower, pressed against the tiles. Needless to say, we spent way more time in the shower than we should have, but I couldn't find it in me to care.

Once we got dressed, Maddox pulled me back downstairs,

and we curled on the couch together.

"Now, keep in mind that this is far from finished, but..."

"Maddox, I'm sorry to disappoint you, but I don't know anything about video games. So I'm not sure I'm..." My words trail off as the image pops on the screen. "Is that... a woman?"

It damn sure looks like one, with long hair pulled in a braid, dressed in some kind of armor, and with a bow and arrow strapped to her back.

"Yeah."

I look over my shoulder at him and find him rubbing his neck.

"What did you do?" I ask slowly, unsure of where he's going with this.

"So I was thinking how all the games I always make are designed for boys."

"Okay, and?"

"So I redesigned it and made a girl's version."

"A girl's version?" I repeat, still not sure I understand.

Maddox tilts his head to the side and gives me that stern, no-nonsense look of his. "Girls can play video games too, you know."

The corner of my mouth twitches in amusement. "I didn't say anything. What I don't understand is why would you do that?"

Maddox shrugs. "Well, so one day I can play it with Edie."

I blink, unsure if I heard him correctly.

"You created a girl's version of the game, so you could play it with Edie?" I rasp, my throat feeling suddenly tight from the emotions slowly brewing inside of me.

Maddox looks away, heat rising in his cheeks. "I know it's silly, and there'll be a dozen games until she's old enough to actually play..."

The way he looks away, the blush creeping up his cheeks,

the game... that damn game. Tears prickle my eyes as my insides turn into mush.

Because there is no other man like Maddox, he's one in a million.

"It's not silly; it's sweet." I cup his cheek, turning him, so he faces me. "You're so damn smart; you know that?"

"Are you surprised by it?"

I chuckle, "Not really. I always knew you were smart. Hell, I was surprised when you didn't go to one of the top Ivy League schools."

"I could have."

My head snaps up, eyes fixing on his face. "What?"

Once again, Maddox tries to look away, but I don't let him.

"I could have." He clears his throat and pushes his glasses up his nose. "I got accepted to Harvard and Yale, and... well pretty much any Ivy League school."

My heart speeds up at his confession. Back then, we never talked much about college. I applied to different schools, but Blairwood was my top choice. I still remember the day I got my acceptance letter. I ran over to Maddox's house and told him that I got in, excited to finally get out of my parent's house, ecstatic to be free.

"Then why didn't you? Out of all the schools, why did you choose Blairwood?"

"Ivy League seemed too... stuffy. I wasn't interested in that. But..." His tongue darts out, sliding over his lower lip. "But also, because I knew you wanted to come here. I chose it because I knew we'd be here together if I did."

I sit upright and turn around to face him. "You chose it because of me?" I ask slowly, still unable to grasp the extent of it.

Maddox shrugs. "Yeah."

Tears gather in my eyes. "W-why?"

"Don't you understand it by now, Aly? I'll choose you. Always."

My chest squeezes, and for a moment, it seems like it's hard to breathe. I blink, and a tear slides down my cheek.

"Don't cry." Maddox's his thumb slides over my cheekbone, brushing away the tear. "Why are you crying?"

"I can't help myself. It's these damn hormones."

"You can blame it on the hormones all you want, but I know you, Alyssa. You're one big softy."

I chuckle, brushing away the tears. "Am not."

"Are too."

"Am not," I whisper, wrapping my arms around Maddox's middle. "Thank you."

"What for?"

"For being here. For choosing me, even when I didn't realize it or know how to appreciate it."

"Always, Alyssa." He slips a strand of hair behind my ear. "I mean it."

"I know."

Turning around, I press my mouth against his in a soft kiss. My bump is between us, and the little one chooses this exact moment to kick. Hard.

"Is that..." Maddox pulls back, his eyes falling to my stomach.

"Yes," I place my palm over my belly and give it a slow rub. "I started to feel her recently, but this is the first big one."

Maddox's hands hover over mine, excitement dancing in his brown irises. "Can I?"

"Y-yeah."

Almost instantly, Maddox puts his hands over mine. I pull mine out and cover his with mine, guiding them on the sides of my belly where I can usually feel her kick the hardest.

But then Maddox surprises me even further. I'm not sure

why, since he's shown me time and again how good of a man he is. He crouches down in front of me, his thumbs sliding over my belly. "Giving your momma a hard time already, little one?" he asks affectionately, a smile playing on his lips.

As if she can hear him, she gives another kick to my belly. Maddox chuckles, "A hellion already, and you're not even here."

Another kick.

"She likes it," I whisper, chuckling.

Maddox looks up, his eyes shining brightly. "What?"

"Your voice. She likes it."

"You think?"

As if she wants to prove my point, she delivers another kick.

"I guess you're right. She likes me."

She loves you, just like I do.

The words come out of nowhere, surprising me. If Maddox weren't holding me, I'd probably stagger back. It takes me a moment to wrap my head around it, but when I do, I know it's true.

I'm in love with my best friend while carrying another man's child.

Before I can even get enough time to process everything, we hear the door open. Maddox and I exchange a look before we turn around just in time to see our friends enter the house.

"Oh my God!" Letting go of Maddox's hand, I throw myself at my friends. "You're home early!"

"*Jesus*, easy now," Yasmin chuckles as she wraps her arms around me.

Callie takes a step back to give me a long look. "Did you somehow get bigger in the past week?"

"Me? You're attacking me?" I jab my finger first at Callie, then at Yasmin. "Next time one of you two decides to get hitched, I expect a freaking invite!" I grab their hands and pull them toward the couch. "I want *all* the details."

Chapter 33

MADDOX

"What are you up to?" I sit on the bed behind Aly, my hand sneaking around her waist as I nuzzle into the crook of her neck. She shivers in my arms, her body leaning into my touch as I rub my hand over her stomach and am rewarded with a soft kick.

A slow grin spreads over my face. No matter how many times I've felt the baby move and kick, it's always as exciting as it was that first time Aly guided my hands to her belly.

"Trying to finish this essay, not that either of you is making it easy for me to do it." Aly looks over her shoulder at me and gives me a stern look, or at least she tries to, but I can see the smile tugging at the corner of her mouth.

Two months. We've been dating for two months, and some days it's still hard for me to grasp it. I keep expecting that I'll wake up and things will go back to how they used to be, but then I wake up and find Aly sleeping snuggled into my side, and that happiness, that feeling of completeness, would slam into me all over again.

"Don't you have any work to do?" Aly asks, snapping me out of my thoughts.

"I just got home from class."

"Seriously, considering you're doing your *Master's*, one would think you'd have more work to do."

"It's not that hard." I peek over her shoulder at the screen. "Need some help?"

"I'm almost done with it." I trail my nose over the column of her neck, inhaling her sweet scent. "Or I would have been if you weren't distracting me."

My hand slides lower, just under her belly. The bump is so big now it can fit into my palm just right. "And how am I distracting you?"

"With your hands." I press my mouth on her throat, feeling the steady beat of her pulse under my lips. "M-mouth."

"How about I put that m—"

The doorbell rings loudly, making Aly jump away from me, or she would if I didn't have my arms around her. Coco starts barking and runs toward the door and down the stairs, clearly excited about the company.

"Ignore it." I pull her back into my chest. "It's probably some salesman anyway. Those people are annoying."

"Maddox!" Aly protests, pushing my hands away. "Somebody's at the door. It's probably a delivery since I got the message that the crib will be delivered today."

I fall down onto the mattress and cover my face with my hands, groaning loudly. "Can't they leave it on the porch? We will go down to get it later."

"No, I wanna see it." The bed squeaks as Aly pushes to her feet. I let my hands fall by my sides and look at Aly. She's like a kid on Christmas morning. She tugs her shirt down over her bump and slips into her flip-flops before looking at me just as the doorbell rings for the second time. "You coming or what?"

Nope, not coming. And that's the whole problem.

"Give me a minute," I tell her, but she's already walking out of the room, so I yell after her, "And don't you dare lift that thing."

Pushing to my feet, I readjust myself as best as I can before following after her. Knowing Aly, she'll ignore what I said, try to lift the damn box on her own, and get hurt in the process.

"Hey, sorry for... Mrs. Anderson, hi."

I stop in my tracks on top of the stairs at the sound of Aly's voice. She's holding onto the door, my mother standing on the other side.

Shit.

So much for the delivery.

"Alyssa." Mom takes her in, her gaze lingering on her stomach. "What in God's name..."

"Mom," I interrupt before she can finish whatever she was planning to say. Taking two steps at a time, I descend the stairs and stop next to Alyssa. "I didn't realize you were coming."

Mom's gaze lingers for a moment longer on Aly before she shifts it to me. "Maybe you would have if you actually answered your phone for once." I lean down dutifully so she can brush her mouth against my cheek. "Do you even use that thing?"

"Not very often," Aly looks over her shoulder, giving me a pointed look. "Something I keep telling him. Not that he listens."

Mom tsks. "That one has selective hearing just like his father."

I put my arm around Aly's waist. "Did you need something?"

Mom's eyes narrow at my hand. With another tsk, she brushes past us and into the room. "Does a mother need a reason to see her son? You don't answer our calls. You didn't come to visit during spring break. And now I see that the stories are true, and Alyssa is pregnant." It's just then that the delivery truck stops in front of my house. The guy comes out and goes into the trunk from where he pulls the crib box. "And apparently, she's living here too." Mom shifts her attention back to me. "Is there something I should know?"

"Yes," I say; at the same time, Aly says, "No."

Mom looks to Aly and then back to me. "So, which one is it? Yes or no?"

Ignoring her, I shift my attention to Aly, but she's staring at her feet. What the hell?

"Aly and I are dating, and she's living with me," I explain to my mother, completely done with this conversation.

Aly shifts from one foot to the other. "But the baby isn't Maddox's."

Her words are barely a whisper, but I couldn't hear them any louder if she shouted them from the rooftops.

My whole body stiffens as her words echo in my eardrums. They shouldn't sting; after all, they're the truth. I'm not the baby's biological father, but it seemed like I could be after the last few weeks, especially since we started dating. Because that baby might not have my blood, but in my heart, she is mine as much as Aly is.

"Miss Martinez?" the delivery guy asks from the bottom of the porch.

"That's her," I say, almost on autopilot.

Pulling my hand back, I walk around them to the guy to take the box. I mutter my thanks before picking up the box and carrying it inside the house. The image of the crib that we'd picked together for a baby that's not mine is mocking me from the box.

So much for that.

I lean the box against the wall and run my hand over my face.

What the hell was I thinking? Letting myself get attached like that? Letting myself believe that this might be real when

Aly can't even bring herself to admit that she loves me out loud? It's there, on the tip of her tongue, I can see it, but then for whatever reason, she pulls back at the last moment.

"Maddox?"

My head snaps up at my mom's sharp tone. For a moment, I forgot she was even here.

Aly looks from Mom to me. "I should go back up and finish that essay. It was nice seeing you, Mrs. Anderson." As she walks past me, her hand brushes against my arm. "Thanks for bringing that in."

Because apparently, that's all I'm good for. Stepping in when there's work to be done, only to be brushed off later.

The baby isn't Maddox's.

"No problem." I force out a smile, but my face feels tight, smile fake.

But Aly is already climbing the stairs, away from my mother's judging eyes; she doesn't even notice, nor does she look back once.

It's like somebody has thrown a bucket of cold water over my head. The happiness I was feeling only minutes ago when I came home has completely vanished. The only thing left is this emptiness, this...this void I'm not sure what to do with.

"Can you explain this to me?" Mom crosses her arms over her chest, barely waiting for Aly to disappear before pouncing on me.

I slowly turn to face her. "What exactly isn't clear, Mom?"

"All of this." She uncurls her hands and waves them around.

"Aly is having a rough time, so I told her she should stay here."

Mom's eyes narrow as she watches me. "And when did you two start dating? Because the last I remember, she was dating that other guy."

Of course, she'd remember that. That woman doesn't miss a thing.

"Recently. And it was Chad." Just saying his name leaves a bitter taste on my tongue.

"Irrelevant." Mom waves me off. "Is he the father?"

The muscles in my jaw ticks; I clench my teeth together. "He's the sperm donor."

Aly might not consider me father material, but damn it if I'm going to call her ex, of all people, the father.

"Then why isn't he taking care of her and the baby? Isn't that the father's job?"

Not every father's job, apparently.

I pinch the bridge of my nose, tired of this conversation. "He isn't taking care of her because they broke up. And before you ask, no, he doesn't want the baby. Can you just let it go? I don't see how this is rele—"

"And you just happened to start dating after that?" Mom interrupts before I can even finish. "How convenient."

My hand falls down. "What are you trying to say, Mom?"

"I'm not trying to say anything, Maddox." She lifts her chin and gives me a pointed look. "I'm just pointing out that you have a good heart, and you shouldn't let people take advantage of it."

Take advantage of it?

She can't be serious. But watching her, I can clearly see that she is.

"Aly isn't taking advantage of me!"

Just the idea is laughable. Not only has Aly been my friend for years, but she's also made it a point not to accept any kind of help except for the bare minimum since she found out she's pregnant.

"Isn't she? I'm not blind, Maddox. I know you've been in love with her for years. *Years,*" she repeats as if I needed a reminder. "But she conveniently gave you a chance now that she's pregnant and alone? Just think about it."

"There's nothing to think about," I grit through clenched teeth. "You're wrong. And you should know better than that."

"All I know is that my son is dating a girl who's pregnant with another man's baby."

"This is Alyssa!" I yell, unable to hold it in. "It's not just some random girl."

If it were anybody else, I might have understood it. If it was some random girl I just met, maybe, but not my best friend.

"It doesn't matter who it is! I don't want you to get stuck with a child that's not yours."

The baby isn't Maddox's.

I take a step back, my lips pressed in a tight line. There are those words. Again. As if I haven't heard them enough times; Been hurt by them enough times.

My fingers ball into fists by my sides as I try to hold onto my sanity. "Haven't you heard? That won't be an issue."

Mom tilts her head to the side and watches me for a moment. I'm not sure what she sees on my face, she has to see something because her face softens, and she takes a step closer. "Maddox..."

I shake my head, done with this conversation. "Was there something you needed?"

"I—" She opens her mouth as if she'll protest but changes her mind at the last moment. "I wanted to remind you about the charity gala coming the first Saturday in May. Your dad could really use your support there."

Of course, he could. It's always about my dad's campaign and supporting his political career.

"I don't know, Mom. It's just before finals, and I'm not..."

"It's just one night, Maddox. I'm sure you can find a few hours."

I let out a long breath. "Fine. I'll talk to Aly."

Mom opens her mouth to protest, but I lift my hand to stop her. "Aly and I are dating. And if I remember correctly, the last time you dragged me to the gala, you were complaining I never brought dates."

"This is not what I had in mind when I told you to get a girlfriend."

"Well, one way or the other, Alyssa is my girlfriend. We come as a package deal. You can take it or leave it."

The silence settles over us. I can see Mom doesn't like it one bit, but I'm not about to back down on this. Finally, she nods, although she doesn't even try to hide her displeasure about the whole situation. Good, that makes two of us.

"Fine, although I still think you're making a mistake."

"Duly noted."

Mom places her hands on my shoulders. "I just want you to be happy. That's the only thing I've ever wanted."

"Aly makes me happy," I say softly, although I'm feeling anything but happy right now.

The baby isn't Maddox's.

I raise my hand and rub the middle of my chest.

With a sigh and a shake of her head, Mom takes a step back. "Okay then."

She starts walking toward the door, and I follow her to her car. Unlocking her car, she turns to face me. "I'll see you in a few weeks?"

"I'll let you know."

Mom gives me a stern look.

"I'll try to make it," I promise, and then add, "With Alyssa."

"I just hope you know what you're doing." Mom gives her head a shake and slides into her car.

I do, or at least I thought I did, but...

The baby isn't Maddox's.

I watch my mother drive away; Aly's words are still ringing in my mind.

How did everything get so royally screwed up so quickly? Not even fifteen minutes ago, I came home hoping to spend some time with my girlfriend, and now it's like the rug has been pulled from under my feet. My whole world has been turned on its axis because of one sentence.

One damn sentence that broke my heart.

I make my way back into the house. My eyes fall on the crib that's still leaning against the wall. I could still remember the day we finally ordered it. How excited I was at the idea of moving some things around the room to make enough space for it and putting it together.

The baby isn't Maddox's.

Turning my back on the crib, I climb the stairs almost on autopilot.

Aly looks up from her laptop when I enter the room. "Your mom left already?"

"Yeah," I nod and go to the desk, turning on my computer.

"That was fast."

Not fast enough.

"You know my mom," I shrug. "She wanted to make sure I'll be at some charity gala in May. Dad's campaigning again. You know how it goes."

The words feel clipped, almost like I'm detached from it all.

"I didn't realize it's that time of year again."

"It's always that time of year; just one of the charms of being in politics. I told her we'd think about it. Knowing these events, your parents will also be there..."

"You have to go support your dad," Aly says before I can finish.

"I don't want to put you in an uncomfortable position."

The words slip out easily; after all, they're true. Always

thinking of Aly, always putting her first, that's how it's been our whole lives, hasn't it? I haven't minded. I never regretted it, but...

The baby isn't Maddox's.

"You're not," she touches my shoulder.

My whole body goes stiff at her touch. I hadn't expected it, hadn't heard her get up from the bed or move closer.

"Maddox?" Aly asks tentatively.

This was a bad idea. I should have stayed away until I got a hold of myself and figured out what to do about this whole situation—figured out how to face her after what just happened downstairs.

"So you wanna go?" I keep my gaze on the screen, knowing that if I look at her now, she'll know something's wrong. She'll see that I'm hurt, and I'll have to explain why.

Or maybe she won't see. A little voice at the back of my head taunts me. *After all, she didn't see how you had felt all these years. Why would now be any different? And isn't that the real thing you're afraid of?*

Aly shifts behind me. "I mean if you want me to. I'll go with you."

"What about your parents?"

"Nothing." Aly shrugs and leans against the table. "I'll keep my distance from them, and that's it. They made their choice, and I made mine."

And how do I fall into your choices, Aly? Where do I fit in? Am I your friend? Your boy toy while you figure this out? What am I?

Her hand covers mine. A knot forms in my throat, and I shift my attention down to our joined hands. Her thumb slides over my knuckles. My heart is beating a mile a minute as I slowly lift my gaze to hers to find her observing me.

"You've been by my side all this time. If you want me to be

there with you, I'll be there," she smiles tentatively and gives my hand a squeeze. "But if you'd rather I'm not, that's fine too. The last thing I want is to ruin that night for you and your family."

You'll be there, but you won't openly admit to your feelings.

I give my head a little shake. "Thanks. I guess I should get some work done now."

Aly smiles and starts to push from the desk but stops.

"I just remembered. I have a doctor's appointment next week. You wanna come?"

"I-I..."

The baby isn't Maddox's.

"I have a meeting with my advisor," the lie slips easily from my tongue. I should feel bad. I don't think I've ever lied to her before, but I can't go with her into that office and act like everything is fine. Not after today.

"Oh." Aly stops for a moment, clearly surprised by my answer. After all, I've gone with her to her last few appointments. "Okay. Sure. I guess I'll check with the girls to see if they wanna go?"

I nod, shifting my attention back to the screen. "Yeah, maybe that's for the best."

After all, the baby isn't mine.

Chapter 34

ALYSSA

"Alyssa Martinez?"

My head snaps up at the sound of my name. I look to my right, the chair where Maddox would always sit, but find it empty.

I stare at it for a heartbeat longer before forcing a smile out and getting to my feet.

"No company today?" the nurse asks, smiling at me as I close the door behind me.

"It's just me," I say, dropping my things into the chair, so that I can get on the scale. "Maddox had some school stuff to get done."

"That's unfortunate."

"Yeah," I whisper absent-mindedly as I get off the scale and sit down to have my blood pressure measured.

Being with Maddox was so effortless that I didn't even realize how much I depended on him until he said he wasn't able to come.

At first, I thought I'd ask one of the girls to go with me, but I couldn't do it. Maddox has gone to every appointment with me since the one where we found out I'm carrying a girl. In a way, it was our thing, and if he couldn't come, I didn't want anybody else here.

"Hmm..." The nurse frowns as she looks down at the pressure gauge.

I blink myself out of my thoughts and turn my attention to her. There's something about the tone of her voice that makes me weary. "What? Is something wrong?"

The nurse gives me a kind smile. "Your blood pressure is elevated."

A knot forms in my throat, making it hard to breathe.

Easy, Aly, I chastise, forcing my lungs to open and pushing the words out: "Is that bad?"

"Not necessarily, but it's something we like to monitor to make sure both mom and the baby are doing okay. How about I double-check it just in case?" she smiles, but something is placating about the gesture.

"Yeah, sure," But even as I say it, I know it won't be any different. I can feel my heart beat faster as the panic sets in.

What does this whole thing mean? Is my baby okay? Did I do something wrong? Did...

The nurse purses her lips as she reads the levels on the machine before pulling the velcro and freeing my hand. "How have you been feeling lately?"

"I—" I tug the sleeve of my shirt down. "Okay, I guess."

"Nothing out of the ordinary? A stressful situation?"

I run my shaky fingers through my hair and push it away from my face. "It's almost the end of the school year, and I'm a senior on top of being pregnant and working. It feels like everything I do these days is stressful."

The nurse nods at me. "Well, it's best if you discuss it with Doctor Jeremy. She'll tell you what to do, but do try to take it easy, okay?"

Easy? Yeah, right. Still, I nod because is there another choice? "Yeah, thanks."

"You can go on inside and wait for the doctor."

"Sure thing, thank you."

I slowly get to my feet and make my way to the back office, almost in a daze. My throat grows tight, the nurse's words still ringing in my mind.

It's something we like to monitor.

Is it me? Did I do something wrong? Did I cause this somehow? What if—

My hand slides to my stomach, rubbing the bump, and I'm rewarded with a kick. Tears gather, blurring my vision. I shut my eyes for a moment. The knot inside my belly loosens a little bit, and all the emotions come rushing out. I didn't even realize how much I needed to feel Edie move until this very moment. Because if she's moving, that means she's okay, right?

"Calm down, Aly," I mutter to myself as I walk to the examination table and hoist myself up. "You need to calm down. You heard the nurse. This isn't good for the baby."

Laying down, I close my eyes and take a few deep inhales to calm my ragged breathing.

In and out, I time each breath with one of Edie's kicks.

She's good.

That's the only thing that matters. She's good.

"I'll do right by you, little one," I whisper to the empty room, rubbing the side of my belly where I can feel her kick the hardest. "I promise you."

Just then, the door opens, and Doctor Jeremy enters the room, a smile on her face. "Hey, Alyssa, how are you doing today?"

"Apparently, not that good."

The doctor's face turns serious as she takes her chair and opens my chart. "How so?"

"My blood pressure is elevated?"

"I can see that." She scans the papers, her lips pressing together. "And there was protein in your urine."

"Protein?" I curl my fingers around the edge of the table.

"Not an alarming amount," she explains quickly. "But definitely elevated compared to your previous visits."

"What does that mean?" I ask softly, biting the inside of my cheek. Protein in urine?

"It can mean a number of things. Did you have any other symptoms lately? Something that's not usual?"

"My head's been hurting," I shrug. "But like I said to the nurse, it's not unusual considering that the end of the year is just around the corner, and there's a lot to do before graduation."

Doctor Jeremy nods. "I understand. How about we do the ultrasound, and then we'll talk a little bit more?"

Ultrasound. I can do an ultrasound.

I push my shirt up, exposing my belly.

"I felt her move." I suck in a breath as Doctor Jeremy puts gel on my stomach and starts spreading it with her wand. "That's good, right?"

She glances at me for a second. "Feeling the baby move is always good."

I let out a long breath, my back relaxing, if only slightly. I need good news. I needed it yesterday.

Doctor Jeremy turns on the sound machine, and that fast-paced flutter fills the room and my heart. This. This is what I needed.

"Everything seems okay," Doctor Jeremy says as she turns the ultrasound off and removes her gloves. "But I'm still wary of that blood pressure. Like I said, it could be just the stress of school, but it could also be a sign of preeclampsia."

My throat bobs as I swallow. "Preeclampsia?"

"Yes, it's a pregnancy complication." She gives me a serious look. "I'm not going to lie to you, it's an extremely high risk, and there's no cure for it except for delivery."

Delivery?

"I can't deliver my baby now," I shake my head. "It's too early."

Doctor Jeremy nods, her hand covering mine. "Considering you still have about ten weeks to go, and your blood pressure and protein are toeing the concerning levels, I think inducing labor now would do more harm than good. But I need you to take things easy. Try to rest as much as possible and drink more water. I'll also prescribe you medicine for your blood pressure. Okay?"

"Okay," I nod, my mind swirling with all the information I've heard.

"Try not to worry too much, but if anything, and I do mean anything, feels off, you come to me, or you go to the hospital, got it?"

I'm not sure if Dr. Jeremy realizes how contradictive that statement is. How can I not worry when she just told me to look out for any sign that something might not be right?

I can't.

"Hey there!" I look up to find Yasmin and Callie watching me from the couch. "We were wondering where you might be."

I'm not even sure I realized I was home until this moment, which is dangerous, but I couldn't get out of my head what Dr. Jeremy told me earlier. My brain was still processing every detail I'd heard, which wasn't much really, and trying to come up with some kind of solution.

"Aly?" Callie tilts her head to the side; brows pulled together. "Are you okay?"

"Yeah." I run my fingers through my hair. "Just spacing out."

Dropping my backpack on the floor, I join my friends in the living room. "What are you two up to?"

"Just chatting and enjoying the peace and quiet while it lasts."

"Where is everybody?" I ask, sitting down in the armchair and pulling my legs under me.

"Nixon is in class. Zane is probably off somewhere with Rei."

"And Hayden is upstairs. He's talking to his agent on the phone. They're discussing his move and the beginning of training camp, I think." Callie shakes her head. "Some days, it's still hard to believe he did it. He's a professional football player, and he's going to stay here in Boston."

The house was packed the day of the draft. I think the whole football team, and then some, were here to watch and see where Hayden would end up going. I swear I can still hear the roar of approval when none other than the *Patriots* called out Hayden's name. A first-round draft pick. I don't know much about football, but apparently, it's a big deal. I was just happy to see Callie relax a little bit after everything was done.

"Did you decide what you'll do next year?"

"I'll stay here if Maddox will have me. It makes the most sense since I don't want to lose time commuting. Besides, I think Hayden should concentrate on football when he's in Boston, and we can commute on weekends and holidays." Callie shrugs. "We'll figure it out. I'm just happy that he's home."

"The better question is, what are you going to do next year?" Yasmin wiggles her brows.

"I don't know."

Her smile falls. "You don't know? You and Maddox haven't talked about it?"

"No," I shrug, trying to play it off. "There's always something, you know? Between the disaster that was the beginning of this year and then us getting together, it's like it was never the right time."

And not only that, Maddox has been acting...weird lately. Distant. He was still here, but more often than not, I'd catch him looking in the distance. His body was present, but it's like his mind was miles away.

I tried to reassure myself that's normal, all things considered. With the last-minute projects due and exams approaching, every student is going a little bit crazy, but this is Maddox.

Plus, I couldn't forget when that sudden change occurred...

"I guess that makes sense."

My eyes dart toward the stairs. "Did he come home?"

Maybe it was needy, but I wanted to see him. I wanted Maddox to pull me in his arms and reassure me that everything was going to be okay. That...

Yasmin's brows pull together. "Come home?"

"Yes, Maddox said he had a meeting with his advisor."

Callie and Yasmin exchange a look that has the fine hair at my nape rising.

"What?" I ask carefully because something about that look has me on edge.

"Maddox was home this whole time."

I blink, unsure if I heard her correctly. "Maddox was home?"

There's a soft buzzing in my ears as my words echo in the quiet room. Too quiet.

"Maybe the meeting was canceled?" Callie offers with a hopeful smile.

"Yeah," I whisper, not at all convinced. "Maybe."

His mother's unexpected visit flashes in front of my eyes. The way she took me in, her eyes narrowing when she got to my stomach.

And you just happened to start dating after that? How convenient.

I left for the upstairs but not before I heard her hurtful words; her assumption. I knew it would happen sooner or later. I knew somebody would think I was using Maddox for his money and influence. I just never thought the accusation would come from a woman who's known me my whole life. A woman who I've seen as a second mother in some way.

"Aly?" Yas gets up and comes to me. "Are you okay? You seem a bit pale."

"Fine," I look away, avoiding her gaze. "I'm just tired. I think I'll go lie down for a bit."

"Are you sure?"

I push to my feet with that buzzing still ringing in my ears. "Yeah, I'm sure. I'll see you two later?"

"Sure. Yell if you need something, okay?"

With a nod, I walk past her. Grabbing my backpack, I hold onto the railing as I slowly climb the stairs and come to my room.

Maddox's room.

I press my palm against the door and just stand there for a moment.

He was here this whole time? Was he here when he said he had things to do?

Was Callie right? Was his meeting canceled last minute?

No, if that were the case, Maddox would have called and met me at the doctor's office.

My tongue darts out, sliding over my dry lips before I push the door open.

Maddox is lying on the bed, his back pressed against the headboard with a book, and Coco curled at his feet. They both look up at the same time. Coco jumps off the bed and runs toward me, barking in greeting.

"Hey, pretty girl," I coo, and although it's getting harder by the day, I crouch down and rub behind her ears. "What were you up to all day?"

"She was sleeping when I got home."

I slowly push to my feet and find Maddox's dark eyes watching me quietly.

"A shocker, really." Turning my back on him, I go to the desk and drop my backpack to the floor before asking casually: "What about you? How did the meeting with your advisor go?"

There's a beat of silence, and I swear my heart is going to burst out of my chest as I wait for an answer. I unclasp my watch, my heartbeat echoing in my eardrums so loudly I can barely hear Maddox when he finally answers me.

"Good, she's happy with the essay I was working on, and we even brought up the topic of my dissertation."

My whole body goes still as his words register in my mind.

Callie was wrong. There was no confusion, no canceled meeting, no meeting at all.

Maddox lied to me.

And you just happened to start dating after that? How convenient.

Pulling the watch off my wrist, I slowly put it on top of the dresser. I can feel Maddox's eyes on me as I stare at the wall, trying to collect myself before facing him.

"Aly?"

I force out a smile before turning around to look at him. "That's great."

Get out. I need to get out of here.

I start toward the bathroom when Maddox's next words stop me in my tracks.

"How was the doctor's appointment?"

"I—" *Your blood pressure and protein are toeing the concerning levels... inducing the labor... But I need you to take things easy.* "Good. It went good." Although it pains me, I turn around to look at him. "I think I'm going to take a shower."

He opens his mouth, but before he can say anything else, I duck into the bathroom. I close the door behind me, pressing my back to the hardwood. My breathing is labored, and I have to grip the counter to keep steady as one thought keeps ringing in my mind.

Maddox just lied to me.

Chapter 35

MADDOX

"Seriously, what idiot packed this thing?" I mutter to myself as I look through the parts scattered around me, searching for a freaking screw that's not in the damn box.

"Who're you talking to?" Zane asks, peeking through the doorway.

"Myself."

"I mean, I knew you were weird, but that's taking it to the next level, dude."

I glare at him. "If you don't have anything smart to say, please shut up."

Zane's brows shoot up. "Who pissed in your cheerios this morning?"

"Nobody." I return my attention back to the floor and move a few of the boards to the side. I swear if I don't find those screws, I'll...

Entirely unfazed by my poor mood, Zane enters the room.

"You looking for these?" Zane asks, pulling out a bag of screws from under the cardboard box I threw to the side.

I grab the bag out of his hand. "Thanks."

Zane tips his chin toward the parts scattered on the floor. "What is this anyway?"

"Crib. Or at least parts of it. Let's just hope it's all there."

Zane sits down on the floor next to me and looks at the instruction manual. Not like the damn thing is useful. "Damn, already? Isn't it kind of early?"

"The baby will be here in two months, so," I shrug. "I mean, the package got here earlier this week, might as well put it together." I look over the boards and grab the one that seems like the bottom one. "Otherwise, the box is just taking up space."

"I guess that makes sense." Zane looks up at me. "You want help?"

I open my mouth to say no but change my mind at the last moment. "You hold, I'll screw it together?"

"Sounds good to me."

Thankfully, he doesn't say anything else, and we work mostly in quiet. Ignoring the instructions, I have Zane hold the crib's frame as I put the screws in and tighten them. Once that's done, I put together the drawer that goes beneath the mattress.

"It looks nice," Zane says, dusting off his hands against the side of his leg as we both look at the final product.

In the end, Aly decided on the plain white crib without the attached changing space. I still wasn't sure about the railings, but I guess it wasn't really my choice, was it?

Zane gives me a side glance. "Why are you frowning like that?"

"No reason. It's nothing."

Turning my back on the crib, I crouch down to pick up the mess.

"It doesn't look like nothing. I would have thought you'd be happy now that you and Alyssa are finally together, and things are working out."

I crumple the cardboard with more force than necessary.

Why is he insisting on talking about this? Can't he just let the subject drop?

"Things are working out?"

"Sure." I stand up, cardboard in my hands, and tip my chin toward the toolbox on the floor, changing the subject. "Can you pick that up and take it to the garage?"

"I've got it." Zane grabs the box and follows after me. "Seriously, what's going on with you?"

"I told you, nothing's going on. Can't you just leave it be?"

"Why would I? If I remember correctly, you didn't let me be when I was acting like an asshole."

"I don't remember acting like an asshole."

I wait for him to open the front door. Once outside, I go straight for the garbage can and drop all the cardboard inside.

"Maybe not an asshole exactly, but it seems like you have your panties in a twist," Zane continues as we make our way back inside.

"You're imagining things."

I look up and find Aly sitting at the kitchen counter. I didn't even realize she was home. But I guess that was our new normal these days. She's nibbling at her lower lip, her attention on the laptop in front of her.

Almost on autopilot, I walk toward her. Even when I'm angry at her, I can't resist the pull of that invisible string that's connecting us.

Whatever she's doing has her complete focus because Alyssa doesn't move a muscle as I enter the kitchen.

"I didn't realize you were home."

"Shit!" Aly jumps at the sound of my voice, her hand flying to cover her chest. "You scared me."

Zane looks from me to Aly, brows raised in a silent question, before going to the fridge and pulling out a bottle of water.

"We weren't really quiet when we came in." I glance toward her computer. "What were you looking at?"

Aly quickly closes her laptop. "Nothing important, just something for class." She looks down at her wrist. "I should probably take Coco out before I go to work."

Aly slides out of the chair and grabs her laptop.

"Everything's fine, huh?" Zane asks, leaning against the counter.

I glare at him. "Back off, Zane. I'm not in the mood."

Zane lifts his arms in the air. "Whatever you say, dude. Whatever you say."

Shaking my head, I turn around and follow after Aly. When I climb the stairs, I see her standing in the doorway.

She must hear me approach because she turns around to look at me, her hand covering her mouth. "You put it together."

I stop behind her and look at the crib. "Yeah, did you want to do it?"

"Are you serious? I'm not even sure I'd be able to do it with instructions."

"Those are usually useless anyway, so…"

Aly walks inside, her fingers tracing the railing. "It's so pretty." She grabs that stuffed bunny I got for Edie and looks at it for a moment before putting it back down and turning to me. "Thank you for putting it together for me."

"Anytime."

With another smile, she walks to the desk where she leaves the laptop and glances at the bed where Coco is sleeping. "C'mon, Coco. It's time for a walk."

The dog gets to her feet and shakes before jumping off.

Before Aly can hurry past me, something that she's gotten pretty good at the last few days, I step in her way.

"About this weekend…"

Aly looks up at me for a split second before her eyes dart

away. That smile that was on her lips only seconds ago is now gone. "What about it?"

Wrong. Wrong. Wrong.

This whole thing is wrong.

Look at me. I want to demand but can't bring myself to voice the words out loud. *Just look at me.*

"Do you still want to go with me? To the gala?"

Aly's head jerks upright, those blue eyes finally meeting mine. "Do you want me to go?"

"I invited you, didn't I?"

Her throat bobs as she swallows. "Okay."

"Okay?"

She nods.

We just stare at one another for what feels like forever. My hand itches to rise and tuck a strand of her hair behind her ear, cup her cheek, and press my mouth against hers.

Damn this distance. Damn the uncertainty. Damn the words that were spoken.

But before I can do it, Aly gives me a small smile and takes a step back. She walks around me, Coco on her heels, and I let her.

My eyes follow her as she leaves our bedroom, that knot in my stomach growing tighter by the second. It feels like everything is falling apart, and I don't know how to fix it.

Chapter 36

MADDOX

"Aly, are you…"

The words die on my lips when she turns around to face me. She shifts from one foot to the other. "Is this okay?"

She bites the inside of her cheek and smooths her hand over the skirt of her dress nervously.

The dark blue dress helps accentuate the blue of her irises. The material clings to one shoulder and hugs her every curve as it drapes down to the floor.

A wave of heat slams into me, my muscles tensing at the sight of her.

God, she looks stunning. So stunning, the only thing I can do is stare at her while every cell in my body screams one word over and over again. Mine.

I tug at my collar, hoping it'll help me breathe easier, but fat chance of that happening. "You look beautiful."

"You think?" Aly turns around so she can look at her reflection in the mirror. "I tried to find a dress that wouldn't be so revealing, but they made me look like a sack of potatoes."

"I highly doubt that," I chuckle at the mere idea. There's no way anything could ever make her look like a sack of potatoes.

"You weren't there." I move closer and place my hands on her shoulders, turning her to face me. "I swear shopping while pregnant is the worst thing ever. Nothing ever fits, and those things that do, make you feel like you're three times your usual size, probably because you are, and..."

I lean down and press my mouth against hers to stop her from nervously babbling. The movement is so instinctual I don't even realize what I'm doing until a jolt of electricity spreads through my body. The kiss is supposed to be soft, but one touch of my mouth against hers isn't nearly enough. It has never been, so I'm not sure why I'm even surprised.

Things have been so awkward between us lately, but holding her, kissing her, it's like everything in my world is aligning once again.

Right.

Being with Aly feels right. It always has.

With one last swipe of my mouth over hers, I pull back and whisper against her mouth: "You look stunning."

Aly lets out a shaky breath and presses her forehead against mine. "Sorry, I'm nervous."

I brush one of her curls behind her ear. "I can see that. Is there a particular reason for it or...?"

Aly pulls back. "I haven't been to one of these since Christmas, and we both know how that one turned out."

Her hand slides over her stomach.

"We can stay if you don't want to go." The last thing I want is to make her feel more anxious about the whole thing.

"And have your mom hate me even more because you didn't go support your dad because of me?" Aly shakes her head and starts to readjust my tie. "I think not."

"My mom doesn't hate you."

Aly quirks her brow. "She doesn't like me much either."

I open my mouth to protest, but Aly takes a step back and

looks at her handiwork. "You look handsome." She swipes her thumb over my lower lip. "Kind of like Clark Kent. Should I expect you to rip your shirt?"

"You'd be disappointed."

The corner of Aly's mouth rises in a smile. A first real one in what feels like days. "I don't know about that."

"You ready to go?"

"They're all staring," Aly whispers as she moves closer to me. I slide my hand to the small of her back, pulling her into my side.

She's not wrong about it either. The ballroom was packed when we finally got to the venue. Everybody who's somebody in the state, the country even, is here, mingling around and chatting, all in the name of the charity. Politicians, celebrities, you name it, they're here. And it seems all the heads are turning in our direction.

I nod at the mayor of Boston, who's chatting with a few other politicians as we pass him by.

"That's because you're gorgeous."

"Or maybe because I'm so obviously pregnant."

As if she can hear her words, an older woman from across the room looks at us, her eyes narrowing on Aly's stomach.

"I knew I should have gone with the potato sack."

"Just ignore them." I turn around, so I'm standing in front of Aly, shielding her from unwanted attention. "They don't have anything better to do than talk. That's why they're here after all."

"I guess so." But even as she says it, Aly's looking around, taking in her surroundings, her fingers clasping around her bag so tightly her knuckles have turned white.

She's nervous, I realize.

"Aly, if you want to..."

"Maddox," Mom interrupts me, stopping by our side. "You're late."

Aly gives me a small smile that does nothing to reassure me, before turning toward her. "Hey, Mrs. Anderson, that would be my fault. I had a hard time figuring out what to wear."

Mom slowly shifts her attention to Aly and gives her a once-over, her lips tightening. "And you settled on *that*?"

"Mom," I warn. "We're here now, isn't that what matters?"

"Couldn't she have worn something less revealing?"

Aly's whole body stiffens next to me at Mom's cruel words. I pull her closer to my side and wrap my arm around her, but there's no shielding her from my mom's hard stare and even harsher words. "Seriously?"

"Yes, Maddox, seriously." A smile is plastered on her face, but the lines around her mouth are tight. "Do you know how many times I have been asked on my way here when I'm going to be a grandmother, and why have I kept quiet about it?"

"I'm sorry, I..." Aly takes a step back, slipping out of my arms.

"Aly..."

She gives her head a little shake. "I have to go to the lady's room."

Before Aly gives me a chance to say anything, she's already walking away.

I pinch the bridge of my nose. "Fuck."

"Maddox!" Mom chastises. "Watch your language."

I slowly turn toward her. "Maybe if you listened to your own advice, nothing like this would have happened."

Mom tilts her chin upward. "I just told the truth. She should have been more mindful about the event. Her poor mother..."

"Her poor mother is why she's in this situation in the first place," I hiss softly. The last thing I want is to draw any more attention to us, but I'm not just going to let her walk away without saying anything. "I seriously expected more from you."

I shake my head and start to pull back.

I need to go and find Alyssa. Make sure she's all right.

Before I take a step, Mom's fingers wrap around my wrist, and she tugs me back. "Maddox, what are you…"

"I'm going to look for Alyssa. I told you before, and I'm telling you again, we're a package deal. If you don't want that, just say the word."

Mom's mouth falls open. "You don't mean that."

"I do."

Gently disentangling her fingers from my wrist, I turn on the balls of my feet and follow after Alyssa, but I barely get to take a few steps before I'm stopped by one of Dad's old colleagues.

"Maddox, it's good to see you."

"Mr. O'Neil," I force a smile out. "How are you doing?"

"I'm good, can't complain." The man smiles and slaps me on the back. "And no need for that mister bullshit, call me Rick. I didn't realize you were coming."

"My girlfriend and I just got here," I say absentmindedly, scanning the room for any sign of Aly, but she's nowhere to be seen. "The traffic was bad."

"Ain't it always." He shakes his head. I open my mouth to excuse myself, but he just keeps ongoing. "I keep saying that we need to do something about the crazy traffic in this city. Not like anybody's listening…"

Great, just what I needed.

ALYSSA

I turn on the cold water and wash my hands. Shaking the excess water off I place my cooled fingers on my neck, not that it helps take away the embarrassment.

Couldn't she have worn something less revealing?

A shiver runs down my spine, leaving an unsettling feeling behind. I swear I can still feel everybody's eyes on me. If I thought I'd been judged around campus, it has nothing on tonight. Nobody knows how to judge better than the people who pretend they're too high and mighty to notice these kinds of things in the first place.

This was such a bad idea.

I should have known better. I should have never come here and put Maddox in this situation. Never make him choose between standing by my side or his mother's.

Baby chooses that moment to kick me against my ribs.

I turn off the water and grab a few towels to dry my hands before pressing my palm against the spot and giving it a small rub.

"I know, baby. This definitely wasn't one of my smartest moves."

I glance at the door, but just the idea of going back out there and facing everybody has the bile rising up my throat. So, instead, I pick up the clutch from the counter and pull out my phone.

Me: This is a disaster.

I barely press send when the three little bubbles appear on the screen.

Callie: What?

Yasmin: Whose ass do we have to kick?

God bless my friends. I seriously don't know how I would have survived this year without them.

Me: Mine.

Turning my back to the mirrors, I lean against the counter and continue typing, or I would have if Edie didn't decide this was the perfect moment to practice kick-boxing.

"Seriously?" I look down at my stomach, where I can see her tiny hands and feet kick against it. "Can't you give me a break? Just for a few hours?" I ask, rubbing my belly with my free hand.

Callie: Why? What happened?

Me: I should have gone for the stupid potato sack dress.

Me: Now everybody knows that I'm pregnant, and of course, they think it's Maddox's.

Yasmin: So?

Yasmin: Since when do we care about what other people think?

Callie: I second that.

Me: Since Maddox's mom is giving him a hard time about it.

Yasmin: What does Maddox think?

Callie: That she's freaking beautiful.

Callie: And that's a direct quote. I heard it when I was passing by their room when they were getting ready.

Yasmin: See? Who cares what his mom thinks?

Me: Maddox.

Callie: Hard to believe. That boy loves you.

Yasmin: Where are you anyway?

Me: Bathroom.

Callie: Why?

**Me: I wasn't in the mood to stay there and listen

to her tell me how much trouble I put them in because of my "condition."

Yasmin: Screw her. You're freaking Alyssa Martinez, go out there with your head held high because you have nothing to be ashamed of and have fun.

I'm not sure if it's their words or because I've already been feeling emotional as it is, but my eyes burn with unshed tears. I close them, taking one deep breath through my nose and holding it in until the tears are at bay.

Me: Thanks, girls.

Callie: What are friends for?

Yasmin: Go dance, and kiss that boy of yours in the middle of the dance floor, so everybody knows who he belongs to.

Chuckling at Yasmin's words, I stash my phone back in my purse, and I turn around. My reflection stares back at me. The gorgeous woman in the mirror has nothing to do with the scared girl that's hiding inside my heart. When did that happen? How? I was never as insecure as I've been these last few weeks.

No more.

I'm going out there, finding Maddox, and we'll dance, and then I'll pull him out and demand to know what's been going on between us lately.

Lifting my chin higher, I give myself one final look before turning on my toes only to crash into somebody coming in. I grab her hand, trying to steady myself.

"I'm so so—" The words die on my lips when I see none other than my mother standing in front of me. "Mom."

"Alyssa." She takes a step back, and I let my hand fall to my side. She observes me, her gaze lingering on my stomach. "What are you doing here?"

No, how are you? Or, God forbid, are you doing okay? Not with my mother. But seriously, did I expect anything different?

"Maddox invited me." I shake my head and walk around her. "I should go back. He's waiting for me."

"And you had to come? Don't you think it's embarrassing for the Andersons to have to explain all of this?" She waves her hand in my direction.

Just then, the door opens again. This time it's Maddox's mother who's at the door. She glances from me to my mom and back.

Seriously, how is this happening to me?

"I don't know, Mom. But Mrs. Anderson is here, so I'm sure you can discuss how big of an embarrassment I am for both families. But don't expect me to stand here and listen to it."

"Alyssa..." Mrs. Anderson calls after me, but I don't bother turning around.

I had one person already tell me what a disappointment I am; I don't need to hear the same thing thrown in my face from my own mother, no less. I walk as fast as I can on my Jimmy Choo's, the only pair I couldn't bring myself to part with when I was selling off my life, only slowing down once I'm in the ballroom.

I walk around the people, scanning the space for Maddox. I'm just about to call it quits when I spot him near the bar, talking to two older guys. He shifts from one foot to the other, clearly wanting to be anywhere but here. At least here, I can help.

I make my way across the room. One of the men Maddox is talking to notices me first. I smile at him as I join in on the conversation.

"Hey, do you mind if I steal him for a moment?" I slide my arm through Maddox's and look up at him. His whole body relaxes, a look of relief passing over his face when he realizes it's me. "I think you owe me a dance." I shift my attention to his companions. "You won't mind, right?"

"Of course not," the guy with the mustache says. "You kids go and have fun."

The other guy slaps Maddox on the shoulder. "It was nice talking to you, Maddox. Say hi to your old man if I don't see him tonight."

Maddox nods and pushes his glasses up his nose. "Will do."

"Who were those two?" I ask softly as we make our way to the dance floor.

Maddox turns me around when we find a spot, and I wrap my arms around his neck, swaying softly to the music.

"Mayor of Boston and one of my dad's lawyer friends. They cornered me once I left Mom to go look for you."

I look away, embarrassed. "Sorry about that. I shouldn't have run away like that; it's just…" I shrug, not knowing how to finish that sentence without sounding like an overly sensitive princess.

"You have nothing to be sorry about," Maddox says, his voice clipped. "Mom is the one who should be sorry."

But, don't I?

If I weren't here, none of this would have happened. Maddox and his mother wouldn't be fighting, and Maddox wouldn't have been getting these weird looks behind his back for bringing a pregnant girl to an event that's important to his father.

I glance at him, only to find him looking over my shoulder. His eyes are hard; his jaw pressed tight.

"Maddox, I…"

He shakes his head. "Let's just dance, okay?"

His muscles feel tight under my fingers. He is angry; he just doesn't want to say it out loud so as not to hurt my feelings.

I bite the inside of my cheek and nod, letting him lead me over the dance floor.

Later.

Maddox's hands tighten around me as he pulls me closer. I stop resisting it and let my body relax against his strong one as we slowly sway to the quartet playing in the background.

We'll talk about this later because I don't think I can go on one more day wondering what's going on between us. If he finally realized he made a mistake and wants to leave, I'll let him go.

My stomach sinks, bile rising in my throat. I slide my hand over his shoulders, holding on just a little tighter.

But for now, I'll let myself enjoy being in his arms because it might be the last time.

MADDOX

She fits in my arms like she was made for me. I've always known that, and the thought only cemented itself in my brain since we started dating.

Why can't you see it, Aly?

Why can't you see you belong with me?

The need to put my hands on her shoulder and shake some sense into her is overwhelming. But I can't do it. Not here, not now, not like this. So I hold her instead, tightening my grip around her and hoping that it might be enough.

As I lead her over the dance floor, I can see the curious eyes on us. Some are familiar, but most of them I'm not even sure I've met.

I've seen both my parents working the room, and I caught a glimpse of Aly's mom when she slipped back into the ballroom, her gaze falling on her daughter instantly. I pull Aly closer to me, knowing I can't protect her from their judgment, but still willing to do anything to simply try.

Regardless of what she might say, regardless of the fact that this baby isn't mine, I'll do anything in my power to protect the two of them. Because that's what you do for the people you love; you protect them with all you have until there's nothing else left of you to give.

The song slowly dies down, and we come to a stop. Reluctantly, I loosen my hold on Aly, and she takes a step back.

She looks around as if she's waking up from a dream. "Can we get out of here for a bit?"

"Sure."

She nods and turns around.

My fingers clench at my side as I watch her walk away. Giving my head a shake, I follow after her. The fresh night air hits me in the face, making me realize how stuffy the ballroom is. The door shuts softly behind us, dulling the noises from the party inside.

Aly walks to the railing, leaning against it, and looks at the backyard.

Standing here feels like déjà vu. It's the same hotel we were in for the Christmas gala, not even six months ago. How can life change so drastically in such a short period of time and yet, feel like we've made a full circle? Because that's exactly what I feel. Like we're back at the beginning, the distance between us bigger than ever.

"Are you angry with me?"

Aly's soft question snaps me out of my thoughts.

"What?" I look up just in time to see Aly turn around to face me. I furrow my brow. "Why would you ask that? Is this because of what my mother said about the dress?"

"No. Yes." Her gaze darts toward the ballroom behind me. "In a way." She lets out a long sigh. "You've been acting strange these past few weeks."

"I've not been acting strange," the protest comes out quickly.

Too quickly. And she knows it too.

"Seriously?" Aly curls her finger around the railing. "You've been distant ever since your mother came to your house. You barely talk to me. You always keep to yourself. You didn't want to go to my doctor's appointment. Not just that, you *lied* to me. You said you had that thing with your professor when you were actually home the whole time, so excuse me if it seems to me that you're angry with me. If you've changed your mind..."

"You still don't get it, do you?" I chuckle, rubbing my hand over my face.

If you've changed your mind...

All this time and she still doesn't see it.

Aly blinks, clearly confused. "Get what?"

"Fuck yeah, I'm angry," I yell, unable to hold it in any longer.

"W-what?" Aly staggers back, thrown off guard by my outburst. But I don't have it in me to care. It's like the dam broke, and all the feelings, all the frustration I've been pushing back is coming out in the open.

"I'm angry that even after all this time, you don't know me." I shake my head. "Even after everything I've told you, you don't believe my words, but assume what you want to assume."

"What are you talking about? The girls saw you were home when you clearly told me you had other obligations! And it's fine. You don't have to lie, Maddox. I get it; you didn't sign up for this. It's..."

"*The baby isn't Maddox's,*" I throw her words back at her. Aly jerks back as if I slapped her, but I don't have it in me to feel bad about it because I'm pissed. "Didn't you say it?"

"Yeah, but..."

"But what, Aly? But what?"

Aly wraps her arms around herself protectively. "What do you mean?"

"What do I mean?" I chuckle and run my hand through my hair. "What do I mean? What do *you* mean?" I point my finger at her. "Because I've been there, Aly. Since the day you found out you were pregnant. I held you when you cried because you didn't know what to do. I offered you a place to stay when you had nowhere to go. I went with you to the doctor's appointments. I've listened to the baby's heartbeat. I was there when you found out you're having a girl. I bought her her first stuffed animal. I helped you choose her crib. I felt her kick against my hands. I love her. I love her as much as I love you. So don't you tell me she doesn't belong to me as much as she does to you. Don't you dare tell me that."

By the time everything is out in the open, my breathing is ragged, my heart beating a mile a minute as the words echo in my eardrums from the shouting.

Aly covers her mouth, but it doesn't stop the sob from coming out. "Maddox, I..."

I take a step back and blink, pushing away the blurriness clouding my eyes.

Those familiar blue irises are wide and red-rimmed, looking at me with the anguish that matches the one inside my heart.

I want to take her into my arms. Pull her to my chest and wrap my arms around her. Tell her everything will be alright.

But I can't.

I can't have her touch me. Not now. Because if she does, it'll be game over for me. My resolve will crumble, and I'll give her everything she wants, be everything she needs just so I can keep her regardless of the consequences to my heart.

So instead, I shake my head and take a step back. "I need some space."

With that, I turn my back to the only woman I've ever loved and do what's best for me.

Leave.

Chapter 37

ALYSSA

Shit. Shit. Shit.

My hand falls down by my side as I watch Maddox walk away from me. I should probably go after him, beg him to stop and listen, but I can't seem to get my legs to move.

So don't you tell me she doesn't belong to me as much as she does to you. Don't you dare tell me that.

What the hell have I done?

Maddox is the best thing that has ever happened to me. How could I be so blind? How could I hurt somebody I love so much without even realizing it?

I close my eyes, letting the hot tears fall down my cheeks.

A sharp pain pierces my mid-section, knocking the air out of my lungs and leaving me breathless. I suck in a breath, pressing my palm against my belly. My feet feel heavy, unsteady, and I sway back as the pain grows more intense. I grab onto the railing to hold myself up.

What the...

"You had to be here, didn't you?"

Fighting through the pain, I look up and find Chad

watching me from the doorway. When did he get here? And why is he here?

"Chad," I breathe, cold sweat washing over me. "I really don't..."

But, of course, he doesn't listen. Now that I think about it, he rarely ever did.

"My parents are here." His fingers clench into fists. "Their friends. Do you know how embarrassing it is for me to have to explain to everybody how my girlfriend..."

"*Ex*," I grit through clenched teeth. "Ex-girlfriend."

He continues like I didn't say a word. "Is walking around on another man's arm while she's clearly pregnant?"

"I don't see how that has anything to do with me. I already told you I..."

A sharp pain in my belly makes me double over. I press my hand against my abdomen as I try to suck in a breath.

Something is wrong.

So, so wrong.

"What are you..." A shadow falls over me.

I look up, my world tilting on its axis. I blink, trying to bring Chad's face into focus, but it's blurry.

"Alyssa?"

Chad tries to reach for me. Gritting my teeth as I fight through nausea and pain, I lift my hand to push him away, far, far away from me, but I feel weak. So damn weak. Chad's fingers wrap around my wrist, stopping me from touching him.

"B-blood?"

The pounding in my ears turns harder, and it takes me a moment to register what he said.

Blood?

"W-what...?" I look down at my hand. I blink once, twice, trying to understand what I'm seeing, but the image doesn't go away. My hands are trembling, or maybe *I'm* the one trembling, a dark smear spreading over the blue dress almost imperceptible if it weren't for the red coating my forearms, my finger.

My heart speeds up as I curl my fingers around the railing, trying to hold myself up when my whole body sways with the motion. Sweat coats my skin as I stare and stare at the smear of red on my palm.

"N-no."

My vision turns blurry.

No. No. No.

I press my hand against my stomach.

This can't be happening.

Maybe if I can hold her tightly enough, everything will be okay.

It can't...

Maybe...

Not her. God, anybody but her.

My legs feel wobbly; I try to grip tighter, to hold on, but I'm too weak.

Too freaking weak...

Maddox...

"Alyssa?"

MADDOX

"Where is Alyssa?"

At the sound of my mother's voice, my fingers tighten around the glass of scotch in my hand, making the amber liquid swirl around the crystal glass. "If you're here to complain about the way she's dressed..."

"I came here to apologize." She takes the stool next to mine. "Are you drinking?"

"I'm thinking about it."

Maybe that'll help me dull the roaring in my ears. God knows that moving away from Aly didn't do shit. I could still see the confused look on her face, hear the hurt in her voice as she called after me, and I walked away from her.

Dammit, she's the one in the wrong, not me.

Yes, I might have lied, but the only reason I did it was because she's afraid to admit her feelings; the one afraid to let me in and be there for her.

But did you really have to yell at her like that?

"What's wrong with you?" Mom pulls the glass out of my hand, and I don't even bother protesting. "You shouldn't be drinking. Not only are you underage, but you're also driving home later tonight. Do you want to get in an accident?"

"No, you're right." I pull my glasses off and rub my hand over my face. What had I been thinking?

"Did something happen? The last I saw you, you were dancing with Aly, but then you were gone."

"We went out to talk."

My gaze darts to the windows. Is Aly still somewhere out there? Is she crying?

"Did you guys have a fight?"

"I..." I run my fingers through my hair before sliding my glasses on. "We had a disagreement, that's all."

"I hope it's not because of what I said."

"No, it's not because of you. It's because..." I shake my head, not wanting to talk about it with my mother. "It doesn't even matter." I push the chair back and stand up.

Mom places her hand on my forearm, stopping me from leaving. "Maddox, don't be too hard on her."

I raise my brows. "And that comes from you of all people?"

"I told you, I came here to apologize. I was watching you two earlier, and I was wrong. Alyssa is vulnerable right now.

Being pregnant can be the most exciting but also the scariest time of your life. Give her some time."

If time was our only enemy.

"I just want her to let me in."

"She did." Mom smiles softly, a real smile this time. She reaches up, and runs her fingers through my hair, putting the unruly strands back in place. "But that doesn't mean the fear will just magically go away."

I swallow, forcing the lump in my throat down. "I should probably go check in on her."

"I'll walk with you." She slides off the chair and hooks her arm through mine.

I look down at her. "What made you change your mind?"

Something flashes over Mom's face, but she schools her features quickly. "I overheard a conversation I wasn't supposed to hear."

My whole being freezes for a moment. "What conversation?"

Her arm tightens around mine as she continues as if I didn't say anything. "But I also saw the way she looks at you. When you were dancing." She tilts her head back. "I was wrong. She does love you. She might not have said it, but it's there, written all over her face."

Mom gives me a little squeeze on the hand before pulling away. I look through the window, that lump firmly in my throat, making it hard to breathe.

I need to go back to her. I need to...

I blink, my eyes narrowing on the two figures standing on the balcony. The one is crouching...

"Aly?" I push open the door. "Aly!"

"Maddox?"

Ignoring Mom's worried voice, I run outside to Aly. Her

unmoving body is lying on the ground, Chad crouching over her.

I look from him to Aly's bloodless face. Too pale, she's way too pale.

"What the hell did you do?" I push him back as I fall to my knees next to her.

"She just fell!" Chad protests. "I caught her before she hit the floor."

Boiling rage simmers inside me, fighting with the ever-growing fear.

"No, no, no." I push her hair back, but her eyes are closed. This can't be happening. "Aly, c'mon, baby, open your eyes."

I hold her cheek, my hands roaming over her body as I try to assess what happened.

"How the hell did she fall?"

"I don't know, dude! We were talking, and then she just... fell."

This can't be happening. It can't—

"Maddox, what's... Oh my God."

I look over my shoulder to find Mom standing, her mouth open as she stares at us. "She was fine. Five minutes ago, she was fine, and now..."

The words die on my lips as my fingers touch something warm and sticky.

One second my heart is hammering in my ribcage; the next, it feels like everything is moving in slow motion. I look down at my hand, my eyes going wide as I slowly turn it around and gape at my fingers.

Blood.

My gaze falls to Aly.

The blood soaked through her dress, but since it was dark, you could barely notice it.

I shake my head. "No, no, no."

Mom's fingers dig into my shoulder. "I'm calling the ambulance."

I nod, pulling Alyssa into my lap and pressing my hand gently against her stomach, hoping to feel... something. Anything. But there's nothing.

A fear like I've never known spreads through my body, paralyzing me.

This can't be happening. I bury my face into the crook of Aly's neck. *It's not real. She was fine. They were both fine just moments ago.*

"Aly, wake up, please." I tighten my arms around her. If only I didn't leave. If only I hadn't yelled and left her all alone, none of this would have happened. But I did, and now it's too late. "I'm so sorry. Please, just come back to me."

Chapter 38

ALYSSA

I'm so sorry. Please, just come back to me.

I'm not sure if it's the words or the soft pleading in that voice I love so much that brings me back to full awareness. Or maybe it's the sudden warmth surrounding me like a blanket in the middle of the icy storm. Whatever it is, I hold onto it tightly as I cling to the here and now.

"M-Maddox?" I rasp, trying to pry my eyes open.

What's wrong with him? Why does he sound so sad? What happe—

"Aly?" Maddox pulls back, taking away his warmth. I want to protest, tell him to come back and hold me tighter, but my tongue feels heavy in my mouth.

"Aly, you're awake. Thank God..."

I blink, trying to focus on his face, beautiful even with the worry lines marring his forehead. Maddox's mom, of all people, appears over his shoulder, her equally worried eyes watching me carefully. "The ambulance is on its way. They should be here in a few minutes."

"Ambulance?" I try to push up, but pain spreads through

my whole body, chaining me to the ground. If I weren't lying down, I'd probably fall. "What..."

Then everything comes rushing back.

The fight.

Maddox walking away.

Pain.

So much pain.

And blood.

Maddox cradles my face in his hands as if he can sense my panic. "It's going to be okay. You heard Mom. The ambulance will be here any minute now, and they'll take care of you."

"N-no..." I shake my head, tears falling down my cheeks.

"I'm so sorry, Aly." Maddox presses his forehead against mine, tears filling his eyes. "I'm so damn sorry. I should have never..."

"It's not your fault."

It's mine.

I did this. I did this with my carelessness. If anything happens to my baby, it's going to be nobody's fault but mine. I should have taken better care of her. I should have...

"She's here."

Paramedics come rushing up the stairs and crouch down next to me. That familiar warmth disappears as they push Maddox away from me. I want to protest, but they surround me from both sides.

"What's your name?" the female asks as she starts looking over me.

I blink, trying to focus my vision, but it's all blurry.

"A-Alyssa," I wheeze, fighting for breath. The woman gives me an encouraging smile that I don't feel. I grab her hand. "Please... s-save... b-baby."

"I'll try my best, Alyssa. Now, do you remember what happened here?"

"We were talking, and she just fell."

I look around at the sound of Chad's voice to find him standing on the side, watching me with wide eyes. "I caught her before she fell." His swallows audibly. "Will she... will she lose the kid?"

The need to scream at him is overwhelming, but the best I can come up with is coughing in protest.

"Fuck you." Before anybody can see it happening or try to stop it, Maddox is on his feet, his clenched fist connecting with Chad's face.

Somebody screams, I'm not sure who, as Chad's head snaps to the side, his hand covering his bleeding nose.

"She's not losing the baby. Now get the hell out of here because you have nothing," Maddox jabs his finger into Chad's chest. "*Nothing*, you hear me, to do here. You gave that right away when you turned your back on Aly months ago."

"Maddox!" Mrs. Anderson chastises, gripping Maddox's forearms and pulling him back. "This is not helping."

Chad spits on the floor, rubbing his bloody nose with the back of his hand. "Fuck you. You're all crazy."

His eyes meet mine for a split second before he walks away without uttering another word.

"Her blood pressure is elevated," one of the paramedics says, snapping velcro from my arm.

The female nods, her serious eyes meeting mine. "How far along are you?"

"I..." I suck in a breath, trying to force the words out. "Thi—"

"She's thirty-two weeks pregnant," Maddox chimes in, crouching down above me. Gently, so freaking gently, he pushes my hair back. "I'm so sorry, Aly. It's going to be fine. She's going to be fine."

"Does it hurt anywhere, Alyssa?" the paramedic asks.

I nod. Sinking my teeth into my lower lip to stop it from wobbling, I press my hand to the right side of my stomach.

"You most likely have a condition called eclampsia. Do you know what that is?"

My eyes fall shut, and I nod once again.

"We have to take you into the hospital now."

Before I can say anything, the paramedics have me lying on a stretcher and ushering me toward the ambulance.

For a moment, I lose sight of Maddox. I look over my shoulder, trying to find him. I need him. I need him to be with me because I don't think I can do this by myself. But he's not there. My vision is too blurry, and my entire body hurts so much I can't concentrate.

My eyes burn from the unshed tears as a wave of fear crashes into me.

I can't do this by myself. I can't...

"I'm here." Maddox grabs my hand as he climbs into the ambulance with me. "I've got you."

The door to the ambulance closes with a loud *bang,* and before the echo is over, the wailing of the sirens fills the night.

"M-Maddox," my voice trembles as the panic spreads through me, my finger gripping his as tightly as I can.

"Shh... it's going to be okay."

But it's not.

I'd read about it after Doctor Jeremy told me the possibility of getting preeclampsia. I've heard all the horror stories. Sometimes things do turn out okay, but sometimes...

My throat bobs as I swallow. "You have to pick her," the words come out in a rush as the panic gets the better of me. This is not how it was supposed to go. "Promise me. Promise me that no matter what happens, you'll choose her."

"Aly..." Maddox shakes his head, his tear-filled eyes meeting mine. He's trying to hold it together, for me, but he's losing the battle.

I grip his wrist tighter, my nails digging into his skin. "Promise me, Maddox."

Another shake of his head. "I can't."

"You *have* to." I put our joined hands over my stomach just as another stab of pain spreads through me.

It's too soon.

Too soon.

Too soon.

"S-she comes first." I look up at Maddox. His face is blurry, but knowing he's here is enough. If the worst happens, he'll be there. Edie won't be alone because he'll be there, for better or for worse. "A-always. Promise me, Maddox. Whatever happens, you'll choose her."

Maddox presses his forehead against mine. "Aly, I..."

"One minute out." One of the medics' yells.

"Promise me." I blink, one lone tear falling down my cheek. "Promise me you'll choose her."

Finally, he nods. "I promise. God help me, but I promise."

A tear starts to roll down his cheek, but I brush it away and press my mouth against his. The kiss is hard, all-consuming. I try to put all my fear, frustration, and love into it. Hoping it'll be enough. But it's short. Way too short. Just like the time we had together.

"I love you, Maddox."

"Don't say it like that." He cups my cheek, holding me close. "Don't say it like it's a goodbye."

But it might be.

Want to admit it or not, it might be, and I'm not risking leaving this earth without Maddox knowing how much he means to me.

The door to the ambulance bursts open, breaking us out of

the bubble we've been wrapped in and pulling us out into the frenzy.

Somebody pushes Maddox away from me, pulling the stretcher I'm on out of the ambulance.

"Aly!"

I try to look over my shoulder, try to catch one last glimpse of the man who's been my best friend, my lover, my daughter's father in all the ways that matter, and pray that it's not the last time.

Chapter 39

MADDOX

You most likely have a condition called eclampsia.

My feet pound against the floor in tune with my racing heart as I rush after the paramedics.

We have to take you into the hospital now.

The door to the ER slides open, and I rush inside. It's like I've stepped into another world. Most of the seats are filled, and the place is buzzing with activity: TV is on, people shouting, a baby is crying.

Ignoring it all, I go straight for the nurse's station.

"I'm here with Alyssa Martinez," I pant, leaning my hands against the counter as I try to catch my breath. "They just brought her in. Can you tell me what's going on?"

You most likely have a condition called eclampsia.

God, let her be all right.

She has to be fine.

They both do.

The nurse slowly finishes typing before she finally lifts her gaze from the computer and meets mine. "Are you family?"

I grit my teeth. How can she be so calm about the whole

situation? They just rushed Alyssa into the hospital covered in blood, and she's just a little over thirty-two weeks pregnant.

Too soon.

It's way too soon.

Panic makes my throat tighten. Helpless. I'm completely and utterly helpless. My fingers curl around the counter harder, knuckles turning white.

"I'm her boyfriend."

Pity flashes on her face. "I'm sorry, but that's not..."

"I'm the only family she has," I rush out before she can finish. "I'm..." I gulp the lump in my throat. "I'm the father of her baby."

The words slip off my tongue easily. I meant what I told Alyssa earlier. Her baby might not be mine biologically, but I've loved that baby since the very first moment I found out about her existence. From the first time, I saw that flutter of gray on the screen. From the first moment, I heard her heartbeat. From the first time, I felt her kick. I love her in all the ways a father can love his daughter. But really, is it even surprising? She's Aly's, so nothing else was ever an option, not really.

My eyes burn with unshed tears.

If something happens to either of them...

I shake my head, pushing those thoughts firmly away.

Nothing will happen. They're going to be okay. They have to.

Fight, Aly. Fight.

Blinking the nurse into focus, I fix my gaze on her. "Please. The love of my life and my daughter are somewhere behind that door, and I need to know they're all right. She's only thirty-two weeks pregnant, and she was bleeding when they picked her up. Just... *please*."

The nurse observes me quietly, a serious expression on her

face. She's probably seen it all by now, so nothing fazes her anymore, but I have to at least try to get her on my side.

My Adam's apple bobs as I swallow, my nerves getting the better of me.

Why didn't I lie? Why didn't I tell her Alyssa is my wife? Then she'd have to let me inside. She'd *have* to...

"He's there. Maddox!"

I turn around and find my parents rushing inside. "What's going on? Where's Alyssa?"

"I don't know," I shake my head. "They won't tell..."

Mom turns toward the nurse. "Now listen to me, my son needs to know what's going on with his girlfriend and their baby, so you better..."

"I'm sorry, ma'am, but there's a hospital policy, and I need to follow it."

"I don't care about the hospital policy!" I yell, losing the little patience I had left. I turn my attention back to the nurse. "The life of the woman I love and our baby is on the line. I need to know how she's doing." Mom wraps her arm around me as my voice breaks. "Please? I need to know they're okay."

I'll beg. I'll do whatever I have to just as long as I find out what's going on with them. My girls. My heart. That's what they are; my heart. And if something were to happen to either of them...

The nurse must see something on my face because she lets out a long sigh. "I'll see what I can find out."

"Thank you," I breathe out, my eyes falling shut as the relief slams into me.

The nurse starts typing once again, her grim gaze fixed on the screen. "She's in the OR. The doctors are currently working on her."

"OR?"

She can't mean...

"Operation room." Her brows pull closer. "You said she was bleeding?"

"Yes, the paramedic mentioned eclampsia, but I'm not sure what it is."

The nurse's face softens a little bit. "Eclampsia is a pregnancy complication. It's usually characterized by high blood pressure and protein in the urine, which can result in damage to the liver and kidneys."

"How serious is it?" Mom asks, her hands tightening around me.

"Quite serious. The only cure for preeclampsia is delivery, so the doctors will most likely have to do an emergency c-section."

C-section?

"No, they can't." I shake my head. "It's too soon."

Aly wasn't supposed to give birth until summer.

"I understand that this is scary, but performing an emergency c-section is the safest choice for both mom and the baby. Now please sit down in the waiting room. Somebody will come and tell you if there's any news."

"But..." I try to protest, but Mom tightens her arm around me. "C'mon, Maddox. Let's sit down."

I don't bother pointing out that I don't want to sit down. I just want to be with Aly and make sure that she is alright.

Still, I let my parents pull me away, my mind still on what little information I got. She's in the operation room. All alone. Going through a c-section.

"What if..." I croak out, my voice coming out rough.

"Don't." Mom stops me before I can even finish. She slips her finger under my chin and forces me to look at her. "Don't think like that. She's going to be okay. They're *both* going to be okay."

"Your mother is right," Dad adds, as Mom pulls me down

into a plastic chair. "Alyssa is young and strong. She can make it."

But what if they're not going to be okay? What if it has nothing to do with her strength? What if it's all too much, and they don't make it?

I look down at my clasped hands. They're covered in dried blood. Some Aly's and some probably of that jackass of her ex.

My eyes fall shut, and the image of Aly lying down on the floor flashes in my mind. I want to push it back but can't because that's the only thing I have left.

There was blood. So much blood. Too much.

"Maddox!"

My head snaps up at the sound of Yasmin's voice. It takes me a moment to realize it's not all in my head, but that my friends are actually here.

"How?"

Mom gives my hand a squeeze. "Aly's bag was left on the ground. I heard the phone ring and answered, so I told them about Aly."

"What happened?" Yasmin asks as she comes to a stop in front of me, Callie and Hayden hot on her heels.

"How are they?" Callie pants. She grabs my forearm, her fingers digging into my skin as she starts throwing question after question at me. "Is everything okay? Is the baby..."

Hayden stops behind Callie, placing his hand over her shoulder. "Breathe, Angel, and let him speak."

Seeing them like that makes the bile rise in my stomach. Jealous. I'm jealous of my best friends because they have each other...

She's going to be okay. She's not gone yet.

"They t-think..." I stop and clear my throat. "They think it's eclampsia."

"E-what?" Nixon asks joining us too.

"Eclampsia. The nurse couldn't tell me much since they had just brought her in, but the paramedic was certain it was eclampsia. Her blood pressure was high, and she was bleeding..."

Yasmin swears softly in Spanish.

I look up at my friends. "Did she tell any one of you that she's not feeling well? That something might be off?"

Callie shakes her head. "Not to us. Do you think she knew something was off and didn't want to tell us?"

You've been distant ever since your mother came to your house. You barely talk to me. You always keep to yourself. You didn't want to go to my doctor's appointment... If you've changed your mind...

Is that it? Did she know something was wrong? Did the doctor tell her something at her last appointment, and she didn't want to tell me—tell anybody?—because she thought I'd changed my mind about her? About us?

Yasmin leans her head against Callie's shoulder. "She did seem off. Distant maybe? I figured she was busy with studying and stuff. I never... Dammit, Aly."

"Maybe if we pushed harder..."

I shake my head. "It's not your fault. It's mine."

I should have been there with her at that appointment, but I was too stubborn, too prideful to go with her. I should have taken better care of her.

"If something happens to either of them..."

I'll never be able to forgive myself.

Hands fall on my shoulders, snapping me out of my mind.

"Look at me, Maddox." When I don't do it quickly enough, Hayden gives me a firm shake. "Look at me."

Gulping down the lump in my throat, I force myself to lift my gaze and meet the cold green eyes of one of my best friends.

"Aly is going to be alright. She's going to fight like hell to make it through. She has too much to lose otherwise."

"S-she..." The word comes out as a low stutter. I clear my throat and try again. "She knew about the preeclampsia. She knew, and she told me to take care of her. She told me if it comes to it, I have to choose the baby." I see the look my friends exchange, and I don't miss the worry in their eyes. The pit in my stomach grows more prominent, my fingers clenching into fists. "She made me p-promise. She made me promise I'd choose the baby. How am I..." I shake my head, unable to finish the sentence. Unable to say it out loud.

I just can't.

If I do, if I voice the words out loud, there'll be no taking them back.

Callie sits in the chair next to mine and presses her hand against my shoulder, rubbing my back. "Don't think about it. There's time. I'm sure the doctors will do everything they can to help them both."

I know she's right. I know there's no sense in thinking about what-ifs. But it's stronger than me because this isn't just anybody we're talking about here. It's Aly.

"She's going to fight. I know she will, Maddox. She loves you and that baby too much to simply give up."

I nod, unable to form words. Unable to push my dark thoughts away. Because, what if it's not up to her at all?

Chapter 40

MADDOX

Nobody tells you how differently time passes when you're in the emergency room waiting to hear news about the people you love.

It's like everything is moving in slow motion, and you're watching from the outside, waiting for the other shoe to drop.

And through the stillness, people continue coming and going. Regular folks like us are either waiting for their turn to be examined or waiting on news about their loved ones. The doctors and nurses are moving in a frenzy, trying to do the job the best they can in the cacophony that's the waiting room.

Every time the door to the back room opens, my heart tightly squeezes as I look up, dread and anticipation battling inside me. I want answers, but at the same time, I'm not sure I'm ready to hear them either.

At some point, more of our friends joined us. Somebody must have called them, although I'm not sure who. Zane, Rei, and Jade come first, followed by Spencer, Prescott, Grace and Mason, Emmett and Kate.

They're softly talking around me, adding to the background

noise surrounding me while all of my attention is fixed on that damn double-door.

Are they okay? Why is nobody saying anything? Are they alive? What is happening in there? What...

"Alyssa Martinez's family?"

I blink, my eyes focusing on an older doctor as he enters the waiting room. I stand up abruptly, almost losing my balance, but someone places their hand on my shoulder, steadying me.

"That's me!" I say quickly, hurrying toward the doctor. "Where is she? Are they okay? Is..."

The doctor looks at me and then behind my shoulder, making me realize my parents and friends have followed after me.

You're not alone in this.

Somebody's hand lands on my shoulder, giving it a firm squeeze, and Callie ducks under my arm, wrapping her arm around my middle.

"W-we're her family. Is she..." *Alive?* I want to ask but can't say the word out loud. "Is she okay?"

The doctor looks over the group, his eyes settling on me. "You're the father?"

I nod, my throat bobbing as I swallow. Not that it helps. The knot that's been growing in my throat ever since I saw Aly is stuck there, unmoving.

"Miss Martinez had come in with eclampsia. It's the onset of seizures in a woman with preeclampsia."

"Preeclampsia?"

"It's a pregnancy complication with a multisystem progressive disorder characterized by the new onset of hypertension and proteinuria."

"What does that even mean?" Yasmin asks.

"That means that she came in with extremely high blood pressure and failing kidneys, which resulted in a partial placental abruption. She was losing a lot of blood, so we had to perform an emergency cesarean in hopes of saving both mother and the baby."

In hopes...

Those two words echo in my mind repeatedly, growing louder and louder as my vision turns blurry, legs weak.

That means...

The doctor's eyes meet mine. "We've managed to save them both."

As one, the group lets out a loud sigh of relief. My knees buckle underneath me, and it's only thanks to my friends that I keep standing upright.

"They're still in danger, and the next twenty-four hours will be critical. The baby was born prematurely as you already know, but so far, she's doing okay. Out of precaution, we've put her in the NICU. Miss Martinez has lost a lot of blood, so we had to do a transfusion, and she's currently transferring to the ICU so that we can monitor her closely for the next few days."

She's alive.

Aly is alive.

She lost some blood, but she's still alive. She'll get through this. She has to; nothing else is an option.

She's alive.

That's the only thing that matters.

She's alive, and she's breathing.

"Didn't you say the next twenty-four hours?" Yasmin asks.

"The first twenty-four hours are always the most important. Normally, preeclampsia goes away after birth. That being said, it's an unpredictable condition, and it can come back in the post-partum stage of the pregnancy. Closely having her monitored will help us if it comes to that."

It can come back again?

My blood turns cold at the mere idea of it. Of going through something like this all over again and possibly losing Aly...

"Miss Martinez and her baby were very fortunate to be found when they were and brought to the hospital on time."

"When can I see them?" I somehow manage to croak the words out.

"Miss Martinez should be settled in her room soon, then you can see her." Once again, his attention drifts over my shoulder. "Since she's in ICU, she can only have two people at a time for no longer than ten minutes. But if you want, the nurse can take you to see the baby."

"I..."

My mouth hangs open as my need to see Aly battles with honoring the promise I'd made her.

Promise me, Aly's earlier words ring in my mind. The desperation in her voice as she asked the impossible of me. *Promise me you'll choose her.*

As if she can sense my hesitation, Callie turns around to face me. "Go to her, Maddox. Go see your baby, and we'll go to Aly as soon as they let us and stay until you come back."

"I..." *Promise me.* I close my eyes and nod. "T-thanks."

Nixon slaps me over the shoulder, his other arm wrapped around Yasmin. "We've got your back, man. Go."

Just then, a young nurse comes toward me. Her hair is braided, and with a face free of makeup, she looks too young to be working this job. Still, she gives me an encouraging smile. "C'mon, let me take you to see your baby."

My baby.

I follow on autopilot, walking down different hallways, and passing by people, barely registering what's happening around me until we come to a new set of doors.

"We need to scrub up before entering inside since these little ones are extremely sensitive."

The nurse goes to the sink, and I watch her as she pushes her sleeves up her arms and grabs the soap. She scrubs all the way to her elbows, making sure every inch of skin is completely covered in the soap before rinsing and drying her hands with a towel and then adding more disinfectant on her hands for good measure.

When she takes a step back, I move to the sink. The smell of disinfectant is even more powerful up close. Pushing my sleeves up, I repeat her movements. Slowly and thoroughly, I rub my skin until it itches before rinsing.

With a nod of approval from the nurse, I dry off, and then we enter the NICU.

As soon as we pass the threshold, the consistent *beep-beep-beep* of the monitors greets us. My heart starts to race, and I can hear the echo of my heartbeat in my ears as I slowly follow the nurse to the incubator.

I suck in a breath as I come to a stop a few feet away.

There are four incubators in a row, but I know which one is Edie as soon as I lay my eyes on her.

It's like I've been hit with a sledgehammer to the gut. There's no other way to describe it. I let out a loud breath, my chest squeezing tightly as I just stared at her.

She's so tiny.

Too tiny.

Her skin is pinkish and all wrinkled. They put a diaper on her and a knitted hat with a big pink bow on top. Different wires and tubes connect to her small body.

I step closer, my fingers touching the glass of the incubator. "She's so tiny."

"She is, but she's been holding on pretty well, all things considered." The nurse checks a few monitors, writing down something on the chart before she turns to me. "Would you like to hold her?"

"W-what?" She can't be serious, can she? She's too fragile, too vulnerable. I swear, she could fit in my palms and be completely cozy. "But, the wires... I don't..."

"It's going to be okay." The nurse places her hand on my arm and gives me an encouraging smile. "Skin-to-skin care is actually encouraged as soon as possible if the baby is born after thirty weeks."

I look skeptically toward the incubator and the small bundle lying inside. There is no way I can do this; I don't know how, and she's so teeny it's...

"It's safe, I promise. And she'll benefit more from your touch than most of these things."

"I..." I gulp down. "Okay. If you're sure."

"Great." The smile she flashes me is so bright it's almost blinding. "Take your shirt off..."

I blink, unsure if I heard her correctly. "What?!"

At this, she genuinely laughs. "You need to take your shirt off. It's called kangaroo care for a reason. Babies can't keep their body temperature steady; that's why we put them in incubators and encourage parents to do skin-to-skin care to help regulate their body temperature."

"Oh." I guess that does make sense. "Okay."

I remove my glasses and pull my shirt over my head, letting it drop on the chair in the corner before putting my glasses back in place.

"Now relax in that recliner."

The leather creaks as I sit down. It feels cold to my touch, making me shiver. I bite the inside of my cheek, forcing myself to stay still. The nurse coos softly as she gently wraps her arms around the baby and lifts her out of the incubator, mindful, so she doesn't disrupt any of the wires. I watch her like a hawk, my heart in my throat as she crosses the few steps between the incubator and the recliner and slowly, oh-so-slowly, places the baby on my chest.

I suck in a breath as her skin touches mine, and my hands go instinctively to wrap around her so she doesn't move or fall.

"That's it," the nurse encourages softly, checking that all the wires are still in place. "You're doing great. Make sure to hold her head and butt, so she doesn't move."

Once I do as she asked, the nurse pulls back and grabs one large blanket that she puts over the two of us, gently tucking us in.

"Just like that, all snuggled in." With one final pat, she pulls away. "You feeling good?"

I look down at my chest, at that little bundle that's holding onto me like I'm her lifeline.

"Yeah." I slowly let out the breath that I'd been holding. My body is still tense, and I don't know what the hell I'm doing, but just the fact that she's in my arms is enough. "Yeah, I feel good."

At the sound of my voice, her fair eyelashes start to flutter. Taking her time, she blinks her eyes open, and a pair of dark blue eyes fix on me.

If I thought I was losing it before, it has nothing, absolutely nothing, at this very moment. Because as soon as she looks at me with those big blues, I'm a goner.

Anything she wants. Anything she needs. Anything at all, is hers for the taking.

I'm hers, and I'll do everything in my power to keep this little girl safe and sound.

I lean down and press my lips against the top of her head. The cap slides to the side, revealing a little patch of bright orange hair.

"Just like your mommy," I whisper, pulling the hat back in place.

The nurse must hear me because she looks up from the

other incubator where she's checking on the baby. "Did you and your wife decide on a name?"

My wife.

No, Aly isn't my wife, but after all of this is done, I'm sure as hell going to make certain she is.

"Edie," I whisper softly. "Edie Mae Anderson."

Chapter 41

ALYSSA

I shift in the bed as I slowly wake up from a deep sleep. A groan forms at the back of my throat as a searing pain spreads through my body. I try to open my eyes, but they feel heavy with sleep.

Holy shit. What did I do?

The events of the previous night—was it even the previous night?—flash in my mind. Getting ready for the gala. The disappointed look on Mrs. Anderson's face. All the prying eyes directed at me. Seeing my mother. Dancing with Maddox. Our fight. The sudden pain. Chad. Blood.

So much blood.

Edie.

My hands clench around my stomach as my eyes fly open, but instantly, I'm blinded by the bright light.

God, Edie. Tears prickle my eyes as I frantically grip my stomach tighter, only to come up empty. My heart starts racing violently. *No, no, no... Please tell me she's okay. If something happened to her...*

"Aly..." The muffled groan gets my attention. I blink a few times, trying to clear my vision. My eyes burn from the brightness of the room. I squint through the narrowed slits, taking in the room. The bright walls. Blinding lights. Machines with the constant beeping.

Hospital. I'm in a...

Maddox's head appears in front of my face. His glasses are nowhere in sight, leaving his face bare.

"M-Maddox."

His skin is pale, dark circles under his eyes. One cheek is wrinkled and slightly red, probably from sleeping, and his dark curls are mussed as if he ran his fingers through it a thousand times.

I run my hand over my belly. My very flat, very empty, very painful belly.

That *beep-beep-beeping* sound grows stronger by the second.

"E-Edie..." I croak, my voice weak. "Is s-she..."

I try looking around. Try to find a crib to see my baby, but she's not there.

She's not there.

"Baby, please, calm down." Maddox pushes my hair back, his hands cradling my face. "She's okay. She's fine. They put her into the NICU, but she's fine."

NICU.

"S-she..." I suck in a breath, fighting to breathe. "F-fine?"

"Edie is fine." He presses his forehead against mine. "And she's beautiful, Aly. So damn beautiful. With big blue eyes and your ginger hair. She's your mini-me in every way, just like I knew she'd be."

My eyes fall shut as sweet relief washes over me. "P-promise?" I croak, my voice breaking.

"I promise, baby. Edie is fine. I was with her earlier, and I got to hold her. She's so freaking tiny, but she's a fighter. She's going to come through this. You both are."

I let out a shaky breath.

She's fine.

My baby is fine.

I blink, focusing my attention on the man standing in front of me. Through the blurriness, I can see the tears in his eyes.

"God, Aly, I was so freaking worried. There was so much blood," he shakes his head as a tear falls down, leaving a wet trail on my cheek. "I thought I lost you. I thought I lost you both. I would have never forgiven myself if that had happened."

"Maddox, no." I cup his cheek, brushing the tears away. "It's not your f-fault."

"Yes, it is. If I'd have gone with you to that damn doctor's appointment like I should have, none of this would have happened."

"You can't blame your—"

"But I can. If I weren't so absorbed in what I wanted and needed, none of this would have happened. If I knew, I would have never yelled at you like that. I would have never left you. It was stupid, and selfish and..." Another shake of his head. "I could have *lost* you. I almost lost you." He pulls back and presses his lips against my forehead gently. "But you're fine. You're both fine."

I close my eyes, tears sliding down my cheeks.

"Promise me, Aly. I love you two too much. If I lost you..." His thumb swipes under my eyes. I look at him, taking in my fill. He isn't the only one who almost lost people he loves. I did too. I almost lost him; almost lost Edie. "I wouldn't have survived it."

"L-love..." I try to hold onto him, but my hand feels too heavy. Maddox takes it gently into his palm, careful of the IV, and brings it to his mouth, his lips brushing against my palm. "Y-you."

"I love you too, Alyssa. More than life itself. Don't you ever scare me like that again."

I press my mouth against his in a soft kiss. "P-promise."

That was one promise I was more than happy to keep.

"I love you." Maddox holds my face and kisses me once again. My mouth. My cheeks. My forehead. Each kiss is almost feather-light as he makes his way back to my mouth. "And never again am I letting go of you."

This time, the kiss is longer, harder. I cling to Maddox as hard as I can, needing this connection, needing to know this is real, that he's here, and we're alive and well.

With one final swipe of his mouth over mine, Maddox pulls back, and I'm grateful that I'm lying in bed because my whole body feels unsteady.

"She's truly okay?" I ask once again.

Maddox pulls back. Wiping at his cheeks with the back of his hand, he pulls the phone out of his pocket and turns it toward me.

I let out a shaky breath as I stare at the screen. A photo of a shirtless Maddox lying with a small bundle on his chest kicks the air out of my lungs.

"One of the nurses took it yesterday while I was there and sent it to me. She's beautiful, Aly."

"She's so small," I whisper, tracing the image of my daughter. I pull the image up, and Maddox's face appears on the screen. The way he holds her, the protective look in his eyes... No, not my daughter, *our* daughter. Because Maddox was right, he's Edie's dad, for all intents and purposes.

Maddox takes my hand in his and gives it a firm squeeze. "She might be small, but she's fierce. And she'll get through this. You both will, and then we're going back home, and I'm not going to let you out of my sight for the next thirty years."

"Just thirty years?" I chuckle, although the idea of being with Maddox for the next thirty years, or however long I can get, doesn't sound bad at all.

"You're right. Probably better make it fifty, just to be sure."

"Just to be sure."

"I'm going to call the doctor and let everybody know you're awake. They have been worried about you."

"I could have walked, you know," I look over my shoulder at Maddox, who's pushing my wheelchair down the hallway.

"You could barely stand for more than ten seconds. I'm not taking my chances." He smiles at one of the nurses we pass by, and I swear the woman beams at him.

"You're familiar with the staff."

"That's because I'm here a lot, so I'm pretty sure I met all the nurses."

That's Maddox for you, making sure to meet all the staff that's helping the people he loves. I'm pretty sure Maddox didn't leave the hospital at all. Our friends brought him a change of clothes every time somebody came to visit, which was often, but Maddox was always here, either with Edie or with me.

"Plus, I'm quite certain that Mom bribed the whole floor to make sure everybody was taking good care of you."

That wouldn't surprise me at all. I'm not sure what happened, but Mrs. Anderson did a complete one-eighty. When she came to visit, she apologized for what she said when she was at our house and later at the gala. Also, Maddox told me what she did the night I ended up in the hospital. How she called the ambulance and stayed with him until I was out of surgery. The same couldn't be said about my mom. Mrs. Anderson has sent her a message informing her what has happened, but so far, neither of my parents showed up or even tried to call.

"She's something else, alright."

"She's just trying to make up for what happened."

Maddox pulls us to a stop in front of the double doors.

"There's nothing to make up for."

"I know that, and you know that." He walks around the wheelchair and crouches in front of me. "Are you ready?"

My gaze darts to the door, my heart stuck in my throat.

"I think so." I let out a shaky breath, my fingers curling around the armrests. "I'm just so anxious to finally meet her."

The doctors didn't want to let me get up straight away because they were still worried about postpartum preeclampsia, and they couldn't bring Edie to me because she still needed to be in the NICU. But after two days, I finally drew the line. I'd rather die than stay one more day in bed without seeing my daughter.

I knew she was safe and well cared for. I knew that Maddox went in to see her every day, and he showed me photos, but it wasn't nearly the same.

"I know." Maddox leans in and presses his mouth to mine. "Just don't let all the wires scare you. She's been doing much better."

"Okay," I nod, although there's nothing okay about the whole situation. This isn't how this was supposed to go. Then again, I wasn't supposed to get pregnant before finishing college, and look how well that turned out. "I trust you. That's the only reason why I've stayed in my bed up until now. Because I know you'll do what's best for Edie."

"Always." Maddox presses his mouth against the top of my head before pushing to his feet. "Let's go meet our baby."

My throat tightens as I swallow, my palms turning sweaty from nerves because right behind that door is my daughter, and I'm finally going to meet her.

Chapter 42

MADDOX

After showing Aly how to scrub her hands, I do the same. I open the door and slowly push her inside the warm room. I can hear her sharp intake of breath; see the way her whole body goes still as she first sees the line of incubators in the middle of the room.

I can't even begin to imagine how she must be feeling after not being able to see her daughter. I'm away for just a few minutes, and there's this need inside of me urging me to go back and make sure that Edie's alright, even though I've just been there and held her. Rationally, I know she's safe.

I brush my hand over her shoulder reassuringly as I push her closer to where Edie's sleeping.

"She's so small," Aly whispers, almost in awe as we come to a stop just next to the incubator, her fingers gently touching the glass. "You weren't joking when you said she's tiny."

Her lip wobbles, eyes filling with tears zeroed in on the little bundle laying in the middle of her bed.

I place my hands on Aly's shoulder, rubbing at her stiff muscles. "No, I wasn't."

Aly shakes her head. "If I'd just been more careful, none of this would have happened…"

What?

She can't be serious about this, can she?

I turn her around and crouch in front of her, so we're eye to eye. "It's not your fault Aly. You did good. She's here, and she'll get better, grow stronger. You'll see. Before we can blink, Edie will be running around causing all kinds of havoc."

"I know." Aly looks to the incubator. "But knowing it doesn't change the fact that we could have lost her, Maddox."

She's not the only one. I could have lost you both.

I slide my finger under her chin and turn her toward me. Her tear-stained eyes undo something inside of me. "But we haven't. She's here, and she'll get better." I caress her cheeks by swiping my thumbs over her cheekbones to brush away the tears. "And then we'll bring her home with us—where she belongs."

"Home..." Aly returns her attention back to Edie. "That's the only thing I want, to bring you back home."

Aly's gaze falls on the name tag on the incubator. She blinks, her fingers tracing the letters written on the carton, her face turning serious. "Edie Mae Anderson."

Shit, I totally forgot about that.

"They asked me about her name, and I just..." My words trail off. I should have probably thought about it before, warned Aly of what I'd done, but there was just so much going on. I swallow the lump in my throat. "I'm sorry. I know I should have asked you first, but... we can have it changed."

"No."

I open my mouth but stop when her word registers in my head.

"No?" I repeat, unsure if I heard her correctly. Because she can't mean she wants Edie to keep my last name, can she?

"No. I don't want to change it."

"Aly..."

"No," she interrupts me, once again, before I can say anything else. "I meant what I said. I don't want to change it." Aly turns to me. She grabs my hand in hers, intertwining our fingers. "There was so much going on these last few days I never got a chance..." She shakes her head. "I'm so sorry for what I said that night, Maddox. So, so sorry. You were right; it wasn't fair. Not after everything you've done for me. For *us*. You showed me how much you love me in so many little ways. I should have trusted you on that. I should have trusted you when you said you wanted this, wanted *us*, but after everything that has happened with Chad and my parents, it was just easier to doubt you. Easier to believe there's going to come a time when you'll open your eyes and realize you made a mistake when it comes to us."

I cup her face, holding her gaze, so she knows I'm serious. "Never. I could never look at you or Edie as a mistake."

Aly places her hands over mine. "And deep down, I know that. I've known that this whole time because I know *you*. I know the kind of man you are. That's why I feel even worse for saying Edie's not yours. Because you've shown me over and over just how much you love her."

"I might not share her blood, but she owns my heart, Aly," I whisper, brushing her hair away from her face. "Well, one part of my heart at least, because the other one belongs to you. I've loved you from the moment I'd known what love meant, and nothing will ever be able to change that."

"I know that." Aly nods, her tongue darts out, sliding over her lips. "And I'm sorry it took me so long to say it back because I do love you, Maddox. I love your big heart. I love the fact that you always put others first. I love that you love my daughter so much that you'd make her a video game just so you could play it together. I love how you make me laugh and always, *always* put me first. Even when that means walking away from me to do right by her, one day, Edie will be honored to call you her dad. If you'll have us."

"If?" I let out a chuckle. As if that was ever a question. "There is no if, Aly." I bring our joined hands to my mouth and press a kiss against her knuckles. "You and Edie are all I've ever wanted, all I ever needed, even before I myself realized it. But there's one thing you're wrong about, though."

Aly pulls her brows together, uncertainty flashing on her face. "What?"

Leaning closer, I press my forehead against hers.

"I'll be the one honored if she calls me Dad, not the other way around."

Aly sniffs, a tear falling down her cheek. "And when I thought I couldn't love you more, you show me just exactly how wrong I am."

She burrows her head in my neck and cries—actual, gut-wrenching sobs.

"Hey, now. It's okay." I crouch down and wrap my arms around her, pulling her to me, her body shaking. The position is uncomfortable as all hell, so I hold her tightly as I get up and walk us to the recliner. I sit down, Aly in my lap as I hold her to me. "Shh... it's okay. You're both okay. I have you."

I smooth my hand over her back, just holding onto her as she lets it all out. All the fear, frustration, and panic that she's been holding in, even before she ended up in the hospital.

I'm not sure how long we're sitting there like that when the door opens, and Lily, the nurse that was there the night Edie was born, enters the room.

"Hey, Mad—," Lily's eyes go wide as she sees Aly. "Is everything okay? Do I need to call the doctor?"

"Everything's fine," I reassure her, pressing my lips against the top of Aly's head. "We're just a little emotional."

Lily nods her head in understanding. "That's to be

expected, but there is no need to worry. Edie has been doing really great so far."

I run my hand down her back, and push a strand of hair out of her face. "You hear that, Aly? Our baby girl is a fighter."

"You must be Mom," Lily says as she stops by the recliner.

"What gave it away?" Aly asks, wiping away her tears. "The ugly gown or mental breakdown?"

"The gown, actually," Lily smiles. "But don't you worry about me. You've been through a lot. It's normal that things get a bit emotional."

"It's just... a lot. But I needed to see her. Needed to reassure myself that she's alright." Aly tries to shift, but the movement causes her to wince.

"Be still; you're still healing yourself," I chastise. "You won't be of any help to Edie if you have to stay in the hospital longer."

"Maddox is right. Edie has been doing really well, and your husband has been really great with her."

Aly's eyes widen at the label, mouth falling open. Before she can say anything, Lily asks: "Would you like to hold her?"

"I..." A small smile appears on Aly's face. "Yes. Yes, I would."

I start to get up.

"No, it's fine like this," Lily throws over her shoulder, already walking toward the incubator.

"Are you sure?" The chair is barely enough to fit the two of us, and with all the wires still connected to Edie...

Lily tilts her head to the side. "Maybe move to the side a little, so she's lying down on the recliner fully."

I do as instructed. It's a tight fit, but ask me if I care. I should have probably gotten up and let Aly have this moment for herself. But I don't want to. Call me selfish, but I want to share this moment with my two girls. "You good?"

Aly nods, her eyes on Lily, who's expertly taking Edie from

the incubator. Seriously, there's nothing like watching a nurse pick up this tiny human that's connected to dozens of machines out of the incubator. It's like they have spidey senses or something. They make it look so effortless when just the mere idea of it makes my stomach unsettled.

Lily murmurs something to Edie as she brings her over.

"Can you help her loosen the gown a little?"

"Sure." I slide my hand under Aly's back, tugging at the strings holding her gown in place. The material gives in easily, and I tug it down.

"Great," Lily says and places Edie on Aly's chest. "There you go."

Aly's eyes grow wide as she stares at the little bundle, tears filling her eyes all over again. Her hands go around Edie's back, holding her close.

"You were right," Aly whispers, taking one small hand in hers. "She's perfect."

"She is," I agree, my voice hoarse with emotion. "Just like I knew she would be."

Edie grabs Aly's finger, digging her tiny nails into the flesh as she slowly blinks her eyes open at the sound of her voice. Those big, blue eyes stare at us with wonder, and my chest suddenly feels too tight.

"Hey there, little one," Aly whispers, sniffling softly. "Mommy and Daddy are here."

I place my hand over Aly's.

The two most important women in my life are here, safely tucked in my arms, and nothing will ever touch them.

Leaning down, I press my lips against the top of Edie's head before doing the same to Aly and whisper: "You did good, Aly."

"No," she tilts her head back, her eyes meeting mine. "*We* did good. I love you, Maddox."

I shake my head, my throat tight with emotions. "I don't think I'll ever get enough of hearing you say it."

"Good, because I'll be saying it a lot."

I tighten my arms around them. "I love you, too."

Aly smiles and snuggles closer, looking down at our daughter. "You were wrong, though."

"About?"

"We're home." She tilts her head back, a smile curling her lips. "You're our home, Maddox."

Epilogue

MADDOX

Three weeks later

"And you're just going to let us take her?" I ask Lily for what feels like the hundredth time in the last thirty minutes.

The nurse chuckles, "That's usually how it works."

"Just like that? We could be serial killers for all you know."

This time she does laugh. I'm glad that at least one of us finds this whole situation funny. "Well, we've gotten to know you better than we do most of the parents who give birth in this hospital, so I'd say you were good."

I shake my head, still unable to believe it. How can they just let people walk out of the hospital with the babies before making sure they're going to be taken care of properly? Who decided that was wise?

"I still think it's a stupid idea."

Lily pats me on the shoulder as she passes by. "You'll do fine. I've seen you with that baby girl, and I know she couldn't be in better hands."

"He's just panicking, has been since the doctor told us we'd be taking Edie home. I swear, last night, he baby-proofed the whole house." Aly gives me a pointed look. "That's already been baby-proofed."

"Hey, I'm just making sure everything is set in place. The last thing we need is to come back here." I glance at the nurses apologetically. "Not that we don't appreciate all you did for us, but..."

"Don't stress about it," Hilda, one of the senior nurses who's been taking care of Edie, gives me a reassuring smile. "We also don't want to see you back here if it's possible, so baby-proof away."

"See? I told you."

Aly pulls the bottle from the baby's lips. I take it from her and watch her turn a dozing Edie in her arms so she can burp her. She murmurs softly as she pats the baby's back and sways from side to side until Edie lets out a belch worthy of a grown man.

Seriously, the noises that come out of that petite thing.

"Here are your discharge papers. You should schedule an appointment with your pediatrician as soon as possible to keep her on track and make sure she gets all her shots."

I take the papers from her. "Thank you so much. We really appreciate everything you've done for us."

"That's our job. You just take care of that baby girl now."

"Will do."

I slide the papers in the baby's bag just as Aly places Edie back in her carrier.

"Take this?" I hand her the bag and double-check that she's strapped in properly before pulling the blanket tightly around her and picking her up.

"You ready?" I ask, turning around to Aly. She's nibbling at her lip and looks highly amused for some reason. "What?"

"Nothing." She tries to make a serious face, but the corners of her mouth keep twitching upward, amusement twinkling in her blue irises. "Just watching you, that's all."

I push my glasses up my nose. "Then why are you laughing?"

"I'm not laughing."

I tilt my head to the side and stare at her because, seriously, who is she trying to fool?

"What? I'm not." She schools her features and intertwines her fingers with mine. "I just think it's sweet."

"What's sweet?"

"You. How you double-check everything to make sure she's safe." One corner of her mouth lifts upward. "A little paranoid, but sweet."

"I'm not paranoid," I protest. "I just don't want her to fall."

"She's not going to drop anywhere." Aly wraps her free hand around my neck and pulls me in for a kiss. One soft kiss turns into two, and before I know it, my tongue is in her mouth, and I feel slightly breathless. I'm not the only one either.

Aly sways a little as she breaks the kiss, her voice raspy, "Let's go home."

ALYSSA

"Seriously, where are those keys?" I mutter as I dig through the baby bag, trying to find the keys. "I swear..." Just then, my fingers wrap around the metal ring. "Finally."

I pull them out and put them into the lock. "One more second, and I would have turned the whole thing upside down."

"You should put them in the front pocket next time," Maddox says, entering the house with Edie in his arms.

"They were in the front pocket." Dropping the bag by the door, I turn toward Maddox. "Wanna come to Mommy?"

Edie woke up almost as soon as the car stopped and started fussing until Maddox got her out of the carrier. I swear, that baby has him wrapped around her little finger. She just has to look at him, and he'll do anything. It's good she can't talk because the moment she does, he's doomed.

"She's all snuggled and happy," Maddox protests, looking down at Edie. "Right, Princess? You don't wanna be disturbed right now?"

I roll my eyes at him but, in reality, my heart melts a little bit every time I see Maddox with Edie. "You're only saying that because you don't want to give her up."

"I just don't want to make her cry."

I prop my hands on my hips. "That baby barely ever cries."

Just then, a rush of small feet comes our way. Coco whines when she sees us, and she jumps, leaning against my leg. "Hey, pretty girl. We're home, and we brought company."

As if she understands my words, or maybe she can smell her, the dog goes straight for Maddox, who looks at me with uncertainty. "Should I?"

Schooling my features, I crouch down and pat Coco behind her ears. My stomach still hurts where they did the cesarian, but Coco is too overwhelmed to do this later. "You wanna meet your sister?" I motion for Maddox to get to our level, holding onto Coco's collar so she wouldn't jump on the baby.

The whining grows louder, and her entire body is shaking as she looks with wide eyes at the bundle in Maddox's arms. I soothe my hand down her back, hoping to calm her down. "Look at her, Coco. Isn't she beautiful?"

Coco sniffs Edie's head that's covered with a tiny hat, her tongue darting out and licking the baby's cheek.

Edie lifts her little hand in protest. I chuckle as Coco

produces a distressed sound wanting to go to the baby. I tug her back as Maddox gets to his feet.

"Hey now, we'll have you two hang out a little bit later, okay? She's not going anywhere."

With one final rub between her ears, I push to my feet.

Maddox's hand jots out to steady me. "You good?"

"I'm fine, don't worry." I tug Edie's hat down. "Can I have her now?"

Maddox takes a step back, making me chuckle.

"Fine, have it your way." I start walking toward the kitchen, Coco following after me. "We'll see how long it'll last once the gi—"

"Surprise!"

I yelp, my hand flying to cover my rapidly beating heart as I turn around and face our friends.

"You scared me shitless!" I protest, my heart still racing.

And I'm not the only one because Edie chooses that exact moment to start crying loudly.

"Are you insane?" Maddox hisses at our friends, covering Edie's ear with his palm and swaying softly. "You scared her. Seriously, whose smart idea was this?"

All heads turn to Nixon, who just rubs the back of his neck. "In my defense, it's what you do when you throw a surprise party."

"Not for a baby," Yasmin gives him a warning look as she comes closer. "Look at her, poor baby."

"No need to cry, pretty girl," Callie coos at Edie.

"It's fine," Yasmin says, picking her out of Maddox's arms and into hers. "Your uncle Nixon just doesn't know what's appropriate for babies. You'll have to forgive him."

"Hey, I was..." Maddox starts to protest, but both girls give him a death glare.

"You had more than enough time. Now it's our turn."

"Exactly!" Callie agrees. "How will she know who's the best aunt if we don't get any quality time with her?"

I lift my brows at them. "You do know she's my baby, right?"

Yasmin pokes her tongue out at me. "Get in line."

Shaking my head, I turn around and take in the room. When we left a couple of hours ago there was nobody home, but now all our friends are here, and the whole place is decorated in baby pink and pale yellow. The kitchen is filled with balloons and flowers, and there's a big banner with "Welcome home, Edie Mae" hanging on the wall. Wrapped boxes and gift bags fill the dining table, and there's even a cake.

"You guys didn't have to do all of this," I sniff softly.

Although things have calmed down a little lately, I'm still one big emotional wreck half the time. Any little thing can get a reaction out of me these days, and happy or sad, I'll most likely burst into tears.

"Of course, we did," Yasmin protests. She looks up at me from where she's sitting at the table, Edie tucked in the crook of her arm.

"We were planning a baby shower for you, but you had to go and ruin it by giving birth early," Callie rolls her eyes at me before turning her attention to Yas and extending her arms. "My turn now."

"Fine," Yas huffs and carefully transfers the baby to Callie.

My heart stops while I watch them maneuver my daughter around. Will this ever get any easier? "Next time, I'll try to keep the baby in until you guys throw us a baby shower."

Nixon stops with the cupcake halfway to his mouth and looks between Maddox and me. "Are you already thinking about the next time?"

"God no," Maddox says instantly, eyes wide. "We've had enough excitement for a while now."

Hayden looks over Callie's shoulder and tickles Edie's belly.

"You hear that, Edie? You brought enough excitement to your parents. No more, missy."

Edie purses her lips, a crease appearing between her brows as if she's concentrating. By now, I know that look very well.

Hayden sniffs the air, and his nose furrows. "What's that smell?"

Nixon stops by his side and does the same before gagging. "It smells like an atomic bomb just exploded."

"Is that *her*?" Prescott asks, pinching the bridge of his nose. "It can't be her. Can it?"

I go to the foyer where I left the bag and grab it before returning to the kitchen. I let the bag dangle from my finger as I offer it to the room and smile sweetly. "Who's on diaper duty?"

All the boys take a step back as if they're waiting for Edie to explode, and I can't help but burst into laughter.

Shaking his head, Maddox grabs the bag from my hand and tosses it over his shoulder. "So much for the best aunts and uncles," he says to Edie as he picks her up and brushes his lips against her cheek. "They like you just fine when you're all pretty and clean, but not so much once you turn into a smelly mess."

Nixon lifts his hands in the air. "Hey, we're *fun* uncles. We can play games, teach her how to throw a football or a punch, give her junk food, and buy her toys that'll drive you mad. Dirty diapers, on the other hand, are a dad's job."

"You hear that, Edie? You're lucky I like you even when you're smelly."

The two of them leave the kitchen, and I can hear Maddox still talking to Edie as they climb the stairs so he can change her.

Yasmin nudges me with her hip. "You're swooning."

"Maybe just a little," I admit.

Callie chuckles, "More like a lot."

"Fine, a lot. But can you blame me? Seeing Maddox with Edie is making my ovaries explode."

"I don't blame you at all," Yas lets out a sigh. "Maddox is a good dad, not that I'm really surprised."

No, me neither.

"He's the best."

Pulling open the bathroom door, I stop in my tracks at the image in front of me. Maddox is lying shirtless on the bed, Edie on his chest, her little butt sticking in the air. Coco is lying on the side; her hawk-like eyes focused on every move the baby makes.

"...and they lived happily ever after."

Maddox closes the book and presses a kiss on top of Edie's head.

"Isn't she too little for books?" I whisper softly so as not to wake her.

Maddox looks up, his gaze meeting mine.

"One's never too little for stories." He puts the book on the nightstand and gently scoops Edie into his arms. Coco gets up instantly, too. I lean against the door and watch Maddox transfer her to the crib. He really is a natural with her.

Coco jumps off the bed and goes after him, peeking into the crib to make sure Edie is okay before lying down in front of it.

"That dog is something else," I shake my head.

"I think we should probably move Coco's bed closer to the crib, or she'll sleep on the floor."

He's right. Coco has been obsessed with the baby and so protective of her. Seriously, nobody can even look at Edie without her going into protective mode. I'm not sure if it's a dog thing or a Coco thing.

"I think you're right." Pushing from the doorway, I cross the room and wrap my arm around his middle. "Whenever I think I can't love you more, I see you with her, and I fall a little harder."

Maddox turns around, pulling me closer to him. "Is that a bad thing?"

I push a strand of his hair behind his ear. "No, it's not. Just a little bit scary and sometimes overwhelming."

"That's how I feel too, but I never want to stop. I don't want to know the world in which I don't love you, and I never want to go back to the world where you're not mine. Both of you."

Seriously, how could anybody resist him? It's impossible.

"I'm not going anywhere. You and I, we belong together."

Maddox's serious eyes stare at me with such intensity I can feel a shiver run down my spine.

"Good." He nods, his fingers lifting my chin. He leans down, his lips brushing against mine. "Because I'm not letting you go."

Thank you so much for reading Kiss To Belong! I hope you enjoyed Maddox and Alyssa's story. If you're not ready to say goodbye to them yet (I know I'm not), you can grab their bonus epilogue here.

If you have a moment, please consider leaving a short review. I'd really appreciate it.

Do you wonder what happened during spring break when the Blairwood gang left for Hawaii? Great, because *Kiss Me Forever*, a Blairwood University novella, is coming soon! Pre-order now to find out which one of the couples got hitched!

New to Blairwood University? All of Maddox's roommates already have their story out: Kiss Me First (Emmett and Kate), Kiss To Conquer (Hayden and Callie), Kiss To Forget (Nixon and Yasmin), and Kiss To Defy (Zane and Rei)!

Bloggers, bookstagrammers and booktokers join Anna's share team to be the first to know about her upcoming releases and sales.

Want to stay in touch with Anna? Join her reader's group Anna's Bookmantics, or sign up for Anna's newsletter.

ACKNOWLEDGMENTS

I think Kiss To Belong has been one of the most requested stories I've got. I guess what they say is true. It's always the quiet ones, right? I fell in love with Maddox the first time I introduced him in Kiss To Conquer. He was this cute, shy kid that was so desperately in love with his best friend, but she just didn't see it. And I think everybody can relate to that if only a little bit. Aly... There is so much more to her than meets the eyes. I loved writing their story and exploring their relationship, watching it grow from something new and fragile into this beautiful, strong relationship. And Maddox. Well, I don't have words for this guy. Every girl out there deserves her Maddox. Somebody who'll love us despite everything and put us first.

I want to say a huge thank you to my team. To my lovely alpha readers—Carrie, Nina, and Melody—who I couldn't have been able to do this without. I swear, these girls keep me sane on most days. To my cover designer Najla Qamber and her team for giving us another stunning cover to add to Blairwood University. To my models Haylie and Caleb for being my perfect Alyssa and Maddox, and to Braadyn for bringing them to life. To my editor Kate, who always makes some room for me, even though it's sometimes last minute. And of course, thank you to my supporting and loving street team, who helps me promote my books every single day.

Most of all, THANK YOU, my readers, for loving this story, these characters as much as you do.

Until the next book,
   Anna

PLAYLIST

The Rasmus - Holy Grail
Maddi & Tae - Friends Don't
Caleb & Kelsey - Hand to Hold
Olivia Lane - You've Got Me
Cassadee Pope - If My Heart Had A Heart
Rachel Platten - You Belong
Franni Rae Cash - Feelings
Emily James - Never Chase a Boy
Levi Hummon - I Still Do
Morgan Evans (feat. Kelsea Ballerini) - Dance with Me
Tryon - Come Kiss Me
Blue October - I Hope You're Happy
Apocalyptica, Ed Sheeran - I Was Made For Loving You
Tate McRae - that way
Ally Barron - Just Friends
5 Seconds of Summer - Lover Of Mine
Tyler Shaw - To the Man Who Let Her Go
Haley Mae Campbell - Never Been in Love
Noah Schnacky - Hello Beautiful

PLAYLIST

Duncan Laurence - Arcade
Chris Moreno - Running in Place
Jessie Murph - Always Been You
Tyler Shaw - Love You Still (abcdefu romantic version)

OTHER BOOKS BY ANNA B. DOE

New York Knights

NA/adult sports romance

Lost & Found

Until

Forever

Greyford High

YA/NA sports romance

Lines

Habits

Rules

The Penalty Box

The Stand-In Boyfriend

Blairwood University

College sports romance

Kiss Me First

Kiss To Conquer

Kiss To Forget

Kiss To Defy

Kiss Before Midnight

Kiss To Remember

Kiss To Belong

Kiss Me Forever

Kiss To Salvage

Standalone

YA modern fairytale retelling

Underwater

Box Set Editions

Greyford High (book #1 - #3)

The Anabel & William Duet

ABOUT THE AUTHOR

Anna B. Doe is a young adult and new adult contemporary romance author. She writes real-life romance that is equal parts sweet and sexy. She's a coffee and chocolate addict. Like her characters, she loves those two things dark, sweet and with little extra spice.

When she's not working for a living or writing her newest book you can find her reading books or binge-watching TV shows. Originally from Croatia, she is always planning her next trip because wanderlust is in her blood.

She is currently working on various projects. Some more secret than others.

Find more about Anna on her website: www.annabdoe.com

Join Anna's Reader's Group Anna's Bookmantics on Facebook.

Printed in Great Britain
by Amazon